PASSED BALL

LO EVERETT

DEDICATION

For all you single daddy hoes—this one wears baseball pants,
and I wrote him just for you. Enjoy.

AUTHOR'S NOTE

This is the fifth and last book in the Mile High Hearts series which follows the Denver Bandits baseball team. It can be read as a standalone, but to fully appreciate the dynamic of the group, I recommend reading it as a series.

Xavier and Vivienne's story starts with a bad first impression. *Passed Ball* has plenty of cinnamon roll energy, found family vibes that I love to write, and there are plenty of steamy moments to get lost in, too. But I'd be remiss if I didn't share insight into the heavier topics as well.

Content Warnings: *Passed Ball* touches on topics of parental neglect, loss of a parent/loved one, and grief. Alcoholism and sobriety are also discussed. There is on-page alcohol use in social settings. The topics of IVF and fertility challenges are discussed in relation to a side character, along with fatal complications during childbirth, that made a lasting impact on our heroine and her family.

Nothing matters more than your mental health. Please use care when reading about topics that may be triggering.

PROLOGUE

XAVIER

The text is still there, glaring up at me from the screen—a stark reminder of all the changes coming. Reading it a dozen times in the last two days hasn't made it lose its impact. It still hits like a punch to the gut, stealing the air from me.

There's so much missing from the brief exchange that it leaves me grappling with the unknown just like it did the day I got it, two weeks ago.

Now, I'm planted at a wobbly table in a too-loud coffee shop, waiting for the only person who can give me answers.

And right now? All I have are questions, with no idea how to face the biggest one of all: How the hell am *I* supposed to raise a baby?

Two months isn't enough time to prepare for fatherhood—not with the baseball season looming and no support from family.

I skim the text from Kristy, my ex-girlfriend, one more time, looking for something that isn't there.

KRISTY:

I'm pregnant.

XAVIER:

Congratulations?

KRISTY:

It's yours. I'm due in two months.

That's it. That's the whole damn exchange. It may seem callous, but Kristy and I haven't spoken in months, and she made no secret of the fact that she was moving up and on.

That was the last I'd heard from her.

When her text came through, my teammates and I were helping at a massive volunteer fair that Indie, our third baseman's wife, organized to bolster the support of our local nonprofits. It was unexpected, and there were so many questions, but it wasn't exactly a conversation I was eager to have surrounded by strangers.

So, I didn't push for more information despite the shocking due date—how the fuck was I just finding out?

Instead, I finished the event, and when I was home, I called Kristy to make plans to meet and figure all of this out—face to face.

Now, I'm sitting here, with the matcha I know she drinks in front of me, while I wait for her in a random coffee shop. It's dark and dusty, unlike Buns & Roses, the coffee shop my teammate's wife, Lilah, owns, but Kristy picked a neutral location to send a clear message—we're doing this on her terms.

Whatever. All I care about is figuring out what the hell is next.

The door swings open and Kristy struts in. She's conventionally pretty, with blonde hair that falls to her waist and a slim figure that I know she spends hours maintaining with a trainer at a gym. One that, up until a few months ago, was coming out of *my* paycheck.

Her makeup is done perfectly and hair gleams like she spent hours on it. When we were together, we couldn't leave the house for anything if she wasn't photo ready—her words, not mine. The woman lived in fear of non-existent paparazzi following me around Denver and snapping an unflattering shot of her.

It didn't matter that I told her I had only had my photo taken in public by a photographer a handful of times, and only ever when I was with teammates.

"Everyone with a phone is paparazzi, and I refuse to be immortalized looking like a hag," she had said, her nose wrinkling as if the mere thought was offensive.

The only thing that's changed is the rounded bump that's barely noticeable under her oversized sweater. I know better than to comment on a woman's body, even though I have a rogue thought that her bump is smaller than I expected, and that realization causes an unpleasant tightness in my chest.

What if she's lying to me and this baby isn't mine? Or worse, what if something's wrong with the baby? This might be unexpected, but part of me was immediately thrilled at the prospect of becoming a parent. The logistics, not so much, but the actual baby—yeah, I could get on board with that.

Or maybe I'm just a guy who's fucking clueless about what to expect when his ex is unexpectedly . . . expecting.

God, this is going to be a disaster.

For peace of mind alone, I need a paternity test and a clean bill of health from a doctor as soon as possible, because I really am clueless when it comes to pregnancy. I'm an only child with no living family, so this is all uncharted waters.

Standing, I meet her at the edge of the table, awkward as fuck.

Do I shake her hand? Hug her? What's the protocol here?

Kristy's chair makes the hair on the back of my neck stand as it scrapes over the outdated tile floor. She doesn't wait for me, grabbing the chair herself and plopping into it, scowling at me, arms crossed.

Still, I push her chair in and take my seat across from her. Giving her my best disarming smile, I hand over the green drink. Neither does anything to soothe her mood, so I clear my throat and go for it. "It's good to see you."

She lifts the cup, sniffing, little lines popping up on the bridge of her nose, then she pushes it away. "Cut the crap, Xavier. You can't be any happier to be here than I am."

Choosing violence today, I see.

Ignoring her comment I ask, "How are you doing? Feeling okay?"

There's a slightly crazed edge to her responding laugh, and panic wells inside me at the possibility that something could actually be wrong with her, or the baby.

"It's a little late to pretend you care."

My brows draw together, unsure what to make of that. The problem with Kristy and I was never that I didn't care, it was that we wanted different things, and I got sick of her trying to bully me into giving her things I wasn't ready for.

"I can tell you're upset, but I do care about your health, and the baby's."

That makes her nostrils flare. "Upset," she seethes, repeating the offensive word back at me.

Oh, yep. Poor word choice.. "I mean—"

"I'm seven-fucking-months pregnant with *your* kid, my bra is too tight, and I can't have sushi but it's all I'm craving."

"Seven months!" I blurt out. Knowing she was due soon and hearing it said aloud are two different things. It makes me realize how much I've already missed: ultrasounds, the baby moving, months to prepare . . .

At least, I think that's all I've missed. I need to stop at a bookstore immediately, because I *should* know these things.

"No shit. Let's hope she gets my brains instead of yours," Kristy retorts, malice dripping from her tone.

The blow doesn't land—it can't touch me, not after what she just said. My hand rakes through my hair.

A fucking girl.

I'm going to be a dad in a few months . . . and it's a girl.

Kristy pushes a black-and-white photo across the table—our daughter's ultrasound. "At least she's got my lips," she says so offhandedly I can't tell if it's genuine. But I hang on to it because it's the only thing she's said since she walked in the door that makes me think parenting with her won't be a complete nightmare.

"A girl," is all I can manage, I stop counting toes, lifting my eyes from the picture to my ex. My gaze drops to her stomach. "How long have you known?"

"Since I got the ultrasound in the emergency room where I found out I was pregnant about a month ago."

"And you waited all this time to tell me?" I can't hold back the bite of accusation.

Her shoulders fold in, her air of confidence falling away. It's unnerving; I've never seen her like this before. Even when I ended things, she never let anything but anger show. I reach out to cover her hand with mine, an apology forming. She pulls her hand back, toying with her necklace.

"I'm not ready." Her fingers twist and untwist her necklace, stopping when she realizes what she's doing and dropping her hand. "This isn't how I saw my life playing out, and I wasn't sure what to do."

Her honesty has me pausing before I ask, "And do you know now?"

She rolls her eyes, all the attitude that I'm used to back, like it never left. "What I've wanted never mattered before, but I can see you've gone all mushy over a grainy picture. This baby already means more to you than I ever did."

I won't lie to protect her feelings. "I'm ecstatic about this baby. It wasn't my plan either, but I want a chance to give our little girl the childhood I never had. I know this isn't only my decision, though. It's one we need to make together."

She perks up, leaning closer, her hand drifting back to the table, resting between us. The urge to take it and soothe her is gone. "You would raise this baby with me?"

Alarm bells go off in my head. Taking a drink from my cold brew, I weigh my words.

"We can work out a way to co-parent together." I force a smile that I hope conveys warmth, because the same conniving hope I saw so often towards the end of our relationship glitters in her ice-blue eyes.

"So, not *together*," she says too slowly.

"Parenting together, yes." I rub my neck, searching for words to defuse the situation. "But I want to be very clear about where we stand. I'm not interested in a relationship beyond this baby. We can be friends and raise her as a unit, but nothing more."

Her bottom lip pushes out and her arms cross over her chest. "Why the hell not? She's our daughter. You said it yourself, she deserves a chance at a family. Don't I deserve that after all . . . this?" She gestures to her body.

"I will always be grateful to you for giving me a daughter." I hold her gaze. "I'll take care of her, and I'll take care of you too, because I know that's what you're really asking for. But we're not good together. Trying to force this for her sake would only hurt all of us."

I pause, softening my tone as I lean forward. "Take a paternity test, include me in the appointments, and I'll make sure you're both taken care of. I'll help you get your own place, and my lawyer can help us figure out an agreement that works for everyone."

"What's wrong with my apartment?" she scoffs.

"Your roommates don't seem like the kind to tolerate a baby crying in the middle of the night."

Her lip curls like she doesn't like the sound of being woken up, either.

"And what about a nanny?" she asks.

"If you want to keep working, I'll get a nanny to help during the season."

Her lips pucker, souring her face further. "You expect me to work?"

"That's not what I said." The pressure in my head builds, and I press my temples to reveal the ache.

"You said, if I want help, I have to work. I'm not an idiot."

"Kristy," I bark. Nothing has changed since she left, and the back and forth is making me weary. To her, this baby is a pawn to get the lifestyle I wouldn't give her when we were still together. "You will not use this baby to manipulate me."

"Whatever, Xavier." She stands, pushing back from the table to leave.

"Where are you going?" I move to follow her because this conversation is nowhere near over.

"To my apartment. I'm tired, and you're not helping." She stops short of the door and when she looks up, I can see it. The dark circles are covered by her makeup, but it can't hide the dullness in her blue irises. Behind the mask, she's struggling.

And I don't want to make it worse. "Should I have a realtor look for a place for you near my house?"

"Yes, fine. Send me the listings and I'll let you know what I like."

"We're doing this, then?" I ask, fighting the rise of my mouth.

"Don't look so damn happy. I still have to grow this kid for the next two months. Not to mention everything after . . ."

I reach out carefully, my hand brushing her elbow. Her cold blue gaze meets mine, full of pain and distrust. "If you don't want to raise her, that's okay. I can do this on my own."

Her laugh is bitter. "And then what? All your promises to take care of me go up in smoke?" Her voice rises and I glance around, relieved the coffee shop is mostly empty. "Not a chance. You do your part, and I'll do mine."

This is not how I imagined myself becoming a dad. I thought it would happen after retirement, with someone who wanted it as much as I did. This is going to be messy. Kristy's body is stiff as she waits for me to hit back, but I won't. "I never meant to hurt you. We'll figure this out."

"Don't give me that savior bullshit. I know you, Xavier. We're the same. We both came from nothing and I'm not fucking going back. Call the agent, send me the houses. We can both get what we want and at least this time I won't have to pretend to find you interesting."

Tirade finished, she yanks her arm free, her ponytail lashing angrily as she opens the door and walks away again. Only this time, despite her exit and us not being together, she's a permanent part of my life.

CHAPTER 1

XAVIER

I'd never felt more clueless than the moment a nurse placed my seven-pound baby girl in my arms and said, "Congratulations."

Holding my daughter for the first time upended my entire world, and everything I thought I knew about myself was erased. All that remained was her: Holland Áine Kingsley—my daughter, my purpose, my everything.

The paternity test confirmed it weeks ago, but one look at her and anyone can see she's mine.

A thick tuft of red hair peeks out from under her pink hat and her wide, impossibly blue eyes stare up at me. And when her lip starts quivering and she pouts, well, I realize she already has me wrapped around her tiny fingers.

For a few precious minutes, holding her lets me forget the chaos waiting for us. Her mother leaving, my own messed-up childhood, returning to the diamond—I let it all fade as I pace the living room.

I still have no idea what I'm doing and I have no help—no family, no nanny, no Kristy.

But everything I need, I'm holding in my arms.

My daughter has become the driving force behind my entire existence; there is nothing I wouldn't do for her. Nothing that could change my love for her. Since that first moment I held her, wrapped in the teal blanket I bought for her—Bandits teal, of course—she's owned my entire heart.

Unfortunately, I know that's not always the case. My dad never wanted kids—he only agreed to make my mom happy, assuming she'd always be there to take care of me. It was selfish, a lie he told to keep her, putting his fear of losing her above everything else. In the end, it hurt all of us, and we lost her anyway.

"I'll never hurt you like that," I whisper to my sleeping daughter. I should lay her down and put away the piles of clothes that have accumulated over the last few days, but I can't pull myself away. "Never."

History has a cruel way of repeating itself. Only this time, it's not a father refusing to step up, it's a mother walking away. I don't blame Kristy for that; not everyone is meant to be a parent. But her leaving still hits the same raw nerve, reopening old wounds.

Kristy and I had a plan. She said she was staying, and I was going to help her however I could. But the moment Holland was born, I saw it written all over her face—dread, not joy. She let me pick a name, signed the birth certificate, handed me our daughter, and walked out of the hospital a day later without so much as a goodbye.

The only thing keeping her here was the life I could give her. She admitted as much when we met at the coffee shop, but I ignored my gut.

I'm listening now.

Whether Kristy needs time to adjust or can't do this at all, I don't know. What I do know is that I won't let her drift in and out of Holland's life, leaving scars the way my dad did. My daughter deserves better. I want her to grow up surrounded by love, not instability. But doing this alone? It terrifies me.

How the hell am I going to be enough for her?

I know I'll never fail at loving her. It's everything else I'm afraid of.

Endless scenarios swirl in my head, each one more frightening than the last. The parenting books I blew through all said intrusive thoughts are normal. Surviving, let alone thriving, with these nonstop grenades of terror being launched at you by your own subconscious, every second of every day, seems too daunting to be normal.

It's not limited to the fear of keeping her alive. It's the existential questions plaguing me on top of the primal fears.

Would she be better off if Kristy came back and wanted to be in her life? And will she hate me if I deny her that?

Will I be warm enough to raise a child when my memories of having a parent who cared are tainted and distant?

How will I do it all with baseball? And if I can't manage, how the hell will I support her?

Bile crawls up my throat as my mind spins, weaving a future where Holland hates me, where I'm not the father she needs. Or worse, the unthinkable happens and our car plummets off a bridge into water, but I can't unbuckle her car seat fast enough to save her.

I cross the living room again, wearing a path in the carpet. My arms shake with my daughter in them and then I remember my promise to myself: to do everything I can to ensure this little girl is safe and loved—to give her enough so she's never missing out.

There's a metric fuck ton I don't know about being a dad. But one thing I do know is Holland deserves so much more than the upbringing I had, and nothing will stop me from making sure she never knows the pain and heartbreak I've experienced.

Not at the hands of me, or her mother.

Her hot breath puffs against my chest and her eyes part enough to give me a peak at those dark blues as she stretches out, yawning as if to say, *"You're thinking too loud, Daddy."*

There's something hopeful about the way my daughter looks up at me, like she knows she can trust me.

Which is ridiculous because, at four days old, she can barely see me. She can't possibly know that. *I* don't even know if she should trust me. I have no role models, no experience. Only an idiot would bet on me.

I sink into the corner of the couch, doubt weighing me down.

In two weeks, I have to return to playing baseball with no help in sight now that her mother is MIA. It's not how I envisioned my season going, but I wouldn't give this up for anything.

Cactus league games have already started, and while most of my teammates are exhausted from readjusting to the pace of the season, I'm wiped out from late night feedings and being on constant alert since Holland came home.

I let my eyelids fall closed for a minute. Just to rest them.

A soft knock at the door has them popping open as I practically jump, startling Holland. "Shh . . . It's okay, Áine."

I settle my daughter against my chest, murmuring her middle name—the same as my mom's. Irish for radiance. As I gently bounce her, I shuffle through the house toward the door and open it.

At first, all I see are the stacks of neatly wrapped boxes, Tupperware containers, and four sets of legs sticking out from the bottom of the pile of gifts on the other side of the door. They shuffle a few things around, revealing Poppy's long red braid and Indie's wild curls.

"Can we come in and set all this down so we can meet her properly?" Mia asks, peering around a pink gift bag which is starting to slide off the casserole dish she's balancing it on. My catcher's reflexes kick in, and I grab it before it hits the floor. "And that's why they pay you the big bucks."

"Come on in," I say, stepping out of the way. My teammates' significant others step through the door, a blur of energy and excitement. It makes me want a nap.

Lilah breezes past me, her growing baby bump leading the way to the kitchen. "There are energy bites in here." She holds up a bakery box for a split second before she shelves it in the fridge. "These are breakfast sandwiches—you can reheat them as needed. And this . . ."

"Is your vanilla cold brew?" My mouth waters at the sight of the Buns & Roses to-go carafe fit for a construction crew . . . or a newly minted single dad.

"It is. All for you," Lilah confirms sweetly.

"You're my favorite, don't tell the others," I whisper, conspiratorially.

Poppy drops her gifts on the counter and then joins her friend at the fridge. "Continuing the food parade, this is a spaghetti bake that you can pop in the oven, and Indie brought prepped, chicken fajitas bowls," Hendrix's fiancée says as she passes the food to Lilah. Each dish follows the last, filling the empty space.

"And I made Dean's favorite chicken tortilla soup," Mia says, setting down the rest of the food. "Oh, and he picked out our present. He said having a baby isn't an excuse to skip leg day. It's a baby carrier and an infant insert."

"Harsh." Indie laughs. "He really is only nice to you, isn't he?"

"Don't worry, I withheld phone sex on your behalf. You deserve a few weeks without worrying about workouts to care for this little cutie."

"Mhmm. I'm glad I'm not there to deal with his cranky ass."

It dawns on me that this is only the second conversation I've had with someone who can talk back to me in two days.

The only other being a brief phone call with my friend Edward, but that call was cut short when I had to change a diaper. He had called to check in after I sent him a picture of Holland. The older man befriended me when he found me wandering around the planetarium he works at. I was overwhelmed after finding out about the pregnancy and he listened. We've kept in touch since. But we talked yesterday, which means that, until five minutes ago, I hadn't talked to another adult today.

"He tried to cover his ass when he realized what an asinine comment it was." Mia blushes, her cheeks going pink when she mumbles, "But holding out on him is more fun . . . for both of us."

"I don't need details, Mia," I say.

Sex hasn't been on my radar since the last time Kristy and I slept together, back in July. Sex and relationships—anything that doesn't involve baseball or my baby—is not a priority.

Right now, my priority is figuring out how to do this alone, and what's next. My lawyer's advice: file for full custody to protect myself and my daughter in the event Kristy shows back up. He also let me know that the lovely state of Colorado requires a walk-away parent to be absent for a significant amount of time before the primary parent can be granted full custody. But, fun fact, there's no amount of time specified before it's considered abandonment. I guess the courts work off whims, just like my ex.

If, at the six-month mark Kristy hasn't shown back up, the court will *probably* consider that a sufficient amount of time to petition for termination of parental rights.

So now, on top of everything else, I have to prepare for the possibility that I'll be going to court soon.

Yeah, sex and relationships are the least of my worries.

A throat clears, dragging me out of my thoughts. "I don't mean to be an asshole, I'd rather leave that title to Dean, but why don't you give me sweet little Holland and go shower? You stink, and I'm pretty sure you were just sleeping standing up," Poppy says, stopping in front of me, nose wrinkled, hands out, and green eyes glued to my daughter.

"Do not," I argue weakly. She might be right about me sleeping standing up though.

Unfortunately, when I dip my nose towards my pits, the smell rudely wakes me the hell up. I hand over my sleeping daughter to the strong-willed women converging on me. All four of them soften to puddles at the sight of Holland bringing her fist to her face as I pass her to Poppy.

"You really do. But it's okay, you've got us. Go shower and I'll heat up some food for you." Lilah runs her thumb over the back of Holland's tiny fist. "Poor girl, he had your cute little nose right by those nasty pits. We're lucky it didn't shrivel off," she croons.

With a glance over my shoulder, I watch my friends fussing over my baby girl, welcoming her to the Bandits family. For the first time since I found out I was going to be a father, things seem like they might be okay and the tightness in my chest eases a little. I might not have a family by blood, but this family, is pretty fucking incredible.

The suffocating smell I discover when I strip my shirt over my head proves that Poppy was right and that I'll need extra time scrubbing. But knowing that Holland is safe and cared for doesn't stop me from rushing through a quick wash, rinse, and repeat.

It should honestly be a crime that I let it get this bad in only two days, but I was fucking terrified to leave her side for even a minute to shower. Which is something I'm going to need to figure out because, after a thorough washing, I nearly feel like a functioning human again. Who knew water and soap had those kinds of superpowers?

Not me.

Grabbing a fresh pair of joggers and a shirt without spit up crusted to the shoulder, I find my house buzzing with activity.

Most notable is the smell of a homemade pizza cooking from the kitchen where Lilah is working on a salad. I'm about to tell her how unnecessary it is, but everywhere I look, something is getting done without prompting.

Mia's sitting on my living room floor folding Holland's tiny clothes, and Indie's singing softly while she changes a diaper. Beside her, Poppy is putting together a bouncer that I don't recognize.

My feet stop moving of their own accord, and my throat tightens. "What's going on?" I croak, dumbly.

"Now you can bring her to the bathroom with you when you shower, and your teammates won't have to suffer from the smell of armpits and sour formula." Poppy shrugs like it's the most obvious thing in the world. "I hope you don't mind that you didn't get to rip the paper off yourself, but the situation was out of hand."

"And you've gotta eat. The Bandits expect you at one-hundred percent when you report back." Lilah opens the oven and the smell of bacon and cheese hits me, making my stomach growl loudly, proving her point.

"Speaking of baseball, what exactly is your plan?" Indie runs her hand over my daughter's head.

It's the million-dollar question. One I've gone over hundreds of times, and am still as uncertain of the answer as I was the first time. Kristy and I were supposed to split time based on my schedule. She'd have her when I was playing, on the road, or practicing. I'd have her anytime I wasn't. It gave us time to find a nanny. But she blew that up when she walked away, leaving me with no one to care for my daughter.

"I don't fucking know. How the hell am I supposed to trust someone else to watch her while I travel after . . ." My teeth grind together, halting the frustration that was about to spill. Regardless of my relationship, I won't poison my daughter with the anger I have for her mother.

Until I can process my feelings, I'll shut the fuck up. "A service sent over a few profiles for nannies. I have it narrowed down to two and I'll make my decision after I interview them."

"You know we will help as much as we can," Lilah says, over her shoulder. Her smile is sweet and reassuring, not at all pitying.

I swallow around the heavy lump stuck in my throat. "Yeah, I know," comes out on a croak that I don't try to hide. "Thank you. I'm not sure what I did to deserve this, but I appreciate it more than I can say."

They showed up not knowing how lonely this all is.

This is what I want for my daughter, to be surrounded by this kind of love. To be safe and cherished—everything a child should be.

Nothing like the way I was raised.

CHAPTER 2

VIVIENNE

There's no way . . .

I stop in my tracks, blinking. I've never hallucinated before, but there's a first time for everything. Either the man in front of me is a figment of my imagination, or Xavier Kingsley is a hot mess. Neither makes sense. The Bandits' catcher is always composed, polished, and maddeningly perfect.

Even in the unwelcome cameos he makes in my subconscious, he's infuriatingly sexy and unflappable. It's the one redeeming thing about him.

If he's going to drive me insane with his cocky arrogance, at least he does it while looking like a sex god.

But it's definitely him. Those broad shoulders and that unruly red hair are unmistakable. Nobody else fills out their baseball uniform quite like number seven. It's tragically unfair for him to have all that *and* mesmerizing blue eyes, a sharp jawline, and freckles that manage to be both rugged and charming at the same time.

Since he waltzed into my life a year ago, acting like an arrogant prick, he's been everywhere—billboards, interviews, and—unfortunately—back at my camp, again.

The universe is mocking me. Throwing the presumptuous baseball player that I'd love to fuck in my face.

Wait, what?

Forget. I definitely meant *forget*.

Especially considering the first time we met, he wrongly assumed I was some star-struck fan wanting to bask in his greatness. Little did he know, being pushed around and outnumbered by my brothers prepared me to put men like him in their place.

He straightened up fast when I told him I was the Director of Operations at Double Play, the organization running this camp for youth from under-resourced backgrounds.

But first impressions stick, and his was as damning as it gets.

Today, though, his cocksure attitude is pointedly missing, replaced with messy red waves that look sloppy in a way the man I met would never allow, and the gray shirt he's wearing is wrinkled, as if it came straight out of the hamper after barely passing a smell test.

When he turns to face me, any thought that I might be imagining things evaporates. It's him, but it's no longer the disheveled appearance that has my mouth hanging open.

It's the infant in his arms.

Who's baby is that, and why did he bring her to the stadium when he's supposed to be volunteering?

I scan the area, waiting for someone to step forward and claim the baby, but then I notice the dark circles under Xavier's eyes, and everything clicks. The wrinkled shirt, the shoes, the haggard appearance, it's all a dead giveaway. No one's coming for that baby.

I've seen that look on all of my older brothers as new dads. Leo, who's twenty years older than me, was a walking zombie when his wife had my niece Tenley. She might be in college now and living under my roof, but I'll never forget how she shifted my brother's life. He went from wild and invincible to a barely functioning, lovesick dad overnight.

Xavier's dull blue gaze sweeps the arena, almost helpless, before they land on me. The pitiful look in them knocks the wind out of me. He quickly drops his gaze to the baby, brushing a kiss on the fluff of red hair sticking up from her teal headband.

I shake off the distraction, turning toward the dugout where the other players are gathered, all ready to start. Well, everyone but the man with the baby, who looks like a lost child himself.

"What's the plan for today?" Dean Harrison, the Bandit's first baseman and a Double Play board member, asks when I reach the dugout railing.

"The bus should be here any minute. The kids will start with a tour before they come out onto the field for the camp," I explain.

Dean nods, adding, "We have five stations for them to rotate through. Cruz, Dom, Hendrix, Xavier, and I will each lead a group. The rest of the guys will float around and help as needed."

"Are you sure about that? Your catcher seems a little preoccupied at the moment."

Dean scratches his jaw, his focus falling on his teammate, who's still standing around like he's waiting for something.

"Are you going to deal with that, or am I?" I ask, leveling Dean with a glare I honed from years of solving everyone else's problems.

His attention shifts from me, back to the train wreck standing behind me. "He's been through a hell of a lot in the last two months. Cut him a little slack."

"That's fresh, you telling me to be nice. He's supposed to be coaching my kids, that's hard to do with a baby in his arms. I'm sorry he's going through it, but I have dozens of kids on that bus who've been looking forward to this for months."

My job is to be concerned about them first.

I've been taking care of other people since I was old enough to make mac and cheese. But babysitting grown men with kids of their own? That's where I draw the line.

Dean blows out an exasperated breath. "I'll see what's going on. His nanny was here to help earlier."

He jogs over to his teammate and I watch as they start talking, Dean patient and Xavier agitated, running a hand through his messy red hair. I should give them privacy, but my curiosity keeps me rooted in place. His lips press into a thin line as he shakes his head at whatever Dean says. Honestly, I feel bad. I'm still not sure what his deal is, but he's obviously stressed.

When he shifts the baby in his arms, his sleeves pull tight as he bounces on his feet. I'm impressed she's still asleep with how tense he is. Not even his movements can ease the tension in his jaw as his gaze darts around the stadium, searching for something—or someone—that isn't there.

But we need to get started, and if I can't rely on him, I'll have to bring someone else up to speed. I push off the wall and walk toward the two men, stopping next to Dean so we can figure it out.

"Can someone fill me in on what's going on?" Against my better judgment, my eyes trail over Xavier. There's a vulnerable look on his face I never expected to see him wear. His eyes wrinkle in the corner and he looks from his teammate to me.

"My um . . ." He makes one more slow sweep of the field. "My nanny disappeared."

I pinch the bridge of my nose. "Did she go to the bathroom or something? Nannies don't just vanish."

His jaw ticks and I can't tell if he's annoyed with me or the situation. "I don't know. She was here and now she's gone. That's the definition of disappearing."

"Is she coming back?" I look around, half expecting a woman to appear out of thin air.

"I have no fu—" His mouth slams shut and his eyes squeeze closed. His shoulders rise with his deep intake of breath and his lips move as he silently counts to three. "I couldn't tell you."

"Where'd the hot nanny go?" Braxton Hayes, the Bandits' resident troublemaker, shouts from the dugout, a shit-eating grin on his face.

Xavier whips around to face him, clearly pissed.

"We're going to take a walk while you figure this out," Dean says, lifting the baby from Xavier's arms without waiting for permission.

"What the hell do you know about it, Hayes?" Xavier snaps, once his daughter is out of earshot.

"I know *all* about Carly. She's fun. You take her for a spin yet, old man?"

My stomach churns at the way Braxton talks about a woman I don't even know.

Xavier steps forward, bumping against my arm as he does. "You've gotta be kidding me. What the hell did you do to her?"

"Nothing she didn't ask me to. In fact, she wanted more . . ." He clicks his tongue. "But I don't do repeats, which I told her when she cornered me outside the locker room earlier."

Xavier lunges forward and my hand shoots out before I can stop it, my fingers clasping around his wrist to stop him. "Don't. He's not worth it."

"Shit," he growls from somewhere deep in his chest, pressing the heel of his other hand into his eye.

This is a mess. The last thing I need is the kids witnessing a fight between two players they idolize. I spring into action, dropping my hand from Xavier's arm to grab my phone. "Hey, Tenley," I say when my niece answers on the first ring. "Are you busy?" After Braxton's stunt, I don't want him near my kids. I'll take Xavier and his terrible choice in nannies over that asshole.

"Can you come to the Bandit's stadium? I need help with an event today . . . Thanks, I owe you." I hang up and turn to Xavier, who's still as shell-shocked as he was when he realized no one was there to watch his daughter.

"No more drama today," I say firmly. "I know it's not your fault, but I have to consider what's best for my campers."

I stand my ground, trying to be firm, but then he looks at me wearing that lost expression, and tiny cracks form in my resolve.

As quick as I notice the fracture, I reinforce the walls I've built to protect myself. His problems aren't mine to fix—I've done that my whole life. And now that I'm finally living on my terms—away from my family's vineyard and embracing the freedom I love, I refuse to get sucked back into being a people pleaser.

"I hear you." His shoulders slump. He looks so contrite, so utterly defeated. It's heartbreaking, but it's not my problem.

Straightening my spine, I stand tall. "Glad we're on the same page. My niece will be here in twenty minutes to help. She's great with kids," I add, though she had little choice. When I left for college she stepped in to help with younger siblings and cousins, just like I had before her.

"I know I'm not in a position to make demands, but she stays here with Holland. I'm sure she's capable, but I don't know you or your niece well enough to let her walk away with the most important thing in my world."

Some of the cockiness I remember bubbles to the surface as he asserts himself. Damn it, why does my pulse quicken seeing him advocate for his daughter like that? I shove the unwanted attraction down.

"You're not in a position to negotiate. Either take the help I'm offering, or I'll find another volunteer. But if it makes you feel better, Holland and Tenley aren't going anywhere. She'll stay here with her while we run the camp, if that works for you."

"Yeah. That's fine." A weak cry comes from Dean's arms, where he's pacing the baseline with Holland. Xavier tracks his teammate as he adjusts his daughter. "And, uh, thanks for the help. I . . . um . . . owe you." Xavier's voice is distracted.

"You do. But I doubt you have anything I'm interested in," I call back.

CHAPTER 3

XAVIER

How the hell did I manage to make a complete ass of myself in front of Vivienne Cardoza again? Every time I see her something goes wrong, or my brain short-circuits and all my blood rushes to the wrong place.

At this point, there's no way Vivienne doesn't hate me, and I don't blame her.

She might be wrong about me, but she's right about one thing: she saved my ass. Only now, I'm drowning in the mess Braxton left behind, scrambling to find a new nanny and figure out how to repay Vivienne.

I want to knock him on his ass for what went down with Carly, but I can't take any more heat for my own problems today.

Vivi rolls her lips, watching me for a beat like she wants to say more, before turning sharply toward the dugout. She leans against the far side of the railing, studying the guys like she's bored, but I catch the curl of a manicured finger as she zeros in on Braxton. "Over here, rookie."

"Me?" He smirks, hopping off the bench. "I'm no rookie, but I reckon you can call me whatever you want."

"Huh, the way you act, I'd never have guessed you had much experience with being a teammate. Either way, you're free to go." Braxton laughs like it's a joke, but Vivi stands there, shoulders pulled back, eyeing her nails, barely sparing him a glance. "Think I'm funny, Hayes? You're the last person I want around my kids. From what I've seen, you're a shit teammate and a poor excuse for a human. That's not behavior we want to model at Double Play." She finally looks up at him, her gaze frigid. "If you're not going to listen to me, you can explain to your captain why Xavier's nanny left him high and dry."

A chill races up my spine. Vivi is bold, unyielding, and tough as nails.

And she might hate Braxton more than me.

My scorned teammate's mouth hangs open a moment too long, looking as dumbfounded as I felt when Vivi put me in my place last year. He recovers with a huff of laughter. "Fine by me."

He takes the dugout steps, disappearing into the tunnel below.

When he's gone, Vivi turns back to me. "Being pissed at him doesn't mean I've forgotten about you. Are you sure you're in the right headspace for this today? These kids need someone reliable and stable."

Forget what I said. She still hates me. Her words settle deep in the pit of my stomach, joining the weight of everything else.

"I've got it." It's not a claim I'm confident enough to make. I'm no better than a pile of hot trash at the moment, failing at nearly everything because I'm stretched so thin that I can't do any single thing well.

For fuck's sake, I forgot to pack diapers yesterday when I took Holland for a walk.

And that's nothing compared to the fact that, somehow, my nanny and teammate were fucking around after only a week on the job and I had no clue.

Dean strolls back, Holland fast asleep in his arms, and passes her off seamlessly. He makes it seem so easy, yet every time I try to set her down, she's wide awake the second I think about moving. I'd give anything to be half as good at this as he is.

"How'd you do that?" I ask, trying to sound casual.

"I got lucky is all." He pats my back, his pity making me flinch.

I might not have the hang of this dad thing, but I'm not suffering, not in the traditional sense. Having Holland is the furthest thing from misfortune. Pity has no place in my life.

I stand off to the side, useless as my teammates and Vivi go over the plan for the day. Doubt creeps in while they set up the stations. Someone else taking my spot would have been better for these kids, for Holland, for Vivi.

The longer I stand there, the worse it gets. My annoyance builds with every passing minute, until I realize I'm pacing, my teeth grinding together, jaw aching, and head throbbing. A whimper from Holland snaps me out of it.

My tension doesn't only affect me anymore, so I take three deep breaths, forcing my shoulders down. When I look up, there's a girl with dark hair and green eyes—not unlike Vivi's—bouncing over from where Vivi stands. She can't be more than nineteen, barely old enough to take care of herself.

"I'm Tenley, Vivi's niece, and you look like you could use help." She extends her hands expectantly.

"Are you infant CPR certified?"

"Sure am. I'm in nursing school. Don't worry, I'm not going anywhere. We'll take a quick walk behind the net, away from the flying balls and bats, and find a seat." She points to the safety of the area behind the dugout. "Promise."

I glance around, as if another option will magically appear—an experienced older woman with a whipped cream mask, perhaps. But all I see is Vivi tapping her foot, gaze narrowing in on me.

Right.

"Here's her bag. I'll be over there." I point to the station behind home plate. Grabbing the diaper bag, I lead Tenley to the seats. "Sit."

"You know I've carried a baby before, right?"

"I don't particularly care." My nerves are frayed and I'm being an ass, but all my control has been stripped away. "Look, I'm sure you're fine."

"*Fine,*" she scoffs. "Okay. I get the new dad stress, I've watched my uncles go through the same thing. The whole protective, scared thing? On brand. I sympathize. But here's the deal, you either trust that I can handle your baby for a couple hours—maybe feed her, change her—or you deal with *her.*"

She rises on her tiptoes, glancing over my shoulder. I don't need to turn around. I can feel Vivi's eyes burning into me. Tenley's grimace when she drops back down to the concrete confirms it. She's my only option.

"Oof . . . That vein on her temple is pulsing. That's when you know you're in trouble. Quick, hand me the baby for safekeeping because she's seconds from kicking your ass. You don't mess with her kids."

Tenley lips curve into a sugary sweet grin and she plops into the seat, arms extended, lashes fluttering up at me.

"Don't make me regret this," I threaten before folding like a cheap card table.

"You made the right choice. She'll be fine with me. You, I'm still a tad nervous for." Her thumb and pointer finger pinch together displaying a sliver of space between them as she smirks more brazenly now.

I sound as tired as I am when I say, "She's right behind me, isn't she?"

"Yep." Tenley pops the *P* dramatically.

"Is there a problem over here?" Vivi's emerald gaze rakes over me, heavy on the annoyance.

"Nope."

At the same time, her niece mutters, "Meh," with an indifferent shrug of her shoulder. The apple certainly didn't fall far from that tree. Both of the Cardoza women seem to enjoy putting me in my place.

"Then get your gear on and get out there." Vivi points to my station.

"It's in the locker room. I'll be right out."

She can't be more than five-foot-three, maybe five-four on a good day, but when she throws her hands in the air and pushes her finger into my chest, she towers over all six feet four inches of me. I've never been more terrified of someone so short in my entire life.

"Strike three is so damn close."

"Wh—"

Her fingers fly across her lips in a zipper motion. I shut up on instinct alone.

"You have two minutes. Grab your gear and come back out ready to coach. This stadium might be your house, but these are *my* kids, and for the next two hours, I'm *your* landlord. I know you have your own things going on, but I need your focus until we load the buses back up. Last chance to back out."

"I'm staying. Just give me a minute."

"Good." She smiles, and holy shit, I think it's real. "The kids are done with their tour and heading down the tunnel."

A curtain of espresso-colored hair swishes around her shoulders when she spins on her wedge heels and marches back down the stairs to the field.

Taking her lecture to heart, I break into a run, casting a backward glance to ensure Holland is settled. I duck through the dugout and head for the locker room. Once I'm beneath the stadium, I let out a ragged breath. Giving myself a second to breathe before I change, I make it my mission to get through the rest of the day without disappointing anyone else.

My daughter is at the top of that list, followed closely by Vivienne Cardoza, her kids from Double Play, and my teammates.

How a spitfire of a woman I barely know managed to wrangle her way onto that list is something I'm too exhausted to give any further thought to today. Seems like a problem for future Xavier, in eight to ten months, when I'm getting more than two hours of sleep at a time. Then I'll be rested enough to sort through why I care what Vivi thinks of me.

CHAPTER 4

VIVIENNE

After the chaos of today's camp, I need chocolate and an orgasm. Preferably in that order. Neither has ever failed me—at least, not when I'm the one in charge of them—and I need that kind of consistency right now.

Nothing kills the mood like crappy chocolate or those delightful tingles fading before they even have a chance to peak because your partner rolls over and gets up. Or worse, mutters the fatal words: *"You're good, right?"*

No, I'm not good, you nitwit. You've been diddling my left labia for ten minutes.

In comparison, today wasn't all bad. The camp was a success, despite the fact that I spent more time babysitting grown men than working with my kids. But after wrangling one stressed-out single dad and laying down the law with Braxton Hayes, I've earned a little self-care.

Intent on indulging in everything I deserve, I tug my silk blouse over my head—a small luxury from my "treat myself" era. Halfway off, the condo door slams closed.

"Aunty Vi!" Tenley's voice rings out, brimming with excitement. "I know you're home!"

I can't help the twitch of a smile as her steps grow louder. "In here, getting changed." Any second now, she'll launch herself onto the couch, dark chocolate in hand, waiting for me to join her and gush about her day. It's been our thing since she moved in, and I love it.

She's been my universe since the moment she took her first breath.

Our bond is unshakable. I'm part-big sister, with only ten years between us, part-best friend, because I was her only confidant in a house full of boys, and part-guardian, though I could never replace her mother.

Tenley was only two when Erica passed away at twenty years old. Complications during her brother, Cade's, delivery stole her mother before she ever really knew her. Buried in grief, my brother threw himself into work, leaving a void I stepped into without even realizing it. At twelve, I didn't think about the weight of what I was doing, I just wanted Tenley to be okay.

While Mom took care of Cade, I spent every free minute loving my niece— devoted to making her laugh when she cried for her mom, and holding her hand so she wouldn't be alone. Over time, as my older brothers added more kids to the mix and everyone struggled to keep up with the growth of the vineyard, I naturally became the family shepherd. My teenage years weren't spent at parties or dances—they were filled with diapers, feedings, and refereeing fights between siblings and cousins.

I swap my blouse for a crop top, pull on my rattiest sweatpants, and head to join Tenley because she still has me wrapped around her finger.

"I see you've donned your uniform." She's upside down on the couch, legs propped against the back, a bag of dark chocolate morsels resting on her stomach. Her phone dips as she gives me a once-over.

Tenley still looks adorable in the skirt and sweater she wore to the stadium— youthful, cute, and undeniably *her*. Growing up on a vineyard, I lived in boots and jeans. Now, a good dress or skirt makes me feel unstoppable at work. But outside the office? Comfort wins.

"You'll have to pry these sweats from my cold, dead hands."

"So . . . I take it you're staying in?" She flips, taking the chocolate with her and rearranges herself on the couch, giving me *the look*.

Avoiding her critical stare, I duck into the kitchen, grabbing two spoons and a jar of peanut butter.

"Yes. I'm all people-d out."

"I'm people."

I drop down on the couch next to her, holding out a spoon.

"But you're *my* people. And besides, I'm pretty sure you're half angel."

The laugh that bursts free from her sounds anything but angelic. "Far from it."

I tilt my head, pretending to consider. "You have your moments. Like today, helping with Kingsley's childcare emergency. I shouldn't have called you, but I was in a pinch." Pressing chocolate chips into the peanut butter piled on my spoon, I use the bite to silence myself before guilt drives me into over-apologizing.

Asking Tenley to step in felt a lot like crossing a boundary. Taking care of my younger nieces and nephews left me jaded and hypersensitive to asking for help, especially from family. But Tenley doesn't know how much it shaped me—and she never will. The last thing I want is for her to think she's a burden, then or now, when she's anything but.

"Are you kidding? Holland was perfect. If anyone's an angel, it's her. Best. Day. Ever!" Tenley squeals.

"That's great, but I'm sure it was inconvenient." My chest tightens. I love her kind heart, but I've seen it taken advantage of too often. I owe it to her to protect this slice of independence she got when she moved here for college—not just from guys like Braxton Hayes or Xavier Kingsley, but from me, too.

Tenley shifts, dipping her spoon into the peanut butter. "Not at all. Do you know if he still needs a nanny? I'm not taking any classes this summer. I could help." She's beaming, giddy at the prospect.

Giving it some thought, I stall, taking a spoonful of heaven for myself. "Are you sure that's a good idea? Shouldn't be focused on finding a summer job in your field and enjoying your time in college."

"Are you kidding? I'm literally going to school to be a pediatric nurse and all my friends are working this summer. Besides, I love kids, and the extra cash would let me get my own place next year."

The thick peanut butter sticks in my throat. Struggling to clear it, I ask, "What's wrong with staying here?"

"Nothing. I mean, I love you, Vi. There's no one I would rather be roomies with, but . . . Don't you want some space to . . . I don't know, bring home a date once in a while?"

"Dating is overrated. I have other things I want to accomplish, and I'm too busy to pretend all the mediocre men I meet are interesting."

"Why are you spending any time with mediocre men to begin with? Those aren't the kind we strive for." She waves her peanut butter covered spoon around as she continues her rant. "But if you don't want to date, you could host a party here, make new friends. The girls you worked with on the volunteer fair a few months ago, Lara and Indie, must know people they can introduce you to," she suggests, and I know she's grasping at straws because she's never even met Lara or Indie.

I scrunch my nose, offended. "I have friends."

"Harlow lives ten hours away. Your FaceTime chats hardly count as having company over."

My niece flashes that same crooked smile I've known since before she could walk—a clear signal of trouble. When she rubs her hands together, I brace myself, already knowing a setup is coming. This month alone, I've already turned down a barista, a random guy from the grocery store, and the new trainer at the campus gym that she swears are all perfect for me.

"I still think you should try dating. It doesn't have to be serious. Please let me set you up. I have this one professor—so hot." She scrunches her nose adorably. "Too old for me, but perfect for you. Or I could make you a dating profile. You millennials love your apps."

"Seriously? I'm barely a millennial. And no, you're not setting me up with your hot professor—wait, how hot are we talking? No. Never mind." I manage to sound serious instead of intrigued.

Her smile turns feral.

Dammit, he must be really hot.

"Say yes, please." She bounces on her knees. "I hate that you're alone."

I haven't been alone since the day I was born. "If I wanted to date, I would. It's not a priority for me."

And I certainly wouldn't use dating apps. Been there, done that. It's a swamp of men looking to hook up. Which would be fine if any of them showed even a bit of consideration for the women they were sleeping with. The algorithm only sends me guys who think the clit works like a doorbell. Press it once and someone comes.

"Make it one. You've never had a real boyfriend, and it's been a long time since you've even been on a date. It's just . . . tragic."

"Um . . . ouch. I've had a real boyfriend." Two, actually, my freshman year of college. Neither was serious, but I tried dating. All it did was take away from time I should've been studying. When it became clear that they couldn't handle not being my only focus, I cut them loose. Since then, it's only been casual dating and hook-ups. Both have left me unimpressed.

"This decade?" She deadpans.

My laugh sputters out. "Ten, you're relentless tonight. What's this about?"

"It's those sweatpants, they're making me mean. But seriously it's a Friday night, there's good dick out there, and you're here like a spinster instead of the hottie you are."

"Ten!"

"What? Everyone needs it."

I almost tell her I'm getting what I need. It's not like anyone's ever fucked me better than I can myself. Sure, there are things I miss, like the rough scrape of a man's hands against my hips, the look in his eye when he likes what he sees, the heat of a body against mine for post-sex snuggles. Companionship is nice, even if the sex is boring.

"No dating app, no professors," I say firmly.

"Whatever. You'll get bored when I move out."

"Are you trying to hurt me tonight?"

"Of course not." Tenley snuggles closer, her dark hair tickling my neck as she makes herself comfortable, setting her head on my shoulder. Then she shifts, turning those pleading green irises up at me.

They're a shade darker than mine and so much like her mother's. It's almost like Erica's with us when she looks at me like this. My beautiful sister-in-law was magnetic. Even as a child, I was drawn to her. Erica was part of our family from the first time she stepped foot on the vineyard.

She would *hate* that I haven't dated or made any real friends outside of work since moving here.

A choked laugh comes out of me. "You remind me so much of her, you know. She'd be so proud of you—for a lot of things—but this would make her the most proud. You, meddling in my life, making sure I'm okay, that was her thing. She was always fussing over me, but she was nicer about it." It's hard to believe that Tenley is almost the same age Erica was when we lost her.

Her eyes twinkle, and she kisses my cheek.

"What am I going to do with you?" I inhale the scent of her strawberry shampoo, letting it momentarily take me back to when she was little enough to crawl into my lap for a bedtime story.

"You could find out if Xavier still needs a nanny for me? Please." She bats those thick brown lashes knowing damn well it's my weakness.

"And how am I supposed to do that? I don't even have his number." Not entirely true. I have access to it through Double Play, but I would never abuse my position like that.

"You're the smartest person I know. I'm sure you'll figure it out."

Fucking menace, using praise against me like I don't know exactly what she's doing.

"We'll see."

She pumps her fist silently.

"That wasn't a yes," I remind her, holding out the peanut butter.

"Coming from you, it's as good as one."

I guess that's the thing about knowing her better than she knows herself—it goes both ways.

CHAPTER 5

XAVIER

The sudden jerk of my leg sends sparks of pain shooting through my toes. I curl in on myself, groaning when my forehead thuds against something hard.

"Fuck!" Dizzy, I fumble around, trying to make sense of the mess I've found myself in. Slowly, the room comes into focus, followed by pain.

My toe, my head, my hips—everything hurts. I suck in a deep breath and then the smell hits me. Sour, burning, potent—

Oh god, what is that?

Holland.

I'm on the floor of her room, having spent the night trying to settle her fussy little self.

Gagging, I push myself up, and before I can even process what's happening, a tiny whimper turns into a full-blown howl. Ignoring my pulsating toe and the bump I'm sure is forming on my head I bend over the crib to grab my daughter.

Oh, no. No. No. No.

Panic rises as I realize the smell is coming from her. I guess that explains the gas pains she had earlier.

I will not puke on my daughter.

I might screw everything else up, but that's the bare minimum I can do for her.

I rush into the bathroom, slamming my elbow into the light switch. Fight-or-flight kicks in with a shit-covered baby in my arms, and I spin in a circle.

What the fuck do I do? It's *everywhere.*

There's no way around it; I'm getting dirtier before either of us gets clean.

Now would be an excellent time to not be doing this alone, to have someone to hand me a towel or start the shower for me.

I hold my breath, cradling her against my chest as the liquid seeps through her onesie, coating my arms. The reheated chicken carbonara Hendrix dropped off threatens to make a reappearance.

Moving as swiftly as I can, I lay a towel in front of the tub and flip on the shower. Holland's screams bounce off the tile, each cry deepening the sinking sensation in my chest. Frantically, I strip her out of the ruined clothes and toss them straight into the garbage. Every cry cuts through me, leaving a mark on my heart.

"I know, Áine. I'm trying." Those two words are my constant refrain. Most days, I feel like I'm failing—like I'm not enough.

Something's wrong, and I'm more sure than ever that I'm screwing this all up.

It's isolating, beyond anything I've ever felt. To make it worse, Kristy won't answer my calls or texts. When she walked away, I thought she'd at least communicate with me. Instead, she blocked me on all social media and disappeared. What stings the most is that she left without discussing what's next, and I don't know if she ever plans to come back.

I step out of my sweatpants and check the water temperature, adjusting the nozzle until it's lukewarm.

She's so slippery. Please don't let me drop her.

I clean both of us up, but it does nothing to soothe Holland.

Running on so little sleep should be illegal, especially before sunrise.

After our shower, Holland squirms and fusses until dawn, then lets out a series of impressive farts and passes out on my chest.

I'm just starting to fall asleep again when Mia arrives with coffee and to relieve me so I can get to practice.

I make it to the stadium later than I'd like, and as I drag myself through the parking lot, the effects of last night linger.

Without my friends and their significant others, I'd be screwed. I've tried finding another nanny, but my trust is non-existent at this point. People have let me down my whole life—Kristy and Carly being the latest examples—and I can't take it anymore.

And seeing the effortless connection between Tenley and Holland . . . I want that. Someone calm with her when she's fussy, someone focused on her needs, someone not distracted by my job or teammates. A nanny who isn't afraid to call me out when I'm being overbearing. No one else is right.

"You look like shit." Worry etches a deep line between Hendrick's brows as he holds the door to the Bandit's stadium open for me. "Is everything okay?"

"Okay is a relative term right now. I spent my night on the floor next to my daughter's crib because she was fussy and woke up to a literal shitstorm." The dull ache that starts at my tight shoulder and wraps its way around my neck is a reminder of the toll doing this alone is taking on my body. I wince when I reach for the locker room door, holding it for my teammate.

"Nothing about that sounds okay. You need to find a nanny."

"Fuck, I know. I have an interview tomorrow," I say, following him to our lockers.

"Don't try to find something wrong with this one," Cruz chimes in from where he's tying his cleats. Dean and Dom come through the door behind me, each taking their spots to get ready for practice.

"I can't wait to remind you of that when you're looking for someone to help take care of your little guy in a few months." The all-business expression he was wearing melts away at the mention of his own baby.

"How's Lilah doing? My sister was miserable by this point in her pregnancy with Clayton." Dean's nephew was born a few weeks before Holland.

"She's amazing." Cruz beams, proud as hell and as awestruck with his wife as he's been since they realized there was more there than friendship. "Being able to stand the smell of coffee now that she's further along certainly helps."

"Have you guys started looking for someone to help when Lilah goes back to work?"

"Not really. Willa has a friend that's interested—we're kind of banking on that. And our parents will both come out to help for a few weeks." Lilah has a community beyond the team that I don't, including family and her employees at Buns & Roses, like Willa. I envy that kind of support.

"What about Vivi's niece?" Dom asks.

Dom voices an idea that's crossed my mind a few times since the camp. But Tenley's a college student. I need a permanent solution, not a short-term fix for the summer. But damn she was great with Holland. Finding someone like her, full-time, seems impossible.

"I'm sure my interview tomorrow will be fine." There's less conviction in my tone than ever.

Miller Murphy, our new manager who took over after Wilson retired, claps his hands. "I know you guys love to chat, but let's wrap it up and start practice, all right?"

"He's always so polite when he threatens us," Dom whispers a little too loudly.

"Would you rather I yell like I do at the delinquents?" Murphy responds, referring to the new guys who joined last year—Braxton Hayes included. They've made a name for themselves, not only because of their skills on the field, but also for their attitude and off-field drama.

"They deserve it," I say under my breath, still bitter that Braxton cost me my nanny.

"Did you tell Xavier yet?" Murphy asks Dean.

"Not yet. I figured I'd let him get dressed first."

"Tell me what?" I glance between the two.

"You took off so fast after yesterday's game you missed the team bonding while everyone signed the items for the gala auction. So I need you to stop by Double Play to do it this week." Murphy's half-smile fades as he adds, "And try not to piss off Vivi. The Bandits value our nonprofit partners."

"You got it, Coach." Fantastic. I'll find time for that.

Every year the Bandits host a gala to raise money for Double Play. All the players are required to attend.

Dean claps me on the shoulder. "I don't envy you."

"Yeah, thanks." I mentally tally my week, wondering when I'll make time for it.

It's not until the next morning, slightly more rested, that I realize I can swing by Double Play after my interview. I'm learning to multitask, but this shit is hard, and not enough people are honest about it.

"Morning, my little Áine. Did my girl have sweet dreams?" I lift Holland from the crib. She looks so much like my mom, with red hair and fair skin thanks to those strong Irish genes. The resemblance takes my breath away—a bittersweet reminder of what I've lost and what I have.

I push away the memories, focusing on the present. Baby-soft hairs tickle my nose as I kiss the top of her head. If you'd told me a year ago that inhaling her new baby scent would be my favorite way to start the day, I would've called you mad. Yet, here we are.

"We're going to find you a nanny who won't disappear on us today," I say, amazed at how much I talk to her like this.

After compulsively checking the diaper bag, Holland and I head out—only five minutes late, which might be a record.

Twenty minutes later, I'm praying the bell at Buns & Roses doesn't wake Holland as I wrestle the stroller through the door and into the warmth. I yank off my beanie, running my fingers through my matted hair as I scan the coffee shop.

A young couple is huddled in the corner—definitely not my nanny. There's a guy working on his laptop, a grandma with two grandkids, and a teenager waiting in line.

A whimper from the stroller reminds me to move, but I'm not sure where to go. There's no one here who fits the bill of the twenty-six-year-old nanny I'm supposed to interview.

"Did you bring Holland to see me, or is she keeping you up all night again and you're just here for my coffee?" Lilah steps out from behind the counter, peeking into Holland's stroller with a grin. "She's the sweetest."

"Mhmmm, especially when she sleeps well, like she did last night."

Lilah straightens, hand resting atop her stomach. "So, a regular amount of caffeine today? No need for an IV drip?"

"Let's not go crazy. I'm still a single parent." I glance back to the seating area, hoping my interviewee showed up while I was talking. No such luck. The same crowd is here, but now the couple in the booth is kissing, coffee forgotten.

"You didn't happen to have anyone stop in looking lost or asking for me. I'm supposed to meet a potential nanny here for an interview."

"I didn't see anyone. Want me to check with Willa? She's in the back, but was helping customers earlier."

"No. I'll send her a text. It's possible we got our times mixed up." Like a beacon of disappointment, I look at my phone to see a text preview showing a message from Teddy.

TEDDY SINCLAIR:

Sorry for the late notice, but I have to cancel our interview. The family I used to work for let me know they're expecting again and looking for help. I hope you understand.

"Son of a . . . biscotti." I catch myself at the last minute.

"Everything okay?" Lilah asks, her nose scrunching because she already knows the answer.

"No, I guess we'll be taking that coffee to go. Back to the drawing board with nannies. On the bright side, I have plenty of time to get to Double Play now."

"So, a double shot of espresso, then."

"Why the heck not?" I agree, following her to the counter where she works on the opposite side, making my drink.

She hums as she works, her back to me, and I realize whatever she's doing is more involved than my macchiato. Spinning around with a flourish, she hands me a brown bag and sets down two drinks.

Wincing, she grabs her stomach. "Oh, that one hurt."

Panic hits. "Shit, Lilah, is it contractions? Do I need to call Cruz?"

Her hand closes over mine, pulling it across the counter. Despite the discomfort, she looks overjoyed. "Just an elbow or foot. See?" She waits a beat, then places my hand on her bump. "We're fine."

"Oh, wow." I pull my hand back, rubbing my neck, my gaze shifting to Holland. "That's . . . wow."

"Kristy never—*really*?" Her smile falls.

"Things weren't good when she came back. She could barely stand to be around me, and there was a lot of animosity. I missed out on a lot." Without realizing it, I've started rocking the stroller back and forth, a habit I picked up to soothe Holland. Only right now, I'm not doing it for her sake.

Her hand lands on my forearm. "I'm so sorry, Xavier."

I shrug. I'm not okay with how things went down—how things continue to be—but there's not much I can do about it.

Instead of explaining my very complicated feelings, I point to the bag. This is more caffeine and sugar than even I need.

"One for you and one for Vivi. Plus some treats, in case you need to earn some brownie points."

"Does everyone know she hates me?"

"Hate's a strong word . . . lacks patience might be more accurate." Tapping her finger against her chin she pulls the bag back before I can take it, adding two cookies. "In case your third impression fails as badly as your first two."

"Your husband's a gossip," I tease, taking the bag from her before she can add in her famous sticky buns. I'm not that hopeless.

I don't think.

CHAPTER 6

VIVIENNE

There's a DILF staring at me with sad eyes for the second time this week, and it makes something twist uncomfortably in my chest. It's like the universe knows my weakness and is exploiting it. I can't help the way it pulls at my people-pleasing heartstrings.

He's standing in my office doorway looking so . . . wholesome. Like he's genuinely trying to make up for everything that's gone wrong between us, and that's part of the problem.

"Xavier," I greet him, keeping it cool. My attention flicks to the stroller, the two coffees, and the bag from Buns & Rose. If he's going to interrupt my workday, at least he didn't come empty-handed.

"Hey, Vivi." His voice is gravelly, like it's been raked over the coals. It's probably how he sounds first thing in the morning. Damn it. Even tired and sad, he's attractive. I hate that it makes me want to fix everything for him.

"Murphy told me to stop by and sign some things for the gala auction." Xavier ducks his head looking almost . . . embarrassed. "I guess I missed out the other night when I rushed home to relieve Mia from watching Holland."

A wave of guilt ripples through me. He's still without a nanny—no wonder he's tired. How long can this go on?

Tenley's face flashes in my mind—the way she lit up when she was talking about her time with Holland. Even though it was short, the little girl made an impact on my niece.

I force the mask I've perfected over the years into place, keeping it professional, but not letting him see the cracks in my resolve to keep him at a distance. "Over there," I say, pointing to the table with the papers. "I'll grab you a Sharpie and some pens."

My resistance is slipping, and I hate that it feels so natural.

It takes longer than expected to find Sharpies. The container at the front desk is empty, so I head to the supply closet. Distracted by my phone, I almost walk into the doorframe as I return to my office. But it's not the door that stops me.

Perhaps it's Tenley's recent push for me to date, but I'm suddenly questioning why I'm drawn to Xavier. He stands with his back to me, bent over the stroller, feeding his daughter. The softness in his voice as he whispers to her melts me, and the sight of him—ruggedly handsome with red hair sticking up from the beanie he was wearing—makes it clear he's completely devoted to Holland.

What a way to be loved, I think.

But standing here, watching Xavier, feels wrong. My neck prickles uncomfortably with my reaction to him. It's unlike anything I've felt before. Normally, I can shut my emotions down and focus, but with him around, everything blurs.

As much as I hate to admit it, Tenley was right: I need to get laid. Well and quickly.

And he looks like just the man for the job.

My vagina needs to calm down and stop shouting. I'm the one in charge here.

For some asinine reason, I cross my legs, like he might actually hear my wicked subconscious. "Sorry about that," I say, like I haven't been lurking. "The markers went missing. I had to go track some down."

Excellent, now I'm rambling, which I don't do.

He looks over his shoulder and his lips curve, giving me the sense that he knows how off-balance I am right now. It annoys me to no end that he's having this effect on me right now. I don't like feeling flustered and out of control, especially not at work.

"That's okay. I've got nowhere else to be . . ."

He pauses long enough for me to cut in. "Can I get you a chair?" I'm not sure if he was done, but I'm so desperate to keep things moving that I don't care all that much if my social etiquette is borderline rude, so I settle for professionally accommodating.

"Nah. She won't let me sit long anyway, and I'd probably doze off if she did." The weak laugh he gives me tells me there's truth behind that statement.

"Okay. Let me know if you need anything." I keep my distance, dropping everything on the table. "Water, more pens, and markers. You know, the necessities for signing."

For a second, I'm grateful he's too busy with feeding Holland to notice my clipped tone.

"I'll be quick and get out of your way so you can work."

Guilt twists my stomach. I want to apologize, but I want him out of here more.

CHAPTER 7

XAVIER

I wouldn't say I know Vivi well, but I can tell she's uncomfortable. Professional composure can't hide what her stiff body language is screaming. She wants me out of her office. After our last two interactions, I'm not surprised. Every time she sees me, I'm a walking disaster.

Her back is ramrod straight as she stands beside her desk, shuffling things around needlessly. So I do the one thing I can to make her more comfortable, uncap a pen and grab one of the balls waiting to be signed. Before picking up the next one, I risk a glance over my shoulder, catching sight of Vivi stretching to reach her phone on the opposite side of the desk.

My foot that's rocking the stroller falters at the sight of her bent over the desk. She has to push up on the toe of one of her black heels to reach the device, and the green dress she's wearing pulls tight across her heart-shaped ass. For the first time in a long while, I take a moment to appreciate her beauty—like really appreciate it—because you can't be in the same room and not notice Vivi. She's got it all. She's sharp, focused, and has really distracting curves.

In another life, I'd have already made a move. But I'm not that guy anymore. I'm surviving, not thriving. And until I can carve out more time, relationships will have to wait.

I'm halfway through the pile of memorabilia when a cry comes from the stroller. Holland only got a fraction of her bottle earlier, and the half-ass job I'm doing of rocking the stroller while I sign isn't cutting it.

I've learned to do a lot one-handed over the past month. If I can manage a shit-covered shower without dropping her, I can finish signing this stuff while I hold her.

Unbuckling Holland, I scoop her out of the stroller and cradle her against my chest, suddenly wishing I had taken Vivi up on that chair.

There's an audible sigh from behind me, and when I turn towards Vivi, her eyes are closed and she's muttering under her breath. I don't get the impression that it's directed at me, but I've misread her before.

This seems like the worst possible time to interrupt her, but I ask anyway. "Um. Do you think I could get that chair?"

Her eyes open and she pushes back, but doesn't look up at me. "The chair is really the least of your worries, isn't it?" Or at least I think that's what she says, but I can't be sure. She might be talking to herself with the way she's rambling.

I fight a chuckle I know she wouldn't appreciate.

"Let me take Holland so you can focus on signing, and I can get back to work."

I hesitate, unable to pinpoint why. It's not a matter of trust, it's a matter of wanting to prove I can do this.

"That's not—no. I'll take the chair. I can sign while I hold her—"

"Xavier, stop. I know you can, but I need you out of my office at some point today. Please let me help."

I sigh, running a hand through my hair before conceding. "You're sure?"

"So sure. I know I'm not as warm as Tenley, but I promise you I don't hate babies."

Her self-deprecating comparison to her niece bothers me more than anything else she's said. She can be blunt, but to hear her think that about herself sparks a protective instinct in me I've only felt for a few others.

Holding Holland close, I walk over to Vivi, bending to her level. I look her in the eye and say, "Whoever made you think you weren't warm was a fucking idiot." I let the obscenity slip in front of my daughter because it's important Vivi knows how serious I am.

Her green irises meet mine, their softness stirring something inside me. I'm not sure I deserve the tenderness she's offering, and the irony isn't lost on me—I'm about to give her a lesson on her own worth.

"I know cold—I've seen it firsthand, and you're so far from it . . ." I shake my head. She doesn't need my tragic past, so I focus on what I've learned about her. "You can't run this place without having a selfless heart. Anyone who's spent even a minute with you in the presence of Tenley or the kids you work with every day can see the protective fire in your eyes. You're not just warm. You'd burn down the world to make sure the people you love have everything they deserve. Hell, you even stood up for me and you don't even like me."

"Did not."

There's the heat I was talking about, dancing wildly as she tips her chin up at me.

"You *so* did." She didn't have to save my ass. She could have sent me home, but she didn't. "There's very few people that would stand tall in front of Braxton and professionally tell him to pound sand, but you did, for me."

She licks her lips and I trace the movement, all too aware of how close we are right now.

"No, I did that for me. I really didn't want to work with Braxton."

I shake my head. "Whatever you say. I like my version better."

When I get an eye roll in return, it feels like the closest thing to a win.

Vivi doesn't wait for me to pass Holland off, taking her from me like she's done it thousands of times before. "Go sign things. We can't have you disappointing all of your *fans*."

"Was that—Are you teasing me?"

She hums, her teeth pinning her lip, holding back what I know would be a stunning smile. "Let me tell you about the first time I met your dad. Doesn't that sound like fun, Estrela?" She rolls the *r* so effortlessly that I can tell it's an endearment she's comfortable with.

I want to ask her what it means. But I don't get the chance because her voice shifts to a sweet whisper as she rats me out to my daughter with the embarrassing story of the time she rightfully handed me my ass when I assumed she was a fan, not just a woman doing her job.

A lump forms in my throat as I step back and I can't explain why. The simplest answer is fear—fear over Holland not having her mother in her life. But there's something deeper, something about seeing someone else look at her the way I do, as if she's everything pure and good in this world. She deserves that.

The air in the office is too thick, and I'm more determined than ever to get this over with and leave. I block out the sound of Vivi's chair squeaking, and the gentle hum of her voice as she talks to Holland. I focus on signing one ball after another, then move on to bats and jerseys, trying to drown out the pull in my chest.

By the time I cap the Sharpie and turn around, I'm raw. As if one glance from Vivi could strip me bare and reveal all my shortcomings.

With every intention of getting the hell out of here, I turn toward her desk, finding Holland asleep in her arms. Like a natural, Vivi taps at her phone, using the thumb of her free hand. It's funny, I would've never described Vivi as cold, but the way she looks right now is more serene than anything I could have pictured.

The room seems to expand around me, and the suffocating tension I felt a moment ago lifts. I sit on the table, watching her finish the message, one eyebrow raised, but otherwise completely at ease.

"Want me to take a selfie so you can stare some more?"

A soft chuckle rumbles out of me, but I don't hate that idea nearly as much as I should considering she didn't correct me when I pointed out that she doesn't like me. "You'd have to have my number to send it to me."

"Too bad." She hums, her mouth curving and revealing a dimple I hadn't noticed before. She lifts her chin, and the softness in her expression vanishes, replaced by the professional demeanor I'm more familiar with. "It's none of my business, but what are you going to do about a nanny for her?"

I scratch at the stubble on my jaw. These days, shaving only happens when it becomes unbearable, or when Holland finally goes down for the night without too much fuss. Vivi follows the movement, studying me with quiet attention.

"Some of the wives and girlfriends are helping, but I can't keep relying on them. It's not fair—they've got their own lives. And Cruz and Lilah are going to need help too when their baby arrives."

"So, you're going to find another nanny?"

I let out a frustrated laugh, tipping my head back and staring at the ceiling for a moment. I'm doing everything I can, but it still feels like I'm falling short, and I don't need a reminder of that.

She must sense the misstep because she quickly adds, "The only reason I'm asking is because Tenley really enjoyed spending time with Holland. She hasn't found a summer job yet." Her voice falters a little now. "This might be a terrible idea, but she asked if you were still looking for someone. I'd never hear the end of it if she found out I saw you and didn't check."

That's not at all where I expected this conversation to go.

Her face and her words don't match; I can read the hesitation written all over her pursed lips. "Listen, you don't seem sure about this. If you have doubts about Tenley watching Holland, maybe it's not the best idea. Besides, how would it work with her school schedule this fall?" I ask.

"It's not about Tenley's ability—there's no one more caring. She'll treat Holland like her own."

Vivi's gaze drops to Holland before returning to me. Her brows are drawn together, and her expression is serious, studying me like I'm the threat. It's the same protective instinct I have for my daughter.

"There would need to be rules, clear expectations. When school starts again, Tenley is a student first and a nanny second. Her hours would cut back, drastically. She can only be a piece of the solution, not the whole answer. If this impacts her studies—"

"It's over," I answer for her.

"She can stay when you're out of town, but no moving her in. She's young, and needs time for friends—distance from the job when she's off—a life outside of work."

Her protective instincts are on full display now, laying down boundaries. The implication that she's calling the shots on my childcare doesn't sit well.

Sadly, I'm all too aware that I'm out of options and time.

"Anything else?" I try to mask my annoyance.

"Not right now, but I reserve the right to change my mind."

My tongue rolls against my cheek. "I wouldn't have it any other way."

"I need to talk to her, make sure she still wants to do this. You two can meet and work out the details after that."

Do I want a woman that doesn't like me calling shots on my business? No, but Tenley is my best option. "She's lucky to have you."

It's true, even if it's just my way of smoothing things over.

"Listen, I know it sounds crazy, but in my family, if you don't go to college, you work for the family business, and I want her to have options." Vivi stands, gathering Holland into the stroller with one last lingering look. She straps her in, then turns to me. "Now, get out of my office so I can do my job."

"I think you're forgetting something." I adjust the buckle on Holland's chest, even though it's fine.

"Doubtful," she volleys back, but the corner of her lip twitches up a little.

Grabbing a Post-It and pen, I scribble my number down, then place it in the center of her computer screen where she can't miss it. "My number, so Tenley can reach out to set up a time to talk. *If* she's interested."

Vivi plants herself behind the desk, her fingers digging into the back of her leather chair. Her tongue rolls over her teeth, trying to keep quiet.

"I let you set your rules, and I respect where you are coming from, but I'm going to set some of my own. First, she has to want to do this. I can't go through another nanny that's going to walk away. And you both need to understand where my daughter is concerned, I am in charge. You can't be in the middle of this all the time. I'll do everything you asked because I'm a decent person, but I don't want you trying to dictate things. Tenley would be my employee. End of story."

"Fine," she says, pulling the sticky note from her screen and dropping into her chair, dismissing me from her office.

CHAPTER 8

VIVIENNE

I stand in the middle of my blissfully silent living room looking between the knockoff Peloton I bought with my first big girl check and the book sitting on the arm of the comfiest chair known to man.

It's a tug-of-war between what I should do and what I want to do.

The school year is almost over, and preparations for our programming to switch over from after school to day camp are well underway. Which means I've been extra busy with staffing and planning on top of everything else, like the six-foot-four catcher taking up space in my office a few days ago.

My teeth seesaw over my lip as I take a tentative step toward the bike. I could always read later, but when I give the embossed flowers on the cover one last parting glance, the switch flips and I think *fuck it*. What the hell was the point of moving out here, building this life for myself, if I don't do what I really want to?

The bike can wait. I *want* the serotonin that comes from reading a romance novel.

Channeling the same energy the kids had earlier, I dive into the chair, crack open the pages, and try to ignore the fact that I keep picturing the male lead with red hair even though it's brown.

I'm lost in the story, doing my very best version of male narration—extra bravado coloring my voice with the building tension. I'm so focused on my amazing cowboy impression when I say, "Hands on the hay bail, darlin'," that I don't hear the door open.

I tilt my head back and laugh at how ridiculous I sound, but it's abruptly cut off by the scream I let loose when I find Tenley staring down at me from where she's standing behind the chair, barely containing her laughter.

"What the hell, Ten! Why are you creeping around?"

"Don't stop, it was just getting hot. And you know I love a cowboy romance." Tenley leaps into the oversized chair next to me, sticking her nose right in my book. "Oh shit. That's, like, really good. Should I leave you alone?" She thumbs over her shoulder.

I slam the book shut, my cheeks already flushed from the reading. "No. This can wait. Tell me about your day."

"I got the job!"

The joy vibrates off of her, and even though I might not have been thrilled with the idea of her nannying for Xavier, there's no chance I'd stand in the way. She's beaming, her big smile glowing brightly, so instead of warning her about all the ways this could go wrong, I wrap my arms around her.

"Congrats. I'm happy for you." Stifling her by placing my own expectations on her would trap her in the same way I felt trapped when I was younger. I still have concerns about how this is going to work during the school year, but for now, I'll stay quiet.

"I start next week. He's going to have me watch Holland during the gala."

How had I forgotten that I'd have to see him at the gala and why is he suddenly everywhere I am? Tenley bumps my shoulder, sensing my tension, and I relax.

"Speaking of the gala . . ."

I groan in exasperation, knowing exactly where this is going.

"Do you have a date?"

"It's a work thing, not a social outing," I justify.

Tenley rolls her eyes, scoffing. "Do you at least have a semi-unprofessional dress? It is still a gala. You can't wear a high-neck sheath dress."

"Can't I?"

"Not unless you want to look like you get a monthly clothing allowance from Ann Taylor. And is that really the look you're going for? Think about all the potential sugar daddies . . ." She hums. "Baseball players and wealthy donors."

I cock my head in confusion. "And why the hell would I want a sugar daddy?"

"You made it pretty clear you don't want to date, but I thought you might enjoy a mutually beneficial pairing." She says it like it's a totally normal suggestion.

While I've succeeded in raising her to be a functioning adult, society and social media said, "Hold my beer and watch this."

"Has anyone ever told you that you're slightly unhinged?"

"Nope. But my aunt nurtured my creative imagination growing up. So, who's really to blame for the way I turned out?"

"I have no regrets." Truthfully, she's the coolest person I know, even if she sometimes lacks boundaries.

"So you'll let me pick out your dress?" We bump into each other as she bounces next to me, half-turned in my direction and hands clasped in front of her chest.

"That's a bold leap."

"But will you?" Cue the puppy dog eyes.

"Fine."

Her smile widens, and she falls back against the cushions dramatically. I never planned to say no, but it's more fun to make her think it's a possibility.

When she's done making a show of sighing in relief, her grin turns from elated to devious. "And hair and makeup? Wait and see. You're going to look so hot when I'm done with you."

"Hey, that was rude."

"Don't act all hurt. You know as well as I do that you always look gorgeous. I'm just going to help you kick it up a notch—do a full beat. Oh! Some shimmery green eyeliner on the inside corners. Yes, that's what you need."

As she skips off to her bedroom to make a list, I mentally prepare myself for the hours of prep she's going to put me through.

Although, doing something lavish for myself sounds nice, I'll give her that.

Tenley's To Do's:

Help Vi find a dress that slays
Pick up a new eye shadow palette from Sephora before the gala
Search Tik Tok for hair inspo
Pick up mints to slip in her purse
Buy 27 Matte Forest Green for Vi
Cut bangs???

CHAPTER 9

XAVIER

Going to this gala is absolutely the last thing I want to do tonight.

As far as managers go, Murphy has given me more flexibility than most would. But tonight is mandatory for all players and I'm not interested in ending up on his, or the front office's shit list for ditching.

Coincidentally, it's also the perfect opportunity to give Tenley a test run before she watches Holland during games and practices where I'm less accessible.

The doorbell rings, and when I open it and find Tenley, alone, my eyebrows pull together. Vivienne was supposed to come with her and then we were going to ride together. Tenley insisted it was practical since she doesn't have a car. We agreed she'd use one of mine moving forward.

"Look at you, giving off main character energy in that suit. You're a solid seven."

"Seven?"

"With the suit on," she repeats slowly, letting the veiled meaning sink in.

"You remember I'm your boss, right?"

"And you remember the last nanny you had diddled and dipped, right? Would you prefer I had an unhealthy attraction to older baseball players?"

Yeah, that's a fair point—one I can't contest. I look to my side, catching my gaze in the mirror. "It's the dark circles I'm sporting, isn't it?"

"Sure. If that makes you feel better. Where's Holland?"

She flits past me, breezing through the house like she owns it, while I stand in the doorway, confused. "Holland's in the swing, in the living room!" I yell at her back, still standing at the open door. I swing it shut as I move to follow her and figure out what's going on when something stops the door from closing all the way.

"You almost took my toenail off and that definitely would have been strike three."

Vivi's sweet voice sounds lighter and more relaxed than when she usually talks to me. I turn, finding her framed in a halo of light from the setting sun, making her look like an angel standing on my front porch.

I already know she's pretty, but nothing could have prepared me for seeing her in something other than her professional wardrobe. It sucks the air from my lungs, leaving me completely defenseless.

Her dress is black with threads of gold that make it look like it's woven from stars. The bodice clings to her curves, giving her cleavage that makes me weak in the knees, and layers of sheer fabric fall in panels, giving way to a slit that hits high on her thigh.

This dress was made to highlight all the dangers her body poses to my sanity, but it's outmaneuvered by the woman wearing it.

Her dark hair is pinned in an elegant twist, leaving the long column of her throat exposed. Her eyes glitter like emeralds, accentuated by a flick of iridescent green liner. I've never paid this much attention to a woman's makeup before, but I'm mesmerized.

What's even more ridiculous, I can't stop staring at her neck. Her hair is usually down in perfect waves, hiding it from view. Now, with it bared, it feels intimate—like she's inviting me to lean closer, to catch the scent of her shampoo.

I force myself to meet her gaze and open my mouth, but nothing comes out. There's only so long I can stand here gawking before it gets awkward for both of us, so my gaze drifts over her one last time, trailing lazily up her body.

Stepping aside, I gesture for her to come in. With her back to me, I take a steadying breath and lick my lips, ready to try again. Taking a calculated risk, I rest my hand on her lower back, guiding her toward Tenley in the living room. She doesn't slap it away, and that small mercy gives me the courage to speak.

"Vivienne, you look incredible."

She tilts her chin up, curiosity flickering across her face and sending my thoughts into chaos.

"I mean, you always look great, but tonight—wow—you know?" I run a hand through my hair, a habit I've picked up lately, and then quickly drop it, remembering I'm supposed to look presentable tonight, not like an exhausted dad.

She chuckles softly, and I can't even be embarrassed, not even when it's clear she's laughing at me. Because for once, she doesn't look annoyed or like she wants to murder me. Instead, her eyes sparkle with amusement, and I soak up every second of it like a man starved.

"Thanks." She lifts a finger, tracing the outline of my jacket lapel without touching it. "You look . . ." She takes a shaky breath, and I swear I see her shiver before dropping her hand. "You look really nice too, Xavier."

A little flustered by her attention, I smooth a hand over my jaw.

The irritation I'd felt earlier about going, fades. Tonight might not be so bad. For a few hours, I can be something more than just a dad—starting now.

I lead Vivi to the living room, where we find Tenley, lying on her side, deep in play with Holland, who's gurgling up at her. The sight melts away some of the dread over leaving.

"You know, Tenley told me I was a seven. At least one of you has some sense," I say, playfully.

"I told you, you were a seven *with* the fancy suit. Don't overinflate my praise." She doesn't even bother looking up from my daughter as she insults me *again*.

Vivi hums thoughtfully, her gaze sweeping over me, and for the first time since learning I was going to be a dad, I care about something unrelated to my daughter, or baseball. I want her to dispute that and tell me that a seven is way too low.

"Are you hearing this? And I'm supposed to walk out the door and trust her with my daughter after that?"

Vivi looks between us, holding back her laughter as if she's trying not to encourage us while we lob snarky remarks back and forth. It's the most like myself I've felt in months.

"You might be mid on a good day, Big Red, but your daughter is perfect everyday. Me and my new bestie will be just fine here tonight while you two kids get up to whatever it is you do at these stuffy galas." Tenley waves us off, her focus remaining on my daughter the whole time.

"We really should get going before we're late to the stuffy gala," Vivienne says, all business again.

I cross the room and scoop Holland up, pressing a kiss to her head. "Love you, Áine." Looking from my daughter to Tenley, I hesitate. "You've got your phone, right?"

She waves it between us. "Your number is programmed in there, and I can call Vi."

"She's got a fresh diaper on and I fed her right before you got here. She'll need another bottle before we get home. I left everything out where it's easy to find. The bottles and formula are on the counter and there's a fire extinguisher under the sink . . ."

Tenley rolls her lips together and I stop, realizing I'm spiraling.

"Breathe, we've got this." She models taking a deep calming breath and, without thinking, I mimic her.

This is hard, harder than leaving her with the girls, but Tenley stares me down, waiting patiently until I hand my baby back and rejoin Vivi. "Shall we?"

When I reach the edge of the living room, I glance back to check if she's following. She's still standing in the middle of the room, not paying me any attention, mouthing *"mid"* to my nanny with a raised eyebrow.

Tenley catches me but doesn't give me away. Instead, she smirks at her aunt and shrugs.

Yeah, Tenley and I are going to get along fine. It's her aunt that has me thoroughly perplexed.

CHAPTER 10

VIVIENNE

I've come to the realization that red-headed men are a terribly underappreciated demographic. Not that I think this particular man has ever been lacking female attention, but the way he looks in his tux, hair styled and a hint less messy than I'm used to, is something to be appreciated.

He walks around to the passenger side of a flashy sports car that looks like it costs more than I make in a year.

Our arms brush when he opens the door and I have to suppress a shiver. "I hope you don't mind if we take this." His rich, masculine scent wraps around me. It's deep and timeless, like well-worn leather, and I want to know if it's cologne or him, but it's so subtle that it's gone before I can place it.

I look over my shoulder. "*Oh no*, please don't make me ride in your fancy sports car."

An endearing blush creeps up his cheeks, almost like he's embarrassed to have something so nice.

"Holland's car seat is in the other car, so I want to leave it here for Tenley." He's talking about the very nice, albeit less flashy, Cadillac SUV parked next to the Audi.

"Really, this is fine," I assure him.

Xavier's hand lands on the back of my neck, gently helping to guide me so I don't wreck my hair by bumping it on the low door frame. If he wasn't flustered, it might come off overbearing. Instead, it's painfully sweet.

Looking at my lap, I busy myself, getting situated against the soft leather. Xavier leans in, more brazen, like the man I first met, making a breath catch in my chest. "Say the word and I'll drop you off and circle the block before I park and get out so that you aren't photographed with a seven."

The velvety warmth of his words wash over me, and it's my turn to blush. I might have hated it the first time he hit on me, but I can't help but find his self-deprecating sense of humor tonight endearing.

Perhaps that's why I give into my impulse to tease him back. "She was wrong, you know. You're at least an eight in that tux." Flirting with him feels good, so I add, "It's very flattering."

With that, he smirks, shutting the door and jogging around to the other side.

He joins me in the car and stretches his arm behind my seat, turning to put the car in reverse without using the camera, making him somehow hotter.

Competency kink unlocked.

It takes me a minute to get a hold of myself as we make the mostly quiet drive to the hotel. The air between us is still and heavy.

Work with the Bandits aside, Tenley watching Holland means that we'll probably be bumping into each other more. So, instead of letting the stifling silence continue, I break it. "Are you excited about having a night out? I imagine those have been scarce."

His knuckles flash white as he flexes his fingers around the steering wheel. "Not in the slightest."

"Oh." I'm not really sure how to process that. The Xavier I first met was cocky—arrogant, even. The second time I saw him, he was beyond flustered. Tonight, he's vacillating in-between—going from teasing to shy. All of those versions of him are true, but I don't think any of them are *really* him, and I wonder what he's like when he's able to relax and just be himself.

"I hate leaving Holland behind when I already spend so much time away from her during the season." His eyes shift from the road to me. "Sorry. I know this night means a lot to Double Play, and to you, but they'd raise as much money without me."

We would and the baseball season is long. He's going to miss a lot.

From what Dean has said, Xavier is Holland's primary parent. It's none of my business, but now that Tenley's involved, I can't help my curiosity. Or at least, that's how I justify why I care. "This shouldn't all be on you. What about her mom?"

"Not in the picture at the moment." His words are sharp, bitten off like they taste sour.

The hardened tone catches me off guard. I've never seen him mad like this. The pain in his voice is pointed and new questions ricochet through my head. *At the moment? How much more is he facing that I'm not aware of?*

It's humbling and the regrets about how I've reacted to him in the past are immediate. So I say the one thing he probably wants to hear more than an overdue *I'm sorry*. "If you want to leave early, I can catch an Uber home."

"Nah. I should stay. It'll make Murphy happy, and it gives Holland time to get used to Tenley." He sighs, then adds, "Besides, my friends have been hounding me to take time for myself. Hopefully tonight will shut them up."

"Being the only parent isn't easy. And they say you can't pour from an empty cup." Vulnerability clogs my throat because I might not know what Xavier is dealing with, but I think I know how he feels. I've always struggled with balance. It's why Tenley keeps trying to get me to date and make more friends.

"Technically, I'm not."

"Not what?" I ask, confused by my drifting thoughts.

"The only parent." He sighs. "Kristy, Holland's mom, left, and I don't know if she plans to come back. But you're wrong about the empty cup. Holland fills my cup, baseball fills my cup, my friends fill my cup. My cup is full."

That pulls my focus back inside the car. I watched my three older brothers manage life as single parents, all for different reasons, so I know a thing or two about how much dedication it takes to do it well. "That might be the most sincere thing I've ever heard you say."

He laughs. "Well, you don't think very highly of me, so I'm not surprised."

"Keep showing me this side of you instead of the guy I met the first time you volunteered for Double Play and you might change my mind."

"Yeah, that guy was a jackass." He smirks, but it doesn't light up his face the way it should. "Kristy and I had fought, and I was frustrated with the situation, but it's no excuse for how I talked to you. I was feeling sorry for myself—that I'd let someone who treated me so poorly have such a big piece of me. But that's not who I am. Not really."

"Can I let you in on a secret? A man that takes accountability when he's wrong is actually a pretty big turn on for a lot of women."

"Is that so?" His eyes sweep over my body.

"Well, I mean, I don't want to speak for my entire gender, but I appreciate the apology."

"In that case, do you think tonight can be our fresh start?"

"Hmmm." I tap my chin, pretending to consider his proposal for a moment. We've both had moments we wish we could take back. But with Tenley watching Holland and life throwing us together, a fresh start is exactly what we need. "Yeah, I think it can."

"Does that mean you're willing to walk in with an eight?"

That makes me laugh. He sounds so serious, but the light is back in his eyes, shining like a beacon in the dark car. "With a heartfelt apology like that, you elevated yourself to at least an eight and a quarter."

He holds my gaze, granting me a crooked smirk that makes my inside sizzle. "I'll be a ten before the night is over."

"Don't be so sure about that." It's strange that I'm so at ease, teasing him like this.

I'm shocked to admit that Xavier Kingsley's not half bad. And he's sure as hell no eight, not even close. He's been at least an eleven since I saw him in his tux.

But I like that he has no idea how he's affecting me.

CHAPTER 11

VIVIENNE

This is not my first gala. It is, however, the first time I'm arriving on the arm of a player, and I'm trying not to think too hard about the fact that I've dropped my professional wall enough tonight to allow it.

For one night, the glitz and glamor of Hollywood is set against the majestic backdrop of the Rocky mountains.

Xavier eases up to the curb, putting the car in park, and when I reach for my door handle he tsks. "Don't move."

"That's not really—"

"I'm working my way up to a ten and you're not about to ruin it by refusing to let me open your door like a gentleman."

Before I can answer, he's out of the car and rounding it, and I use the seconds alone to pull myself together.

Confidence looks good on Xavier. Seeing him playful and demanding does something to me I didn't expect. The cocky catcher who's always grated on my nerves is stirring something else entirely tonight.

It's too bad Xavier's not the kind of guy I can hook up with and forget. Our lives are too tangled. And like I keep telling Tenley, I'm not interested in dating. Dating leads to serious relationships, the kind that take over your life, and I need more time to live life on my terms.

In a perfect world, I'd find the consistency of someone who cares about my experience, without the obligation of more. I've had enough of frustrating one-night stands. Still, I can't help but think that if *more* were on the table, Xavier doesn't strike me as a man who leaves the job unfinished.

He opens the door and holds out his hand to help me out of the car. Warmth floods me, turning my insides to mush. I can almost feel his hand gripping my hip, guiding me down the red carpet. The rough scrape of his calluses against my skin, the firm, claiming hold . . . it's too easy to imagine.

"Are you just gonna stare at it?" His low chuckle pulls me from my spiral. I glance down at his hand, then back up at him. He raises an eyebrow, silently teasing. *It's only a hand.*

I learned long ago how to take care of myself, but the slide of Xavier's rough palm against mine as he helps me out of the car is a startling reminder of how long it's been since someone *else* made me feel anything.

He hands his keys to the waiting valet. And then it's not just my hand in his, it's his fingertips searing me through the fabric of my dress where they rest lightly at the small of my back. Then he's guiding me away from the car. If Tenley had talked me into wearing the backless dress she loved so much, I'd be in all kinds of trouble.

It's not until he pauses in the middle of the red carpet that I realize the photographers are about to take our picture together, looking very cozy.

"Oh, um, I'll just—" I gesture toward the door. "I can head inside."

His face falls, and the sight makes my chest pinch. I rush to add, "You don't really want your picture taken with me. You're just being nice to make it up to me."

"Don't tell me what I want." His voice is firm but gentle as he nudges me closer. "I'd be an idiot not to want you at my side. You're the star of the show, and you shine like it tonight. Stunning and bright."

And just like that, I relent. Letting him pull me against his side, I look up at him and I can't stop the way my lips curve as the cameras' flashes ignite around us.

"That wasn't so bad, was it? I didn't even break anyone's camera."

"An impressive feat for an eight and a quarter."

He holds the door for me and I catch him doing a fist pump in the lobby mirror.

The ballroom is already humming with conversation and laughter when we walk in. It doesn't take long to spot our table. Dean, Mia, Dom, Indie, Hendrix, Poppy, Cruz, and Lilah are gathered there—the women seated together on one side, laughing loudly, while their partners linger on the opposite side with drinks in hand.

Dean specifically asked me to sit here to highlight Double Play's growing partnership with the team. But even knowing that, I still feel out of place. My relationship with the guys is strictly professional. And, aside from Indie, I've barely spent any time with their partners.

Xavier leans in close, pulling out my chair. His breath caresses my ear when he asks, "Can I grab you a drink?"

I open my mouth to tell him he doesn't have to do that, but he cuts me off.

"I'll just grab you a glass of champagne. I can tell by the way you stiffened you were about to give me the brush off again." We're so close as he pushes in my chair that I doubt anyone can hear us over the music, especially when his next words are so low they're almost a whisper. "You should probably know I don't do anything I don't want to. If I'm offering you something, I mean it."

His raspy, confident voice sends a jolt through me, and I can't help but imagine what other ways I'd submit to him if he used that tone differently.

"Champagne sounds perfect." I force myself to look unaffected by the hot current that runs up my spine.

"Thanks for making that easy."

"I aim to please," I say with a light laugh, a sentiment that used to be all too true. This time, though, it feels like a choice.

I watch as Xavier joins the guys, noticing how easily they greet each other—like family—exchanging hearty pats on the back. Everyone except Dom, who pulls Xavier into a full-bodied hug.

It's only when Xavier's back is swallowed up by the crowd that I realize the laughter and chatter at the table has quieted. I turn to find the attention of my tablemates on me.

Lilah, rubbing a hand over her belly with a knowing smile, speaks first. "You came with Xavier and you don't look like you want to strangle him."

"And I'd heard you were the sweet one in the bunch." I laugh.

Indie, sitting opposite me, nods. "Don't let her fool you. She's sweet but nosey."

"It's really a lethal combination. She puts you at ease with that sweet face and then, bam, you're spilling your life story to her," Poppy adds, lowering her voice as if sharing a secret. "If I'm honest, it's gotten worse during pregnancy. Now that she's only got a few months left, she's almost all momma bear."

"Awe, I love when you share our origin story," Lilah jokes, giving Poppy a playful bump with her elbow before turning her focus back to me. "But I'm more interested in hearing about what's going on with *you*."

I'm grateful when Mia cuts in, saving me from the interrogation. "Are you excited? Tonight's a big deal for Double Play!"

I nod. "We've been working hard to get ready and I can't wait to see that all pay off."

"God. You're such a badass, pulling all of this together *and* giving a speech in front of all these people. I'd throw up all over the stage. But you're always so poised up there. I'm honestly a little jealous," Lilah says, squeezing my arm in a show of support.

"Do you ever picture the audience in their underwear, or is that advice as useless as it sounds?" Mia asks, scanning the room and pausing when she catches sight of her boyfriend.

I laugh, at ease with these women as they welcome me into the fold.

"Can't say I've ever tried that trick." Although, I might tonight. My gaze is drawn to where Xavier is standing with his back to me at the bar before I turn to Mia again and add, "I don't mind the speech. It's better than rubbing elbows with the donors by myself all night."

"Somehow, I doubt you'll be doing anything alone tonight," Indie says, her focus off in the distance. I turn my head to find her staring at the place I was. This time, Xavier and Dean are both leaning against the bar, watching us while the others wait for their drinks.

"I'm sure Dean will do his fair share of schmoozing—it's the one time he's not the grump. He lets his Beacon Hill blood shine through when it counts."

Mia shakes her head, smirking. "She wasn't talking about Dean."

I'm being ganged up on in the friendliest way possible, but I'm still not sure how to react. I glance back at the bar. Hendrix is still waiting for his drinks with the four others watching and waiting. With all the attention on me, I feel like I'm under a microscope.

"Our catcher hasn't taken his eyes off you since you walked in. There's no way he's leaving your side tonight."

"That's ridiculous. He gave me a ride because Tenley is watching Holland. Nothing more."

Mia cocks an eyebrow at me. "Sounds practical."

"It was," I assert. "I get it, you guys all are matched up with hunky baseball players, but that's not what's happening here. We agreed to a fresh start for Tenley and Holland's sake, but that's all."

"That's too bad, because he's walking back over here and the way he's looking at you is anything but friendly."

"I love it when Dom looks at me like that." Indie's get a dreamy look on her face as she talks about her husband. It's the first time I've seen her like this—the definition of smitten. Our relationship is professional, but friendly. This side of her, though, is different, softer.

"God, yes. The sex is always hot. Always. But when they get all possessive . . ." Poppy's bare shoulders tremble. "Especially after a game. There's nothing like it."

Four heads nod along with her, sly smiles tipping up all of their lips.

I laugh loudly. "As happy as I'm for you guys, that's not something I can relate to. At best, sex has always been mediocre for me"

"Mediocre . . . like you've never come?" Indie whispers, her shock widening her eyes.

"Not without a self-assist," I admit, shrugging it off.

Just then, the roughness of a warm palm brushes over my shoulder.

"Thank you," I squeak out, praying he didn't overhear. Considering we were on shaky ground until a few hours ago, that's definitely more information than I want him to know. Besides, I'm sure a man like him can't possibly relate to my mediocre sex life.

"Dance with me, wife," Dom says, pulling Indie from her seat.

"I don't know . . . dancing with you only leads to trouble." Her voice is playful, but she looks up at her husband with so much admiration. It's an intimate moment between the two, but when she doesn't immediately stand, he hauls her out of the chair and into his arms.

Two by two, the table empties until Xavier and I are alone.

"You know what's great for forging new friendships?" Xavier asks, leaning over the back of my chair so his lips are close to my ear. He's everywhere I look— one arm braced on the table in front of me, the other brushing my shoulder. God, he's big when he surrounds me like this.

"Well, if you're anything like my best friend Harlowe, it's a spit handshake."

His chuckle rumbles through me, warming my body with each vibration. Xavier's got an incredible laugh—deep and smoky, a little mysterious, and I like earning that sound from him.

"Maybe we save the spit for when we know each other better . . . but I'd really like to share a dance with you."

Heat crawls up my cheeks. My conversation with the girls has hot, dirty sex on the brain, and his voice so close to my ear isn't helping. It's all too much, making my already-heated blood boil.

"Dancing could be nice," I finally say, praying the walk to the floor is enough of a reprieve to get myself under control.

Xavier pulls my chair out and I stand, following him as we weave through the crowd. I remind myself that he's just trying to make up for the first impression he made and give us a fresh start. It helps me regain some composure, and by the time we reach an open spot on the floor, I'm a little steadier.

At least, until Alexander Nate's "save this dance for me" starts up. The soulful beat and Xavier's arm sliding around my back so his palm lands on my hip make for a potent combination.

There's an intimacy in his hold as he easily glides us around the floor. I'm surprised at his grace when he spins me around only to pull me close, like the lyrics describe. His sure movements exude confidence and I choose to focus on the fact that I'm oddly proud of him for finding his footing after the camp, and not the way dancing with him has my whole body tingling.

As if he can sense I need a second, Xavier pulls his gaze from me. After a long moment, his eyes settle back on mine. "I know I already told you this, but it bears repeating. You're beautiful."

Not "you look beautiful," or "your dress is pretty." This gorgeous man thinks *I'm* beautiful, and he's not shy about telling me.

His words settle over me like a warm blanket and a flutter stirs low in my stomach, a combination of nervousness and something else. I open my mouth, ready to thank him, but he's not done.

"Seriously, you took my breath away when I saw you standing at my door." He fingers the strap at my shoulder, making that ripple in my belly turn into a full-blown earthquake.

His sapphire eyes are filled with intense earnestness as he focuses on me, like he's watching to make sure I really hear him.

No one's ever looked at me with such intensity. All I can do is whisper a "Thank you" before I hide my face in his lapel to escape for a moment.

For the second time tonight, his rich scent fills my senses, and it does nothing to help my scattered thoughts. Instead, it's like a drug, melting my resolve further with every breath I take. My head spins, and my pulse quickens, and for a second, all I can think about is how badly I want to be closer to him, swallowed up in that warmth and intoxicating smell.

The dance ends too soon, but the effect lingers. We stand there, as the music fades, the MC's voice a distant hum I can't focus on. Xavier stares down at me, lifting a hand to brush a strand of hair from my cheek. The moment seems suspended in time, and I wish it could last all night.

"Stunning," he whispers, looping the strand behind my ear. Goosebumps break out on my neck and chest as his fingers brush down the length of my neck. "Thank you for the dance."

I clear my throat, blinking up at him as I try to make sense of how a simple touch affects me so deeply. "Of course. How could I say no to someone who's so clearly a nine?" I joke, trying to ease the nerves prickling through me.

"One more to go." His velvet laugh washes over me, and it's almost too much on top of our proximity, especially after that dance.

The floor around us has emptied, so I step back, breaking our connection in an attempt to preserve what's left of my sanity. "I could use some water before my speech."

He doesn't call me on my cop-out.

Instead of ordering a drink like I expect him to, he grabs water for himself as well. It didn't go unnoticed that he came back empty-handed when he grabbed my champagne earlier, too. Curiosity wins out as I say, "Just because I'm having water doesn't mean you can't have something else."

His measured exhale lands softly between us as the server hands him my water, and he slides it to me. "I've never been much of a drinker, but since Holland was born, it's lost its appeal . . ." A pause stretches out before he continues. "My dad was an alcoholic, and I never want my daughter to see me like that—or not be able to care for her because I've had a drink."

I'm not sure what to say to that, other than the truth. "I'm sorry you had to go through that, but I'm glad you're breaking the cycle."

His shoulders rise and fall in an indifferent shrug. "She will always come first."

It's so matter-of-fact and I don't think he understands what a big deal it is, but I've seen it time and time again at Double Play—parents not putting their children first. "You're a good dad, Xavier. Dare I say a solid ten?"

He doesn't boast or pump his fist. Instead, he gives me a small smile and a heartfelt, "Thank you."

CHAPTER 12

XAVIER

The only sounds filling the dark nursery are the soft gliding of the chair and the gentle sucking as Holland drinks her three a.m. bottle. That, and the noise in my head—the thoughts that started after the gala and have only gotten louder since.

Vivi's a puzzle and I've spent five nights trying to piece her together. She's breathtakingly beautiful, willfully strong, stubborn as hell, and kindhearted in a way that makes everyone she meets want to be better. And she's brilliant. I saw it firsthand during her speech and after in the way she could connect with anyone and everyone.

But then, there's that conversation at the table. That admission she made to the girls about her mediocre experiences with men. I can't wrap my head around it. Vivi Cardoza—a woman any man would be lucky to have—hasn't had a single, memorable, sexual encounter? It's a fucking crime.

And my cock is more than willing to be the one to change that.

But that's where we hit a wall. My priorities are clear. It's Holland— always Holland. No matter how much I want Vivi, no matter how badly I want to be the one to show her what she's been missing, I won't put anyone ahead of my daughter.

Until I get a handle on being a single parent, my dick can wait. But that's where things get uncomfortable because it means someone else is going to take the job from me. My body riots at that thought, like it goes against every fiber of my being.

"It's really a fuc—freaking problem," I whisper into the darkness. The only thing I can come up with to explain why that bothers me, is that Vivi brings out the parts of me that have been dormant since Holland was born.

For a few hours with her, I let my guard down and wasn't just Holland's dad. Dancing with her, earning her laugh—it brought back the playful side I feared was gone.

But somehow, Vivi and the flimsy truce we formed seem to be the missing piece to that puzzle.

This is a riddle better solved when I'm fully awake.

Tenley's been here every day since the gala, helping with Holland while I'm at practice or games. We're still finding our routine, but it's incredible how much the extra help has improved things. I'm not on the edge of drowning anymore. Now, when I leave, I can breathe easy knowing Holland is being cared for the way she deserves.

The sucking noise I've been surrounded by stops and I look down to find the bottle empty. Propping Holland against my shoulder, I pat her back until I get a good burp out of her.

"That's my girl," I whisper, my voice raspy. "Back to bed, Áine." I settle her on her back, swaddling her tightly, the way she likes, before I drag myself back to my room.

I've barely fallen asleep when my alarm goes off a few hours later. Pulling the monitor from the nightstand I see Holland still sound asleep. After throwing on a pair of shorts, I head to the kitchen and grab the premade smoothie I thawed last night. Tenley researched how to make them ahead of time so my mornings are easier and she's been keeping my freezer stocked. With the drink in hand I head downstairs for a quick workout.

I keep it light since we play this afternoon, checking the monitor between sets. I'm almost done with my last set when Holland starts fussing, ending my workout.

With Holland happily strapped to my chest, I pop my breakfast in the microwave, making her bottle as she sucks contentedly on her pacifier.

When the timer goes off, I bring our meals to the living room. Unstrapping her from the carrier, I settle next to the rocker, my breakfast burrito on the coffee table. Pre-making food I can eat with one hand has been the key to success in the morning.

"Teamwork makes the dream work, right, baby girl?" At first, talking to her felt ridiculous, but now it's better than the lonely silence when I don't.

It's not long before she's finished her bottle and I'm pushing off the floor to take our dishes to the kitchen. I glance over at her before grabbing the notebook Tenley brought on her second day.

She sat me down and said, "Communication is a vibe, Xav, and I need you to get it together." Then she showed me how to log Holland's bottles and diapers to keep her on a consistent schedule between the two of us. The parenting books taught me the basics, but my new nanny's methods are practical for keeping us organized.

Basically, this notebook is my new best friend.

Another thing I've learned is that the bouncer Poppy and Hendrix got me is a godsend. Bringing it to the bathroom when I shower has been the best parenting advice so far.

I'm realizing that accepting help, even when it's uncomfortable, doesn't make me a failure.

Fresh from my shower, I walk into the living room, shirt flung over my shoulder and Holland in my arms to find Tenley walking through the door.

"Are you ready, my little starlight? You're going to help me write an essay for my advisor while your dad beats the Roadrunners into the ground," she singsongs as she takes Holland from me. "And tell your dad to wear a shirt, his nipples make me uncomfortable."

"Sorry." My apology is muffled by the shirt I'm quickly pulling over my head.

"Oh, don't worry, it's not in like a sexual harassment way. Your unkempt smattering of chest hair makes me sad for you and no one likes a sad nanny."

My laugh catches me so off guard that I snort, loudly, startling Holland and making her cry.

"See what I mean. You've made her cry with how depressing it is."

"It's not like I have a ton of time on my hands," I remind her, pulling my collar back when Tenley's too distracted to glance down at my chest.

The hair I normally trim is longer than I used to let it get, but I didn't think it looked bad. I thought it was rugged, manly.

I find myself wondering what a certain brunette would prefer.

Shaking away the wayward thought away, I look up to find Tenley staring at me, dumbfounded.

Thankfully, she lifts her gaze to the ceiling, letting me off the hook. "Well, I'm here early today, so bump grooming that to the top of your to-do list, Ginger Daddy."

I cringe. "Nope. Do not call me that."

"Yeah, you're right. You can't pull it off."

"On that note, I'm going to grab my bag and head to the stadium before you abuse me further."

"It's not abuse, it's caring. Stop and grab yourself a cup of coffee. You look tired," she says, taking Holland down the hallway towards her room. When she gets to the door, she spins back toward me, a grin splitting her face. "Actually, I follow Buns & Roses on my socials and I saw they had a special on sticky buns today."

Insult aside, that actually sounds really fucking good. Lilah makes the best pastries, and there's nothing like a coffee fresh from Buns & Roses.

Tenley and my daughter disappear and I can hear her singing a song that has to be made up because it contains all sorts of complex sounding medical terms in lullaby form.

On my way out the door, I grab the signed paperwork my lawyer needs to have the private investigator track down Kristy and serve her a court summons because nothing with the custody case can move forward until they find her. It's stressing me the hell out.

I'm still unsure what I'll do once we find her. All signs point to her not wanting to have any part in Holland's life, but I owe it to my daughter to find out for sure before filing to terminate her mother's rights in a few short months.

It all makes me sad, and a sticky bun can't cure it, but it won't hurt either, so I head to Lilah's coffee shop, dropping my notarized paperwork in the mail on the way.

And when I walk into Buns & Roses, sitting right there with her head bent over her laptop among the crowd of people buzzing around the shop is the woman that's been haunting me ever since I overheard her imply that she's never had good sex.

STUDY ABROAD: MASTER PLAN

- Convince Vi to start dating
- Figure out how to get Ginger Daddy and Aunt Vi together
- Get Transcripts
- Scheduling a meeting with Advisor
- Write essay
- Get letters of recommendations
- Complete application by Nov 1st
- Save money from nannying
- Tell Vi about Spain
- Have Vi help me tell Dad

CHAPTER 13

VIVIENNE

I'm not one of those people who thrive on working remotely—I never have been. And most days my job doesn't accommodate it because we have volunteers and kids in and out all week. But today, I don't have a choice. There's a small construction project happening, and they needed to turn off the power for most of the day.

At least coffee tastes better when I don't have to make it. This morning, when I was bitching about not being able to work from the office, Tenley suggested making Buns & Roses my office and the deal on sticky buns sealed my fate.

I've been parked at a corner table all morning, working on finalizing the volunteer scheduling for summer camps. The coffee shop is alive with its usual soundtrack—a hum of conversation, the grind of espresso machines, and the clink of mugs against saucers. It's chaotic, but it doesn't bother me. People are always in and out of my office at Double Play.

When a shadow falls across my table, I assume it's someone passing by, so I keep my head down and finish what I'm working on. But the person doesn't move on.

I glance up to find a tall, broad baseball player standing over me. He looks good—rested, even. Tenley watching Holland seems to have done wonders for Xavier. The dark circles under his eyes have faded and his smile comes more easily. As long as there are no issues with it taking away from her life outside of work—namely, school—I'm happy it's working out.

"Xavier," I say in acknowledgment.

"Are you here for the sticky buns too?" He drops in the seat across from me, a coffee in one hand as he slides a bakery box across the table toward me. He pops the lid open, revealing fluffy pastries glazed in gooey sweetness.

"There's a small remodel happening at the office; I'm working here against my will. But the promise of a sticky bun as a reward was the tipping point," I explain, my mouth watering at the sugary smell invading my nostrils.

"I'm a big fan of the dessert first theory. Why deny yourself something so good?" he asks, his voice dripping with innuendo, and I can't help but wonder if we are still talking about sticky buns.

He adds two forks to the box.

I bite my lip, stopping myself from reaching out and taking one of the forks. "What are you doing here?"

"I stopped to grab coffee on my way to the stadium and I couldn't resist the two-for-one deal."

"Yes, but what are you doing at my table?"

"Two sticky buns sounded like a good idea. But now I'm not sure I'll be able to eat both of them." He sighs like it's a real tragedy and glances over his shoulder at Lilah, lowering his voice. "And I won't be able to throw it away. I would feel too bad."

My stomach growls loudly, halting the half-hearted brush-off I was about to give him. He holds out the fork for me, and I take it.

"Besides, if you don't help me eat them I'll end up taking it to the stadium with me and the guys will fight over it. We can't have that kind of petty energy in the clubhouse." Without missing a beat, Xavier digs in, pulling a piece of the sticky bun off and popping it in his mouth, chewing before he says, "Have I told you that your niece is terrifying? I think it's the Gen Z in her; she gives zero fucks about offending me. I can't even imagine how badly she'd roast me if I didn't feed you."

"She's someone you want on your side, that's for sure." I press my fork down into the doughy creation and I cut off a small piece for myself—savoring the bite and the break from work.

He takes another piece, chewing slowly, and I find myself oddly mesmerized by the way his throat works as he chases it down with a sip of cold brew. "Somehow, her lack of filter and strong meter for bullshit make me more comfortable leaving Holland with her."

"She'd burn the world down before she let anything happen to your daughter," I say, meaning every word.

"Seriously, you should be proud of her. Despite not knowing what's going to come out of her mouth half the time, she's an amazing person, and she's going to make a great nurse."

It's one of the few things he could say to render me speechless. Pride wells up, tightening my throat until it's hard to swallow. The emotion is too much, and I'm afraid of what might slip out if I try to speak.

I grab the fork instead, tearing off a piece of sticky bun and chewing slowly.

We're barely friends, and he's Tenley's boss. Sharing that I more or less raised her—and why—is too personal. Like revealing a scar I'm not ready to show.

The obscene moan that pours out of me when I bite into the gooey center of the sticky bun is the accidental distraction I need. I'd be mortified if there wasn't a tiny orgasm happening in my mouth. It's honestly the closest I've come to heaven in a while.

Across the table a throat clears, Xavier's knuckles are white and the veins in his forearms pop as he grips the fork in his own hand. When my eyes lift to his, they're squarely on my mouth. I reach for the napkin and dab at the corner, but it comes away clean.

"So . . ." I take my time pulling another piece of the airy dough off. "Things are going okay with Tenley?"

"Ah . . . yeah. She was singing Holland a song about the absorption and metabolization of drugs when I left. My baby is going to be smarter than me by the time she's six months old."

"She'll be ready to rule the world before she's out of diapers. That's how Tenley was—she could have run an entire country by the time she was five."

He laughs, but it's the kind of knowing laugh that makes me think he's picturing it. "I kind of like it. Maybe her time with Tenley will stick with her and she can do something more meaningful with her life than catching and hitting a ball for a living."

"What you do is meaningful," I assert.

He scoffs at me and it makes me angry because I see the impact athletes have on kids every day.

"You don't believe me? Stop by Double Play. You'll find dozens of kids that idolize you because the game means everything to them. It gives them hope and a goal to work toward where they otherwise might not have it. It gives them an escape when things aren't great at home. That's why I was so annoyed when your nanny up and left. Those kids deserve the best and the drama with Braxton was not it."

"Yeah. It was bullshit." His voice drops, rough and raw. "I know better than anyone how much your kids rely on Double Play. My mom died when I was young, and after that . . . baseball was all I had. It saved my life." He exhales, a hand raking through his hair. "You had every right to be frustrated with the situation. It might not have been directly my fault, but I'm sorry it made your job harder."

Silence hangs between us. I'm not sure how to respond to the revelation that Xavier's childhood wasn't so different from the kids I work with every day. I knew his dad was an alcoholic but I just assumed his mom was around.

It explains so much—his need to do things on his own but also why he tolerated the way his ex treated him.

"It's water under the bridge," I say, bringing us back to his apology.

"I hope you didn't think I was minimizing what you do. Double Play fills such an important need, but sometimes I get so focused on giving Holland the childhood I didn't have that I lose perspective."

"Xavier, it's fine." I place my hand on his arm, a small gesture meant to reassure him. "It'd take a lot more than that to hurt my feelings." His gaze flicks to where our hands connect, so I pull back, adding, "I get it, though—the drive to give someone you love more opportunities. I'm the same with Tenley."

He nods slowly. "Did you mean it, about stopping by Double Play?"

"Of course. The kids love when players drop in. Help with homework, play a little catch—they'd lose it over a new face. Between us, Dean's around so much he's lost his sparkle."

He looks down at his phone, his face changing from relaxed to tense when he sees the time. "Shit, I lost track of time. I've got to get to the stadium, but it was good to see you."

"Good luck tonight."

"Who needs luck when I got a full four hours of uninterrupted sleep last night?" he jokes, standing from the table.

My teeth roll over my lip as I watch him go. It's the honest to god truth that catchers have the nicest asses. Forcing my eyes back to my computer is nearly impossible, but the fear of him catching me checking him out is enough to have me dropping my gaze and hiding my heat-stained cheeks.

Just then, my phone buzzes with a text from the contractor that power is back on in the office.

Looks like my field trip is over.

HOLLAND'S DAILY LOG:

11:30 – 4 oz bottle

11:45 – Poopy Diaper

Napped for 2.5 hours

2:15 – 4oz bottle while she watched some baseball game

2:30 – Blow out during your at-bat.

I think she was mad you struck out. Do better.

3:50 – Wet Diaper

4:00 – Went for a walk

4:25 – 4oz bottle

5:15 – Wet Diaper

VIVI'S NUMBER IN CASE OF EMERGENCY: 720-370-6019

CHAPTER 14

XAVIER

"You're sure you're okay with her overnight?" I ask Tenley for the hundredth time.

She taps her foot impatiently. To be fair, I've lost patience with myself too. Logically, I know Holland is in good hands and will be totally fine with Tenley for the three-day road trip, but I can't help it.

In my defense, I was the same way leaving her with the girls when they were helping me right after she was born. Nothing prepared me for how terrifying this part of being a new dad is. *Nothing.*

"We've got this. You have Vivi's number in case of an emergency, and I have the contact information for the entire Bandit's organization, their spouses, the front office, and her pediatrician."

"Yeah, okay." But nothing feels okay. I hate leaving her.

"Does it make you feel better if I tell you Vivi is coming over to watch a movie tonight? So there will be an even adultier adult with us."

"A little," I admit.

"I mean, she basically raised me, so we know she can't make it worse."

I lean in, momentarily distracted from the pit in my stomach by Tenley's insight. It explains a lot about her aunt's protectiveness and makes me sad for Vivi, who would've been a kid herself when Tenley was born. But now's not the time to unpack it, especially with a plane waiting on me.

"That's not the confidence builder you think it is," I say with a frown, the pit back and deeper than ever at the reminder that I have to get on a plane and fly away from my daughter.

"Was that a joke?" Tenley fakes shock, looking down at Holland. "Say goodbye to the comedian, Holland. If he doesn't leave, the traffic on I-70 will make him miss his flight."

"Point taken. I'm leaving." I drop a kiss on Holland's head and grab my bag, looking back when I get to the door. "And Tenley, please don't forget to—"

"Don't worry, Ginger Daddy, I'm going to send you all the pictures and texts."

I let loose a sign of relief, ignoring the nickname for once, muttering a relieved, "Thanks."

It's irritating how often Tenley's right. Especially with how smug she is about, well, everything. If I hadn't left when I did, Murphy would've been blowing up my phone. As it stands, I'm the last one on board.

The crew wastes no time finalizing prep and securing the cabin. Sliding past the coaching staff, I take the empty seat across the aisle from Hendrix, Cruz, Dean, and Dom, who are already buckled in and deep in conversation.

As we taxi, the engine's roar drowns out the ding of my phone. I catch the notification pop up and grab the phone from the armrest while fastening my seatbelt. It's a picture of Holland doing tummy time with the message, "Be prepared to be sick of me," punctuated by the smiling devil face emoji.

"That's fucking cute," Hendrix says, leaning over to see the picture on my phone. "How are you holding up?"

I shake my head, unable to lie. "I'm a mess."

"That's not true. We've seen you when you're a mess," Cruz cuts in. "This seems pretty normal for a new dad leaving his kid with a new nanny, for the first time." His forehead creases, and I can see the realization hit him—he's going to be in my shoes soon.

Dean smirks, glancing at Cruz's pale face. "And we're going all the way this year, too. You better take notes from that football player who flew his wife's doctor out to postseason games."

"That's actually brilliant," Dom adds, clapping Dean on the shoulder. "Ideas like that are why we keep your grumpy ass around."

"Too bad you gave up your rights to that private plane," Cruz says with a faint smirk. "Would've come in handy."

Hendrix clears his throat, pulling everyone's attention. "Speaking of babies, how would you and Lilah feel about bringing a one-month-old to a wedding? Say, early October during the break before the postseason."

One by one, my friends' faces transform from puzzled to pleased.

Cruz's grin spreads so wide it's a wonder it fits on his face. If we weren't still climbing to cruising altitude, I have no doubt he'd already be out of his seat and pulling Hendrix into a bear hug. "You and Poppy set a date?"

"Yeah," Hendrix says, a little sheepish but clearly proud. "I want to celebrate winning the World Series with my wife."

"That sounds perfect," Cruz replies. "I'll have to check with Delilah, but I can't imagine she'd miss it for the world."

"It's really important to us that you guys are there," Hendrix adds, looking each of us in the eye. "I can't get married without my groomsmen."

"No fucking way. Are you serious?" Dom nearly jumps out of his seat, practically vibrating with excitement. "Don't play with me!"

Dom starts humming the wedding march, and a choking laugh bursts from Hendrix. "Why do I know I'm going to regret this?"

I watch it all unfold, like I'm on the outside looking in as the four of them celebrate.

Then Hendrix's gaze shifts to me, and the smile fades. His lips press into a thin line as he swallows hard. It's a look I'm not used to seeing on him. Usually, he's the picture of confidence—a veteran on the team who's earned every bit of it. But right now, he looks nervous.

"You're in too, right? I want you there beside me with these fools. Everything will be as baby friendly as possible so that Holland can be there, if you're okay with that."

I assumed Hendrix was talking to the others when he asked them to stand with him. They've always included me, and we've grown closer over the years, but I've still felt like I'm on the fringe of the group.

Being included in something this important makes me feel worthy.

"Yeah, man. I'm there," I say to Hendrix.

The rest of the flight passes without any more dramatic declarations of friendship. When we deplane, I'm greeted by seven new pictures from Tenley, including three from a spa-themed photoshoot. Holland is swaddled in two fluffy white towels—one wrapped around her tiny body and the other perched on her head like a turban—complete with cucumber slices on her eyelids.

XAVIER:

I see you're taking this seriously.

TENLEY:

Baby skin care is a passion of mine.

TENLEY:

Also, the cucumbers are totally baby safe.
It's backed by the science of Google.

XAVIER:

Thanks for the pictures. Enjoy your movie night.

I'm not sure if she does it on purpose or if it's solely her personality, but Tenley's antics ease some of my nerves. The ridiculousness of it all forces me to relax a little. And later that night it helps me play better than I have all season.

After the game, I'm back in my hotel room getting ready to call it night when my phone buzzes again.

TENLEY:

Look at these amateurs. Who falls asleep before the infamous "love fern" scene.

The image of Vivi and my daughter sleeping peacefully together is a little dark and grainy, but that doesn't stop me from saving it. I tell myself it's for no reason other than I miss my daughter, but that's a lie.

XAVIER:

If you let my daughter watch How to Lose a Guy in Ten Days without me we are going to have a problem.

Three dots appear and disappear several times before I put her out of her misery.

XAVIER:

It was a joke, Tenley.

TENLEY:

Sometimes it's hard to tell since you're not usually funny.

TENLEY:

Kidding.

XAVIER:

No you're not.

TENLEY:

Look, safe and sound in bed.

A second picture comes through this one of Holland in her crib, and I save that one too.

XAVIER:

Thanks for all the pictures today. I'm sorry I gave you such a hard time before I left.

TENLEY:

I'd be more worried if you hadn't.

I don't sleep through the night, but it's not because I wake up with worry, it's because it's what my body is conditioned to do after weeks of doing this on my own.

CHAPTER 15

XAVIER

I'm elbow deep in a diaper change before our night game at home against the Los Angeles Diablos. Holland's tiny feet kick the air, making my work more challenging. After last week's road trip, we've really hit our stride. The chaos that used to run my life has smoothed out into something calmer—or at least as close to it as you can get with a baby.

Since the day I ran into Vivi at Buns & Roses, Tenley's gotten in the habit of coming over an hour or so earlier than she needs to, so I can get other things done. Sometimes, it's just stopping for coffee; yesterday I got a haircut. Vivi was right when she said I'd be a better dad if I wasn't running on fumes—little changes, big differences. For the first time, I think I'm getting this dad thing down.

"Hey, Baby Daddy. I'm here!" Tenley hollers as the door slams closed behind her.

The new nickname is her favorite way to torment me this week. "How many times have I told you not to call me that?" I bark from the nursery where I'm finishing up.

"But it's so much fun to see how it makes you squirm."

Holland gurgles, her mouth parted and the corners pulling up. It almost looks like a smile. I wouldn't put it past Tenley to have won my daughter over so thoroughly that she would be amused by her dad's discomfort.

"She can't even see me," I grumble to my daughter.

Lifting Holland I turn to find Tenley in the door frame. "I don't need to see you to know you're in here scowling and giving yourself wrinkles over it." "She just woke up from a nap. I haven't fed her yet."

"That's fine, I've got her. But I need you to do something for me."

I raise my brow at her, hesitant to agree without knowing more, but she stares impatiently, waiting for me to agree.

"What is it, Ten?" I finally ask, bored with the stare off. Her smile falls, like she thought I might hold out in the odd battle of wills she had me locked in.

"There's a bag on the counter. Can you drop it off at Double Play on your way to the stadium? It's for Vivi. She's having a really shitty day. I meant to drop it off on my way from the library, but forgot. Normally I wouldn't ask, but it's on your drive and she could really use it today." It all comes out in one long string of words.

A frown pulls at my lips. I'm thrown off by how vulnerable she seems. It's out of character for her, but I agree without hesitation. The thought of Vivienne having a bad day unsettles me, and if whatever Tenley has can help, I'm in.

"Yeah, sure. It's not a problem at all."

Her smile brightens. "Thank you so much. You're sure you can drop it off before the game? It's her favorite red velvet cake. I grabbed it from a bakery on campus after a meeting, but I was so excited to see this little one that I drove straight here and forgot to stop."

"Are you sure it wasn't me you were excited to see?" I deadpan.

And just like that her smile slides off her face and is replaced with an exaggerated look of disgust. "We talked about the dad jokes—they're lame. Do you want to be lame, Xavier?"

"Like I told you last week, I couldn't care less. The dad jokes come with the baby—it's a package deal."

♥

Consider me puzzled, and slightly aroused. Which admittedly is a strange combination.

I stand in the doorway of Vivi's office, the bag from Tenley hanging from my hand, my jaw nearly hitting the floor. I can't tear my eyes away from the scene in front of me, even though I know I should.

There she is, on her knees in the middle of her office, skirt pulled taut over her ass, her upper body stretched forward in a thread-the-needle yoga pose. My only saving grace is that her head is turned away from me. She deepens the stretch, reaching further with the arm threaded under her torso, releasing a soft moan. I shut my eyes, but it's no use—my body responds, and I go half-hard at the sound.

This is wrong. So *so* wrong.

She's having a rough day, and here I am, drooling over her like a pervert. I take a step back, shaking my head as if that could shake the image loose. Regaining my composure, I move forward, knocking as if I've just arrived.

Vivi pushes up on her hands, eyes wide with surprise when she sees me behind her. "Oh hey, didn't expect you." She quickly stands, smoothing down her skirt and adjusting her top as she turns to face me.

Why am I here again? My mind goes blank, the image of Vivi's sinful ass the only thing that sticks. My fingers flex involuntarily, and I glance down at the crinkling bag in my hand. "Tenley said you were having a bad day . . . She, uh, asked me to drop this off." I shove the bag toward her like a total idiot.

"Oh god. Is that from Sugar Slice?"

I can tell by the awe in her voice that "yes" is the only acceptable answer.

It seems like a rhetorical question, but like I said, I'm dumbstruck. So, like an actual moron, I hold up the bag, checking the label. "Sure is. That's the place near campus?"

Jesus, I'm a riveting conversationalist.

"Allison's cake is better than sex, and I missed lunch today, so this is the perfect midday pick me up."

That wakes me the hell up. My throat tightens as I swallow hard, trying—and failing—to ignore the effect her casual words have on me. The semi I'm already sporting isn't going away anytime soon. It demands that I be the one to show her how good it can be. The heat in my body spikes, and I tug at the collar of my shirt to cool off.

But the patience I've learned as a dad kicks in. I force myself to stay in control, choosing the safer route instead of acting on the impulse. "She said it was your favorite. Is, um . . . everything okay?"

"Oh yeah. Fine." She rubs her neck and winces.

Clearly it's not fine. "Your neck is bothering you," I state.

When Tenley said she was having a bad day and needed cake, I expected to find her upset, not hurting. But other than the obvious discomfort, she seems fine, happy even.

"It's nothing." She waves me off.

"So you weren't stretching because you're hurt?"

She laughs crossing the office and stopping halfway to me, holding her head at an uncomfortable angle the whole time. "I don't have time to be hurt."

I glance at my watch—I don't need to head to the stadium yet. Instead of handing her the bag, I set it down on the corner of her desk and perch on the edge.

"Come here." I widen my legs to make room for her to step in. She looks at me, raising an eyebrow.

"Trust me. Our trainers work on sore muscles all the time. I've picked up a thing or two."

She hesitates, standing still in the middle of her office, biting her lip, looking more nervous than I've ever seen her.

"Vivienne. You're in pain and I can help. Please let me."

CHAPTER 16

VIVIENNE

Having reliable judgment is usually my strongest ally, but right now, it's not working. Xavier perches on the edge of my desk, thick thighs spread daring me to make a terrible decision.

The cake isn't the most tempting thing he brought into my office.

Stepping between his legs and letting him put those strong hands on me is a surefire way to unravel every ounce of self-control I have left. Ever since the gala, my thoughts have been a traitorous mess, thanks to him in that tuxedo and the girls filling my head with vivid, ridiculous ideas about athletes and their stamina. Now, my body has decided it's horny for this man and this man only, urging me to do far more than accept an innocent shoulder rub.

It's a bad idea. I need to be able to work with him and even if it's not against the rules, it feels like crossing a line. Besides, I don't do relationships. If he's even looking for a relationship it should be with someone more willing to give up pieces of themselves. That's not me.

There are a million reasons to tell him no. But I don't.

Blame it on the exhaustion or the ache in my shoulder that started after I fell asleep holding Holland during movie night last week. Either way, I'm not at my strongest right now.

No matter the reason, it all boils down to one thing: I'm a weak woman desperate for relief. With my neck aching the way it is, I'm not picky about how I get it. Xavier might not be able to give me the orgasm my body is begging for, but maybe if he can loosen up the tension in my shoulders and neck, it'll help ease this constant strain.

I step between his legs, turning so my back is to him, my body framed by his long legs. My focus fixates on how they stretch out beside mine, lean and powerful. They're undeniably close, caging me in. But no matter where I direct my attention, I'm all too aware of how precariously close I am to being in his lap.

God, if I had to face him right now, I'd completely fall apart. I'm too unsteady, too wound up, and he's too near. It's dizzying and thrilling all at once, and my pulse flutters wildly as I stand there, waiting for him to do something. *Anything*.

The seconds stretch on. My body is hypersensitive. I close my eyes, trying—and failing—to calm my racing heart. He's got to be able to feel it pounding out of control.

I'm seconds away from begging when he shifts closer, sending a shiver down my spine.

"Can I touch you, Vivienne?"

Oh my god. There's a raw edge to his request that makes me think this isn't all in my head. That simple, powerful question goes straight to my core. It should be embarrassing, but I'm too far gone to care.

"Yes." My permission is entangled in a shaky exhale.

His fingers brush my bare shoulder as he moves my hair to one side. It's June, and hot as hell, but I wish I would've worn a blazer or something thicker than the thin sleeveless knit turtleneck. Without that barrier, I'm exposed, feeling nearly naked.

"You'll tell me if anything I do bothers it." It's a gentle demand.

Which is *perfect* because I'm an absolute tramp for the way he's walking me through this. I want him to do it under very different circumstances. The kind where he gives me what I really need. *Him.*

I nod. Or, at least, I think I do.

"With your words. I can't see your face and I don't want to hurt you."

Again with the soft commands. He's seconds away from unraveling me without doing a damn thing. It's absurd.

I can't do this. Nope, I'm not strong enough. I'm about to step away when a hand ghosts up my rib cage, sending goosebumps racing down my arms. He holds me in place with the hand that's dangerously close to the bottom of my breast.

If I slouch a little—nope, bad Vi.

His other palm cups the side of my neck, his thumb cautiously sweeping over the muscle there. "Is this where you need me?"

Not even close!

I nod again, and when his hand freezes, I remember my words. "Yeah, it's been bothering me since I fell asleep holding Holland. I can't get rid of the knot."

"Tenley sent me a picture. You both looked very cozy." I can hear the smile in his voice and can't help me to do the same.

"Of course she d-did." He hits a sore spot and my words stutter.

"Sorry." He continues working my shoulder and up to my neck. "Is this okay?"

I drop my head, forcing my shoulders away from my ears as he works his thumb in circles along the edge of my shoulder blade, increasing the pressure.

His thumb rolls over the tight muscle.

"God, yes." He hits another sensitive spot. Now that it's loosened up, the pain is mixed with incredible bliss. My hands fall to the tops of his hard thighs, bracing myself because I think I might collapse. "Your hands are pure magic."

I swear I hear him swallow. "Um, it's kind of what I'm known for."

My mind is sluggish, too hazy from this weird massage induced lust that I'm lost in. But he pops a foggy bubble when he adds, "Because I'm a catcher."

I don't know what to say or do—I'm out of my damn mind. And while I could blame my lack of good sex for my current state, Xavier deserves some of the credit too. We got off to a rocky start, but each new thing I learn about him leaves me pleasantly surprised and hungry to know more.

The hand on my waist slides up my spine, igniting a trail of warmth with every inch it covers. When his palm settles between my shoulder blades, it starts working in sync with his other hand, skillfully kneading the tension from my muscles. Each stroke pulls me further into a haze, and I stop thinking about anything except the way he's touching me.

It's not until there's a knock at the door that I realize I'm in Xavier's lap. At some point, I must have let go, completely, my weight sinking into him. Heat floods my cheeks as I leap up, probably undoing all the progress he made on my shoulders.

When I glance toward the door, and see Dean's standing there, my stomach sinks. He looks way too amused and smug for my liking.

"Didn't mean to startle you. I was stopping in to drop off the check from the auction proceeds at the gala. The team wants a photo op." An oversized check appears from the hallway.

"And they sent you?" Xavier asks.

I say a silent thank you that he's offering a distraction by giving Dean a hard time.

"Oh, okay," I say, my professional mask firmly back in place. "Would you mind taking a picture?" I grab my phone, pushing it into Xavier's hands before he can respond.

We rearrange ourselves so Dean and I are in front of the double play logo painted on my office wall and he holds out the fake check, both of us smiling for the camera.

When we've got what we need, I send the pictures off to Piper, the Bandit's PR director. Looking up from my email I find Dean staring a hole into the side of Xavier's head.

"Are you heading into the stadium?" he asks.

"Yeah. I should probably get going."

Xavier follows his teammate to the door. When Dean disappears into the hall, Xavier turns back to me and says, "Hope that cake lives up to the hype." And then he winks and I hear the faint sound of my vagina calling out for him to come back. She's clearly not done with him.

CHAPTER 17

XAVIER

Dean's timing couldn't be worse. I'd finally gotten Vivi to relax, to let me help her for once, and then he had to walk in and interrupt.

Now, instead of enjoying a few more minutes with my hands on her skin and convincing her to eat the damn cake Tenley sent, I'm here, trudging toward my car with Dean's hand on my shoulder and questions written in the set of his jaw when he looks over at me.

"Is there anything going on with you and the director of my non-profit?" Dean asks, like I owe him an explanation.

"Is it really *your* non-profit?"

"Stop dodging the question." He cuts to the chase.

I let out a sharp sigh. "There's nothing to tell. Tenley's her niece, so the universe keeps throwing Vivi and me together, but that's all it is."

Dean stops walking, turning to look at me like he's waiting for more. "That's it?"

"We're friends. What else do you want me to say?" I snap, throwing up my hands. I'm annoyed that he interrupted us. Annoyed that I don't believe the answers I'm giving him. Just fucking annoyed.

He narrows his eyes. "You remember how things went down when Mia and I tried to hide our relationship, right? Collateral damage all over the place—Hendrix, my game, Mia herself."

"Yeah, Dean, I remember," I say through gritted teeth.

"Listen, if there's something going on, you can tell me. There are no rules that say she can't be involved with a player. I'm just making sure, if there is something going on, you aren't hiding it because of her job."

"Like I said, we're friends." Each time he forces me to repeat it, I grow more agitated. Having Vivienne in my lap minutes ago didn't feel friendly—not by a long shot. I wanted to keep her there and pull her closer so she could understand how *unfriendly* touching her made me feel.

My teeth grind together. "I brought her a treat from Tenley because she was having a shitty day. I'm not interested in a relationship right now, and I don't know when I'll be ready."

Except that isn't entirely true. If I were looking for more with someone, Vivi would be the only name on that list. And selfishly, I want to figure out a way I steal pieces of her without having to sacrifice the little time I have.

He studies me for a moment longer. "You don't look at her like a friend does. If you decide to go for it, don't make the same mistakes I did. I'd hate to see either of you get hurt."

Yeah, I don't want that either.

CHAPTER 18

VIVIENNE

The sugar rush from the cake Xavier brought earlier is long gone, but the ghost of his hands lingers on my shoulders, leaving me calm and loose for the first time in days. My body is lighter, my thoughts are clearer, and for once, grocery shopping after work isn't a chore.

My phone vibrates in the cart's cup holder, and I spot Tenley's name flashing on the screen. Tension snaps back in an instant.

My niece never calls. She claims shorthand text messages that start with "Hey, fam" are her love language. Which is so fucking confusing because I'm only one person. But when I questioned it, she patted my arm like I was tragically uncool and said, "It's not that deep, Vi. 'Fam' is a vibe, not a headcount."

So, when I see her name now, I know something's wrong. I swipe to answer, pinning the phone between my ear and shoulder as I steer my cart to the side of the aisle.

"Hey, Ten—"

"Mayday, Vi. No time for greetings," she groans into my ear.

Her broken voice stops me in my tracks. I'm blocking the aisle, but I don't really care. "What's wrong?"

"So, so much. But the nonstop pooping while I hurl into a trash can is the biggest bummer."

"Oh, sweetie, I'll be right there. Is Holland okay?" I abandon my grocery list on the spot, veering toward the pharmacy aisle to grab some Pepto before heading to the checkout.

The Bandits are playing at home tonight; it'll be hours before Xavier's home to relieve Tenley. She can't wait that long.

"She's probably traumatized from watching me from the hallway, but yeah, she seems fine." Tenley's voice wavers, followed by a groan that tugs at my heartstrings. "I'm pretty sure it's food poisoning, but I didn't want her too close—just in case."

"Can I bring you anything else?"

"Just let me perish," she groans dramatically, treating me to another pained moan.

That seals it—sports drinks are definitely in order. I grab a few bottles from the fridge near the checkout.

Tenley might have a flair for theatrics, but she's smart and level-headed. She handles her own problems and doesn't ask for help unless it's serious. If she's reaching out now, I know she really needs me.

I'm antsy as I follow the curve of Xavier's driveway up to his house, my grip tightening on the wheel.

With the bag of medicine and sports drinks cradled in my arms, I jog up to the door.

"Tenley?" I call out when I step into the massive front foyer.

"In the bathroom," Tenley croaks, her voice even more pitiful in person.

I follow her voice to the first-floor bathroom. I'm relieved to find Holland sitting in her fancy bouncer, looking healthy and happy, easing the tightness in my chest.

I step around her and into the bathroom. Tenley, on the other hand, is a pale, crumpled version of her usual self, slumped in front of the toilet.

"Are you the reaper, here to drag me to the afterlife?" She winces, squeezing her eyes shut.

I crouch beside her, smoothing a hand over her hair. "More like your savior, here to tuck you in and take care of the baby."

"You brought me grape Gatorade? You're a real one, Vi." She sniffles, her voice rough.

"Of course—it's always been your favorite. But right now, we need to get you cleaned up and into bed." I help her sit up and loop my arm around her waist, steadying her. "Where am I taking you?"

She nods toward the hallway, weakly guiding me. "There's a guest suite downstairs. It's dark and quiet down there."

I help her down the stairs and settle her into bed. She cradles the electrolytes to her chest and looks up at me, her eyes widening, before she says, "Holland needs a bath."

"I can handle that. Get some rest and I'll check on you later."

Last time I was here, Tenley and I hung out in the living room watching old movies. It's strange navigating his house now, trying to find everything I need so I can bathe Holland.

There's evidence everywhere around his home that suggests the Xavier I first met at Double Play was truly him at his worst. But for a year, I carried the impression of him being this cocky, arrogant player.

Now that I've spent time with him, I've seen firsthand that he's nothing like I imagined. And as I rush through his house, it's clear that this man loves his family over everything else.

The proof is staring back at me in the ultrasound picture stuck to the fridge, and in every adorable detail of Holland's nursery. It's there in the teal baby blanket hanging over the arm of the couch.

But it's not only his love for her that has me convinced. I find it again in the picture of him and his teammates together at the top of a mountain overlook. Giant smiles on everyone's faces as they surround Cruz and Lilah on their wedding day.

Refocusing on the task at hand, I scoop Holland out of the bouncer and we go in search of her bath stuff together. I find it in the bathroom upstairs next to her nursery.

"Okay, sweet girl, let's get you cleaned up for bed. We'll wash away any germs so you don't get whatever Tenley's got if she's wrong about it being food poisoning."

She gurgles back at me, cradled in my arms as I let the water run until it's warm and plug the tub. "Look at this fancy little chair. I bet you love this" Her wide-eyed stare is so innocent that it makes my heart skip. Once she's settled in the chair, I run the washcloth over her legs, making sure to get those chubby little rolls on her thighs. It doesn't take long and by the time we're done, her eyes are heavy.

Carefully, I lift her out of the tub and wrap her in a fluffy towel, but not before I end up soaked from her and the bath water on the edge of the tub. A downfall of having big breasts that get in the way.

Holland goes down easy after changing and feeding her, but my shirt and the waistband of my leggings are soaked through and cold.

Uncomfortable as it is, I take a few minutes to sit in the rocker and bask in the peace that holding her brings me. Eventually I lay her down and leave the room so I can find a change of clothes.

Checking the time on the stainless steel microwave, the glowing numbers tell me I have five minutes before I'm supposed to have my weekly call with my best friend Harlowe. "Shit," I mumble, wrapping my arms around my middle. The air conditioning has my teeth chattering.

I head for the laundry room, going straight for the dryer. I wonder if Xavier is the type to put his clothes away immediately, or if . . . Bingo! I hit the jackpot, finding one of his shirts buried beneath a pile of pink and purple baby clothes.

Stripping off my damp clothes, I toss them in the dryer with the clothes that are still there. I instantly feel better, but my call with Harlowe isn't the naked kind.

Even though it's freshly washed, there's still a hint of Xavier clinging to it when I pull the shirt over my head and I'm not ashamed to admit I soak it in, burying my nose in the black fabric and letting the essence of him envelop me.

He's been on my mind all day and this little hit of him is exactly what I need to soothe my still-frayed nerves from that massage this afternoon.

My phone rattles against the marble countertop, and a picture of Harlowe and me from last year's HarvestFest at the vineyard makes me smile.

"Um, where are you?" Harlowe's voice bursts through as my camera connects.

"At Xavier's. Had to come rescue Tenley. She got food poisoning, and he's got a game tonight, so she called me to help with Holland."

"You're in Ginger Daddy's house?" She leans in closer to the screen. "Is that his shirt?"

"Yes," I say, starting the drier so I can change back into my clothes before Xavier gets home.

"Spill," Harlowe demands as I step out of the laundry room and into the hall.

"Holland, his daughter, needed a bath, and I ended up soaked."

"Here I was hoping it was because you finally broke your dry spell, and he was the reason you were wet." She wiggles her eyebrows at me.

"No . . . but after the massage he gave me today, that's all too plausible."

"Way to bury the lede. You need to recruit that man to help you get off."

A muffled cough pulls my focus from my phone. I expect to find Tenley coming upstairs for something, not the man in question standing stock-still with a Bandits duffle slung over his shoulder and a heated question in his denim blue eyes.

"Um, I'm going to have to call you back," I say to Harlowe, my pulse pounding in my ears as I freeze just a few feet from him.

CHAPTER 19

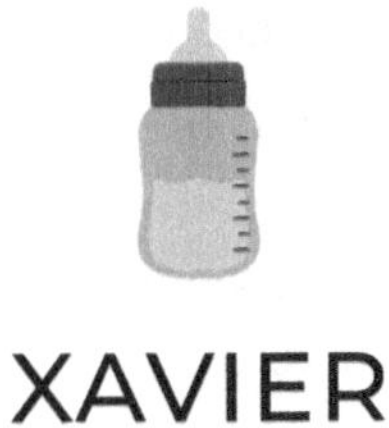

XAVIER

I knew Vivienne would be here. Her text after the game said Tenley was sick and she had called Vivi to come help with Holland. What I didn't expect was to go in search of her and hear her on the phone, mid-conversation with a friend, casually dissecting her sex life. And more importantly, the possibility of *me* giving her what she's missing.

Nothing could've prepared me for the vivid scenarios I've been imagining for weeks to suddenly be within reach. It's a sharp turn from the direction I expected my night to take, but her friend's words loop in my head like a siren's call getting louder with each step I take.

"You need to recruit that man to help you get off."

When I step around the corner and find her in *my* hallway, wearing nothing but one of *my* shirts, my restraint snaps—all reason evaporates. She's here in my house, in my clothes, and for weeks she's all I've seen and it has me hurtling over the edge, reckless and ready to give her exactly what she needs. The reasons I've had for holding back suddenly don't seem unmanageable.

Her eyes lift from the phone and those plump lips part on a trapped inhale. She looks so at home, like she belongs here, and it's sexy as fuck. I vaguely register a hurried goodbye to her friend and the faint sound of the call ending.

Vivi freezes, and her eyes lock on mine as I let my gaze rake down her body. The hem of my shirt barely skims her thighs, leaving enough to the imagination to drive me wild.

I know I should walk away, check on my daughter, shove this ridiculous idea that I could have her out of my head. But I can't move. Not when she's looking at me like she wants me to be the solution to her problem. And not when every part of me is screaming to close the space between us.

Doing the right thing won't erase the memory of her in nothing but my shirt.

Maybe Vivi is the catalyst for me getting my identity back. Whether intentional or not, I can't ignore that any more than I can ignore what I just learned. This could all backfire, but the pull to her is too fucking strong and I'm too fucking weak.

There's risk in getting involved with Vivi, and no one stands to lose more than me and Holland. My daughter already has enough uncertainty in her life with Kristy missing. If Vivienne will allow me to have her the way I want we'll need boundaries and rules to keep *everyone* safe.

My mind made up, I step forward. My fingers find the hem of my shirt sitting high on her thigh. I rub it between my thumb and pointer finger. This close, her scent surrounds me. She reminds me of summer—it's an addicting mix of welcoming honeysuckle and citrus.

Her tongue wets her pink lips. "Did you hear that?"

"Every damn word."

She drops her head, avoiding me. *That won't do.* I cup the side of her neck, hooking her chin and lifting her face. She's flustered and I need to know she understands what she's getting into. "Don't be embarrassed. But I have to know, the night of the gala you said something that bothered me. You said that you've only ever had mediocre sex. Is that true?"

"Yes," she admits, her cheeks turning pink. She's a powerhouse—it's one of the things I respect most about her. But there must be something really wrong with me because the idea that I could be the first to give her what she needs where others have failed has my cock turning to stone in my shorts, begging me to let him show her how good I can make it.

"It's a crime that a woman as remarkable as you hasn't been treated the way she deserves." The words come out gritty with urgency.

"It's fine. I do okay on my own." She shrugs, and it makes my blood pressure spike.

I want her to be as bothered by this as I am. It's like I'm on a damn seesaw that I can't get off, tipping between anger on her behalf and filthy joy at the idea of being the first person to get her off.

It's the last part that has me stepping forward, pinning her to the wall with my hips, giving her proof of what she's doing to me. "Tell me the truth. Does your body ache to be fucked the way you deserve?"

Her mouth drops open at my boldness, and I have to hold myself back from taking it, here and now. She needs to be certain because I'm not offering roses and wine. I don't have that in me—not right now.

"Yes," she croaks, her nipples pebbling against my shirt.

"And would you let me be the person who gives you what you need?"

Her breathing picks up as her eyes shift between mine like a pinball. "Yes."

I'm unable to stop the groan that starts in my throat when she shifts under the weight of my body. I give her my thigh, wedging it between her legs. Her head drops back against the wall at the friction. "We need safeguards. Rules. And I need you to be honest with me about what I'm up against."

"I'm not interested in a relationship," she adds, her voice strained.

"Good," I rasp, nodding. "I can't give you that. My life is crazy and Holland has to come first, always. This would just be sex—me giving you all the orgasms that you've been missing out on," I tell her honestly.

Pushing her shoulders back she asks, "And what do you get out of it?"

I drop my lips to her ear, letting my nose run over the shell. It's all I'll allow myself for the moment, though it's not nearly what I need, and whisper, "Having you will be more than enough."

"Hardly seems fair." I think she means it as a joke, but it comes out in short pants.

"Not fair? You're everything a man could need. I've been out of my mind wanting you for weeks. It would be a fucking privilege to make you come."

She bites on her lower lip, her hands lifting to my chest and using it as leverage. "My life is finally my own and I'm not ready to make room for anyone else. This can't turn into more, Xavier."

"I've got everything I need. Remember? But a brilliant woman once told me I'd be a better dad if my cup was full. This seems like a great way to pour into it."

Her husky laugh is drenched in pleasure as she rocks against my leg. "I think she meant basic human needs, like sleep and food."

I hum thoughtfully. "Let the cup runneth over." I add more pressure, giving her what she's seeking for a moment. "Everyone should have good sex—human connection is a basic need. Sex with the right person goes beyond need. When I'm through with you, you'll understand."

"You make it sound so simple."

"Simple? Not always. Worth it? Yes." Her focus locks on me, full of understanding. I'll try harder than anyone else ever has. "I wish you could write me a list of all the ways you want me to make you come, but you're too needy to stop, aren't you?" I pull my knee back a little and let her sag into me.

"Please don't stop. I can't—talk." Her voice wobbles, but she looks so determined. It's fucking adorable.

I push an inky strand of hair back from her face, bending to eye level and snaring her attention. "You'll come after we talk." She whimpers but doesn't argue. "Has anyone ever made you come?"

She shakes her head slowly. "No. Either they haven't cared enough or haven't paid attention. Sex always feels very focused on my partner's needs versus my own." She sighs like it pains her to admit. "Deep relationships aren't really my thing—I'm too focused on other things. So I never put all that much thought into it."

"And what about when you're on your own? Can you make yourself come, or is that hard too?"

Her eyes light up with mischief and her hands loop around my neck anchoring herself to me. "I'm a pro at making myself come."

"A well-practiced expert." I make a mental note that seeing her make herself come needs to be one of the first things we try. "So you've never come from dry humping?" I ask, giving her my leg back.

Her breath rushes out of her. "No."

"And your fingers are the only ones that have given you an orgasm?"

She nods, and the mental image of her fucking her hand spring up in my mind.

I press my lips to her ear like it's a secret between the two of us, even though we're all alone in this dark hallway. There's a primal part of me that hopes that the next answer is a no. "Has anyone ever licked your needy pussy, Vivienne?"

"Yes, but no one's ever done a good job." Her head falls back against the fall and she adds, "I can't wait for you to try. I know you'll be the first to do it right."

Jesus, her confidence in me is almost enough to have me coming in my pants.

"Fuck, yes, I will." I lick a path up her neck. "And I'm going to enjoy every second of my tongue buried inside you."

Vivi shivers under me, her pulse pounding in her neck as she climbs. She's close and I want to make sure we're on the same page before this goes further.

"And when I fuck you, my cock will be the first you come on."

"God, yes." She cants her hips faster.

"Then this is where we start. Tell me you understand what this is and use me to get yourself off." I palm her breast through my shirt, helping her take what she needs.

"I want you to show me everything—all the ways you can make me feel good. No falling in love, no dating, and no other women. Just orgasms."

"No other men. We stay friends when this is over. You and Tenley don't disappear from our life when this is done." My tone softens. "That part is non-negotiable because of Holland."

Her hands slide up the sides of my neck, holding my face. "I would never take Tenley away from Holland, but I won't lie to her either. She doesn't need the details, but we can't pretend this . . ." Her lips twist as she searches for the right words. "That our situation isn't happening."

I nod. Tenley is too smart for her own good—there's no way she won't notice something, especially now that we've agreed this is a regular thing. "When she asks, you can tell her whatever you're comfortable with. I'm not ashamed of what we're doing, but I don't want to cross any boundaries that make you or her uncomfortable."

Her thumb sweeps over my jaw. "I appreciate that more than you know."

"And when we've crossed everything off our list, I'll find more ways to make you come until we've made up for everything you've missed out on. Then you go on your way, satisfied, and find someone who can give you all the things I can't—a future where you come first in every way."

"Starting now?" She hooks a finger into my waistband, twisting so I can't pull back again.

"Starting now," I agree. "Take this one on your own because the rest of them are mine."

It's a beautiful thing, watching her come into her own and rock over my thigh, riding until she buries her face in my chest, mumbling a string of obscenities.

"Let me see you, Vi." I tilt her chin up. "Get used to being vulnerable with me. It's the only way this works."

Her teeth clamp down on her lip, like she has to concentrate on getting there.

"By the time we are through, I'll have you coming on command. I'm going to get to know your body so well you'll never have to stress about this again."

Like I expected, she responds to the dirty talk. She's so damn sensual, so perfect, she just doesn't know it yet.

"Just let go. Trust me, trust your body. Come all over my thigh."

And she does, crying out, a damp spot soaking through my thin shorts, her eyes rolling back and legs trembling as she comes apart for me, pinned against the wall in the hallway where I found her. Pride swells in my chest. Without even touching her, I was able to give her something no other man ever has.

I let my forehead fall to the wall next to her head, giving us both the minute we need to collect ourselves.

"If that was only the first one, when do I get the next one?" she asks, her pupils unfocused and her voice husky.

There's not a single part of me that doesn't want to drag her upstairs and fuck her into my mattress, but I know that's not what I should do. Vivienne is practical and thoughtful. Nothing about what we just did feels like a mistake, but I want her to sleep on it before we take things further.

"Soon enough." I kiss her forehead. "Make me a wish list of everything you want to try. We'll start there."

"You want me to make an orgasm wish list?"

"Yeah. Don't overthink it, just write down what you want."

CHAPTER 20

VIVIENNE

"Soon enough," I rant under my breath, my forehead falling to the desk in front of me with a thump. "Make me a list."

What the hell was I thinking? What the hell was *he* thinking? He really wants me to write out all the ways I want him to make me come? The other night could have been luck. There's no guarantee that he can do it again.

Chemistry can fizzle—

Who am I kidding? Nothing is going to fizzle. He lit a fire inside me and I don't think anything can put it out.

But a list. I can't do that. "Can I?"

I must look unhinged, talking to myself alone in my office.

"Are we interrupting something?" Indie asks, stepping into my doorway.

Heat rushes to my cheeks.

Jesus, Vi. Get a grip.

And I almost do . . . until Lara pokes her head in.

"You're as red as a tomato."

I wave them in wordlessly. The list has me so caught up that I lost track of time before our meeting. That's not my style.

And we've worked together long enough for them to recognize when something's seriously off. I'm always composed, professional—hell, even when I'm taking arrogant Bandits down a peg, I do it with poise. That version of me is nowhere to be found right now.

Lara pulls the door closed behind the two of them.

Xavier's back on the road and I've had the condo to myself for days with plenty of time to write the list, but I haven't been able to bring myself to do it. Lara and Indie exchange matching looks of concern as they watch me stand from my desk and pace to the window. I'm not ashamed of what Xavier and I are doing, but telling them about our agreement feels very personal. Harlowe is the only person I'd trust with this, but she's unreachable because she's in the backcountry for training.

I bite my thumbnail, turn away from their amused faces, and take another lap across my office.

"Dean's going to be really annoyed when he gets home from New York and finds out he has to replace this carpet," Lara teases.

"You guys are going to think I'm crazy," I huff, sounding as resigned as I feel.

"I doubt that," Lara says.

"Remember the teensy problem that we talked about at the gala?" I start, my stomach flipping anxiously.

"The one where no one has ever given you an orgasm." Indie lays it out there, not an ounce of hesitation.

I drop back into the desk chair, looking anywhere but at the two women sitting across from me. "That's the one."

"Oh, honey," Lara says sweetly. This is new information for her. She was at the gala, but seated at her father's table and I'm sure the mayor and his guests weren't talking about the wonders of athlete-induced orgasms.

"Xavier offered to help me."

When neither of them speaks, I lift my head from the pen I'm playing with. Indie sits there, gaping at me, and Lara has one perfect eyebrow arched.

"I'm going to need one of you to say something."

It's Indie that speaks first. "I'm so damn proud of you."

"When do we get to the crazy part because so far I'm not seeing a problem? The hot daddy wants to give you orgasms. Sounds like a solid plan," Lara says.

Indie drops into the chair next to Lara and I blow out a ragged breath. Having this conversation in my office with these two, who are technically here in a professional capacity, is out of character.

Lara, ever perceptive, leans forward and rubs my forearm. "We're friends first. Anything you tell us stays within the circle of trust. Our meeting doesn't officially start until this conversation is over."

Something's got to give. The tension inside me is unbearable.

They're offering to listen, and maybe it'll help. I've been distracted, completely unlike myself. I let out another shaky breath and begin, starting with his visit to my office. They listen intently as I explain how he found me in the hallway, wearing his shirt, the rules we set, everything.

"He wants me to make an orgasm wish list."

"And he was able to give you one already?" Lara asks.

"Well, technically, I gave it to myself, but I've never been able to do that with someone else . . . So, yeah."

"Why do you think it was so easy with him?" Indie asks, her voice calm but pointed. The question hits me like a punch to the chest. I've been going over the same thing a thousand times and I'm not sure I'm ready to face the answer.

I swallow hard and force the words out before I can second guess them. "I've been thinking about that a lot, actually," I admit, my voice quieter now. "And I think it's because . . . he's the first man I've ever let myself have an emotional connection with—ever."

"A lot of women need that connection to enjoy sex," Lara says, making it sound much less daunting.

"Now that I've had a glimpse of what sex can be like, it's all I can think about. The man has turned me into a wanton hussy who can't focus on anything else." I lean back in my chair, exhaling dramatically. "I've never cared this much about sex, but the anticipation is making me all kinds of crazy."

"There's only one solution for that," Indie says with a smirk.

At the same time, Lara leans in. "Make the damn list."

Their eagerness on my behalf makes me laugh despite myself. "Like now?" I reply, throwing my hands up.

"Yes! Open up the notes app and start typing. You can send it to him tonight," Lara suggests.

"I like this. It's perfect—you get your homework done, and tonight, when you send him the list, you get phone sex."

"She's right. There's no way you don't get an orgasm from the man after sending him a text that dirty."

"I've never done anything like this before."

"Good thing you've got help." Indie wiggles her eyebrows.

Lara pushes my phone toward me. "Unless you prefer paper and pen for your lists."

"Not for this one." A giggle bubbles out of me. I swipe the phone off the desk. "I can't believe I'm doing this."

"The basics have to go on there," Lara starts.

"And you already crossed off dry humping," Indie adds.

"Then there are the obvious ones. Fingers, mouth, penetration."

"I'm not writing penetration."

"Do you prefer fucking?"

I add penetrative sex below the first two.

"Do I include other things on here? Like places?"

"Why the hell not? It's a wish list. If you've ever fantasized about it, add it," Lara encourages.

"It's not like he's going to hold you to it if you change your mind," Indie says.

"I know this is your list, but I love giving as much as receiving," Lara adds.

I put it on the list because the idea of making Xavier lose it is as appealing as anything else we've talked about.

"Um, I think I'm going to finish this later," I say, turning my face down on the desk. It's suddenly too hot in here.

Both Lara and Indie laugh.

"Yeah, you are," Indie teases.

Hours later I'm working on a grant, in bed, because I spent too much of my morning socializing, when Harlowe texts me for an update. On the bright side, even though I'm behind on work, I'm not half as anxious as I was this morning.

HARLOWE:

I'm back in civilization and I need an update. Have you seen the hot baseball player with the nice ass again?

VIVI:

No, but I did make a list of all the things I want him to do to me . . . while at work today.

HARLOWE:

Scandalous.

VIVI:

Not helping.

HARLOWE:

How kinky did you get?

VIVI:

Um . . . I don't know. A few shades darker than vanilla.

HARLOWE:

Tell me you put spanking or breath play on there.

VIVI:

Stop it.

HARLOWE:

Awe. Do you like that idea a little too much?

VIVI:

I hate you. I have to send him this and he's going to rethink his decision.

HARLOWE:

I doubt that.

Hyping myself up, I set aside my computer and take all the advice offered to me today.

I delete and retype three different greetings before I finally settle on using awkward humor to break the ice.

VIVI:

Hey, teach.

XAVIER:

I was wondering when I'd hear from you. Did you do your homework?

The heat rises in my cheeks and I roll over in my bed, burying my face in a pillow. It doesn't matter that he can't see me, he's got me hot with just a text.

VIVI:

I did.

XAVIER:

Send it to me.

VIVI:

[Vivi's Orgasm Wish List Attached]

I press my phone to my chest, heart galloping. It buzzes against my chest, his name flashing on the screen. I answer, breathless, and there he is—leaning against the headboard, his tousled red hair and smoldering blue eyes making my flush deepen. He's shirtless, mostly out of view, but the hint of his toned body is enough to send a thrill through me.

His voice is scratchy, sounding as ready for bed as he looks. "Damn, Vi. You look so pretty it hurts."

I glance down. There's nothing overly sexy about the pajamas I'm wearing—tiny flowers dot the cream set. The ribbed tank top is a thicker, fitted material that gives the girls a little support, but it's not lingerie by any stretch of the imagination. The matching bottoms have slits up the side that keep them from being restrictive. "It's just—these aren't—"

His gaze narrows to a pointed glare, cutting my words off. "Don't brush off my compliments. I'm a single dad to a newborn. Extra energy is in short supply and I'm sure as hell not going to use it to say things I don't mean. So when I tell you that you look like a fucking dream, believe me."

"Thank you," I breathe out, sinking into bed, my head falling back against the pillows.

"I wasn't sure if you'd make the list."

I laugh at the irony of that statement. "The little assignment you gave me has been all I can think about."

"I'd apologize for your suffering, but I'm not sorry." There's heat in his stare when he adds, "Should we open this list together?"

I groan because that might be more than I can handle. "Really?"

"You're not shy about asking for what you want outside the bedroom. Channel that same energy here. I know you can."

"Okay," I say, faking confidence. "Open it."

I wait for a second as he opens the text I sent him.

"Fuck." There's a desperation in his tone that's so unlike him. I've seen him when he's on edge before, but it's always been about his daughter. This is a different kind of urgency, and it tugs at the thread of need between us that's so tight after the last few days. "This list, sweetheart . . ."

"Is it too much?"

"I've been walking around half hard since I made you come in my hallway. My teammates think I'm snorting little blue pills for fun. This list could be a mile long and it wouldn't be too much."

His vehement speech gives me the courage to tell him about this morning. "Lara and Indie know about us. They helped me get started on the list."

"Tell whoever you want—there's no shame in what we're doing. Personally, the more people who know you're off-limits, the happier I am. But I promised to take my cues from you, so I am." His eyes rake over me, making my skin hot.

"This road trip was really inconvenient. When do you get home?"

"Three more days." He rubs his knuckles along his jaw as he watches me. Even over the phone, his attention elicits a riot of goosebumps. "It's too damn long. I don't want to wait to hear your sexy little whimpers. Let me help you cross something off tonight."

Just the rasp in his voice has the heavy heartbeat thrumming between my legs. Having someone dead set on giving me pleasure is unfamiliar territory for me.

There is only one we can cross off tonight. "You want to have phone sex?"

"Don't you? Isn't that why it's on the list?"

"Yes," I croak. Indie's words stuck with me and I added it when I got home, along with a few other things.

"How do you want to come tonight? Will it be on your fingers as you imagine they're mine? Or do you have a toy you want to use like it's my cock?"

"Fingers," I say, surprising myself. Normally I'd reach for my trusty vibrator, but there's something carnal about being able to feel what he would.

Xavier's groan shoots straight to my core, flickering through me like he's right beside me. "Fuck, you're such a filthy girl and no one's ever taken care of you the way you need. But that ends now. You're going to touch yourself and teach me everything you need to get there. When you unravel, I want my name on your lips."

The mouth on this man is everything I didn't know I'd been missing. He's so damn sure of himself. "I can see you're not lacking any confidence tonight."

"Only because I'm determined. Sleep is overrated. I have no problem spending all night talking you through it, if that's what it takes."

Yeah, I don't think that's going to be a problem. Knowing how motivated he is to learn what I like has flipped a switch in me. No one else has ever put in a fraction of the effort he's talking about.

But oh god, where do I start. Verbalizing something so intimate is new to me.

"I'm not sure how to do this," I admit quietly. "Help me get started . . . please?"

CHAPTER 21

XAVIER

Fuck she's pretty when she's nervous. I've never seen her this unsure before and it only makes me want to take care of her more. But I also don't want to push her if she's not comfortable.

I'm about to tell her as much when she adds, "I need this, Xavier. Tell me what to do." She shifts against the pillows, bringing more of her upper body into the frame. There's still a pink tint to her cheeks, but the waver in voice is gone.

"That fucking tank top is going to kill me, Vi." The material is molded to the tempting swell of her breasts and her peaked nipples, making my mouth water. I can't wait to spend hours exploring her body. "Do you even know what you do to me?" I run my hand up my shaft once, to ease the ache—it's all I'll allow myself until for now.

Vivi's lashes flutter against the apples of her cheeks, my praise making her blossom.

"I'm already so damn hard for you. It's going to be a miracle if I make it out of this without cum covering my stomach."

Her chest rises with a shaky inhale. "I'm not opposed to that." She shifts, setting the phone against something so I can see more of her.

"Nah. Tonight is about you, not me. Stick your fingers in your mouth for me and get them nice and wet."

I'm captivated as she lifts two fingers, watching them disappear between her parted lips. "I'd do almost anything to fuck that perfect mouth. Make it my warm, wet home until I'm coming down your throat. You didn't have to put that on the list, but I can't say I'm sad to see it there."

She moans around her fingers and my dick twitches against my stomach.

"You're doing so good. When they're nice and soaked, slip them between your legs for me and play with yourself."

She releases her fingers with a wet plop, saliva gleaming in the dim light of the lamp. And does as I say, her mouth falling open on a silent exhale. All I can do is watch for a minute as she gets more comfortable finding what feels good.

"That's it, now tell me what you need."

"I need more . . . It's so good—too good. Having you talk me through it . . . I can feel it right there." The words fade a bit when she throws her head back and presses the back of her free hand to her cheek. "God, I'm overheated. I should have done this days ago."

Fuck if I'd have known, I'd have called her the day after we made our deal. "I wish you would have called. Next time, let me help you. Don't put it off this long. But it's okay, Vi, we're just going to have to take our time and make sure you get what you need."

"Take my time? Why on earth would I do that? I'm already so damn close." White blooms across her plump bottom lip where her teeth drag across it.

"I can think of a few reasons. If you go slow I can learn what works for you." I'll learn by exploring on my own too, but this will help her learn to speak up. "Plus, drawing it out a little is only going to make you come that much harder and I want you shaking when you finally let go."

She huffs out a frustrated breath. "I know how to edge myself, Xavier."

"That's right, you're a pro at this." I laugh.

Her eyes narrow. "I can hang up this phone and do this without you."

"But you don't want to. Keep your touches light and tell me what gets you there."

"Circles work best." Her breath catches in her throat. "I usually can't finish without them."

"That's it, sweetheart, keep talking."

She's being so honest and open, pride swells in my chest because she's trusting me with her intimate secrets.

"What about your nipples? Do you like having your breasts played with? Because they're fucking perfect and I'm dying to get my mouth on them."

Her unfocused gaze finds me and there's sadness there that breaks my heart. "I've always been self-conscious about their size."

Anger burns through me on her behalf, knowing at some point, someone made her feel that way. "I won't do anything that makes you uncomfortable. Ever. But there is nothing about you that doesn't do it for me. Head to toe, every fucking curve is a masterpiece." I pan my phone down letting her see my erection straining against my gray sweatpants and dark stain where it's already leaking.

When I lift the phone back to my face, she's blinking back awe. "Has anyone ever told you that you're unfairly hot?"

"Never anyone that mattered."

"I don't believe that for a second." Her laugh is warm and content, mirroring the lazy smile she wears.

"It's true. I don't let many people get that close." Except for Kristy. She wore me down, always hanging around and fawning over me. Looking back, it probably should have been a red flag—it was toxic as hell.

Something flashes in her features, sadness or pity, and I don't like it—not when I'm supposed to be focused on her. And not when it skims topics that are too serious for what we're doing.

This agreement with Vivi is perfect because I get someone good like Vivi in my life without the risk of getting hurt again, or losing focus on my priorities. Which are giving Holland a better life than I had, and baseball. It's a reminder I need right now because losing track of why we are doing this would be so easy.

But as long as Vivi is on the same page, we both get what we need and no one gets hurt.

"Ready for more?" I ask, refocused on the moment.

"Please." It's a broken plea, falling off her parted lips.

"I bet you're soaked for me. Slip a finger inside and test that cunt for me." Her pupils flare, like she didn't expect that from me, and damn, I like taking her by surprise.

She surprises me in return when she asks, "Is that what I'm doing? Keeping this pussy warm for you until you get back?"

"Fuck yes," I grit out as I give my cock a squeeze. "Fuck, Vivi, you might not have known where to start but you sure as hell aren't having a hard time keeping up. That mouth is going to kill me."

"Just trying to keep up. Now, tell me I can have a second finger."

"Nice and slow—" The cutest little annoyed growl cuts me off.

"Xavier," she huffs out.

I don't dare laugh. "Take what you need, sweetheart. I won't hold you back." Vivi sinks into the pillow chasing her orgasm in earnest, leaving me enraptured. "That's it. So damn perfect. Fucking stunning with your fingers buried inside you."

"Xav." This time my name is drenched in desire, her release right at the tips of her finger.

"You're as sweet as honey when you say my name like that. Let me hear it again."

"I'm right there, so close." Her lip quivers with a shaky exhale before my name spills out of her again.

"Good girl. Let me see you come for me."

Head thrown back and her tits pressed toward the ceiling, she loses herself to her pleasure.

"Jesus, Vivi. You're even more beautiful when you're coming."

My first thought as I watch her come down from her release is that we need to add more to our list. She's got me hooked and I want to watch her fall apart for me in every way possible.

"That was . . ." She shivers. "I thought last time might have been a fluke. Is this what it's supposed to be like? Because it's never been this good, not even on my own."

"Not that I particularly want to hear about your past experiences, but no, it's not always this good. Chemistry makes it better and we have that in spades." There's something in the back of my brain that tells me I'm giving away too much, but Vivienne deserves to know how she affects me. "I haven't stopped thinking about you for weeks."

Her lips rub together like she's thinking about how much to give in return. "Same. I thought after the hallway it would fade, but it only made it worse. I can't get you out of my head."

"If this gets to be too much or if that changes, you need to tell me. I can't stand the thought of hurting you. When you meet someone else or you don't want to do this anymore, you need to be honest with me."

"*If* that happens, I promise to tell you. But we have a lot of things to cross off our list, unless you've changed your mind."

"Not a chance. I'll be home in three days. When I get back to Denver, you better be ready, because that list doesn't stand a chance. I'm coming for everything on it and then some."

"Mhmmm, can't say I have a problem with that." Vivi's lids are heavy as she snuggles into the pile of pillows behind her. "I know it's not on the list, but there's something I wanted to ask you."

I'm still rock hard in my sweats and heavy with need from watching her come, but it can wait. She's relaxed in every sense of the word and I love that this formidable woman is letting her guard down for me, even if it's because she's lost in her post-orgasm delirium. "What's that, sleepy girl?"

"What's the deal with Holland's mom? Do you think she'll come back?"

That's not the direction I thought she was going to take, but I guess I should know better. Vivienne's in my life because of her connection to Tenley. We might be keeping this within the realm of a situationship, but there's a real friendship forming that I'm not willing to give up. "I wish I knew. It would make my life a lot easier if she would communicate . . . literally anything."

"So you haven't heard from her since . . ." Her voice fades away and I can see her doing the math.

I push my hand through my hair. "Since the day we left the hospital. I grew up with a dad who wasn't . . . fit to be a parent. Kristy wasn't thrilled about the pregnancy or being a mom. Maybe I should have encouraged her to sign away her rights in the hospital, but I wanted her to be sure, for Holland. I thought she'd stay close, let me know what she was thinking, but she just vanished."

She brings the phone closer. There's so much sincerity in her gaze that makes it hard for me to swallow around the lump in my throat.

"It's so unfair to put you and Holland through that. I understand if she's not sure about being a mom, but to drag you along without so much as a text . . ."

"All I can do is wait her out at this point." It's the grim truth of the situation. Until she makes a decision, or a suitable amount of time passes, my daughter is stuck in limbo.

"Holland is lucky to have you." She pauses thoughtfully and adds, "And that's not a dig at your ex but because you've put her above everything else. You have the money and connections to pass off her care and be hands off, but you don't."

Her praise softens the hardness that talking about Kristy brings with it. "I'm glad you think so, but you know what I think?"

"What's that?" She's losing the fight to keep the exhaustion out of her voice.

"That it's time for you to go to sleep." I'm not ready to hang up, but the yawn she covers with the back of her hand tells me she needs sleep more than she needs to hear about the drama in my life.

She stuffs her fist under the pillow and relents. "Have it your way. Inquisition over."

"For now," I add, because I'm not closing the door on getting to know each other. "I'll tell you anything you want to know when you're conscious, because we're friends. Remember?"

Hell, I think I might *need* her to be my friend.

"For now," she agrees.

CHAPTER 22

VIVIENNE

Harlowe Corbin is a saint. Literally—her job is saving lives. She goes into dangerous situations to help people in trouble. But if she doesn't stop texting me for status updates on my sex life my best friend is going to need rescuing from *me*.

It's irrational for me to be this annoyed with her, but I'm already painfully aware of Xavier's absence in my life—at least physically. We've exchanged daily texts and calls since I sent him the list, but we haven't seen each other in person.

That damn list is taunting me. And now, Harlowe's nosey face is popping up on my screen, no longer satisfied with the lack of information.

"Aren't you supposed to be in the middle of nowhere for cadaver training today?" As if on cue, Echo barks.

"Such a clever dog," she gushes and I can picture her ruffling Echo's black and brown fur, his adorably floppy ears bouncing. "He says, 'Hi, Auntie Vi. Tell my mom all about your baseball player.'"

"Let's start with the fact that Xavier is decidedly not *mine*. That's kind of the whole point of what we're doing. I'm not ready to give up my life for someone else." Then I sigh, adding, "He's also out of town, which you know." The wheels of my office chair squeak as I push back from my desk, crossing the office to close my door so I'm not overheard.

"You're a lying liar." She laughs loudly; it's one of my favorite sounds. "You made me hold your Ken doll during every pretend wedding ceremony. I was the host of every imaginary first birthday your hoard of Barbies had for their children growing up. He might not be *yours*, or even *the one,* but I know you still want those things."

She's bold and smart and she knows me too well. But all of that was before I watched my brother lose himself when Erica died. It was before the same pain sucked me into early motherhood for my big family and took the joy out of those childish dreams. Someday, I want more, but for now I'm committed to keeping the autonomy I have over my life.

"Plus, you look too happy for someone that only had one amazing orgasm with a hunky baseball player before going back to Solo-Landia."

Even if she is nosey as hell, she's my person. '"Oh god. Let's not call it that," I groan.

"Would you rather I call it Dry Vag Isle? Or No-Man-to-Mount Mountain."

"Pass—on all of it." My head whips side to side even though she can't see. "Absolutely not."

"Tell me the truth."

"I thought it was Echo that could sniff things out," I grumble. "Fine . . . there may have been some phone sex."

There's a pause and then she switches to FaceTime. A meadow, filled with wildflowers, comes into view behind her. Harlowe's long blonde braids are bright under the afternoon sun. Next to her, Echo lies on a crash pad. "I need to be fully immersed when you tell me this."

"How do you have reception out there?" Normally when she's in the field she's nearly impossible to reach.

"My best guess? Divine luck. Don't leave out the good bits, please. There's not a single man in Timberline Peak or the surrounding countries that interests me. I need this."

If she was anyone else, I'd be alarmed at her insistence. But Xavier's coming back today and I'm antsy to see him. Maybe talking to my best friend will help—like releasing a pressure valve.

So, I tell her *almost* every dirty detail. It ends up lightening my mood but it doesn't touch the nagging desire to see him.

"Xavier and I haven't even had sex yet. It's ridiculous that I'm daydreaming about him coming back and checking off another thing on our list," I rant to my best friend.

Harlowe is breathless with laughter on the other end of the phone when I hear her Team Leader telling her it's time to get back to work.

There's a drawn out sigh, like she's not ready for our conversation to end. My heart is heavy too. Her job and the time difference can make it hard for us to talk as much as we want. The fact that we got to FaceTime twice this week is a miracle.

Only a few more months until I can see her in person when I'm home later this summer for HarvestFest.

My parents host HarvestFest at Serra Brilhante Winery every year; it's a tradition I've never missed. Even in college, I'd come home for a long weekend to celebrate the season. Harlowe comes back too even though she doesn't live there any more.

"Time to go fetch some more body parts."

The cackle that tumbles out of me is unguarded. "Imagine hearing that out of context. Good luck with your limbs."

Harlowe snickers, making Echo lift his head. "Look at us making buried bones the theme. You with how badly you want the hot baseball player's bone, and me digging up femurs with my dog."

"You're depraved, and weird, and I love you."

"Love you too. I can't wait to see you and squeeze you in person. I demand a minimum of two minutes of hugging before I let you go."

That's a lot of hugging, but for her, I'll allow it.

"Let's go, Corbin," I hear Harlowe's supervisor say.

"God he's cranky these days, too much time on the mountain and not enough with his wife. I keep telling him to retire so I can have his job, but no . . ." She sighs dramatically and I know Travis is standing over her shoulder.

"And then you'll be in charge. God help us all," I tease before we hang up.

The rest of my day is a blur of meetings, reviewing grants, and donor outreach. Lunch comes and goes without me stopping to eat, so my head is buried in my purse, searching for a protein bar, a stick of gum, anything to get me through this email before I force myself to take a break and find some real food.

A tap at my office door stops me, I lift my head from my oversized purse, embarrassed to be caught foraging like a trash panda. My gaze climbs up muscular legs dusted with red hair and glee chases away my mortification.

Paper rustles and my stomach groans loudly when I see the bag from Buns & Roses clutched in Xavier's hand.

His feet are moving before I can invite him in. I blink once, twice, three times, not believing my eyes. "You're here."

"And it sounds like I got here right in time. Did you skip lunch, Vi?" I missed the deep tenor of his voice and how it turns soft when he says my name. It's better in person.

"Stop. It wasn't that loud."

"Whatever makes you feel better. Good thing I stopped to grab you a treat on my way. It's not Sugar Slice, but Lilah knows a thing or two about baking."

"You stopped by to bring me a snack?"

A rumble starts deep in his chest. I can almost feel it from across the office. He's closer than we've been in a week and not nearly close enough. "Among other things."

"What kind of things?" My eyes take in his tall frame, corded forearms, and the backward hat with red strands curling out from under it. He seems larger than life standing in my office.

"The kind that requires a locked door."

I laugh because I can't believe he's here. It's not exactly what we agreed to—somehow it's more. But I don't care. And it's not because he brought me food, although it certainly helps. "When did you get in?"

Xavier studies me as he locks the door and circles my desk. "They ended up flying us home overnight. I spent time with Holland this morning, then went into the stadium for physical training this morning after Tenley texted me to let me know there was no rush because Holland was sleeping."

"And you thought you'd spend your rare free time bringing me lunch?" He stops next to my chair, spinning it away from my desk, his hands flexing when he wraps them around the armrests and folds over me. I have to tip my head back to look at him, my throat bone dry as I try to swallow down my excitement. "Or did *someone* sell me out?"

"So, you did skip lunch, *again*." With how close he is, the low din of his words shoots straight to my belly, making it flip before desire settles deeper, reminding me badly I've wanted him close for the past few days.

CHAPTER 23

XAVIER

Twice now I've stopped in her office and found out she hasn't eaten. It makes me wonder how often putting work above herself. Vivienne's stomach gives another echoing lurch and I realize I care more than I should about a grown woman feeding herself.

When Tenley let me know that there was no rush to get home, the pull to see Vivi was too strong to ignore. It just so happened my nanny also let slip that her aunt forgot her lunch. And when Cruz mentioned the brownies Lilah made, it added a pit stop to my agenda.

Stopping to grab her lunch was an easy decision. I get to do something for the woman who takes care of everyone else, and cross something off that wish list of hers at the same time. It's a win-win and I refuse to look deeper than that.

"Consider this a bribe. I thought if I showed up with an incentive, you might let me spend some time distracting you from your work this afternoon."

"Bribes are against the Double Play code of ethics, Mr. Kingsley." She's a brat and it's fucking cute.

I reach for the soft curve of her waist and pull her out of the chair. Damn, I like the press of her body against mine . . . too much. I spin us, making her squeak as I settle her in my lap and steal the chair right out from under her.

Now that I've got my hands on her, there's no way I'm letting her go. With that in mind, I keep one around her waist while the other smooths down her silky skirt. The rough calluses on my palm catch on the smooth material until it ends below her knee.

She's soft and warm under my fingers. I relish in the contrast as my hand slips under the hem of her skirt. Taking my time, I draw circles on her inner thigh until she relaxes into my chest, goosebumps rising on her soft skin. Having this kind of effect on her with such simple touches is powerful.

"I came to cross something off your list." With each word, my touch goes higher. "But now that I know you haven't eaten, I'm going to need you to do something for me first."

I almost feel bad when my hand stills and Vivi deflates, already so needy for me. She peers over her shoulder at me. "This feels a little like quid pro quo, and that goes against my morals."

Holding back my laughter I roll my tongue against my cheek, dropping my hand from her leg and reaching for the brown Buns & Roses bag. "Now hardly seems like the time to debate ethics and morality. Not when I'm about to make you come all over my fingers in your office."

"Fair point. What's the catch?"

"You need to eat—that part is non-negotiable. But I'll let you decide if you want dessert or the meal first." She raises her eyebrow at my audacity to demand she eat, even though I know she damn well wants to. So I smirk, adding a polite, "Please."

With a level of sass that rivals her niece, she takes the bag from where I'm holding it in front of us, giving me free rein to go back to touching her. My palm covers the skin where her skirt is still rucked up from earlier.

She peeks back at me. There's a hint of defiance in the dimple at the corner of her upturned mouth telling me she's fighting the urge to argue with me.

On cue, her stomach growls and she peels the bag open, pushing the sandwich aside to pull out the decadent-looking red velvet brownie. I get a sick sense of satisfaction watching her give in.

"Dessert first," I hum. "I like it."

She moans obscenely around the bite. "Oh—It's so good."

My cock immediately thickens in my shorts and I slide my palm up her thigh. "That's my girl. If you don't take care of yourself, I'll make it my job to do it for you and that'll take time away from the list." There's a playful edge in my voice, but I'm not joking.

I've learned enough about Vivi to know that she's the first to jump in and help others—whether it's her niece, her kids at Double Play, or even me. But I've never seen her slow down and do the same for herself. *She* calls it focus—masquerades it as a product of being independent. *I* call it neglecting her own needs. Limited time or not, maybe this situationship is as much about taking care of her as a whole, not only in bed.

"Would you like some?" She twists her top half and offers the brownie to me. The change in position forces my hand further north and draws a breathy inhale from her.

"No, that's for you. I'm craving a taste of something else." When my knuckles brush the damp lace of her underwear. It takes all my willpower to move slowly, tracing two fingers over her center.

Vivi's chin drops. This time, the noise that tumbles from her mouth has nothing to do with the dessert. Her underwear sticks to her as I continue to play with her through the material.

"You're going to come all over these fingers so I can have my dessert too. This is a trade-off, after all. You get the brownie. I get you."

"Xavier." My name is barely more than an exhale. Soft, sweet and tantalizing. She says it again and again, making me exceptionally hard as I work her over.

Hearing Vivi beg for me like I'm her damn savior is better than winning the lottery. I'm the luckiest guy in the world right now. A fact that crystallizes further when her hand comes up to grip the back of my neck.

She squirms, the friction of her ass rubbing against my length. Each twitch of her hips increases the threat that I'll spill in my pants like an inexperienced teen. "Take another bite, so I can give you what you need," I croak, my throat scratchy.

"It's been seven long days since you've touched me. The teasing won't do it. I need your fingers."

Despite her demand, she plays my game, bringing the brownie to her mouth and taking another bite. My eyes flick from her lips to her throat and as soon as she swallows, I sink two fingers inside her tight channel.

"Fuck, yes. I'm so proud of you for telling me what you need."

She shudders, letting my words fuel her chase.

"More." It's whispered because of where we are, but no less urgent.

Each pump of my fingers makes her rub against me, driving us both closer. This is supposed to be about her but I'm as desperate for her release as she is. She's hot, wet, and so goddamn sexy in my lap. There's no way I'm making it out of this chair without coming all over myself.

I curl my fingers, reaching for the spot inside of her. Each stroke makes her breathing more frantic. Completely lost to her pursuit, the brownie hangs between her fingers, in danger of falling to the floor as she braces herself against me and the chair.

"You're fucking perfect, sweetheart." Saving the sweet treat from certain death I bring it to her lips and say, "You need to take care of yourself so you have enough energy for all the ways I want to fuck you." My lips brush the shell of her ear with each word.

"Shit, Xav—I'm going to—oh, Jesus. Yes." Her fingers tighten on my neck.

"Don't hold back. Give me every single drop so I can lick you off my fingers."

She curses quietly, her head falling to my shoulder as her body tenses. Uneven breaths puff out of her. It's too much, and it's been too damn long since I've been with someone. I press the heel of my hand to her clit, urging her on, holding her to me as she rocks in my lap.

The pressure of her against my cock has me seeing stars and there's no stopping the wave of pleasure that hits me.

I bite down on my lip, hissing as hot cum paints my briefs. Thank fuck I don't lose all awareness of the fact that we're in her office, where anyone could walk past.

"Goddamn, Vivienne," I huff, slowly pulling my fingers from her. She shifts in my lap, rearranging herself, her cheeks flushed and her eyes glassy. I couldn't look away if I wanted to. Her hooded eyes track my fingers as I lift them to my lips, sucking up every bit of her sweetness.

"Your cunt is a fucking treat. Next time I taste it, I want you sitting on my face so I don't miss a drop."

Her eyes widen with shock, but it only lasts a second. "Kiss me."

"You want to taste yourself on my lips?"

She nods, her lip pinched between her teeth.

"If I hadn't just come in my pants that would have made me." I grin wildly at her.

"You did?" Her mouth pops open like she can't fathom that it was just as good for me.

"Fucking right I did. And kissing you will have me walking out of here sticky and hard again."

One thing is certain, the mediocre sex in her past had nothing to do with her. She's fire and passion, curiosity and desire. This woman is hungry for intimacy and none of those fools knew how to give it to her. They didn't listen to her body. They didn't pay attention to *her*. And she wasn't comfortable with them the way she is with me.

They didn't deserve her, and it's their loss because I'm taking note of every little thing that gets her off.

My fist tangles in her hair as I pull her mouth to mine, stopping when our foreheads touch. This almost-kiss is charged with need, unlike anything I've ever felt. I can't imagine not tasting her, not giving her what she's asking for, even though keeping this off the table would probably be smart.

Her thumb traces my bottom lip slowly.

"Why do I feel like you're about to change my life with a kiss, sweetheart?"

"It only seems fair considering you've ruined me for anyone else. No one is ever going to be able to make me come like that."

"That was our deal—I give you what no one else has been able to. If you expect me to apologize, you're going to be disappointed."

The attitude rolls off her in waves as she tugs me closer and nips at my bottom lip before kissing me full-on. She sets the tone, her mouth moving over mine before her tongue sweeps inside. Fudge and tartness from the brownie mix with the taste of her, and the combination is as intoxicating as she is.

I swallow her moan and take over for her, pulling her closer and kissing her until she's panting in my arms and I'm hard again.

Kissing her might be dumb, given the boundaries we set, but fuck, is it fun. And if I don't stop now, I'm going to fuck her right here, on her desk. One of us pulls back, but I'm too dizzy to know who it was.

"We should stop." I punctate the statement with a chaste kiss.

Her unfocused eyes sweep around her office. "Probably smart," she agrees, her hands smoothing down my shirt.

Still, I hold her to me, not ready to get up and leave yet. "So . . . Miss Independent has a praise kink?"

She tucks her chin, looking at her lap, letting a nervous giggle fall between us. "I think it's more of a *you* kink."

"As much as I like the sound of that, you blossom when I talk. Especially when I'm telling you how good—how perfect you are."

"Not all that surprising, considering I was a textbook people-pleaser growing up. Now that you mention it, I'm sure it has something to do with my past lackluster experiences. Part of me would rather fake it with a partner than see them disappointed that I couldn't finish." She shrugs like that isn't the saddest thing I've ever heard.

"Nah. The boys you had before me—yes, *boys*—were the problem, not you. They didn't listen to you or your body. You fucking light up under my touch because I see what makes those pretty greens roll back in your head. I listen to what makes you whimper; I notice the way you shiver for me when you like something. All they had to do was pay attention."

Vivi rolls her lips together and opens her mouth. There's an argument building behind those pretty lips, but I won't hear her make excuses for them, so lift a finger to her lips, silencing her. "I'm done talking about how other men treated you and your body. From now on, the only thing I care about is how *I* treat this body, because until you tell me otherwise, this body is mine."

"And your body is . . ." Her voice fades off, her eyes trailing down me.

"No one has made me come in my pants since I was sixteen, so I think it's safe to say you own every inch of my body, sweetheart."

Pink stains her cheekbones when her gaze falls to my lap. "That kind of makes me a hypocrite for not noticing how much you were enjoying it."

"I prefer to think of it as the greatest compliment. You were focused on your own pleasure for once—just the way I wanted you to be."

She sighs and I know our time together this afternoon is coming to an end. It's for the best; I need to get home to my daughter and she needs to get back to work.

"I should . . ." I thumb over my shoulder.

"Yeah, I should . . ." She nods to her computer, but neither of us moves.

"This is weird, right?" I ask.

"Kind of." She bites her lip and I give her the time she needs to process what's on her mind. "I've only ever had casual sex before."

"Sweetheart, we agreed not to talk about other guys anymore."

"Calm down, caveman. My point is, this is different . . . we aren't that. Without this"—she waves a hand between us—"our paths still cross. There's no avoiding each other. It's not the same as a random hookup from a bar or a dating app. I can live the rest of my life without seeing them again."

"That's why we have rules. I don't want them to stop us from getting to know each other, and I like spending time with you, texting you, but I don't have a relationship in me—not now. Probably not any time soon."

"And I don't want that. My whole life I've been what everyone else needs me to be and I'm finally what *I* need. I won't give that up."

"For the right person, you won't have to."

She reels back like that truth slapped her. "Everyone takes, Xavier. Even when they aren't trying to."

I would take too—I know I would. My life is too chaotic not to. "Do you want to stop—" My voice is cut off by the shake of her head.

"No." The word rushes out of her. "That's not what I'm saying. I enjoy spending time with you, too. I needed to know we were on the same page."

"So it's cool if I keep texting and calling you, even if I'm not sure when I can see you again. Because it might be days or it might be weeks."

"Please," she says, sagging with relief. "And I get it. The season is crazy and you have a daughter."

It's the same way I feel. We might not know what the hell we're doing, but I know I don't want to act like she's nobody to me just because she can't be everything to me.

Holding her hips, I stand from the chair and straighten her skirt. It's a little wrinkled but the pleats hide most of it. Tugging her with me, I walk to her door, stopping with my hand on the knob.

I need one more kiss to hold me over. I pull her to me, spinning her against the door and kiss her goodbye the way I want to. I'm already taking from her and I like it, because kissing her brings me back to life. She makes me forget all the stress and pressure. For a while, I just get to be me.

Her lips are swollen and red, marked with my kiss when I pull back . . . and I like that too.

"I'll text you," I say, and unlike the boys that came before me, I mean it.

CHAPTER 24

VIVIENNE

My head spins as the door shuts with a quiet snick, leaving me alone with my thoughts, and Xavier on his way home. I don't do things like this—not in my office, during the middle of my workday. Is this real life? Because it sure doesn't feel like it.

To be sure, I lift my fingers to my swollen lips. The remnant tingle is real, and so are the wrinkles in my skirt from being bunched up around my waist.

Each time we're together is better than the last. I'm honestly concerned for my well-being. At this rate, by the time he's inside me, I might end up in a sex-induced coma.

The man takes his time. He asks me questions and the way he watches me . . . I suppress the urge to shiver. And the way he talks to me every step of the way—god it's hot. I guess you can take the people pleaser out of the girl, but you're left with a girl with a praise kink.

It requires some effort, but I push him to the back corner of my brain and refocus on the work I need to do for the rest of the afternoon.

Another visitor shows up at my door hours later when the tingles have sadly disappeared from my body.

"Always the overachiever. You're the last one here," Tenley's teases from the door to my office.

"If that's true how'd you get in here?" Clay, the intern who works the front desk, would never leave without locking up.

"Good timing. I came in as he was leaving. Clay locked up on his way out. Could you step away from the email and grab dinner with me."

"Nonna's?" I ask, already knowing her answer.

"Hell yes. I feel like I've hardly seen you the last few weeks."

The guilt that causes is fast and furious. "We do need to catch up and . . ."

"Pasta is love served family-style." We both recite the saying that Nonna, my mom's mother, had cross-stitched on the front of her favorite frilly apron. Pasta was as much a religion in our family as wine was growing up. Each house dotting the vineyard hillside had the same quote, hand-stitched by Nonna, hanging somewhere in their kitchen.

My dad's grandparents immigrated from Portugal and started Serra Brilhante Winery. It's where he was raised, and us after. Generations of Cardoza's have worked the land, including my brother, Tenley's dad.

After my parents met and fell in love, they had an army of kids. My dad's Portuguese heritage blended with my mom's close-knit Sicilian family. Now, decades later, there's no life event, good or bad, big or small, that doesn't call for both wine, pasta, and a whole lot of fussing from both grandmothers.

There was never a shortage of love, food, or noise in our house. There was also an excessive amount of work to go around. We all had roles to fulfill that helped keep the vineyard running, like it or not.

"Dinner sounds perfect." My time with Tenley is slipping away. Before I know it, she'll graduate and move out. I press my laptop closed and I slip it into the bag at my feet.

The corner of her mouth tips up in a knowing smile. "Buns & Roses? Tell me you had an actual lunch and not just a sticky bun."

"There was lunch." And an orgasm. My attention drops to the garbage where the mostly-eaten sandwich resides inside the discarded brown paper bag. Not a crumb of brownie is left.

"Xavier was raving about their red velvet brownie earlier. Said it was so good the taste was going to stick with him for days. What a crazy coincidence."

My gaze shoots back to her. I almost choke on the gulp of air I suck in. She's smiling at me in a way that makes me nervous, like she knows.

Is it bad if I wait to tell her until *after* a glass of wine?

"Crazy indeed." But not for the reason she thinks. "Come on, let's go and we can catch up over dinner."

♥

The first time we ate here after Tenley moved in with me was because of the nostalgia the name evoked in us. My niece was a little homesick and pasta was the perfect cure. We've kept coming back because no one in Denver does Sicilian better, and being here feels like the best part of home.

Every detail, down to the stone walls and bright-patterned plates, remind me of family dinners my nonna used to host weekly in the vineyard's tasting room. It was the one time each week where everything stopped and we all came together. No shop talk, just lots of family. It was the one place I could be me without the expectations that came with being the eldest daughter and caretaker for my gaggle of cousins.

"How were your nursing classes last semester?" the hostess, Carmine, who knows us by name, asks Tenley as she leads us back to our table. Green vines climb the wall next to our favorite table. It's set back in a corner where we can laugh without worrying about disturbing other diners. Our own little family dinners—the two of us.

"Would you like to see the wine list?" Carmine's lips quirk up in a smirk. She knows damn well I don't need a list.

"My father would disown me if I had to peruse the list. If you wanted to adopt me into your family permanently all you had to do was ask."

Tenley snickers across the table. She knows damn well Dad would never.

"You know, I do have a brother." Carmine laughs warmly.

"And you know I don't date." Although I'm not sure that claim holds anymore.

Our favorite hostess shakes her head. "Rosalia will be over to take your drink order shortly."

As Carmine said, her sister stops by within minutes, taking our orders and happily chatting for a minute before she has to rush off to help other tables. Now it's just Tenley and I, plus the elephant in the room—if an elephant were shaped like a hot-as-hell catcher, who makes my body come alive and happens to be my niece's employer.

I swallow dryly, reaching for my wine to wash the nerves down, when my niece saves me from myself. "Vi, I know you didn't leave your desk to get lunch. So, who came through with the Buns & Roses delivery today?"

There's a hint of knowing blossoming at the corner of her lips as she waits. We never stood a chance of hiding things.

"Your boss."

She's wearing a megawatt grin now. "It took you two long enough." There are practically hearts in her eyes as she bounces in her seat.

"Hold on there, crazy lady," I caution before she gets too carried away. "Whatever you think is happening between us, I can guarantee you, it's not that. I can hear the wedding bells going off in your head."

"You literally can't." She laughs back.

"Seriously, I know you better than anyone else. We aren't dating, it's more like a . . ." Sometimes the two of us are more like best friends than aunt and niece, but I draw the line at having an explicit conversation about my sex life with her.

"Awe . . . is he your Netflix and Chill buddy?"

God she's so smug about this. "We're calling it a situationship."

She rolls her eyes so hard I'm astounded she doesn't fall out of her chair from the momentum. "How very Gen Z of you."

"Neither of us are looking for a relationship. I don't want one and he's too busy."

She hums, like the pain in my ass she is. "That's the dumbest thing I've ever heard. But if you need to fake it for awhile I can go along with it."

"No one is faking." I rub my temples, reaching for my glass.

I should have ordered a bottle.

"Why are you so against relationships? Your parents have been married forever and still look at each other like love-struck teens. If it weren't for the *life changes* they'd still be popping out siblings for you."

"Gross. I don't need to think about that."

"Suit yourself, but I hope I find someone that looks at me the way your dad looks at your mom," she gushes, propping her fists under her chin. "And look what they built. They have this incredible, close-knit family, and a thriving vineyard. They've worked side by side everyday and still love each other."

"Did they though?" I ask frustration sneaking into my tone. "*I* raised that close-knit family while *they* were focusing on building that thriving empire."

Tenley blinks like I slapped her and I realize how bitter I sound.

"No," I choke out. "I didn't mean it like that."

She shakes her head, her hands twisting her napkin now. I put that look on her face. *Fuck,* I'm screwing this up. "I'm sorry, Tenley."

She pushes her shoulders back, masking the hurt. "It's fine. I get it."

"I don't think you do. You are the best thing that ever happened to me—my built-in best friend. You healed me when we lost your mom and I don't regret a minute of the time we spent together. We needed each other, Tenley." I search her face through the tears I'm holding back. "But as I got older and more babies were born at the vineyard no one asked me what I wanted. They saw the bond I had with you and thrust the responsibility of caretaker for everyone else on me. There were no day trips to the ocean with my friends like my parents and brothers had. No music festivals in the bay area, no prom. Harlowe was the only friend that didn't abandon me when they realized how little fun I was."

"Do your parents—does my dad know you feel like this?"

I shake my head. Her hurt evaporates and leaves behind sadness and I hate that as much.

"Is that why you picked Maryland for college? Why you stay away and only go home for HarvestFest?" Unshed tears glitter under the dim lights of the dining room.

I lick my lips, not wanting to answer but knowing she deserves it. "Yes. I love and miss them, but I need space to live my own life. If I stayed there, I'd work on the vineyard, never seeing what else I could do."

It's the part I leave unsaid that has the biggest impact: *Like her dad and uncles.*

This time her head shake cracks my chest open. It's like she can't quite fathom how we got here and who this person in front of her is. "My dad stays because he wants to be there, because every memory he has of my mom is tied to that vineyard. Because he loves it as much as he loved her. Because he loves his family."

One hot tear streaks down her face and I can't sit by and watch. My napkin flutters to the ground when I stand and round the table. I drop to one knee and wrap my arms around her middle.

"Tenley, I know. I watched your parents fall in love on that vineyard as they worked together. Their love story was always my favorite one to reenact with my dolls—it gave me my greatest gift. But I'm not your dad, and I'm not your mom."

How do I explain this without doing more damage?

"The vineyard breathed air into them, even before they fell in love, but it suffocated me."

She nods like she understands, but I don't think she does, not really. I let her go, returning to my seat before drawing the attention of the entire restaurant.

"You won't hurt him, will you," she asks.

Ouch, that stings. But she's holding back tears in a restaurant and it's all my fault so I'd say I deserve it.

"No, we agreed to rules. He doesn't want a relationship any more than I do. What we have is physical—convenient."

"I don't think this is a good idea. He was supposed to be . . ." She slams her lips shut, biting it nervously. Before I can ask her what she was going to say, the server brings our food and my niece quickly changes the subject, schooling her expression like the last five minutes never happened and don't have it in my heart to rehash it.

"There's a home game coming up next weekend that I want to take Holland to. It's Saturday afternoon. I thought Xavier might enjoy having her there, but I was going to see if you would go with me. I'd be more comfortable having backup, but I get it if that's weird now."

Hell would have to freeze over for me to say no to her right now, and I'm pretty sure she knows that.

STUDY ABROAD: MASTER PLAN

- Convince Vi to start dating
- Figure out how to get Ginger Daddy and Aunt Vi together
- Get Transcripts
- Scheduling a meeting with Advisor
- Write essay
- Get letters of recommendations
- Complete application by Nov 1st
- Save money from nannying
- Tell Vi about Spain
- Have Vi help me tell Dad
- Make sure Aunt Vivi and Ginger Daddy don't screw this up

CHAPTER 25

VIVIENNE

Before working at Double Play, I'd never been to a baseball game. I grew up in a football family—my brothers played and my dad raised us all to be die-hard Miners fans. To this day, he's still a season ticket holder.

Back then, he claimed the tickets were to entertain business partners, but over the years he's taken my brothers and nephews more than he's ever taken potential distributors or clients.

Since starting this job three years ago, I've been to dozens of Bandits games, but this is the first time I'm going in an unofficial capacity and my stomach is twisted like the pretzels they sell in the concession stands.

Tight knots of nerves and excitement have my stomach flipping and I might vomit all over the peanut-covered concrete. In the days since my emotional dinner with Tenley, I've prioritized time with her, only calling and texting Xavier when she wasn't around. His schedule of back-to-back home games has made it impossible for us to see each other anyway. All his free time has rightfully been spent with his daughter before he goes back on the road.

Tonight, I'll get to see him and even if it's only from the stands while he plays, I can't deny it has me absolutely giddy. Tenley arranged for us to sit with the other Bandits families behind the dugout. Normally the wives sit in the outfield, but with Holland coming, we're sitting behind the protection of the net, and close to her dad.

"It's really early. We should have waited." Tenley nervously chews on her lip, focusing on the field where the players are taking batting practice.

"This is perfect." I pat the seat next to me, coaxing her to sit. My eyes drop to Holland, who's strapped to her chest. "Let's take her out while she's awake so she doesn't get too hot."

Reaching into my small belt bag I grab the surprise I brought.

"Stop! That's adorable. You got her that?" Tenley's excitement is written all over her smug face.

"Just shut up, will you?" I laugh. God, she's impossible. I wanted to do something nice for Xavier. Without his ex in the picture, he doesn't have someone to make moments like this special and, well, he deserves this. "It doesn't mean anything."

"Yeah, of course. Seems legit."

I clutch the tiny teal jersey to my chest, looking around frantically. "Oh screw off, Ten." When I'm sure no one who matters is watching, I set it across my lap, fingers brushing over the tiny letters that spell out Kingsley.

My gaze snags on the number seven and then does a sweep of the field, looking for the other number seven, but I don't find him. My neck prickles with embarrassment when I ask, "Is it too much? Should I just—" I unzip my purse, ready to shove it back inside, when Tenley's hand covers my arm, stopping me.

"It's perfect. He's gonna love it."

Chewing my lips, I check the field again. "Okay, let's change her before he comes out to stretch."

Tenley nods in agreement, quickly unstrapping the baby carrier and laying Holland across her lap so I can slip her tiny arms through the jersey and pull it over the light denim romper she's wearing.

"Oh my god," Poppy says when she catches sight of us, leading the rest of the women down the stairs. "Quick, someone cover Lilah's eyes. This is so cute it might make her spontaneously produce a twin."

I look and find all four of them watching in delight.

"I hate you," Indie says, her lashes glittering with unshed tears. "I'm going to fucking cry when he sees her and I'm absolutely going to blame the egg retrieval hormones."

This *is* too much. Tenley was right. Situationships don't do this. I should leave. The other girls are here and they'll be more than happy to help with Holland. But when I look at Tenley, I know I can't bail on her, especially not after what an asshole I was the other night.

"Ladies, I'm going to need you to chill. She's one comment from a freak out. *It's* not that deep," my niece says, her tone placating and making me feel like one who needs a babysitter.

Thankfully, they take pity on me and don't say another word about the fact that Holland is clad in her dad's number, thanks to me. Instead, they refocus their giddy chatter on the guys who are jogging out onto the field for warm-ups.

Next to me, the girls are gushing over their men, and it stings because I want to join in, but Xavier's not mine. Not really. I rub my knuckles over my breastbone, trying to ease the ache there. I'm as left out now as I was as a teen. Or maybe the sting there is because of the man in question. I don't know and I'm not sure I want to.

All of that is washed away when he steps out of the dugout and spots me in the crowd.

If I was brave enough to claim him publicly, I'd be vocally celebrating the way his pinstripe pants hug his thighs, highlighting the sharp line of his quad muscle that you see through the fabric. There'd be raving about his devotion, not just to his little girl—the same one that's suddenly being thrust into my arms—but to his sport.

"Hold her. He'll want a picture of this."

The look she gives me spells trouble, but it's nothing compared to my ovaries twitching at Xavier's approach. The All-Star catcher eats up the dirt between us with his sure strides. The uniforms alone are hot, but the catcher's gear gives him an edge over everyone else on that field.

His cocky smile fades, replaced with genuine awe when he notices the jersey his daughter is wearing.

Raw emotion paints his face, his hand dragging over his mouth as his steps slow. He looks from his daughter to me and I lick my dry lips, trying to hear anything over the pounding in my ears.

A sound that gets louder when he flips his hat backward as he approaches the net. When he's all but pressed against the black barrier, I step forward, bringing Holland to him.

There's not a functioning brain cell in my body as Xavier reaches through the net with his fingers and takes his daughter's hand. Luckily, for both of us, Indie springs into action, working the zipper on the net free, creating an opening a few seats down.

"Did you do this?" he asks quietly, as he follows me down the row.

"Tenley planned the game, but yeah, the jersey was me. Is that okay?"

"Is it—" He shakes his head in disbelief. "Yeah, it's okay, sweetheart. It's more than okay. No one's ever done something like this for me before."

I look up from where he's scooping a sleeping Holland out of my arms to find wonder glittering in his icy blues. My heart kickstarts in my chest and I know that if I get the chance, I'll keep doing things like this for him because, judging by the way he grabs on to my wrist, squeezing gently, no one else ever has.

"Thank you," he mouths as he dips his head to bury his nose in the crown of red hair that matches his own.

The moment is short but no less sweet as Tenley snaps a few more pictures. There's a shout from behind him and Xavier glances over his shoulder, then back down to his daughter before he leans through the netting and places her back in my arms for safe keeping.

His strong arm comes around my shoulder, nearly throwing me off balance when he pulls both of us to his chest. "Meet me after the game." He nods towards the woman watching behind us. "The girls can help you three get down there."

"We'll do our best, but it's kind of up to this one."

Xavier folds over us brushing a kiss on Holland's cheek. "Be good so daddy can thank Vivi properly after the game." My blood heats at the unspoken meaning behind his statement.

Stepping back, he focuses his attention on Tenley over my shoulder. "I want copies of those pictures. You made my whole season, kid."

"Don't make it weird, Ginger Daddy, it was nothing."

He shakes his head and I cringe at the nickname. Xavier jogs back to his team and an usher comes over to zip the window up. It's a good thing too, because I'm busy watching number seven cross the field, his tight pants giving me the best view in the stadium.

"Don't drool on the baby," Tenley says with a healthy dose of sarcasm, taking her from my arms.

"Ginger Daddy," I mumble to her, my head cocked in question.

"It drives him crazy, and not in the same way it would if it were coming out of your mouth."

I snicker. She's the same way with my brothers, always doing her best to get under their skin. "I bet it does."

She returns to her seat with Holland, looking smug.

"What exactly are your intentions with our catcher?" Poppy asks, leaning over the arm of her seat.

"She's using him for orgasms." Once again, Tenley displays her utter lack of filter.

"Ten!" I whisper-shout.

"Own it, Aunt Vi. That's what it is, a situationship. There's no shame as long as no one gets hurt."

Her warning looms over me and I don't like the way it's becoming a little less possible to not develop feelings for this man with each passing day.

My focus is drawn to where he's stretching on the field only to find him watching me with a lopsided smirk. It packs a punch I know will stick throughout the game and I issue a silent plea that Holland lets me claim that thank you from him.

"Give her a break, Tenley. Your aunt deserves good sex just like the rest of us."

It's on the tip of my tongue to tell them we haven't gotten quite that far yet, when a groan comes from next to me. "I'm all for it. In fact, up until recently I'd been trying to hook her up with my hot professor, but I don't want to hear details."

"Why does it feel like she's babysitting us?" Indie asks from the other side of Poppy.

"Because she's more mature than both of you." Lilah laughs and then adds, seriously, "Tenley, would you consider being cloned before this baby arrives?"

"Cloning is a myth, Mama." We all turn to look at my niece who's bouncing Holland in her arms.

"You're a nursing student, a future medical professional—a scientist," I scoff.

"It's true though, I did this whole deep dive on it. There's no irrefutable proof available to the public that Dolly was ever cloned. And there's no way it's real to the extent the government claims, and not one single bad guy has used it to their advantage yet. I'm not buying it."

I shake my head. There's no point in arguing with her, but even if I wanted to, the announcer's voice breaks up the conversation, asking us to stand for the national anthem.

The first two innings are relatively uneventful, and I get some time to talk to the girls that I don't know as well. Honestly,they're all delightful, and I'd be happy to talk to them all night. But the guys have other plans.

With two outs in the bottom of the second inning, Cruz takes the plate. He's the first of the group to bat this inning and sends the ball sailing over the third baseman's head.

For a pregnant woman in her third trimester, Lilah is still incredibly agile— cheering and jumping up and down when her husband rounds third base. She's practically climbing the netting as he kicks up a cloud of dust, sliding headfirst into home plate right in front of us, and I'm afraid she's going to go into labor when he struts over after the ump signals him safe to place a kiss on her belly and then her lips from the field.

Following Cruz's run, it's a parade of baseball boys showing off for their women. One after another, they shamelessly flirt with their significant others while they play.

"You know they're never going to let us go back to sitting in the outfield now," Mia comments when Dean winks at her from outside the batter's box, making a show of adjusting his pants. It's a seemingly innocent gesture as his hand is nowhere near his dick, until he pulls his helmet down, covering his face for everyone not immediately in front of him and winks at his girlfriend.

"Well, shit, I think Mia just got pregnant," Lilah jokes.

"Can't get pregnant twice," Mia says under her breath, her face morphing from dazed to panicked.

We all turn to look and find Mia and Poppy staring at each other wide-eyed, completely missing the at bat.

"Care to repeat that louder for the rest of us?" Lilah laughs while the sisters-in-law glance back and forth between each other. Mia's jaw tenses with worry. We wait while a silent conversation passes between them, both of them crossing their arms and squaring off.

It's Poppy who speaks first. "I didn't hear anything. Did you, Mia?"

"Nope," she says.

Indie's eyes shift back and forth like they're watching that game they play on the jumbotron with the ball under the hat. Finally, she throws up her hands. "Fine, torture us." Indie's voice turns soft. "Please don't let me stop you from sharing your news." She waves a hand in front of her face. "Fucking hormone shots. I promise these are tears of excitement for any news that may or may not be coming."

Holland's sleeping soundly after her bottle and diaper change during the seventh inning stretch. She's been an absolute doll as we passed her around, taking turns cuddling her, the carrier all but forgotten.

Or at least she's trying to sleep soundly, but things get tense in the ninth and I have to pass her to Tenley, who's the least invested in the outcome of the game.

The rest of us are barely hanging on, clinging to the edge of our seats when the Diablos load the bases up for a potentially game-changing rally. With two outs and only one point behind us, they're in position to take the lead. Every pitch ratchets up my pulse. It looks like the Bandits might be in trouble with a full count on the batter, until he fouls it high in the air.

My fingers wrap around the armrest, and I suck in a nervous breath, the ball climbs and climbs, before turning back towards the earth. Xavier rips off his mask, tossing it to the side. Head tilted back, he tracks the ball as it comes closer. It's a race between him and gravity. Using the dugout railing for leverage, he throws his whole body into it, stretching and snagging the ball before he flips over the railing. I swear my heart stops for a moment, and then, when he pops back up with the ball in his glove, it restarts.

The catch ends the game and I absolutely lose it—much to Xavier's delight. He dusts himself off and smirks at me right before his team swarms him and I lose sight of him in the chaos of the celebration.

We pass the time in our seats talking about the upcoming Fourth of July holiday. When the girls find out I don't have plans, they don't quit until I've agreed to spend the day with them watching the game and lounging in Dom and Indie's pool. The crowd begins to thin and we all head to the family waiting area together.

While everyone else lounges on the couch, looking completely at home, I pace the length of the room.

"You're making me dizzy. Sit down," Indie says from the opposite end of the couch.

I shouldn't be here.

Tenley laughs. "If you don't belong here, I'm definitely out of place."

"It's not the same and you know it." I twirl a lock of hair around my finger, studying it. "You're his nanny and you four are all wives and girlfriends."

"Fiancé," Poppy reminds me cheerfully.

"Right, that's what I mean. I'm nothing."

"Do you want to be here?" Mia asks without judgment.

"Yes," I say on a shaky breath, my feet stopping.

"Then you belong here," Lilah says, like it's the simplest thing in the world.

It's said with such earnestness that I believe her without question.

CHAPTER 26

XAVIER

When you experience as much pain and ugliness as I did after my mom died, you know true beauty when you see it. Vivienne waiting for me outside the locker room, with my daughter in her arms, isn't just another pretty sight, it's breathtaking.

This woman, who barely knows Holland, and has no real ties to her, is holding her like she's a treasured gift. Her green eyes are soft as she whispers calming words. It's such a startling contrast to Holland's own mother.

I can't make Kristy want to be a part of her daughter's life. Choosing not to be a parent is a valid choice, but I want a clean break for Holland and I.

Still, it guts me because I'm all too aware that there is no erasing the pain it will someday cause Holland. It's been over twenty years, and I'm only starting to heal from my childhood with the help of Edward, Holland, Tenley, Vivi, and my teammates. Dread consumes me any time I think about the unknown and navigating that conversation with my daughter gracefully when the time comes.

I stand back, watching Vivi dote on Holland. It tickles something in the back of my brain. It might be the leftover emotions from the shock of them being here. Or maybe it's bigger than that. Tonight has been special, and it wouldn't have been if not for Vivi. Seeing my daughter wearing my jersey for the first time, and having her here, surrounded by people who love her, healed a damaged part of me.

"There we go," Tenley says, standing from where she's crouched over the diaper bag at Vivi's feet, screwing a lid on a bottle. Her attention catches on me, leaning against the door frame, watching this all unfold quietly, but she quickly refocuses on Holland and Vivi.

Her aunt smiles warmly at her, reaching out for the bottle. "I've got it. You hogged her for most of the game."

With all the dramatic flare I've come to expect, my nanny rolls her eyes. Beneath all the sass, there's a sparkle when she releases her hold on the bottle. "That's a boldfaced lie. Are you trying to take my job from me?"

"Nope, my nanny days are behind me, but she's so perfect and I just need a little hit."

Stepping forward, I speak up. "That's what they all say. Next thing you know, you're a junkie, pressing your nose to her head every chance you get." I say it like I'm joking, but there's nothing I wouldn't do for a whiff of that soft smell that clings to Holland.

Vivienne's eyes lift, surprised to find me there, her gaze tracking over the length of me, making me stand a little taller. I'm still in my baseball pants and a form-fitting undershirt. Judging by the way she drags her teeth over her glossed lips, the look does something for her.

Most of the makeup she wears to work is missing, but she looks even prettier with only a touch of mascara and a shine to her plump lips. She's dressed down too, in a pair of leggings and a tank top that molds to her curves.

A throat clears next to me. Tenley watches us with a half smirk. *Busted.*

I run a hand through my hair, pulling my focus from her aunt.

For the past month, Tenley's sole focus has been taking care of my daughter. While she's well compensated and all signs point to her loving the job, it's a lot for anyone, but especially a nineteen-year-old who must miss having a social life.

"So . . . I've got to do press." I rub my palm over my day-old stubble. Murphy pulled me aside before I hit the shower to let me know I was needed for the postgame wrap-up—something they've let me skip for most of the season.

Starting tonight isn't ideal; I had other plans for after the game. One that involved mapping out every inch of Vivienne's body.

Vivi hums thoughtfully, talking to Holland who's happily sucking away on a bottle now. "The heavy burdens of making the play of the day with that catch."

Tenley scoops up the diaper bag, ready to help. "That's fine. I can stay, or we can head home." Every word is genuine, but before she can cross the small space and grab Holland, I step forward, bringing me nearly chest to chest with Vivi. Holland's content, nearly asleep as she eats in her arms.

"No, head out. I can take things from here." I'm looking at Tenley, part of me not ready to give up on the idea of more time with her aunt tonight. It's selfish, stupid, and definitely beyond the bonds of what we agreed to. "You should enjoy what's left of your night."

"That's not—"

I cut her off. "Go have some fun. You deserve the time off."

"Some *responsible* fun," Vivi tacks on.

"If you say so." Tenley holds out the diaper bag and both Vivi and I reach for it at the same time. Her invested gaze snaps between us.

"I'll take the bag. You take the baby," Vivi says, hiking it up her shoulder and stepping in close, giving me a tempting glimpse of her cleavage as she slides Holland into my waiting arms.

Tenley waves and follows the crowd outside leaving us behind.

"You don't need to . . . I'm sure you have plans." The words taste wrong on my tongue, but I force them out.

Vivi crosses her arms under her chest, the swell of her soft breasts straining against her tank top. "Big plans." The corner of her mouth betrays her, twitching, despite her attempt to appear serious.

"Is that so?" Flirting with a baby in my arms is new for me, but the natural give and take between us makes it impossible to stop.

"Oh good! You're still here. I thought you bailed. Time to head to the press room," Piper, the club's manager of media relations, says. "Is Holland coming?"

"Yes," I answer.

"Okay! The female audience will eat that up." She glances at Vivi smiling. "I see you've got the arsenal of supplies. Let's find you a seat in case dad needs backup."

I'm about to protest, when Vivi grins up at me. "I've got faith in you, but an extra set of hands with live cameras never hurts."

There's an extra octave in her voice that's not normally there. She's flirting back and I fucking love it.

God, I hope these postgame remarks are brief.

CHAPTER 27

VIVIENNE

This isn't normal, not for me. Men holding babies have zero effect on me. None. Never have. But the man in front of me, still clad in tight baseball pants and a shirt that clings to every dip and swell of his muscled body, is fueling *so* many fantasies right now.

It's purely a carnal reaction, driven by biology, because there's no other explanation for how I feel watching Xavier fully own this single dad gig. He's got confidence I haven't seen from him since last year—only less boastful and more settled. It has me nearly combusting.

Sitting in the back of the pressroom to listen to his postgame remarks, I'm like Baby in *Dirty Dancing*. If someone asks me why I'm here, the only thing I'd be able to tell them is I carried a diaper bag. That's how dumbfounded I am looking on as he shifts his hold on Holland, commanding the room.

Xavier sits at the long table with a microphone in front him, owning the attention of all the reporters, all while cradling the sweetest baby in his arms. He holds Holland's pacifier in place while answering question after question with witty remarks and thoughtful responses. Piper eats it up next to me, clasping her hands under her chin while he charms the pants off everyone in the room.

"Xavier, how do you like your team's chances at the postseason?" a young reporter in the second row asks.

"Great question, Jack. There's no arguing that we have the talent—the heart is there too. Every guy in that locker room is hungry. We're doing our best to stay healthy and taking it one game at a time. It's all we can do, but yeah, I wouldn't bet against us."

"This is PR gold," Piper whispers when Holland's tiny fist balls up, lifting in solidarity with her dad.

It is, but more than that, Xavier looks at ease and genuinely happy.

Postgame remarks wrap up and he heads straight through the crowd of reporters, blazing a path towards me. I grab the diaper bag at my feet and stand to meet him halfway, because following his lead is all I'm capable of in this state.

Xavier stops in front of me and our height difference has never been more obvious as it is while he smirks down at me, looking pleased as pie. With his daughter in one arm, he takes my chin, tilting it up. It's a simple touch, nothing overtly sexual, yet the claiming nature of it has my tongue darting out to wet my lips.

"Will you tell me more about those big plans you've got for tonight?" Right there, in a room full of reporters, he puts me on my knees for him like it's the easiest thing he's ever done.

There's no hiding my smile back when I tell him, "Well, you see I've got a to-do list a mile long and I was hoping you could help me with that."

He takes me by the hand, leading me to the hallway outside the locker room, giving us space from the media. His muscles strain against his shirt as he leans in close. "Give me a minute to change." He looks from Holland to me and back again. "I want to get to the list as badly as you, but would you mind if I shower when we get back to my place? I want to get you two home."

"Not at all. Do what you need to, we'll be waiting."

He hands off Holland, disappearing into the locker room to change. It only takes minutes before he reappears, and takes Holland back from me. Our arms brush during the transfer and goosebumps scatter everywhere. It's unnerving how one touch can send me reeling. No one else has ever held this much power over me.

I need space before I forget what this is—before the current of the night carries me away with it. I get it on the drive back to his place, him in the SUV with Holland, me driving his Audi.

But it doesn't last long. When we get back to his house, he pours me a glass of red instead of taking me up on my offer to put Holland down so he can shower.

Then he points to the couch, his tone brooking no argument. "Sit. Your only job right now is to relax for a few minutes. I've got this."

The urge to help is ingrained in my marrow. Years of fighting it has yet to erase my people pleasing nature, but I can tell it would be pointless as he pushes the glass of wine into my hand, so I do as he asks.

"Okay, Áine. Stay asleep like the angel I know you are and I'll get you a pony for your first birthday," Xavier whispers, using a light touch to remove Holland from her infant seat.

The first sip of wine washes over me, warming me as much as the meaning behind his words.

"Bold move. Bribing the baby with a pony."

"Worth it." Those two words and one devastatingly playful smirk make me go from warm to burning up under his gaze as he moves towards the stairs.

Fifteen minutes later, I'm halfway through my glass of wine and almost caught up on my social media scrolling when the sound of footsteps has me looking up.

Xavier stops, leaning against the arched entryway into the living room. The light from the hallway casts shadows around him. He's edible in a pair of gray joggers and a black cotton shirt, but he may as well be naked with the way my body reacts.

"Fuck." He draws the word out, stalking towards me slowly. "You have no right to look as tempting as you do simply lounging on my couch."

"Says the barefoot man in gray sweats." The wineglass at my lips catches the words, muting them. "You're basically a thirst trap with a pulse."

"What was that?" he asks, stopping beside the couch and taking the glass from me, setting it on the coffee table. He's imposing and I can't look away.

I bite my lip. "Nothing, ignore me."

"Yeah, there's no way I could ignore you. Since the second I found you standing in my hallway, you've invaded every spare thought." He sinks down on a knee, leaning over me, surrounding me with his fresh scent.

"Has anyone ever told you that you're a shameless flirt?" My hand falls to the knee that's pressed to my hip. His eyes follow the same path, but he doesn't answer and I can't stand the silence. "Thankfully, you've improved because your first attempt at flirting was brutal."

Something between a laugh and a groan shakes his chest. "Here I was hoping you'd forget about that encounter now that you know me."

My secondhand embarrassment threatens to pull a laugh out of me. Feeling bad, my hand flies up to stifle it.

Fingers circle my wrist, catching it. "That smile is too pretty to hide, even if you're laughing at my expense."

I bite my lip, leaning forward and pulling him closer. "Past Xavier kind of deserved it."

"He really did. I've already apologized but I'm still mortified that I spoke to anyone that way, but even more so because it was you," he admits sheepishly.

"And all is forgiven—it has been for a while. But I'm curious, if you could have a do over, what would you have said?"

His heavy sigh fans across my chest when he drops his head between us. "It's hard to say. I'd like to tell you I'd have charmed you, but what if changing your first impression of me means I don't get Holland—that we aren't here right now?"

"Xavier Kingsley believes in the butterfly effect," I muse.

"I'd believe in almost anything if it means I get to keep all the unexpected joy the last few months have brought me." His tone shifts as he crowds me, wedging his thigh between my legs and forcing me back onto the couch.

"Is that so? Tell me more about this joy."

"Right now, I'm focused on enjoying you, and that's something I won't give up. Even if it means you thought I was a jerk for a while, then it was absolutely worth it."

His lips drop to my neck, sucking on my pulse point, causing my breath to hitch.

I've memorized every single thing on my wish list and nerves flutter wildly in my stomach, the beat of their rhythm growing more insistent with every kiss he trails down my neck.

"You taste so fucking good, every goddamn inch of you." His palm covers my breast over my tank and he groans. The appreciative sound does something to me. "And these, I love these, it's a shame I haven't seen them yet."

"No better time than the present." Being an early bloomer made me self-conscious and it took years of positive self-talk for me to change that narrative. I push those old thoughts away, reaching for the hem of my tank, pulling it over my head.

"Jesus, I knew you'd be perfect." He nips at the rounded swell of one, scraping his stubble over it and dragging a whimper out of me. "So sensitive."

Bite.

Lick.

Kiss.

Each swipe of his mouth on my now marked skin drives me higher.

"I have an addendum to our list." His voice is pure gravel. The rough pad of his thumb brushes over the red blossoming across my chest. His hips rock against me before he lowers his mouth to kiss my tender flesh.

I hum, too distracted by the way he consumes me to really respond.

His fingers pull the cups down, pushing my breasts higher. "These deserve to be worshiped—fucked and played with until you're begging me to paint your neck."

Everything spins around me, and I open my mouth to speak—though I don't know why, there are no words, my brain is a blank space filled only with the image he's crafted.

It only short circuits further when he runs his long finger along my collar bone. "You wear pleasure like you were made for it. These marks are merely the beginning." His hand collars my neck, holding it gently, intently watching the spot where he's anchored to me. "Will you let me give you more?"

"Yes, everything," I agree, entranced by the idea of a limitless list. I've spent years not demanding the pleasure I want. The list feels a little like a step toward shedding the old Vivi—the woman more concerned about not hurting her partner's ego than being fulfilled. Xavier's quickly become someone I trust as a friend and he's offering me everything I want—and some things I didn't know I wanted—on a silver platter.

He kisses down my stomach and those nerves disappear. He's got me more worked up than I've ever been.

"These curves haunt me in my sleep, taunting me because I haven't spent enough time exploring them. No one's ever been my type the way you are, Vivi."

Each layer of praise he lays down is another click higher on the rollercoaster he's got me riding. My fingers tangle in his damn strands, holding him to me as much as they urge him forward. "Xavier, I need you."

"What do you need, gorgeous? And be specific." Sharp scrapes of his five o'clock shadow tease my hip where it meets the waistband of my leggings. "Tell me how you want to come tonight."

"On your mouth," I practically shout, making him chuckle, the deep vibrations hotter than any sound I've heard before.

"That's it, sweetheart, don't ever settle for less than you deserve." I lift my hips, helping him as he pulls the material down my legs. "Are you going to sit on my face and soak me?"

I shake my head. "Not this time, please." It's hard enough for me to come like this and I'm not sure I could do it like that.

"We don't do anything you don't want *ever.* Do you understand, Vivienne?" There's something intimate about the way he uses my full name as he ducks his head to make sure I get those vivid blue eyes.

All I can do is nod. I'm putty in his hands. "Another time. I'm not sure I'll be able to enjoy it. I'll be too worried about whether I'll be able to come like that, and don't want anything getting in the way tonight."

"No matter what we do, I'll always make sure it's good for you. But I'm so proud of you for telling me what you need," he praises.

And I preen.

Xavier frees my pants from my ankles, letting them fly some place behind us. On instinct alone, my lids drift shut as his nose drags over the lace of my panties. And then I forget to breathe altogether when he uses the flat of his tongue to press them against my core, tormenting me without actually giving me what I need.

"Is this what you want?"

"No," I whine, my mouth dropping open as he pushes the soaked material inside me. I have no doubt he could get me off like this, but it's not what I want.

His shoulders push me wider, giving him more access as he sucks and nibbles through the fabric.

"Xavier, I need you."

"Need me where, sweetheart? Use that perfect mouth to tell me how I can make this good for you."

"Fuck me with your tongue. I want your mouth on me."

"Say please."

I push up on my elbows, staring him down. His red strands are darker, water from the shower still clinging to them. He looks like a god, propped up between my legs, the muscles and tendons in his shoulders straining. My chest heaves with a mix of annoyance and ample lust.

"If you don't eat me out and make me come all over your stupidly handsome face right this second, I might die. And listen carefully when I tell you, I have no qualms about taking you with me since this is all your fault."

He shifts on the couch and has the audacity to smirk as he tells me, "I think I came in my pants again."

"Seriously?" The question is stolen right from my throat when he hooks my underwear to the side and licks a hot stripe up my center. The cry he forces from me when the tip of his tongue spears me on the second pass is feral—foreign to my ears because no one's ever owned my body the way he does. He doesn't go slowly or ease me into it, he presses his face against me and eats like a man who can't be sated.

"It's a crime that I still don't have you naked, but I can't tear myself away from this sweet pussy long enough to care."

It's erotic, dirty, everything I never thought it could be. He whimpers against my core like having me on his tongue still isn't enough as he feasts on me, making wet sucking noises that only make this all hotter. Then he sucks my clit into his mouth and the world comes into sharp focus.

Two fingers pump inside me, another two reaching up to pinch my pebbled nipple. He's everywhere all at once.

"Don't stop." Twisting my fingers in his hair I hold him to me, rocking against him shamelessly.

"There you go. Take," he commands, curling his fingers and stroking me. My thighs shake, need coiling down my spine so urgently that I'm afraid when I break apart it will be a permanent fracturing of my body.

"Take it all." Xavier hums again, his final warning, before he fastens his lips harshly over my clit.

Pleasure bursts from me. It's an exorcism of sorts. It washes over my limbs, pulses of ecstasy rocking through them, taking those last remaining pieces of the old Vivienne with them.

For years I've forged a life—a future that suits me, where I'm in charge. Every aspect of my life has been carefully crafted to ensure I don't lose myself. Professionally. With my family. Romantically. But sexually, I've held onto the control so tightly that I've never let anyone close enough for a connection. This man might not realize it, but Xavier is teaching me to reclaim my power one orgasm at a time.

With the utmost care, he fixes my ruined underwear in place and lets his head fall to my stomach. His pulse races nearly as fast as mine against my soft belly. Oxygen and blood slowly return to my brain, but the silence between us is easy, peaceful. There's no rush to talk. Instead, I sift my fingers through his messy hair, trying to fix the damage my hands caused as it dried.

He's the first to speak. "Nothing compares to the sight of you uninhibited, claiming the pleasure you deserve. You're a damn masterpiece with my name pouring out of your mouth."

My voice is hoarse when I joke, "This praise kink you're giving me is going to make it impossible for me to move on when this is over."

He lifts his head, icy blues devoid of amusement at my lighthearted comment. "That's not something I want to think about."

Yeah, I don't particularly like the idea of him with anyone else either. It stings in a way I don't expect. "That's what we agreed to, right?"

He nods, his hand drawing circles on my stomach. "We need another rule. No talking about the after."

"Like ever?"

"Ever. I'd rather believe I've ruined you for all men. Let me live with my delusion."

I hold out my pinky finger, waiting. He stares at it. "Never made a pinky promise?" I ask with a raised eyebrow.

"Maybe we should spit on it?" He jokes. "My childhood wasn't the kind filled with Eskimo kisses and pinky promises." He hooks my little finger, pulling it to his mouth and sealing it with a kiss. "It was more beer bottles thrown at the wall and moldy bread."

I knew things were bad, but I didn't know they were that bad.

"Don't give me that look." It's a quiet plea. "I got out in one piece and I've made a pretty good life for myself. Without my past, I wouldn't be the dad that I am."

"I don't believe that for a second." The words are out, hanging between us, but I refuse to take them back.

"He showed me how not to be a father."

"And I've seen you with Holland. The love you have for her is authentic. It's not manufactured by your past. Giving him credit for the father you are isn't fair to you or her. He didn't do that, you did."

He shrugs before he adds. "That girl is my entire world and I'll never let her know the pain of a parent who has given up. She'll always know that I'm there for her. It's something I'm acutely aware of because of him."

I think about earlier and how he sent Tenley home. How he sat me down on the couch with wine instead of letting me help. Since he showed up at the camp a month ago, ragged and stressed, it's been a common thread—guilt over not doing it all.

"Accepting help from the people who care about both of you doesn't mean you've given up. It means you can give her more. You're not alone anymore."

I can practically see him turning the words over in his head.

A cry pierces the air, echoing through the baby monitor on the coffee table, and his head falls to my stomach. Xavier's soft lips brush over my skin. "No, I'm most definitely not alone. I have to get her," he says, pulling me with him as he sits up.

"And I need to get home," I say slowly, unsure if it's what I want.

This time it's him looking at me with a brow cocked in challenge. "Do you?"

Another wail comes from the monitor, and the need to help hits me squarely in the chest. "Yeah, I think I do."

TWO-MONTH EMPLOYEE - REVIEW TENLEY

Boss Daddy,

Since you didn't schedule my review, I decided to write this
self-reflection for my two-month nanny-versary.

Consider it a list of my greatest achievements
during our short time together.

Your Spotify playlist? Straight-up criminal. I took the
liberty of curating a better one and named it "cool dad
vibes." Please stop playing "dope tunes."

It's offensive and your daughter deserves better.

The snacks in your pantry are mid at best. I've used the
provided credit card to level up the selection.

I'm a better person when properly fueled.

Holland is crushing tummy time under my care.

Also, there should be a bonus for not crying when Holland
pooped mid-diaper change four times in one week.

CHAPTER 28

VIVIENNE

There's a knock on my window that has me nearly jumping through the roof of my car. Exhaling deeply I turn to find Poppy looking amused and adorable. She's decked out in the cutest, two piece, red gingham set looking ready to celebrate the holiday.

"You look like you're about to bolt." Her voice is muted by the glass between us, but the message comes through loud and clear.

The thought had crossed my mind. "It's not that I don't want to be here . . ." I step out of the car, joining her in Dom's driveway.

She grins like she's in on a secret. "It's just that you don't want to be here?"

"Kind of. I'm used to being on my own." And honestly intimated, I wouldn't admit it outloud but this day feels like a WAGs only event. And I'm not that.

"You can run and I won't even tell them I caught you."

"No." I roll my eyes, annoyed with myself. "I want to be here, really. It's silly nerves."

"Making friends as an adult is hard. If it gets to be too much, start talking about hippopotamuses and I'll help you fake an emergency."

The absurdity of her suggestion puts me at ease. "Hippopotamuses?"

"Can you think of any real-life situation in which nature's angry marshmallows would come up today?"

"What?" I choke out, now laughing in earnest.

"They're round, squishy-looking, but shockingly ready to charge on a whim—angry marshmallows."

It reminds me of exactly the kind of nonsensical conversation I would have with Tenley. So when Poppy starts walking up the driveway and through the house, I follow her, already less anxious.

"This place is adorable," I comment as she leads me through the kitchen and living room to the back patio.

"Dom is surprisingly domestic," she agrees.

Everyone else is already floating in the pool. The sun is high in the afternoon sky making the pool glitter and the clear view of the mountains a stunning backdrop.

"Holy shit. If I wasn't married already, I'd propose to that bikini," Lilah says when she looks over at me from where she's lounging on a pink floaty. She's the picture of relaxation, her pregnant belly glistening with the sunscreen that she's reapplying.

"I agree. You look like a goddess." Indie hands me a bottle of water and a towel.

"But actually, where did you get it? This baby is making my boobs huge, and that suit is doing things for your girls that would drive Cruz crazy." The slight current in the pool floats her past a sleeping Mia.

"I'll send you the link. There's a blue one that would look amazing with your eyes."

I almost sound like someone who's not emotionally stunted from shutting people out for the last dozen or so years.

Fake it 'til you make it. That's the motto.

Now that Xavier's in my life, I'm doing a lot less faking. And I'm not solely talking about orgasms. There have been more real, cheek pinching smiles in the last few weeks too. They happen first thing in the morning when I find a text waiting, wishing me a good morning. Then again in the afternoon, when he reminds me to take a break for lunch. Or later in the day, when he shares something funny that happened while he was on the road. And even from a random selfie he sent "just because."

Each message makes this independence I fought so hard for feel a little less lonely. Now, when Tenley or Harlowe question how I'm doing, I can honestly say I'm good.

"You're staying for the game, right?" Poppy takes the spot next to me at the edge of the pool. I release the claw clip from the strap of my bikini and twist my hair up, clipping it back because it's already sticking to my neck.

"Yeah, if that's okay. I haven't watched many this season."

"Of course it's okay. I'd probably cry if you left before the game, thinking it was because you were mad at us. These first trimester hormones are a real treat," Mia says, sounding groggy. She's been hiding behind a pair of sunglasses, quietly floating around the pool since I got here.

"I didn't think you were awake over there!" I say, excited to hear about Dean's reaction to their news.

"Honey, I'm barely alive, but sure, let's call this awake," she says with a yawn.

Indie and Poppy laugh, but Lilah looks a bit more sympathetic.

"Did you tell Dean?"

Her beaming smile is an answer in and of itself. She nods excitedly, looking gray as she scoots up on her floatie so she's sitting, propping her sunglasses on top of her head.

"After the game, as soon as we got home. His face was priceless; I wish I had a picture." Her eyes go misty. "At first I thought he might pass out, which was only because I gave him no lead up. The nerves were making the nausea worse, or maybe it was the ninth inning chili dog?" She considers that. "So I just blurted out that I was pregnant while he was taking his shoes off."

A tear slips down her cheek and I have the urge to sink into the water and give her a hug. We don't know each other well, but it's exactly what I would do for Harlowe. My entire adult life has been so focused on outrunning the feeling of being stuck that I never stopped to think about what I was giving up—new friendships. What these four have is rare and fuck, I miss my best friend.

I'd never replace her, but making some friends might not be bad.

"Once he realized what I was telling him, he practically tripped over his shoes trying to get to me. He started spinning me around and I had to tell him to stop because I was about to throw up all over both of us."

Tears glisten on her cheeks and I stop holding myself back, dropping into the warm water and gliding through it until I reach her. "You are going to be an amazing mom. I'm so happy for you guys." She leans over on the floaty and I wrap my arms around her.

"Thanks, Vi."

"What's going on with you and Mr. Play of the Day?" Poppy asks when I let Mia go.

I grimace. "I can't decide if that's better or worse than Tenley calling him 'Ginger Daddy.'"

Poppy throws her head back and cackles, joining us in the pool. "She doesn't."

I nod. "He hates it, which only makes her more enamored with the nickname."

"He does have that *daddy* energy with you." Indie tilts her head thinking about it.

"It's definitely new. With Kristy he was . . ." Lilah's voice trails off like she's weighing her words.

"Not the same?" Mia finishes.

"Not at all," Indie confirms.

"What do you mean?"

Poppy's the first to speak up. "Kristy was awful. And he was quiet, almost concerningly so."

"It was terrible," Lilah agrees, rubbing her stomach. "Truly. And I hate saying that about anyone, but I don't understand how they ended up together."

"He deserves so much better—they both do," I agree, knowing enough about the situation to know that much is true.

"I think he's found that," Indie notes.

My head whips towards Indie who looks pleased with herself.

"You managed to skirt all our questions at the stadium, but Tenley's not here to run interference today, and I think it's safe to say we are all thirsty for details," Mia says, letting me go and going back to lazing on her floatie.

"It's not like that. He's just helping me with the problem from the gala." You would think after making the list with Indie and Lara that I wasn't so awkward about the whole thing. But I fear that's not the case.

"You have to tell them about the list," Indie gushes.

"Wait, how much do you know?" Poppy splashes her aggressively, but it only makes all of us scream with laughter.

The more time I spend with them, the more I think their relationship more closely resembles sisters than friends.

"Shit, that freshly fucked look you're wearing is hotter than the sun," Indie proclaims and I cover my face with my hands.

"We haven't quite gotten there yet—to the fucking." I stammer over my words.

"Isn't that so much better than penetration?" she teases.

I squirm. "Neither feels like a winner when you have to type it out to send it to someone as part of a sex wish list."

"Is this list in some sort of kinky chronological order?" Indie asks.

At that, everyone else gapes. It's Poppy who demands, "Wait, I feel left out here. Fill me on this list and what's on it."

"There's no set order. Things have kind of just unfolded naturally." I explain our agreement, skipping some of the finer details.

"But you still haven't had sex? And you've seen him four times?" Mia asks, perking up.

"Well, technically three. One of those was over the phone."

"Jesus. I'm too pregnant and horny for this," Lilah whines.

"I haven't even seen him naked. He's been incredibly devoted to the Ladies First Philosophy."

"What about him, have you—"

I cut the question from Mia off with a shake of my head. "Very devoted to *my* cause," I repeat. Not willing to share all that much more.

"Are you sure you're not interested in more? That right there is husband material. I mean, you've seen his ass in baseball pants. That's reason enough on its own," Poppy says.

Boy, have I ever. It's a work of art and I'm suddenly irrationally mad that I've never seen him anything but fully clothed in person.

"If I was going to fall for someone, it would be him. But I'm not ready for that." I pray they don't press for why, because all my reasons about wanting to remain independent, focus on my career, and build my own life first grow fuzzier as I spend more time with Xavier.

"I'd mostly sworn off dating for years when Cruz and I got together. Sometimes fate has other plans."

"What made you change your mind?" I ask, telling myself it's simply to get to know Lilah better and has nothing to do with my current situation.

"He's the best thing that ever happened to me and I decided to stop letting my past dictate my future."

"Everyone has baggage," Poppy adds. "Hendrix and I both have trust issues. When you find the right person, getting over those issues is more important."

"The dates I went on before I met Dean were abysmal. We were only supposed to be a winter fling," Mia says.

Defensiveness rears its ugly head, and I want to tell them that's not how it is.

For a moment, guilt flickers and I feel like an asshole for using Xavier, but I shove it aside. He wants this as much as I do. That's why we set the rules and agreed on boundaries in the first place.

Thankfully, before I can dwell on it for too long, the chatter switches to planning Poppy's bridal shower and bachelorette party. Which she insists I come to regardless of how long this situationship with Xavier lasts.

CHAPTER 29

XAVIER

After beating Phoenix, the guys and I agreed to meet in the lobby for a late dinner and, not shockingly, I was the first one down here. I look from the blank screen for the fourth time as my teammates exit the elevator with big, dumb smiles plastered to their faces. I immediately want to punch them.

I know what gave them those dopey looks: they talked to their girls. And I didn't, because technically Vivi is not mine, and that fact gnaws at me, souring the contents of my stomach.

I should have called her, but we talked briefly this morning and I didn't want to seem clingy.

Instead, I'm staring at the lock screen on my phone, willing it to ring. It's the picture Tenley snapped at the game the other day. Holland and I are centered, with Vivi standing at my side, looking down and smiling at my daughter. Her smile is so fucking bright and real, it intensifies the urge to call the woman I can't get out of my head.

Hendrix walks up first, stopping in front of me and pausing my fixation on the picture that has me completely fucked in the head.

"Why don't you ever call me?" I grumble.

"I'm sorry . . ." he draws out, his forehead creasing.

"Do better, man," I say as Dean stops next to him and my attention switches to him. "You too. Would it kill you to pick up the phone once in a while?"

"Yes." There's not a hint of sarcasm in Dean's voice.

"I'll call you, bud. What do you fancy? Good morning, beautiful? Or . . ." Dom taps his chin. "You seem like the kind that prefers a good night call."

"Nope," I say, turning away and leading the four of them into the restaurant.

A sly grin takes over the golden boy's face, and I know I'm going to hate whatever Dom says next. "So fickle. It can only mean one thing: you're all fucked up over Vivienne Cardoza. Don't worry, I can help."

"Say's the man who spent a year pining after a woman that wanted nothing to do with him." I scoff.

Cruz joins us as we make our way to a quiet booth at the back of the bar. "There's no one better to give you advice if you really like her," our captain says, his brow knitting together like he can't believe the words coming out of his mouth.

Three of us turn to him, pausing as we slide into the booth. Dom looks smug as hell.

"Thank you. You've always been my favorite." He pats Cruz on the shoulder.

"What?" Dean grumbles, staring daggers at his best friend.

"Shhhh," Dom soothes, reaching across the table to lay a hand on Dean's arm.

He immediately snatches it away, his scowl deepening as he says, "Actually, you know what? That's fine. You can have him, Cruz."

"There's plenty of me to go around, no need to fight. Xavier needs us to be a united front if we're going to help him with his girl problem." Dom looks completely serious as he props his chin on his hand, staring right at me.

I roll my eyes, trying to remember how I got myself into this mess. "I don't have a girl problem."

A balled up napkin hits me in the face, straight from Hendrix's hand. "Dude, just call her."

"We're talking about Vivi, right?" Cruz asks, looking between the two of us.

"Is it really that obvious?"

My four closest friends stare back at me, blankly.

"You had a photoshoot with her and your daughter in front of a stadium full of fans." Hendrix deadpans. "So yeah, it's obvious."

"Not to mention I caught you leaving her office," Dean adds.

"Yeah, okay," I admit defeat taking over. "Fuck, I don't even know where to start."

I look around the table. Each of these guys has had to navigate some sort of force trying to keep them from their girl to find happiness. In comparison, my problem seems silly.

The server comes up to take our drink order. When she walks away I say, "Vivi and I are hooking up. It's not serious, but I like her. She's cool and we've become friends, but neither of us are interested in a relationship." I pause before continuing. "This wasn't supposed to be complicated, because my life is crazy enough. But the more time I spend with her the more I want—the more I overthink every little thing. We made rules so this wouldn't happen, but the rules didn't stop her from getting under my skin."

They laugh. *All* four of them. *Loudly*.

"You guys are assholes."

Cruz is the only one who looks even a little sorry.

"You can't fuck a girl like Vivi and not catch feelings," Dom says.

I glare at him and he smirks. He's lucky there's a table separating us.

"Explain to me why catching feelings for Vivi would be so bad."

Everyone looks at Dean. No one expected him to speak up a second time.

"When you say it like that, I sound like an asshole. But it's got nothing to do with her. She's . . . Vivienne is incredible, but there's no room in my life for more. I've got Holland and I've got baseball. That's all I can manage."

Dean shakes his head. "Good luck, kid."

He may as well have called me an idiot with the way the sarcasm drips from the moniker.

"Are you sure this doesn't have anything to do with your dad?" Cruz asks.

The waitress chooses that exact moment to bring us our drinks—four beers and my water.

Dom glances from his beer to my water, his face going serious. "You're nothing like him, Xavier. You know that, right?"

The sentiment hits me harder than I expect. "I know, but that doesn't mean ignoring the lessons his example taught me. My daughter will never have to face the things I did because I'll always put her first."

"And each of us admires you for that, but we don't want to see you pass up something good in your life out of fear."

"You're not waiting for Kristy to come back so you can try to be a family for Holland, are you?" Hendrix asks, covering all the bases. Damn, I have a lot of fucking baggage.

"Fuck no," I practically growl. "If Kristy wants to be a mother to Holland, I'll co-parent with her. But our relationship was a train wreck from the beginning, and I have no interest in putting my daughter through that."

"You still haven't heard from her?" Hendrix asks, sounding nearly as angry as me. His mom left him and Mia, never looking back and leaving him to be raised by his grandmother.

I run my tongue along my teeth, shaking my head. "Unfortunately, I think it's going to come down to my lawyer tracking her down to file for full custody and eventually relinquishing her rights." I'd much rather talk about the current woman in my life. "And things with Vivi are good, but we set boundaries and in trying to respect those I'm overthinking things."

"So . . . why are you talking to us about this?" Dean sighs.

"He's right," Hendrix adds. "Talk to Vivi. Whatever you're doubting, just ask. What's the worst that could happen?"

"Things could get weird and I could lose her friendship. I don't want that," I say.

"Or you could come out of it with another person that cares about you and your daughter. Delilah and I talked all the time when I was on the road, even before we got together."

Oddly enough, that makes it better. They might be married now, but for years they were nothing more than friends. And with these four all paired up, Vivi's the closest thing I have to a best friend.

I spin my phone around in my hand thinking it over for a minute before I unlock my screen and text her.

XAVIER:
Can I call you tonight?

VIVI:
Of course. You can call me anytime.

XAVIER:
Okay, I'm having dinner with the guys, but I'll call you after.

XAVIER:
Have you eaten? Or do I need to DoorDash you something?

VIVI:
So bossy. Yes, I've eaten. Had sushi while I talked to Harlowe.

XAVIER:
I can never be sure with you.

CHAPTER 30

VIVIENNE

For the third night in a row, I'm giddy over the prospect of Xavier calling again, like he has since texting me to ask if he could. Only, this time, I'm not home alone, in bed, like I've been for the others.

I'm at his house for a slumber party with Tenley. She's asleep on the couch after watching movies and I'm sneaking away to let her sleep. The back of my neck prickles with awareness as I pass through the hallway where Xavier found me the night we made our agreement.

Kismet strikes, and he picks that moment to call me on FaceTime. I have a split second of doubt when I question my decision to stay here tonight without asking, but I hated the idea of Tenley being alone every night.

"Hello," I say tentatively.

A knowing smile splits his face as he takes in where I am. "Hello to you too."

"So . . ." I let the implication hang between us, which only makes his grin spread.

"Yeah, *so . . .* You're in my house." He's in the same hotel room as last night, lounging in the armchair, the shades to the wall of windows behind home open with the city light glittering behind him. He looks like a god—relaxed, confident, and impossibly handsome. It makes me wish I was somewhere more private instead of where my niece could stumble across us on her way to bed.

"In *our* hallway to be specific. Is that okay?"

"You tell me. Is everything good there?" He leans forward, running a hand through his tousled red hair.

My stomach swoops for an entirely different reason than the butterflies from moments ago. "Oh, god! Yes. Sorry, I didn't mean to worry you."

"Relax. I trust Tenley—and you," he adds softly. "You'd let me know if something was wrong."

"I would," I confirm. Something I didn't plan for when I started messing around with Xavier was falling for his daughter, but the sweet baby girl easily won me over.

"Now that we've established that, go to my bedroom."

"Go to . . ." My brows draw together. "No, that's your space."

"Exactly." He leans back in the chair, propping the phone up on the window ledge, giving me one of the best views I think I've ever seen.

"But . . . why?"

"Seeing you in my bed, preferably in one of my shirts, or naked—ladies' choice—makes the week without you more bearable."

His declaration has me tongue-tied as I push off the wall and follow his instructions. I barely breathe as I make my way through his house, afraid that any noise might wake Holland and put an end to this before it starts.

Although I know where his room is, I've never been inside. My hand stills on the knob and my gaze darts to the phone, checking to make sure he still wants this.

Oh, he wants this all right. His black joggers are already tented, his erection stretching toward his stomach.

I step inside and lock the door behind me, heading straight for his closet. "That was some game tonight," I comment offhandedly, crossing the room to his open closet door. When I get inside, I prop the phone on a shelf, making my way down the row of clothes, dancing my fingers over them.

Toward the back of the closet, there's a selection of jerseys. Thumbing through them I realize they go as far back as high school, I look at the phone, my eyebrow raised as I pull out an alternate Bandits jersey that I recognize from their community service day a few years back.

"No. *When* you wear my jersey, I want to be there to strip it off you in person."

"That sounds awfully serious."

"That's because I feel very strongly about the ways I want to fuck you with my number on your back."

"Shit, that's hot." I tuck the jersey back in, moving to a shelf with a stack of soft and well-worn T-shirts. If I can't have his hands on me, this is the next best option.

With the shirt in hand, I set the phone on the shelf. As I reach for the hem of my oversized crew neck, pulling it over my head, the phone tips, falling face first. A barrage of curse words stream from the phone, making me laugh. It might be a little cruel, but I slip his shirt on before finally picking it up.

"No. No. No," he whines. "I want a do-over."

It only makes me laugh harder. No one's ever been so disappointed by a phone falling before and it's kind of adorable. "I would, but I feel very strongly about all the ways I want you to touch me the first time you see me naked."

"Tease."

"You like it."

"I do. But since you robbed me of seeing your perfect body, go get in my bed."

I want to push his buttons and see where it gets me, but I want to be in his bed surrounded by the smell of him even more. So, I slide my leggings off, enjoying the way the cool sheets feel against my skin as I climb into his bed.

He waits until I'm snuggled against his pillows to ask, "What did my three favorite girls do tonight?"

Those damn butterflies take off, flying circles around my stomach. Reminding myself what this is, and how we got our start, no longer tames them. They just keep swooping.

"Mostly stuffed ourselves with takeout and watched Tenley's favorite movies."

"Excellent. So I should expect my Netflix algorithm to be screwed." His laugh is deep and easy.

I bury my face in the pillow, hiding my smile, because Tenley refused to watch them using her profile and now I know why. "There's a possibility it might be a little skewed."

He hums. It's one of my favorite sounds he makes. "Is the mischievous streak from you, or was she born with it?"

I pull my face from the pillow, not wanting to hide when I tell him the truth. "I wish I could take credit, but her mother was a menace. Erica was the ultimate prankster." Like it always does, the memory of my late sister-in-law leaves a bittersweet ache settling in my chest.

"What happened to her?" he asks.

"Complications with Cade's delivery, Tenley's younger brother. She had a condition called placenta percreta that caused her to hemorrhage after delivery. She was gone less than an hour after she gave birth."

"That's terrible. I'm so sorry your family had to go through that."

"It was a shock. Everyone who knew Erica loved her. Even as a kid, I knew she was special. She was the love of my brother's life and after . . . everything changed. Leo kind of disappeared, working endless hours, letting his grief take over. I let mine take over too." Even if I didn't realize it. Erica was like a big sister to me; I followed her everywhere. When she was gone, she took a piece of me with her.

His lips press into a line, and he rolls them together. "She sounds incredible. Processing a loss like that is devastating but especially when it's so sudden." There's a sadness in his voice that we share. Both of us lost someone we loved before we were ready.

"I'm not sure process is the right word for what I did." My head tips back. That year was so heavy, so painful. "I saw my brother hurting, I was hurting, and there was this sweet little girl who didn't understand any of what was happening. I didn't know how to fix it, so I threw myself into the one thing I could do: distract Tenley." My throat burns with tears fighting to escape.

"Did anyone realize what you were doing? Your parents or brother?" he asks.

"If they did, they never said anything. My brother was . . . not himself. And I think my parents thought it was my way of coping. Then my other brothers started having babies. Not to mention, my younger brothers, the twins, were four and a handful. Somehow, I became a backup guardian for all of them."

Xavier's forehead crinkles, his voice laced with soft understanding as he murmurs, "That doesn't seem fair to you."

"Nothing about it was fair. Cade never got to know his mother, my brother lost the love of his life, and Tenley . . . " My voice cracks on her name. "But yeah, I wish I'd found the courage once time passed to tell them how trapped I felt. Instead, I just ran away the first chance I got."

"You and Tenley obviously stayed close." There's a question buried in there that he doesn't fully voice.

I can't stop the smile that always comes at the mention of my niece. "Yeah. That bond is life long, I'm afraid."

"What about the rest of your family?" His brow knits.

I shrug, unsure how to put what I've always struggled with into words. "Do you think it's possible to be bitter about the circumstances and still really love them?"

"Yeah, I do." Xavier scratches his jaw and I can almost feel the heavy weight of his thoughts, even with the distance between us.

"My mom was incredible. She had terrible taste in men, but she was remarkable . . . this bright light in the world. Before she died, everything was good. After . . ." He blows out a breath. "Not so much. And I'm still mad at her for leaving me with him, but that doesn't mean I love her any less. Parents—family—aren't perfect, but sometimes we love them through that."

"Even your dad?"

He laughs, dark and bitter, a sound that shouldn't come out of the man I know. "Fuck no."

"Do you still talk to him?" I ask, although I'm pretty sure I know the answer.

"He's dead," Xavier says flatly, the weight of what that means undercut by his detached tone.

Aside from Holland, he doesn't have any family. Holland doesn't have any other family with her mother out of the picture, it's her and Xavier.

"Xavier . . ." I breathe, not sure what to say.

He shakes his head. "I hadn't talked to him since the day I graduated high school and I'm positive he was thrilled to be rid of me."

"I can't believe . . ."

"He hated me, Vi." He rolls his lips together. "He drank himself to death. After we lost her, he was never the same. He died right alongside her, even if his body was still here. In the end, I think he got exactly what he wanted."

"How did you—you're so . . ."

"Well adjusted?" he offers.

"I was going to say *good*. You're a good man, Xavier. One of the best I know."

"My coaches and teammates growing up helped. They knew my dad was a piece of shit." He nods towards the phone. "That shirt you're wearing is from the club team I played for in high school. I played on a scholarship that I applied for myself because I knew I needed to get away from him, and baseball was my best shot. The owner gave me a job cleaning after practice, and later, when I got older, he let me coach the younger teams. It helped pay for new equipment and my travel. My teammates' parents were always buying me lunch at tournaments and inviting me home for dinner. I guess what I'm trying to say is I had a village that took care of me."

"I'm grateful you had them." The truth of it nearly chokes me, before I manage to add, "You really should spend more time at Double Play. They could use a role model like you."

"It's not that noble, sweetheart. I was trying to survive."

"And so are some of those kids. Seeing you—hearing about your story might give them hope. You can be the difference they need."

He studies me for a moment, then nods. "Yeah, maybe I will." Shifting the conversation back to me, he shuts the door on the conversation about his childhood. "Have you ever told your parents how you felt about the way you grew up?"

"Not even once." I laugh hollowly, my hair falling forward when I shake it free from its ponytail.

"That surprises me."

"Why? Because I've never been shy about putting you in your place?"

He smiles that crooked, knowing smile at me and I know whatever he says next will undoubtedly make me like him more. A big problem, considering he's only supposed to make my vagina happy, not my heart. "Because you're a warrior with a soft soul. You fight everyone's battles for them. I thought your own would be at the top of your list."

"That's the funny thing about having a soft soul. It can't handle the blow of disappointing the people I love the most."

"How would you disappoint them?"

"You don't think telling my brother and parents that I'm bitter over how the death of their wife and daughter-in-law affected my life sounds horrendously selfish? Because when I say it out loud, I sound incredibly selfish. I left and never looked back. To them, I'm sure it feels like I've snubbed the vineyard—my family. But I just need to break away and figure out who I was without all the obligation at home. There was no freedom to figure that out in California."

"I think they'd rather know than continue to live a lie they're unaware of."

"It's unfair that you're so hot and this insightful," I tease, because it's truly one of my favorite things about him and because I don't want to talk about the past anymore.

He tilts his head slightly, lightness replacing the serious tone. "Tell me more about how hot you think I am."

"Are you fishing for compliments?" I shift in his bed making the sheets fall lower, pulling the conversation back to a more comfortable territory—sex.

"No, I'm fishing for your orgasms, so slip that hand under the covers and play with that pretty little cunt while you tell me how much you like me."

"I said I like the way you look."

"You said more than that and we both know it. Now stop telling lies or I'll edge you," he says.

"Promises, promises."

He licks his lips, blue eyes smoldering over every inch of skin they devour as I kick the sheets down, freeing my bare legs. "Adding that to our list for another night."

CHAPTER 31

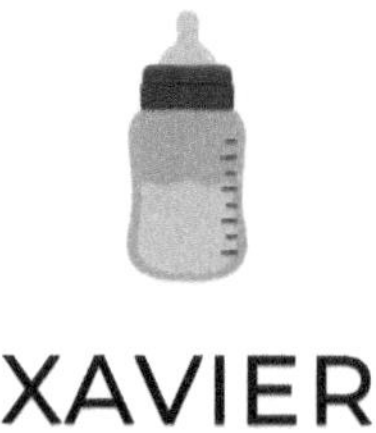

XAVIER

Ten. Eleven. Twelve.

The barbell clatters to the mat with a force that reverberates through the empty weight room, but it's nothing compared to the frantic energy inside me. My hands flex and release before I pick it up again, the ache in my grip almost soothing because it's easy—uncomplicated. I grit my teeth, straining through the last rep of my deadlift.

Dom leans against a bench nearby, wiping sweat from his face with a towel. "What's got you in such a hurry?" he asks, before tipping his head back to squirt some water into his mouth.

I don't answer right away, rolling my shoulders to work out the tension. The state-of-the-art weight room at the Bandits' stadium is empty save for the two of us. Most of the guys went straight home after we got back from our road trip this morning, desperate for downtime in the chaos leading up to the All-Star Break.

I stayed behind to get in my workout now, so when I get home, I can spend my time with Holland before our game tonight. I'm shocked that Dom stuck around with Indie waiting for him, but I think he can sense the bone-deep restlessness I can't shake. Everyone gets antsy during this part of the season, but for me, this year seems worse.

I need the grind of the training because everything in my personal life is about to implode. An update from my lawyer this morning when we got off the plane is merely the tip of the iceberg.

They found Kristy, and she seems to be moving on with life in Florida—getting on without a care in the world and I'm more frustrated than ever. I want Kristy to do what's right for her, because what's right for her is best for my daughter. But disappearing without a word for nearly three months is cruel.

I doubt she'll even show up to the hearing in a few weeks. Serving her the summons should have been a relief. Instead, I find myself needing to work off the foul mood that's been plaguing me since Collin called before going home.

"Just a lot on my mind," I say, not wanting to get into it with Dom, because it's not only the shit with Kristy that's wearing on me.

I grind out another set of deadlifts as Dom leans on the rack next to me, taking a long drink from his water.

Another week slipped away without seeing my girls. I'm used to feeling that way with my daughter, but this time the loneliness seemed to double. I can handle the brutal schedule, the exhaustion from travel, and being a single dad. But there's a sense of doom looming over me because of how missing Vivienne is making me feel. I'm headed for trouble with these rules we set, but I'm too out of control with her to stop it.

It's no longer about just giving her orgasms because no one else ever has. It's about feeding the emotional connection she's starved herself of so she can heal.

The nights we talk for hours while I'm on the road barely touch the way I want her. Even when she lets me get her off over video before we hang up and I come into my hand, I'm left unsatisfied. I don't think it's enough anymore. I want her in my bed, in my life, and in my daughter's life too. What I need is to inject her straight into my veins so I can take her everywhere with me.

My teammate smiles like he knows my secret. "Maybe you'd feel better if you faced what's got you ready to snap instead of trying to avoid it."

"Maybe," I admit, tossing my towel over my shoulder and following him to the door. Or maybe not because telling Vivi how deeply this arrangement is affecting me could backfire. I'm trying to take it slow with her, cross things off her list one at a time—build the connection she seems to need to let herself *feel*. Showing that level of restraint gets harder every day.

Sensing the need for something to take my mind off it Dom fills the walk with questions about the starting pitcher we're facing tonight, and I fire back stats until we walk into the locker room. It's empty aside from the singular voice coming from Murphy's office.

I'm about to pull my shirt over my head and head to the showers when Murphy pops his head out of the door. "Kinglsey, good, you're still here. Can I have a second of your time?"

I groan internally. He might have asked, but no isn't an option.

"Of course, coach." I follow him into the office, dropping into the chair across from his desk as he takes a seat.

"How can I help you today?" My knee bounces below the edge of the desk, the restlessness returning when I think of everything I have waiting for me when I walk out these doors.

"This is more about how I can help you. You've had a lot of change this year. I know the start of the season was . . . trying, but you seemed to have settled in nicely. Is there anything else you need from the organization in the second half of the season to help you stay focused?"

"No, sir. I appreciate the flexibility I was given when Holland was born, but we've got a routine going now, and it's working well."

"What's the plan when your nanny goes back to school in a month?"

I blink back my surprise at how much he knows about my situation and at how fast the summer has gone. "She'll stay on part-time, helping as much as she can between classes. I'm lucky to have really great friends in my teammates and their significant others. They're going to help with the last few weeks of the season."

"We're making the postseason this year. Are you prepared for the extra work that comes along with it?"

"Yes, sir."

With that, he stands from his desk, holding the door for me to exit in front of him. His message is clear: get the hell out. "I don't know about you, but I'm going to get out of here and enjoy a few hours at home." Like his invitation to talk did, this feels like an order.

And thank fuck he doesn't stick around for a long goodbye.

Dom is fresh from the shower with his bag slung over his shoulder and on his way out as well. "Everything good?" Dom asks, stopping and holding the door Murphy disappeared through with a gruff grunt goodbye.

"Yeah, it was nothing. Just checking in on how I'm doing," I tell him, finally stripping my shirt off.

"You told him you were nominated for Dad of the Year, right?"

I push my shorts down my hips and grab my towel. "A title I'm going to lose if I don't get home to my daughter soon."

"Not a chance." He gives me a nod and lets me get to it as he disappears into the hallway.

Barring any more interruptions, I might actually get home before I have to turn around and come back for our game tonight. "Jesus, I need this fucking break," I say aloud, but the only response is the echo of my own words off the tile walls of the empty locker room.

It's quieter than I've ever heard it, I think, and then crank the shower handle, letting the water warm up.

CHAPTER 32

VIVIENNE

With a game scheduled for tonight and the team coming off an away series, the stadium sits in a rare silence.

Other than the front office and a few of the grounds crew milling around, it's still.

Following my meeting with Piper, I'm alone, striding through the quiet halls, when all the peace and silence is shattered. I turn the corner to be greeted by Dom, who's as happy as he always is. "Not-the-nanny! What are you doing here?"

I glance to the side, catching his gaze. "That's not going to be my nickname. But to answer your question, I had a meeting with Piper this morning."

"Interesting. I didn't think anyone else was here besides Xavier and I."

My steps falter and I turn to look at him head on. His smile has gone from sweet to sly. It's a struggle to keep the unbridled excitement under wraps when I ask, "Xavier's here?"

"In the locker room. Murphy just left. It's completely empty." He pauses and looks around. "Want me to walk you out?"

No.

Instead of screaming that at him and *running* to the locker room like I want to, I slip my phone from my purse pretending to check it. "Oh, shoot. I left my notes in Piper's office. I'm going to go grab them."

"Uh, huh." He grins at me like the cheshire fucking cat, all bright white teeth and knowing. "I'll leave you to it then."

Please do, I think. My heartbeat thunders, abusing my ribs, and I fear I might lose my nerve if he doesn't leave right now. And that would be truly tragic.

Dom's back retreats and I forgo the pretense of pretending I'm leaving. There's nothing and no one around but me and my doubts. This is so out of character for me, but it's been a week since I've seen Xavier. Knowing he's here, within my reach, is more than I can handle. I refuse to wait another second to see him.

I wait for the click of the heavy metal doors to signal I'm alone and push through the door to the locker room before I chicken out. The sound of a shower running echoes through the empty space. Stepping further inside, I scan the room. It's as empty as Dom said it would be, save for the one open locker with the name *Kingsley* hanging above it.

With all the grace of a baby giraffe, I fumble with my heels and dress. Goosebumps pebble my skin from the jitters, because as I strip out of my bra and panties, I grab the rolled-up towel on the bench, wrapping it around my body and securing it at my chest. If someone walks in and catches me, there is no explaining this away, but at least I'll keep a shred of my dignity.

What a lie. I'm in the men's locker room, uninvited. There's no saving anything if someone finds me standing here wearing only this pathetic towel and flushed cheeks. All the more reason to hurry the hell up.

I follow the sound of the running water to the far end of the locker room, the tile floor cool on my feet. It's jarring against my otherwise heated skin as I approach the only occupied stall. Steam billows from behind the white curtain.

My fingers curl around the slippery vinyl, pulling it back inch by inch. Water sluices down the lines of Xavier muscled back. Rolling down his spine and over the impressive swell that rounds out at the base. As desperate as I am for him to turn around so I can drink in all of him, I can't deny the appeal of being able to take my time eating up every damn inch of him like this.

God, this man's ass is the stuff of dreams—firm and tight. I want it in my hands.

He tilts his head up and his hands push his hair back, making my knees buckle at the sight. Before I lose my nerve, I untuck the towel, hang it over the hook and join him inside the stall, steam licking at my skin.

Whether it's me stepping closer or the soft swish of the curtain closing behind me that makes him turn to face me, I can't say. Regardless, the sight of him in all his naked, wet glory sucks the air from my lungs.

My gaze drifts up lazily, taking inventory of every dip and curve in his strong legs, the coarse hair on his toned thighs, and when they land on his cock hanging heavy between them, I almost die. Never once have I come across a man that I want to fall to my knees for, but right now, even knowing the tile is going to bruise my skin, I'd crawl to this man if he asked me to.

Forcing my attention from his swelling cock, I follow the trail of hair up the line of his stomach to his impressive chest and then his face. One side of his mouth lifts, as if he's caught off-guard but very pleased about it.

"Vivienne." The rough rasp of his voice saying my name pulls my gaze from where it's fixed on his lips, finding those blue eyes appraising *all* of me.

"Hi," I squeak, suddenly very aware that I'm standing in front of him, naked, for the first time. In a public space, no less.

"What are you doing here?"

His voice is deeper than I ever recall it being. At least I think it is, but it could be the heavy buzzing in my ears making it sound that way.

"I had a meeting with Piper this morning—"

"No, sweetheart. What are you doing here, naked, in my locker room?"

Oh *that*?

It's a good question, but all logic seems to have fled my brain, leaving only need in its place. Any intelligent words refuse to form on my tongue, and even if I could push them out, I'm not sure I have the wherewithal to explain why I felt so drawn to do something I know is reckless.

So I show him, stepping forward until we're chest to chest, lacing my hands behind his neck and pulling him down to meet me. "This."

The first swipe of his tongue against mine eases the part of me that has been unsettled since I last saw him. The second drives me forward, aligning our bodies to perfection. He's hard between us, his thickness pressing against the soft swell of my stomach—hot, long, and tempting. I could kiss him like this for hours if it wasn't for the insistent way he twitches when I moan into his mouth.

Xavier pulls back first, leaving me breathless, and folding over me, resting his forehead against mine. "Fuck, sweetheart. I missed you—these lips, this perfect body, all your curves." His fingers travel over every part of me he praises, his eyes devouring me whole.

When his touch travels lower, dipping between my legs, I remember why I came in here in the first place—something I've been dying to do since Lara convinced me to add it to the list.

It's my turn. I'm addicted to the idea of giving him pleasure as much as receiving it.

I place one hand on his chest, stopping him. His eyebrows knit together in confusion.

"There's something I want from you and I need it now." My fist wraps around his length, forcing a hiss from him. "I'm sick of seeing you over a screen—of not being able to touch you."

"Jesus, Vi," he groans my name as my thumb sweeps over the head of his cock, taking the glistening bead with it. I pump again, mesmerized as another forms. Without a second thought, I kneel at his feet, kissing his tip before the shower can steal away the taste I crave.

Looking up at him from beneath my lashes, my tongue darts out, finding his salty flavor. Like a match strike, his body shudders and his teeth grit. I can see his control slipping with each lap of my tongue against his hot skin.

"Did you come in here because you want me to fill this pretty mouth?"

"Yes."

A strangled sound starts in his chest, and his hand reaches out to brush my damp hair from my face. "Because you want to, or because you feel like you have to?"

It's a question no one ever asked me before and it confirms that he's nothing like my past partners.

"Because I need you."

"Then let me ask you this: Do you want to be in control, or be controlled?"

Fire sparks low in my belly at that. I let my hands drop to my lap and sit back on my heels, considering the choice.

I hadn't given much thought to how I would do this, I only knew that I needed to taste him. Needed to see him come apart at my hands the same way I did at his. That I needed *him*.

He wraps a hand in my hair, forcing my head up to him and giving me a small taste of what it could be like. "I need your words here, sweetheart. If you want me to fuck this throat, you have to say it. But no matter how you take my cock, you're always in control."

The feral look in his eyes seals it for me. This isn't about my confidence—I know how to give head. But I've never trusted anyone the way I trust Xavier. I want him like this, on the edge of restraint, with heat in his gaze as he looks down at me, his hand wrapped tightly around the base of his straining cock.

"Use my mouth. Make me gag on you." It might have been the boldest thing I've ever said to a man, but I mean it with my whole body.

CHAPTER 33

XAVIER

From head to toe, Vivienne is even more stunning than I could have imagined. The makeup that's always perfectly placed is blurring from the spray around us. Somehow, it makes her even more remarkable. But knowing what's waiting lower . . . my eyes start wandering south. Not seeing Vivi naked yet is my only regret about taking things as slow as we are.

She's at my feet, bare for me, leaving me no choice but to drink in every inch of her. A gun to my head couldn't make me pick a favorite part of her body. From the flare of her hips as she rests back on her heels, to the heavy swell of her breasts and tight nipples that tip them, every part of her makes me harder than the last.

She's such a potent mix of submissive and demanding. Hands on her knees with her lips parted, my hand wraps around her long hair, tilting her head back. There's a primal longing in her that shoots straight through me. She confirms it when she tells me, without an ounce of questioning, exactly what she needs. "Use my mouth. Make me gag on you."

And that's the point of this whole thing—giving Vivienne control of her own sexual experiences. If she wants her mouth filled, I'll give her that.

Fuck. With her at my feet, those big green eyes pleading, there's not much I won't do for her. Pride swells in my chest at the undeniable truth—she couldn't resist seeking me out. She was here for work and I made this polished, poised woman shed her professional shell. All so I could ruin her in the best way.

"Say please," I demand, feeding into the fantasy we're building together.

"Please, fuck my mouth."

"Are you going to swallow down every drop of cum I give you, like the perfect little slut this list has turned you into?"

"Y—yes." One word breaks me. I tighten my hand in her hair, stepping closer, running the tip of my painfully hard cock over her lips.

"And if you want me to stop?"

"I'll tell you."

"No you won't. Your mouth will be too full to talk." She whimpers, enjoying this as much as I am. "Tap my thigh twice and I'll stop, no matter what. Understand?"

"Mhmmm." She presses up on her knees, bringing herself to the right height for me to slip inside her waiting mouth.

"Good. Now, feed yourself my cock. I want it sloppy after a week with only my hand and my memories to keep me company."

She wraps her fist around my base, guiding me into her soft mouth. My knees nearly buckle when her warmth envelops me. *Jesus*, if I don't get it together I'm going to spill before either of us is ready. Her silky hair brushes my knuckle as she starts moving, taking more of me. I let her lead, giving her the control to pull back when she starts gagging.

"That's it. Every single inch." Her burgundy lips stretch to take me, and when I hit the back of her throat, every semblance of control I'd been holding onto shatters. The look she shoots me is anything but relaxed. If I had to define it, it's pure determination—and damn, that's hot—but I need her pliant.

"Relax, Vivienne. This mouth was made to take me."

She shifts her thighs, rubbing them together. I slip free of her mouth and she says, "I will if you fuck my face the way you promised."

My tongue runs over my teeth. "You're feisty today. Is that because you've been thinking about my cock all week?"

She nods, her teeth denting the fullness of her lip. "Watching you isn't enough. It's been killing me."

Well, shit, we can't have that. "Hands on your tits, tongue out," I say, taking my cock back from her. "Two taps," I remind her as I shove inside, groaning when she moans around me.

Her eyes water, making a mess of my pretty girl. I love that I'm the only one who gets to see her like this, her perfect edges fraying. It makes me come untethered. My hips snap forward until the blunt head of my cock is wedged as far back as it will go.

"I want you like this again, with your head hanging off a bed—or a table; your perfect body at my fingertips, watching your throat struggle to take me." I pulse in again, pushing her further. "Those tits bouncing with every thrust."

Vivi gags, and I feel it everywhere. It's a miracle that the sound alone doesn't make me flood her throat.

Tears roll down her red cheeks and I pull out with a pop and pinch her chin between my fingers. "Breathe, sweetheart. You're doing so well."

She writhes under my praise, which only makes me want to pour it on thick every time we're together.

"I'm close and I want you right behind me. Touch yourself, but don't finish; that's mine."

When she opens her mouth, I press my crown to her lips, stopping the protest I can see forming there.

"You don't like my rules, you can tap out," I remind her, gliding myself over the velvet of her tongue.

With the water spraying both of us, pieces of hair cling to her face and black streaks of mascara run down her cheeks. She's completely wrecked at the idea of being on her knees like this for me. Watching her press a hand between her thighs while taking me as far back as she can, pushes me to the brink.

I pump in and out, her cheeks hollowing around me, working to keep up the punishing pace. I won't last much longer, but it doesn't matter because I want to see her swallow me down. And then I want a taste of her.

"Fuck, Vivienne, that's it. You're going to drain me dry." The sound of her full name on my lips has me thrusting faster.

Her lashes flirt with her cheekbones as her hand moves faster between her thighs. She gasps, choking on a ragged lungful of air every time I pull back. It's more than I can handle and my dick twitches in her mouth. "Your eyes—give them to me," I grit out, that last thread of control unraveling. "My cum is all for you. Save yours for me," I tell her with my last shuddering breath before the stars edge in and I spill down her throat.

The steady gallop of my heart is still thundering in my ears when I reach down and pull Vivi up, spinning her so her back is against the tile wall and dropping to my knees at her feet. I run my hands up her legs, stopping for a second to rub the red dents the floor left behind. It's sick, but I hope they stick around, a lasting reminder of what she risked for me today.

Her hands go straight to my hair and she holds me the same way I just held her. Like I asked, she's close to the edge but hasn't gone over. Seems like we have that in common—taking pleasure in getting the other off.

There's no wading in. I'm too far gone for her after the sexy stunt she pulled, sneaking in here. My fingers find her seam, spreading it to reveal every perfect pink part of her. I want every sweet drop. Without warning, I lick a stripe up her center, right to where she needs me most.

"I've missed your mouth. Nothing else comes close," she pants.

"This mouth is yours anytime you want it." To prove my point, I dip my tongue inside her, eating her like it's my job until she's a quivering mess and I'm as soaked from the shower spray as I am from her dripping cunt.

"I want it, sweetheart. Let me have it," I coax, kissing the swell of her hip as I circle her clit with two fingers.

She whimpers, her grip momentarily releasing my damp hair as her thumb brushes tenderly across my cheek. "It's yours. Only yours," she whispers softly.

Fuck, I like that. I really, *really* like it.

"Good, give me every last drop," I say.

My tongue flicks in hard strokes, driving her higher. When her legs start shaking, I slide two fingers into her messy center, making her flutter around me. She flies over the brink, crying out wildly and clinging to me with each wave that washes over her.

I don't wait for her to stop trembling before I'm standing, pinning her to the wall with my hips, hard and ready. I breathe her in, letting the beat of her pounding heart remind me why I won't take her here and now. She deserves better than a shower quickie.

Her lips part at the first press of my mouth to hers, and I swallow every moan. This kiss breathes life back into us after a week apart. The taste of me lingers, sharp on her tongue, and I lick into her mouth, blending us together.

"You taste that, right?"

"Mhmm." She chases my lips when I pull back an inch.

Holding her face in my hands I tell her, "That's us. Me and you, together. Nothing has ever been sweeter."

Us. Two letters that sound even better than she tastes. The thought should make me nervous, but has the opposite effect. It makes me want more.

CHAPTER 34

VIVIENNE

Today is the first day of the All-Star Break, which means, for the first time since this thing with Xavier started, he has time off from baseball and I woke up to a picture of two pouty faces. His exaggerated and ridiculous, Holland's forced by his thumb and finger, pulling her lips down.

XAVIER:

Spend the day with us? We miss you.

I tap my finger against the screen. This feels like a breach of our rules. But is it really? We agreed to be friends outside of our extra-curricular activities, and friends hang out.

VIVIENNE:

Using the cute baby as a pawn seems unfair.

XAVIER:

I can live with that if it means I get a whole day with you.

VIVIENNE:

And what do you have planned for this day?

XAVIER:

Does it really matter if you get to see this face?

This time Holland is laying belly down on his bare chest in only a diaper and he's channeling his best blue steel. One eyebrow is cocked, and he goes the extra mile, biting the tip of his pointer finger as his sleepy blue eyes stare intently at me. It's stupid and silly and does it exactly what he'd hoped it would.

I pull the covers over my head and laugh into my pillow knowing damn well that I'm lost to this game he's playing when I kick my feet and reach for my phone again.

VIVIENNE:

Tell me when and where.
I'll grab coffee for us on the way.

One more picture comes through. He's got one big hand covering Holland's back as he pumps his fist in victory. Seeing him like this, playful and relaxed, has me floating on cloud nine. Pride swells at how well he's adapted over the past two months, and despite having support from friends and Tenley helping him, the change in his confidence is all him.

XAVIER:

Meet me at Cherry Creek Park. You bring the caffeine, I'll grab breakfast for us.

VIVIENNE:

You know I'm capable of feeding myself.

XAVIER:

Disagree.

VIVIENNE:

Whatever.

XAVIER:

Such a sassy mouth.
Keep it up and I'll find a better use for it.

VIVIENNE:

It's cute that you think that's a threat.

XAVIER:

And now I'm hard.

VIVIENNE:

Pictures or it didn't happen.

My phone dings again, and I'm disappointed that it's only a notification that Xavier has shared his location with me. Silently chastising myself for being such a needy hussy, I throw the covers off to get ready.

Another ding stops me, steps from the bed, and I dive for my phone. What I see on the screen has me sweating on the spot.

The words *pack an overnight bag* are accompanied by a thirst trap worthy of the drool forming at the corner of my mouth. Xavier's standing in front of his bathroom mirror shirtless, red hair a mess, a touch more stubble than normal along his jaw, and his hand disappearing down the front of the obviously tented basketball shorts. Somehow, it's lewd and cozy all at once.

I save it to keep me company when he's back on the road.

I race through packing my bag, my heart pounding with a dangerous mix of excitement and caution because spending time with the hot single dad who's not supposed to make me feel this way suddenly is like the only thing I want.

CHAPTER 35

XAVIER

You know those slow motion montages that happen in chick flicks where the crowd parts and the guy gets a good look at the girl he's into? That's what it's like when I catch sight of Vivienne as she dodges a group of runners on Cherry Creek Trail.

The dark locks that she normally wears loose are braided to the side. Immediately, I know that I'm going to take liberties with the exposed skin she's giving me access to.

Maybe it's the unspoken promise of what's next on her list and the ease with which she agreed to staying overnight with me, or maybe I'm using that as an excuse because losing my mind over neck skin is humbling enough.

It's hot out and she's in a cute little tennis skirt and a cropped tank top that stretches over her curves. The zipper at her neck opens to give me a peak of cleavage, pushing me toward dangerously turned on.

Not the best timing for that considering we're in a park surrounded by other families, but fuck, this woman does it for me.

Get it together, Xavier. Just because this situationship is the healthiest, most mature relationship you've ever had, doesn't mean you should lose all sense.

This is still temporary—a ray of sunshine in my busy life.

My pep talk doesn't stop me from taking the coffees from her, stowing them in the stroller's cup holders and pulling her against me when she reaches us. I bend to meet her, pressing a kiss to her forehead. "Have I told you how much I appreciate that you're always wearing skirts?"

"Is there a reason for this appreciation?" Her lashes flirt with the tops of her cheekbones when she pulls back to look up at me. She's in tennis shoes, instead of her normal heels, making our height difference more pronounced than normal.

Despite our boundaries and being in public, I have to stop myself from dragging her back against me. "Can't I just like the way they look?"

"You can . . . but in case there's more to the story, you should know this one has built-in shorts." She lifts the edge of her skirt giving me a glimpse of tight spandex encasing her thigh.

"Such a shame."

"Did you want me flashing the rest of the park while I played with your daughter today?"

Warmth spreads through me at how she casually admits she's not only here for me, but also for my daughter. I'm walking a risky line, teetering between knowing how we started and living in a delusional alternate reality where we can be more.

I'm almost certain that's what I want now—more of her.

She stretches, reaching out and rubbing her thumb over my forehead. "Such a serious face for a day at the park. Is something wrong?"

"It's nothing to spoil our day over," I tell her, forcing a smile that's not all fake, even if it's a little dimmer than it was a minute ago. A lot has changed between Vivienne and I since the hallway. She might have agreed to spend the day with us but she's still a step behind me.

"See, we're not going to do that. The rules clearly state that we're friends." She rolls her teeth over her plump bottom lip, which I notice is bare. No makeup and she still takes my fucking breath away.

"Friends, hmmm." I step in close again, because I can't help myself. "You show up in all your friend's showers and get down on your knees for them, sweetheart?"

"I can confidently say that was a first."

"Fuck, you're going to get me arrested for indecent behavior in the park and I'm a single dad, so that would be very, very bad."

"It would be very hard to explain that bat in your pants to the police so you should probably tell me what's on your mind."

And that makes my cock soften immediately. Because the mention of the police makes me think about the upcoming hearing. So I tell her half the truth and give her the other thing that's on my mind.

"The custody hearing is coming up. I'm still not sure Kristy is going to show which will drag this whole thing out."

Vivi bends, letting my daughter grab her finger. "Who'd walk away from this little girl?" She looks up at me and I want her to say more—to add *me* to that statement. She doesn't verbalize it, but I swear it's there in her eyes as they sweep over me.

"Not everyone wants to be a parent, and not everyone should," I say, shrugging. It's a concept I'm all too familiar with. "I'm sad for Holland, but Kristy has to choose this life. It's the uncertainty that kills me."

She nods, like that makes sense. "I guess I can understand that. It's been years and I still have lingering resentment towards my parents and brothers for forcing me to become a parental figure before I was ready. "

I take my hat off, running my hand over my hair. "My dad never wanted to be a parent, let alone a single dad, and when my mom died, he shut down. I basically raised myself. I don't want my daughter to experience the kind of childhood I had."

"And she won't." This time she's the one stepping into me, wrapping her arms around my waist. "Because she's got you."

I'm weak as hell for this girl, so I stand there, letting her comfort me for a minute before I break the hold and grab the coffees she got for us from the cup holder.

The iced coffee is labeled "The Boss" and the other, a cold brew, is labeled "Ginger Daddy" in Lilah's handwriting.

I groan. "Your niece is a menace."

She tilts her head side to side, slowly considering it. "Ahh, but she saved your ass."

"She did," I admit, nodding my head along with her. "And I have you to thank for that . . . and for this coffee," I say, bringing the cup to my lip for that first sip.

"So . . . you've got me here, and I brought the caffeine, now what?"

I push the stroller forward nodding for her to follow. "Now we take this girl on a walk. Then I thought we could head over to the planetarium and check out their newest show."

She falls into step next to me and when I look down she's glancing up at me, her forehead crinkled.

"Not what you expected?"

"Not exactly."

"I had to go to this charity event there to raise money for STEM programs in Denver schools. It was right after Kristy and I had broken up—I wasn't feeling like rubbing elbows, so I wandered off to one of the less crowded displays and walked around, lost in the story of the stars."

Vivienne lays a hand on my arm. "Were you two serious?"

I shake my head. "No. We were always on and off. There was a while where we were exclusive, but it was never healthy. I wasn't sad exactly, at least, not over losing my relationship with Kristy. Down might be a better description. I felt like a failure. Mostly because I spent so much time in a relationship that I knew was toxic. It was self-destructive, and it reminded me of my father."

She stops walking, turning, so she's facing me. "Is what we're doing self-destructive?"

Worry marks her pretty face, as if hurting me is so painful that she can't bear it and it almost breaks me. "Not for me and I hope it's not for you either. Having you in my life has lifted a weight off me that I didn't realize I was carrying. When Kristy walked away, I was hell-bent on doing this on my own."

"I hate to break it to you, but you were kind of a mess. You know, even though you have help now, no one can replace what you do for her."

I like to think that's true and hearing it from her makes me believe it. "I could have fumbled through all the diaper changes and baths, but it was the mental toll of not having anyone to talk to—I was drowning in my own head. Knowing I can call you when I'm feeling isolated or overwhelmed is like a breath of air when you've stayed underwater too long."

She blinks up at me and I'm afraid I've said too much. Then, slowly, her lips curve up into a genuine smile and she starts walking again.

"You know, you're not the only one that's benefitted from this situationship. I don't have many friends, I never have. When I was younger, it was because I was always taking care of one of the kids. After I moved away to college, I was so focused on getting my degree and building a life away from home that friendships fell to the wayside. It's been that way ever since. Other than Tenley and my best friend Harlowe, most of the people in my life are more like acquaintances than friends."

Her hand brushes mine and I have to fight the urge to take it.

"Now that I wake up to good morning texts every day, I'm not sure I could go back to the way I was living before. There's life and there's life worth living. I want more for myself. "

My heart skips a beat. And then she continues. "Like fostering strong friendships with the girls—Lilah, Indie, Poppy, and Mia. I want to do things instead of going home to my apartment every night." She inches closer on the path making room for a biker. "I want to go home with you tonight and see what great feels like and then I want to wake up wrapped in your arms where I'm safe and cherished, even if it's one time."

I'm all over the place as I listen to her talk. I keep getting hung up on this still being temporary, when it's so real to me. To Vivi, I'm a friend giving her what she needs. When we started, this was about sex, but now I can see that there's so much more tangled up in this.

This thing is more than I bargained for, and while I'm not looking for the love of my life or a mother for my daughter, Vivienne's earned a permanent spot in my heart for what she's given me. Knowing that I've been able to give even a fraction of that back to her makes any pain that comes with losing her when this list is complete, worth it. So I tell her in a way that I hope doesn't scare her away.

"You came into my life like a shooting star—unexpected and brilliant. This might be a streak in the sky, but the spark you've left on my heart will last forever. You deserve the same, and if I can give you a hint of that spark, it's yours to take."

"I'm not sure I understand the science behind all that, but I'm pretty sure it was the nicest thing anyone has ever said to me."

"I'll teach you all about the stars while this little one takes a nap later."

"Xavier Kingsley, is part of your plan to ruin dating for me? Because no one else is going to be able to compete."

I point at her seriously. "We don't talk about that. It might make me an asshole, but in my head there's no one after me."

She throws her head back, stretching her neck out in the most enticing way, and laughs. "I've already seen you at your worst, remember that time you thought I was a fan?"

I frown. "Unfortunately. Yet, you still gave me a second chance."

She hums. "I didn't give you anything, you earned a do-over. And now, I'm definitely a fan. In fact, I might be your biggest fan."

"That's funny. I always thought my number one fan would wear my jersey to a game." The words come out of my mouth carelessly, but the vision they sear on the surface of my brain is one I need to make a reality. Before she can respond, I bite my cheek adding, "Something to add to our list."

Her cheeks heat, pink crawling over them. Without the makeup she normally wears to work, it's more obvious than I've ever seen on her, and I really like that too.

She nods silently, her lip trapped between her teeth, and we continue following the path along the river.

CHAPTER 36

VIVIENNE

After winding through the park—pausing for a feeding, a diaper change, and a moment to let Holland stretch out on the grass—we make our way down the trail, following it a few blocks down the river to the planetarium. I've passed the gleaming metal dome before, but this is the first time I've ever been inside.

"This is a satellite location for the U of Denver Observatory. The university owns both, but this is more accessible to the public. They also host a lot of events and field trips where the observatory is more focused on academic research," Xavier explains, one hand holding the door open, the other finding the bare skin at the base of my spine as I push the stroller into the planetarium.

It's dumb luck that I make it through the double doors without bouncing Holland off anything because, with her dad's rough palm warm against my skin, I can barely think, let alone steer his fancy stroller. Every time he's near me lately my brain short circuits.

The lobby is mostly empty when we get inside. Other than a few employees, it seems like we are the only people here. "Are you sure they're open?"

Pure delight lights up his face as he leads the three of us toward the front desk. Behind it, an older man looks up, his gray mustache twitching as a matching smile spreads across his face.

Xavier gives me a slight lift of his shoulders that's too coy for the man who towers over me. "For us they are."

"Xavier Kingsley." I laugh. "What did you do?"

He steps in closer, his lips lowering to brush my ear, and whispers, "Showing you that a man should treat you just as good out of the bedroom as in the bedroom."

Tiny vibrations start in my stomach. The light, fluttering sensation is almost unfamiliar because I haven't felt it in a long time. I lick my lips and whisper, "You realize you've never had me in your bedroom."

The man behind the counter stands and rounds it.

"Semantics," Xavier says, reaching out to take the older man's hand and shake it. "Edward, my man. How have you been?"

"A little depressed, if I'm being honest. You don't visit, you don't call, and then this morning I check the calendar and see that you've got the whole place rented out, but you haven't been bothered to stop by and introduce the little lady to her godfather."

Xavier barks out a laugh, so genuine that those vibrations turn into a rumbling earthquake. "Her godfather . . ." With a shake of his head, he flips his hat backwards and reaches into the stroller. Two gentle hands remove Holland with a fluid precision that is criminally sexy for a reason I don't fully understand.

He brings Holland to his chest so her bottom is resting in the crook of his arm as his other hand supports her upper half, giving Edward a better look at her and me a better look at his biceps.

He handles her with an ease you don't always see in new dads. My body flushes hot . . . this is like *really* doing it for me.

"Edward, this is Holland."

The old man lights up at the mention of the baby nestled against Xavier's chest. It's clear these two are close, and I wonder how much time Xavier has spent here in the last seven months.

His friend reaches out, lifting Holland's tiny arm and stroking a thumb down it.

"Do you want to hold her?" Xavier asks, his voice softer than I've ever heard it.

"Yeah, but let me sit. I'm an old man and she's too precious." Edward's eyes are misty with admiration as the two men cross the space to a couch in the lobby.

Once Edward lowers himself into the corner of the leather couch, Xavier carefully passes his daughter off to him, and I stand to the side and watch as the men exchange an emotional glance.

"You did good there, kid," Edward says.

Xavier's throat works around a swallow. "There have been moments where it all feels impossible and others where it feels like a dream come true."

"You're doing just fine." Edward lets Holland wrap his stubby finger up in her tiny fist. "Isn't he, my angel?"

I'm about to wander away, giving them space so I'm not intruding on a special moment when Xavier clears his throat, glancing over his shoulder and finding me. "There's someone else I'd like you to meet."

"Is this the girl that's got that smile back on your face?" Edward lifts his chin, pulling his attention from Holland and focusing the warmth on me. Only this isn't merely him being nosey—he's genuinely delighted to see me happy.

Xavier closes the gap between us, taking my hand. Dumbfounded, I follow as he leads me to where Edward sits with Holland.

"This is Vivienne Cardoza," Xavier says.

"It's nice to meet you, Vivienne Cardoza," Edward says, before looking back at his friend. "You must've sweet-talked her when the lights were low, huh?"

I snort, caught off guard by the way he flipped from grandfatherly love to teasing so naturally.

"Let's call it luck." Xavier pulls me into his side.

I shift under the weight of his arm, glancing up so the full intensity of his stare is on mine and say, "Luck? Sure, let's call it that. Because who doesn't hit the jackpot on their *third* spin, right?"

Edward coughs out a laugh. "Oh, I like her a lot."

There's a subtle rasp to Xavier's voice, warmth wrapping around each word as he presses his lips to the crown of my head and says, "Yeah, me too."

The reverence in his tone has emotion flooding my chest, rushing up into my throat and making it tighten. Part of me is screaming not to lose myself to him—to this feeling. The other part is begging me to forget all our rules, even if only for a short while.

I whisper over the war waging in my heart. "Guess you've got good taste then."

"Speaking of good taste, your date awaits and someone did a bang-up job of coordinating it, if I do say so myself." Edwards runs his thumb over Holland's cheek.

"Date?" I tilt my head in Xavier's direction. I guess I'm not the only one bucking the rules today.

"His words, but yeah." His fingers reach up, brushing back his tousled red hair, lingering on the back of his neck as if unsure of what to say next. "I guess it is a date . . . if that's okay with you."

Well, that was cute as hell and there's no way I'm saying no to a bashful Xavier.

"Is Little Miss going with you?" Edward asks, sounding a little wistful at the idea of losing his new friend.

"She is." Xavier's smile is so tender, it melts my heart. "But I promise, we'll be back soon and you can come hang with us any day in the off-season."

Xavier steps away from my side, lifting Holland out of Edward's arms and passes her to me. Instead of placing her back in the stroller, I snuggle her close, letting her sweetness distract me from the unexpected turn this day has taken.

Xavier extends a hand to help Edward up, the two of them exchanging a brief but familiar glance. One that tells me the older man hates accepting help like this, but knows better than to refuse it.

Edward leads us to a door that opens up into the planetarium theater. It's dark under the domed roof, but I follow the colored lights illuminating the floor to the center of the room. There's a flutter in my chest as I take in each carefully thought-out detail of the setup. I cling to Holland, letting her ground me.

Xavier stops behind me with the stroller and I cock my brow, gesturing to the blanket, pillows, and snack board laid out in the open space. "This would've been awfully uncomfortable if I hadn't agreed it was a date since that's technically against the rules."

With the confidence that can only come from being an irresistibly handsome, six-foot-four, professional athlete, he smirks. "Screw the rules."

There's a flash of that same cockiness from the first time we met. Only now, knowing his heart, it turns me on, instead of annoying me. He takes care of the people in his life—treats them like gold. That I'm letting him do it for me is what's got him grinning like a fool. Not that he thinks he's entitled to my attention.

He doesn't give me a chance to protest before he launches into the world's hottest lecture. "I told you before, this list isn't just about giving you all the orgasms your body can handle anymore. I'm going to show you how you deserve to be treated *in* and *out* of the bedroom until you tell me to stop."

"Until I tell you to stop," I repeat a little breathlessly. Aside from the date, it's still within the spirit of what we agreed to, but it feels like . . . more.

"Yeah. I can find endless ways to make you scream my name, so until you tell me you've had enough, you get all the benefits of being with me."

He parks the stroller, stepping up and stroking his hand over his daughter's hair, but his attention is all mine. It's painfully intimate to have him looking at me this way, almost to the point where I need to look away. My stomach flips and I tell him the only thing I know with any conviction. "There's no chance I'll get sick of this"—I motion between us—"anytime soon. And thank you for today. It's beyond thoughtful."

He bends to reach my lips, giving me a too-quick kiss before he lifts Holland out of my arms. With his back turned, I press my fingertips to my lips. I close my eyes and try to suck in a calming breath but it doesn't ease the heavy want that sits in my chest any time he's around lately.

Not sure what to do with my emotions, I slip off my shoes, taking a seat on the plush blanket where Holland is getting cozy next to her dad.

Everything is laid out to perfection, setting a cozy and romantic mood. I don't know who gets credit for the setup but this date could make even the most jaded girl swoon.

Xavier leans back on his forearms, crossing his ankles. "I hope you don't mind the third wheel. I thought Tenley earned her time off."

"For putting up with you, definitely," I joke. "But for the record, I never mind my sweet Estrela joining us. Not having to share her with Tenley is nice."

Xavier's tongue darts out, making a hypnotizing sweep over his lips—enough to have me leaning closer, only to stop when, without warning, soft music filters in, surrounding us. I pull back, watching as the lights on the floor go out and the stars above us flicker to life. Holland coos like this show is all for her.

I lean back on my elbows, taking it in. "I can see why you like it here. It's peaceful."

"The guys give me a hard time about how much time I spend looking at fake stars, but the first time I came here it helped me dull the noise." He turns his head to face me, and I think it's the calmest I've ever seen those bright eyes. "When I'm here, I can sort things out in my head better."

"Is there a show, or just . . ." I gesture to the ceiling.

"No narration today. Just us and the stars."

"Is this a silent show, or are we allowed to talk?"

"We're allowed to do anything you want."

"Oh, the possibilities." I laugh.

"Well, almost anything. We should probably keep it PG with our little chaperone here." He nods to his daughter, who's happily kicking her feet between us.

"She's so good. Cade was a nightmare when he was a baby." The memory of my nephew's constant cries are still vivid all these years later. "He *hated* being set down."

"On top of everything else . . ." He blows out a breath, his expression softening. "I can't imagine how difficult it was on everyone."

I shift to one elbow, facing Xavier. "He was only a baby and his mom was gone. Everyone did the best they could."

"Did they really?" he asks, gently, not accusing, as he brushes a strand of hair from my face, tucking it behind my ear. "I'm not blaming anyone, but . . . it sounds like they could have done a better job of seeing your pain."

"My pain wasn't important." For years I've reflexively used the same explanation to defend my family, but right now, with Xavier listening, it feels cheap.

His brows knit together and he leans closer. "I'm not saying your pain should've been the focus in the aftermath of losing Erica. But at some point, someone should have stopped to make sure you were okay, instead of moving on and forgetting that you were a little girl who lost someone you loved too."

Overwhelming grief chokes me, my throat thick. No one, besides Harlowe, has ever seen the burden I've carried for so long, so clearly. But this man, who's not supposed to mean as much as he does to me, understands it completely.

"It was unfair to put the weight of that loss on you."

"It was," I admit.

"Pain like that is a little like the birth of a star," he says, pointing to the twinkling stars above us.

"This sounds very philosophical." I hum thoughtfully.

"It is. Stars don't appear out of nowhere. Their birth is a long, chaotic process. First, there's a collapse—gas and dust imploding under its own gravity. Then, to become a real star, the core has to burn at ten million degrees. It takes millions of years to find its equilibrium."

"That does sound traumatic," I comment.

He nods seriously. "And even after that, the star isn't fully formed. It has to blow away the dust and debris from its birth. Only then can it shine freely. I think people are the same way. After we go through something devastating, we collapse inward, and it takes time and effort to clear away what broke us. But when we do, that's when we find our light again."

"Never change, Xavier," I say, leaning forward, cautious of waking Holland who's now sleeping between us, and kissing him.

"Because you like me?" he asks, his lips moving against mine.

"Mhmmm . . . I like the way you always surprise me."

"Good. I like keeping you on your toes." He reaches for a mini calzone and holds the bite-sized snack between us. The savory scent surrounds me and I know without asking—it's from Nonna's.

"You also seem to have an obsession with feeding me." I open my mouth, and when the savory sauce hits my taste buds I groan. It's so damn delicious.

"Can you blame me? The noises you make . . . you make it damn hard to keep things PG."

"Tell me more about the stars," I say.

He does, and for the next hour we talk about the universe. He asks questions about working for Double Play, growing up on a vineyard, and tells me more about Edward. It's the most comfortable I've ever been on a date and I'm nowhere near ready for this day to end.

CHAPTER 37

XAVIER

Vivi stands at the nursery door swirling the wine in her glass, watching as I get Holland ready for a nap. The one she took at the planetarium was too short and she fussed the whole drive home.

"You already promised her a pony last time. What are you going to bribe her with this time?" she asks playfully.

I chuckle. "You're going to be good and go down easy for me aren't you, Áine." I press a kiss to Holland's head before lifting her from the changing table and laying her down in the crib.

"What was that?"

I glance up from where I'm swaddling my daughter. Vivienne is still in the doorway, her shoulder propped against the frame like she's in this for as long as it takes. "What was what?"

"What you called her: Áine." She does her best to match my inflection. "What does it mean?"

"It's Irish." My hand pauses over Holland's chest, my gaze going back to the door. "It was my mom's middle name. It means radiance and brightness. That's what my mom was to me. That's what Holland is to me."

"Hmmm," Vi hums, letting her glass hang at her side as she pushes off the wall and joins me at the crib.

"Hmmm?" I hum back.

"It fits is all. And it's kind of on-theme with your musings about people and stars earlier."

"Is that all?" I ask, amused. Vivienne is guarded but doesn't hold back her words and I can tell there's more to it. But I like the fact that she's spending time with Holland and me too much to dig into it further.

Vivienne bumps me with her shoulder. "No bribe needed, down like a champ."

"She's a terrible chaperone." I turn towards Vivienne. She's so damn pretty like this—at ease in my space. It makes me want things I have no right to.

"Think of all the trouble we can get into without her supervision." Her arms link around my waist.

"Movie time?" Taking her wine, I back her up toward the door and bring the glass to my nose for a smell. It smells fancy—tastes fancy too.

"Do I get to pick?" she asks, taking the glass from me for a sip of her own.

"Why not. I don't actually plan on watching it."

"Oh really. What exactly do you plan on doing?"

With an arm looped around her waist, I walk us backwards out of the room. "Are you familiar with the age-old tradition of making out?"

"I think I've heard of that before. It's the one with kissing, right."

"Kissing. Pfftt." Pressing her back to the wall I lower my mouth to her ear. "Kissing is for amateurs. This is going to leave you breathless, with swollen lips, and a bone-deep ache for more."

"Sounds fun," she rasps, arching off the wall.

"I'm a big fan." I spin her around and bend to kiss her neck.

"Is making out all you're going to do with me? I don't remember it being on the list." She presses her ass back into me.

This fucking tease.

"Seems like a gross oversight to leave it off," I say.

Pushing her hair to the side, I nip at her pulse point, making her whimper softly when I add, "And no, I have much bigger plans for tonight."

"Care to enlighten me?"

"Later, when we have hours of uninterrupted time, I'm going to spend all night buried inside you, making you come over and over again. On my fingers, on my tongue, on my cock. And when you think you can't take any more, you're going to do it one more time, so I can prove to you that you can."

She sags against me, my dirty promise pulling her under. Her teeth rake over her plump bottom lip.

"So what movie are we watching?" I ask.

"Movie?" she asks, breathlessly.

"What are we going to not-watch while I kiss you senseless?" I suck on the spot below her ear making her shudder beneath me. It's a miracle I don't spill her wine.

"How about the one with that guy."

"I'm going to need more than that, sweetheart."

"You can't honestly expect me to think after *that*," she whines.

"Of course I do. You're so focused and smart, I trust you can come up with something if you put your mind to it."

She growls a cute little frustrated noise and I hold back my chuckle.

"The one where he rents a lake house with his childhood friends. The funny one."

I know the slapstick comedy she's talking about, and it's perfect for tonight because I've seen it before. Still, I can't resist messing with her. "Does this movie have a name?"

"It definitely does." She tilts her head, giving me the access I want.

Taking her hand, I lead her to the living room, setting her wine on the end table and pulling her into my lap. My hand cups her neck, turning it so I can kiss her. Her pulse is frantic against my palm. My lips ghost hers. It's a fraction of the taste I want, red wine heady on her lips. I need more but I force myself to slow.

We have plenty of time, and right now I'm really enjoying teasing her. "The name of the movie? So I can start it."

She huffs out a frustrated sigh. "Um, the name . . . the name is *Growing Old*."

"Hmm. That doesn't sound right." I run my hand up her leg and she lets her head drop to my shoulder. How no other man could see how responsive this woman is baffles me. She blossoms under every touch and I love that it's my hands making her this way.

"*Grown Ups*." Her hand comes up and grips the back of my neck, holding me hostage. "It's called *Grown Ups*. I've seen it a thousand times—the twins love it."

"If you've seen it that many times, why did you pick it?" With each kiss I leave on her neck she melts into me, pining my already hard length between us.

"Because it won't distract me from the making out," she huffs.

Flustered Vivienne is cute.

I lean around her and grab the remote, turning on the TV and starting up the movie. We don't even make it through the funeral before my hand finds its way under her shirt.

"I love making out." A contented sound hums in the back of her throat.

"It's very underrated," I say.

"I wouldn't know. I've never done it—not like this. It was always rushed, with one end in mind."

Our kisses are leisurely and unhurried—there's nothing rushed about them.

"I like taking my time with you."

I pull back. "Tell me you only dated idiots before me, without telling me . . ." She smacks my shoulder and I laugh into the crook of her neck.

"Kissing has always been rushed and a means to an end, but it's different with you. I've never been with someone I cared for . . . not until now," she says, pulling me to her, by the back of my neck, demanding a kiss.

There's so much I want to tell her—that I want to keep caring for her no matter how many orgasms I've given her. That this isn't about the list anymore. That being her friend when this is over might not be enough. That there's more life in my life than I thought and she fits in so perfectly that it must be fate.

But I don't, because that is a surefire way to end this thing here and now, and I'm not ready for that. So I give her what I can: the best make-out session of her life. Kissing her until our lips are raw and Holland's cries blare through the monitor.

CHAPTER 38

VIVIENNE

Dinner was amazing, but watching Xavier confidently maneuver around his kitchen while I snuggled Holland was even better. Add in the "Kiss the Cook" apron he proudly wore—a birthday gift from Dom last year—and it's been the perfect night.

"You know what wasn't on my bingo card this year?" I ask, setting my fork on the empty plate, my stir-fry gone. My lips tingle with the memory of our steamy make out session when I dab them with the napkin, adding that to the plate as well.

"Earth-shattering orgasms from a ridiculously handsome catcher?" Xavier flashes me a sly grin.

"That too," I admit. "But I was going to say having someone who has made it their sole purpose in life to ensure I'm fed."

He shifts Holland in one arm, balancing the baby like a pro while grabbing the plates with the other. It's an oddly perfect picture.

"Is having someone take care of you for once really so bad?" he asks.

Reflexively I stand, pushing my stool back and rounding the island to take the plates from him. "I can help."

"You can," he says, spinning out of reach and depositing the plates in the sink, "but you're not going to."

"Why not?"

"Believe it or not, I like taking care of you, Vivienne." He taps the sink, letting water rinse away the remnants of our dinner. "Your job is literally to care for other people—for the community. Before that, years of your life were dedicated to caring for your family. Someone has to take care of you."

Guilt twists my stomach, threatening to make my dinner reappear. "I love my job. I love my family," I assert because both things are true. I chose this career, and all I wanted was a voice in the family when the role of caretaker for everyone else became too much.

"I know you do," he says, his voice soft. "But I spent so much of my life with no one to care for and no one to care for me. Let me take care of you." He glances down at the dishes, turns off the water with a tap, and adds quietly, "At least for a while."

The impact of those last five words has a wave of dread crashing over me with the stark reminder that this will end.

I huff out an annoyed sigh, going back on to the stool and rolling my eyes. "What if I want to help?" The tone is my voice is borderline petulant, but at least I'm using it.

Xavier's gaze lifts slowly. "Do you want to help, or do you feel like you should?"

I bite my lip nodding. "I hate sitting here being useless. The problem was never that I didn't want to contribute or help my family. I only wanted a say."

He nods taking that in. "You can help. Just tell me what you want to do."

"I can get Holland ready for bed."

He stills in front of the sink, like that wasn't what he was expecting. "I'll be in to join you in a minute. I don't want to miss putting her down, but why don't you get her changed?"

This time, when I round the counter, I don't stop until I'm right in front of him, taking the adorable, babbling baby from his arm. Holland reaches up, pulling on my hair and Xavier, soapy hands and all, works to free it from her grip.

"Damn, she's strong," he says when he struggles to pry open her tiny fingers.

"Good genetics." I eye his long, muscular frame for a minute until Holland squirms in my arms and I pull myself away. The sooner we get this little lady down the sooner I can get my hands on her dad's muscles.

I glance over my shoulder and catch Xavier watching us as I leave the kitchen, heading towards Holland's room.

"Let's go, Estrela. Time for you to get ready for bed," I say.

In her room, I lay her on the changing table, and in no time, she's in a fresh diaper and a soft sleeper decorated with little stars. It seems fitting after the day we had together. Waiting on Xavier, I settle into the plush rocker in the corner. Cradling Holland close, I begin humming the familiar melody of *Brilha, Brilha, Estrelinha*.

Twinkle, Twinkle, Little Star.

"Brilha, brilha, estrelinha, quero ver-te bem brilhar. Lá no alto, a cintilar, parece um diamante a brilhar. Brilha, brilha, estrelinha, quero ver-te bem brilhar."

I'm so focused on the tiny star in my arms, her eyelids growing heavy as I sing, that I don't hear Xavier come in.

"That was beautiful," he says, his voice low, almost reverent.

"My grandmother sang it to me when I was a baby, and I sang it to Tenley." My cheeks flush as I realize I'm rambling, overexplaining why I chose that song.

"Was that Portuguese?" He closes the space between us, crouching behind the rocker, his hand landing on my shoulder. It's the smallest touch yet I feel it everywhere, connecting the three of us in this sweet moment.

"It was. How'd you know?" I crane my neck to see him, careful not to disturb Holland.

This time it's him who blushes. The soft glow of the nightlight casts a halo, it's enough light for me to see the pink spreading over the pale skin between his freckles—the ones I can't stop noticing.

"I might've, uh, read something about the vineyard's history on the website when I ordered a case of wine a few weeks ago." He rubs the back of his neck. "Your grandparents are Portuguese, right?"

"You ordered a whole case? You don't even drink."

"No, but . . ." He hesitates, then meets my gaze, his voice quieter now. "I wanted you to have something from home when you come over."

It's officially time to put this baby down.

I stand from the rocker. "Did you want to take her?" I move slowly, not daring to disturb the peaceful bubble we're wrapped up in.

Xavier shakes his head, an appreciative grin on his lips. "You're doing fine."

He joins me at the side of the crib, and his hand finds the small of my back as I lean over the crib. My heart flutters widely as I slowly lower Holland. I silently pray I haven't lost my touch.

I hold my breath, inching her closer. The transfer goes off without a hitch, her soft breaths unbroken, and I straighten.

"She really is the sweetest," I murmur, my focus lingering on her tiny face. Her lips pucker, and I can't help but smile.

"She's the best thing that's ever happened to me," Xavier says, his voice thick with love. It's not only the words, it's the way he looks at her—the raw, unfiltered adoration brimming in his eyes. It's the kind of love that changes a person, and witnessing it takes my breath away.

The man who once seemed careless and brash was misunderstood. He needed someone to believe in him. Over the last nine weeks he's blossomed right in front of me. This tiny girl has given him the love I think he's been craving since losing his mother. And in moments like this, I can't help but soak in the magic of her presence. She's stitched herself into everyone's world . . . mine too.

"We should let her sleep," I say.

He leads me out of the bedroom, his hand warm around mine, only letting go to pull the door shut behind us. The soft click of the latch barely registers before he spins, turning to face me with an intensity that steals the oxygen from my lungs.

I'm backed against the wall opposite the nursery, my mouth watering. God, the way he's looking at me—it's hot enough to make me burst into flames. One of his hands slides into my hair, the other bracing against the wall beside me, catching my weight before my body can slam against the surface. The air between us is charged, my pounding heart the only sound in the silent house.

"I'm about to sound like a caveman, but watching you with her . . . it fucking does something to me."

"How very unevolved of you," I tease, my hands going to his chest, twisting in his shirt and pulling him closer.

"You want unevolved?"

Before I can respond, his mouth is on mine, the kiss hard and consuming. As I start to lose myself in it, he pulls away, leaving me wanting more. My lips part but the words die in my throat as his hands slide to the back of my legs.

With no warning, he hauls me over his shoulder in one swift motion.

"What are you doing?" I whisper-shout, clinging to him for dear life as he strides down the hall, his grip unrelenting.

He turns toward his room, a wicked grin in his voice as he says, "Hauling you to my cave so I can have my way with you, woman."

I let out a squeal as he releases me, the room spinning before it rights itself, and I bounce on the bed with a laugh.

The sound quickly dies when I push up on my elbows, seeing the hunger in his piercing eyes. Xavier stands out of reach, looking devastatingly handsome as his palm drags down his face. I swallow, reaching out and taking the hand hanging at his side.

He comes willingly, stepping between my legs and bending to meet me. Lifting my hand with his, he places it right over his galloping heart.

"It's beating so fast," I say, my voice filled with wonder.

"Mhmm." He doesn't hide behind a smile or bravado. His tone is raw, unguarded. "I'm desperate for you but I'm trying damn hard to keep it together."

"Why?" I fear I already know the answer. I feel it too. This isn't about the list. This man is my friend. I trust him; I've let him in—something I never do.

He swallows, his hand cupping the side of neck and I melt into the contact. "Because I don't want to scare you."

"A little fear is healthy."

"Like at the top of a roller coaster?" he offers.

I nod. "Yeah. I like roller coasters. They remind you you're alive." I reach for the hem of his shirt, tugging at it.

"Me too," he says, pulling his shirt over his head and dropping it at his feet. "Take your shirt off for me, sweetheart."

He doesn't need to ask me twice. It's over my head and joining his in an instant.

"This time, when I get you naked, I'm going to take my time getting to know every bewitching curve. There's not a part of you I'm not going to explore." His voice is pure gravel.

"Good." I reach for the waistband of his shorts, pushing them down his hips. "I want you to brand me with your touch. Make it so I can't ever forget what this feels like."

"And what does it feel like?" he asks, stepping out of his pants and kicking them to the side.

I'm momentarily struck speechless by the sight of him, my thoughts scattering. Xavier's lips curl up into a smirk, and I realize I've been caught staring.

"Like I'm finally living."

"Then I'm doing my job." He drops to his knees in front of me, his hands smoothing up my legs until he reaches the waistband of my skirt. I lift my hips for him, and each brush of his fingers over my skin as he drags the material down my body leaves behind a spark of need.

Xavier sits back on his heels, his palms coming to my knees like he needs the connection to steady himself. A rough groan comes from deep in his chest. "Jesus, you're the prettiest thing I've ever seen."

I'm addicted to the way he looks at me. I need more of it. Knowing he loves my breasts, I unhook the front clasp, letting them bounce free.

"Fucking hell, Vi." He groans and it's everything I hoped for. "You're going to kill me."

I whimper when he pushes my legs apart—his praise, dizzying, giving me a high that nothing else can touch.

"And this," he says, kissing the inside of my knee, all his focus on the wet spot that grows with each second. "I've been dreaming about this perfect cunt for weeks."

"You have?" I pant.

He nods, kissing the other knee, his hands creeping closer to my apex as he spreads them. "It's been all I can think of. Tell me you're going to let me inside you tonight."

As if that's even a question. Honestly, we deserve a trophy for holding off as long as we have.

"I might die if you don't fuck me tonight." I cry out when he hooks the crotch of my thong with his finger, pulling it and letting it snap back in place. "Fuck," I hiss, not expecting it.

"We'll get there, but first we need to get rid of these." He runs his fingers over my center, tracing the edges until he gets to my hips. With painstaking patience he shimmies them down my legs.

I lick my lips, reaching for him—needing to touch him. "Your turn."

He stands, his thumbs sliding beneath the waistband of his briefs. Impatience has me hooking my leg around him and pulling him forward before he's got them all the way off.

"What's the rush?" He laughs, his arm shooting out to catch himself, stopping his full weight from landing on me.

"Seven days and the promise of multiple orgasms," I remind him.

"You miss me, sweetheart?"

"You're enjoying torturing me aren't you?

He tilts his to the side as if considering it. "A little."

"Why?"

"It's nice to know that I'm not alone in how badly I want you."

Repeating his move from earlier, I lift his hand and bring it to my heart which is pounding out of control. "Not alone. Now, please kiss me."

His lips come down on mine as he drags me up the bed. These kisses are nothing like the ones we shared earlier—they're frenzied and filled with a longing for all the promise tonight holds.

We kiss and fight for control. My hands grip his ass and tug him to me. He drags wet, hot kisses down my neck and across my collarbone. I groan in frustration because he's still not touching me where I need him most.

"Xavier!" I cry out in delirious frustration when his teeth scrape over the swell of my breast. "Please. I need you to touch me."

I squirm as his hand traces a light path up my ribs, trying to get him to touch more of me. But he takes his time before his deft fingers pluck at my nipples. "Here? You want my hands on your perfect breasts?"

Xavier treats my sensitive buds to twists and tugs that are nothing short of exquisite. But it's not what I need and he damn well knows it. I spread my legs, silently beckoning him between them. He shifts his hips away, not giving me the friction I'm searching for.

"No!" I sound untethered. "Please Xav—this day has been the world's hottest, longest edging of my life. Put me out of my misery."

His mouth covers my peaked nipple. My whole body is a live wire and his wet kisses only intensify the current of need coursing through me.

"My girl needs to be filled."

"God yes."

"So demanding. You're supposed to trust me to take care of this body and give you what you need."

"I do." There's not an ounce of shame in the way I beg.

His mouth continues to work me into a frenzy, making my back arch off the mattress and sweat bead at the base of my neck. I'm coming unglued—it feels like I'm floating above my body. It's so mind-altering, so intense that I don't notice his hand moving lower until it's between my legs, with his fingers parting me. He swipes through the wetness gathered at my entrance once, twice, three times, driving me higher.

Unable to take it any longer, I grip his wrist, holding his fingers to me. "Xav."

His icy blue eyes glow with unmistakable heat. "I've got you."

Then he sinks two fingers inside, groaning against my flushed chest as my core clenches, fighting to keep him where I need him.

"You're already fluttering around me," he rasps. "You've been so good, letting me play, I'll fix this for you."

I whimper. "Please. It aches."

The blooming tightness is nearly unbearable as he pumps in and out too slowly. The all-consuming pressure is a product of weeks of buildup—time apart with nothing but phone calls, this entire day and the significance of it, the movie. One moment after another has led us here, where two forces are about to collide.

"Stay with me," he demands, pressing another finger inside, stretching me. Spots creep into my vision, my legs go heavy and numb.

"Fuck—Xavier, I'm . . ." The force of my orgasm as it bursts free steals the words from me.

I barely hear him over the pounding in my ears. "Yeah, you are, and it's remarkable, sweetheart," he whispers, alternating his words with kisses as I float back down to my sweat-soaked body.

Reaching out, I grab the back of his neck, trying and failing to tug him up to me. "Let me touch you, Xavier," I pant.

"Give me one more first." The gravely rasp of his voice is potent as he asks for something I'm not sure if I can give him.

"It's okay, I'm good," I try again to urge him higher, to give me his mouth.

Xavier's eyes glimmer with ferocity in the dim light. "Vivienne, look at me and tell me you don't want another."

Is he crazy? Of course I *want* more of that, but I'm not sure I can get there. He's the first man to give me an orgasm. I already know it will never be as good with anyone else, but multiples are something I've never even attempted on my own.

He must see the answer on my face: *I'm afraid tonight will be ruined if I can't finish again, but I want to try.*

"That's what I thought. Good isn't enough—not for anyone, and sure as hell not for you."

"But, it's just . . . you don't *have* to."

"That's where you're wrong. I absolutely have to. Getting you off isn't a chore, it's a goddamn privilege. Are you going to deny me just because you think it's what you *should* do? The bedroom is no place for a woman to be polite. Tell me what you want, Vivienne. Use those words like you do when you're putting me in my place."

"It's just . . . I'm not sure if I can. This entire day has been . . ." I blow out a breath. "Magical. I don't want to ruin it if my body won't cooperate."

"Forget the idea that you're faulty or broken. You weren't with the right people. You need connection and emotion to be vulnerable with someone. Trust, remember? I can get you there, baby. Trust me."

CHAPTER 39

VIVIENNE

Connection. Vulnerablity. Trust.

All things I have with him. All things this list and Xavier have given me.

But it's the unwavering faith in the way he strokes a hand down my cheek that seals it for me.

No more settling for less than I want to make other people happy.

I nod.

"Ah ah. Tell me and then take it," he scolds.

"I want another." My voice booms with conviction in the quiet room.

He kisses my hip. "That's my girl. We're crossing two things off the list tonight."

"What's that?" I ask.

Xavier kisses a path towards my center, and I push up on my elbows to watch. He looks obscene perched between my legs.

"Multiple orgasms. You're going to come on my tongue and then I'm going to fuck you until you can't take another."

"What if I can't—"

Icy blue pierces me, stopping the doubt that was about to spill free.

"*If* you can't then we'll stop and try something new. Or I'll run you a bath and we can relax together. I've waited long enough and we've got plenty of time. We'll do this right or we won't do it at all."

"Yeah, okay." My shoulders fall back and some of the pressure lifts.

When Xavier parts me and swipes his tongue up my center to circle my swollen clit I collapse into the bed. It's almost too much after coming so hard, bordering on pain as he sucks and tugs at the bundle of nerves. I grip his hair, pulling him away and holding him to me at the same time.

Slowly, the intensity melts into a pulsing pleasure that's barely out of reach.

"Xavier," I huff.

He hums against me but doesn't stop working.

"I need more. I can't—"

His fingers trace my entrance, toying with it.

"Yes," I beg. "That."

One word at a time is all I can manage as his thick fingers tease and torture me, moving in tandem with his mouth. My core clenches, beckoning him in.

"Please."

It's right there—but he won't let me grab it. I groan in frustration. And then he's gone. The room spins as he flips me, putting me on my hands and knees and pushing my chest down to the mattress.

I glance over my shoulder trying to find him, only to fall forward when his mouth covers me again. Putting me in this position is vulnerable. Leaving me so exposed, with every part of me at his mercy.

His tongue presses inside me and he steals every thought in my head about not being able to come like this as he sends me racing towards the finish line. Doing more than I ever thought possible with his mouth as he eats me like I'm his favorite meal.

Xavier's arm snakes around me, fingers finding the spot between my legs that's aching for his touch. The first brush of his fingers against my sensitive clit sends me crashing head first into pleasure without warning. It's a shattering burst of light that he prolongs with deep thrusts of his tongue. I grip the sheets, twisting them with my fingers.

"Shit," I hiss, the sensations becoming too much. "Xavier, I need you."

Those three words are enough to pull him away. His back covers mine, and he crawls up my body to seal his mouth over mine, taking us both down to the mattress in a twisted heap of skin and sheets, rolling us so we end up side-by-side.

"Fuck, Vivienne. You taste like honey and sin. I can't get enough." He presses kisses to my forehead. "Never enough."

My heart skips in my chest, the reverence in his tone heavy.

We're still not close enough, even tangled up like we are. My hand snakes between us, seeking out his hard length where it presses against my leg. "Fuck me, Xavier."

"Give me a second." Hot breath fans my face as he hisses at my fist wrapping around him.

I stroke up his shaft, circling his leaking crown. "I don't want to wait any longer. Get inside me."

"Fuck, Vi. Keep pumping me like that and I'm going to come all over your stomach before I ever get inside of you."

A disbelieving laugh escapes me.

In a flash, Xavier has me rolled to my back, my breasts bouncing with the sudden movement and my hands pinned above my head.

"Something funny?"

I roll my lips together and shake my head. "No, sorry." I might be apologizing, but there's no remorse. I've never been comfortable enough with someone that I laughed freely like this in the middle of a very intimate situation.

His eyes pierce mine. Doing his best to look serious, he cocks an eyebrow at me. "Don't believe me?" He rolls his hip, his hard cock grinding down over my sensitive clit.

"Shit," I groan, shifting my hips back to relieve some of the friction.

With another roll of his hips, his cock slips through my swollen, wet lips, forcing another fractured cry from me.

So fucking good. *How is this man is so fucking good?*

"Which one is it, Vivienne?" he asks, rolling his lips together in amusement.

Did he ask me a question? Am I such a mess that I'm losing time while he plays with my body?

"Were you laughing at me because you don't believe that eating your cunt has me ready to burst? Or are you being mean?"

He slips through me again, dangerously close to being inside me. My hips twitch and Xavier drops his head, his shoulders straining as the head of his cock presses there. I have to stop myself from moving, my body ready to accept him.

"The first one," I admit sheepishly.

"If you walk away from this only knowing one thing, it needs to be that you're the most enchanting woman I've ever met. This body is a dream. Curvy, soft, and all fucking mine." He presses in enough to make his point. "I'm seconds from losing it. This pussy is going to drain me, but you're so much more. You're every fantasy I've ever had, but you're also brilliant and successful—endlessly giving with your time and love. So yeah, I'm struggling here, sweetheart, because I can't believe I get to have you, even if only for a little while."

"Condom," I croak out. Not because we need one—I'm on the pill and I trust this man with my body, with my life even—but the emotion behind his words is too much. If I let him inside my body with nothing between us everything will change.

He stares down at me for one charged second and I think he's about to ask for the one thing I just took off the table. But then he presses up on his hands, stretching to reach for the bedside table.

It gives me a moment to get my racing heart under control before it runs away on me.

The drawer shuts and I hear the crinkle of foil. Xavier sits back on his heels, holding the condom between us.

"Put it on me."

I join him on my knees, taking it from him.

It's more intimate than I expect, his blazing focus on me while my hands work the latex down his hard length. When it's on, his chin dips, lips finding me softly. His tongue sweeps inside my mouth taking long, thorough strokes.

I melt into him, and he cups the back of my head, his other arm going around my waist and leading us backwards until he's on top of me.

With a shudder, Xavier breaks our kiss, resting his forehead against mine. The sound of our ragged pants and pounding hearts fill the space between us.

"Xavier, I can't wait. I need you," I tell him.

"I know, sweetheart." His face is soft with sincerity as he notches himself at my entrance. "Shit, it's so fucking good."

My entire body warms as he pushes inside, filling me like no one else ever has. "Oh god." My fingers dig into his back, urging him forward. It's too slow.

"Your pussy is unreal. Jesus, you're so tight, so soft, so fucking *mine.*"

"Yours," I echo, delirious as he pushes all the way in, hitting a spot I didn't know existed—not like this.

With his arm looped under my back, he pulls me up, shoving a pillow under my back. "Look at us, sweetheart. See how pretty you look taking my cock." His focus bounces from where we're joined back to my face. "You're doing so fucking well."

"God, Xavier." That's all I can manage because being with him is overwhelming in the best way. The rawness of it all as he pumps in and out of me completely enthralls me.

"I can't look away, but I don't want to miss it when you shatter for me. So damn stunning." His stream of affirmation is constant.

I lift further, pulling him closer, needing him near. Each thrust takes a piece of me that I'll never get back. There's no stopping it—no stopping us. It was silly to think we could. Xavier's all but proven this works because of our connection.

And that connection deepens as he kisses me. It's dizzying—the highest high I've ever known as we climb together.

This fall is going to ruin us both.

His hips swivel, grinding against my clit with each deep pulse of his cock, hitting me where I need him. For someone who was unsure about multiples until now, I know I'm going to come again, and hard.

"Vivienne." My name is plea on his lips—sweet and drenched in emotion. "Sweetheart," he grits out. "Tell me you're close."

"So close. Please don't stop." I meet him thrust for thrust, chasing the tendrils of pleasure that are forming again.

"I need you to get there with me. I'm—" His teeth nash together, his jaw stony as he squeezes his eyes close. When he opens them, there's fresh resolve on his face.

Xavier's palm slides under my ass tilting my hips, his other hand going to my pelvis, finding my clit with insistent circles of his thumb.

"That's it," I cry, heat racing down my spine.

"God. Fuck." He groans, snapping his hips, the tendons in his neck popping with the strain of holding himself back. "It's so fucking good. You're so fucking good. Never want to leave this body."

He presses down on my clit and the wave hits, my core clenching tightly around him. "There. Right there."

"Now, Vivienne. Please . . . you're pulling me under. I need you to come with me, now." Each word is more frantic than the last.

"Xavier." His name is fractured, and it does him in. He swells, burying himself right where I need him as he strokes me through it and I come undone right alongside him.

This time, it's deep, slow, drawn-out pulses that ripple out from my center. One long orgasm that washes over me.

His body is draped over mine, both of us still spinning out as his movements slow. This feels right, like where I'm meant to be. He isn't only making a home inside my body, he's making one within my soul. He's given me so much more than the things on our list. He's taught me how to let him in. It's a feeling I'll never recover from.

The bed dips with his weight as he crawls back in next to me, after he takes care of the condom. And all I can think as his solid chest presses against my back, lulling me to sleep, is that *someday* more might be nice.

CHAPTER 40

XAVIER

Panic strikes when I realize I'm alone. It's eerily quiet for the first time in three months. There's no crying baby and there is an empty spot that should be filled with a beautiful brunette.

The sheets are a mess from last night, barely hanging on to my bed. Still gaining my bearings, I yawn, grabbing a pair of shorts and slipping them on before I make my way down the hallway.

Wordlessly, I step over the threshold of my daughter's room and pause. The moment unfolding is too sacred to interrupt. I lift my phone, thankful I grabbed it, just as Holland peeks over Vivienne's shoulder as they sway back-and-forth while Vivienne murmurs sweetly to her in nothing but my shirt.

I snap the picture as she turns her head, kiss-swollen lips from when I woke her in the middle of the night pressing to fine, red, baby hairs.

She spots me out of the corner of her eye and says, "Hate to break it to you, Estrela, but your dad is a bit of a creep."

"And how long have you two been in here conspiring against me?" Stepping up behind my girls, I kiss the crown of Holland's head first, then turn and take Vivienne's mouth with a soft kiss.

She leans against my chest and her contented sigh blankets me. "Conspiring has such a negative connotation. I prefer gabbing. This sweet girl was telling me she wants eggs Benedict for breakfast."

"Is that so? Good taste for a three-month-old."

"Right? You'd think she'd be satisfied with a bottle, but no. Such a refined palate."

"Hmmm. Lucky for her, I know a place. But since Holland can't eat it yet, you could come and help her out. I know you're hungry after last night." The phone in my hands vibrates, and when I drop my eyes to it, there's a barrage of text messages already waiting and more coming through.

DOM:

We need to start an All Star Break tradition.

HENDRIX:

I'm not moving up my wedding.

DOM:

Xavier. I need you to do me a solid.

HENDRIX:

You can't marry him off for the sake of tradition.

DOM:

He's our only option.

DEAN:

Um . . . Hello?

HENDRIX:

Something you need to tell me?

DEAN:

. . .

CRUZ:

Brunch. The tradition can be brunch.

DEAN:

Finally, the voice of reason.

DOM:

Weddings are cooler but I guess brunch could work.

CRUZ:

Anywhere but Buns & Roses. My wife doesn't need to get sucked into working.

Looking up from the chaos unfolding on my screen I ask, "How would you feel about a little company at brunch?"

"What kind of company?"

"My teammates and their spouses. Most of them already know we're doing *this*." I suck *that* spot on her neck and she sags into my hold. "Plus, there'll be eggs Benedict." I hold up the screen so Vivienne can see the conversation.

XAVIER:

I'm in, but only if I get to pick the place.

"No, you don't have to do that. It was a joke," she says, her cheeks darkening a shade.

I turn her in my arms, tipping her chin up between fingers. "Sweetheart, do you want eggs Benedict?"

Her lip vanishes between her teeth. The war waging inside her is visible as she fidgets, before answering. "Yes, but . . ."

"No, buts. You *can* ask for what *you* want," I remind her.

XAVIER:

Five Friends Kitchen

DOM:

How very à propos.

DEAN:

Words I never thought I'd hear Dom use for 1,000.

HENDRIX:

I bet you watch Jeopardy! in a robe with your feet kicked up in your favorite recliner every night in the offseason.

DOM:

Only when he's not boning your sister in that remote cabin of his.

HENDRIX:

You're dead.

DEAN:

My sister can defend you and I'll testify on your behalf. Entirely justifiable.

"Are they always this ridiculous?"

"Always."

"I kind of love it—the way you guys act more like a family than teammates or friends. The support you have." Wistfulness bleeds into her voice.

"*We* have," I correct.

She stiffens. Like with the eggs Benedict and her orgasms last night, she's about to make herself smaller. I want to rage on her behalf.

"It's not the same."

It could be, a voice inside of me says. "You and the girls get along. They've invited you to hang out a couple times." I soften the tone as we get to the real issue here. "Beyond the list and everything that comes with it, we're friends."

I *know* we are. I could feel it in the way she trusted me last night.

She rolls her lips together. "We are."

"Good, because there's no one else I want to spend my free time with." I rub the back of my neck, the motion doing little to ease the tension building inside me. Nervously I add, "You're my best friend."

Her face transforms from tentative to radiant, a wide smile lifting her mouth.

"Don't tell Tenley this, but, same . . . How did we get here?" There's disbelief in the way she asks.

I take Holland and pull Vivienne into my side. "Can you imagine? I would never hear the end if she thought I ousted her as your bestie."

"You could never. It's a tie." She laughs

"And I don't want to, but I think we both needed this. My teammates are great, but they've all got their own thing going on. I've always felt a little on the outside, and being a single parent is isolating, even with all the support I have."

"Hey, Xavier." Her hands smooth up my back.

"Yeah."

"You're doing great. Holland is lucky to have such an incredible dad in her life."

Coming from her, that sentiment has my heart bursting with pride. I'm trying to give Holland everything she needs. To be a father and a mother, to give her stability and support, to keep it all together for her.

My throat tightens with emotion. "Thanks," I croak.

She ducks her head, burying it in my chest, her voice less sure when she speaks again. "Thank you for being the friend I didn't realize I needed."

Mixed emotions clash in my heart. I at the end of this being her friend might be all I ever get out of Vivienne, but after last night it doesn't feel like that's going to be enough.

"You want the shower first and I'll give this one her bottle?" I ask.

Heat flares in her eyes and I know she's remembering our shower last night. I'd had every intention of cleaning her up after I coaxed that last orgasm out of her, but soaping her up was too damn much for either of us to take. It took every bit of willpower to keep me from sliding into her bare. And when she dropped to her knees in front of me, I was too weak to say no. I returned the favor a few minutes later and then we both passed out, hard.

"That works," she says, rushing for the door.

Before she gets away I snag her arm. "Think of me while you're in there, but don't take too long, we need to leave in an hour." I love the way it makes her shiver.

"You're the worst. There's a baby in the room, sir." She playfully shoves at me, breaking my hold.

"The worst? I thought you were my biggest fan, especially with how you screamed my name four times."

"No one likes a show-off!" she hollers back, disappearing down the hall.

"Don't listen to her. She likes this show-off," I tell Holland.

When Vivienne comes back freshly showered, we switch places. The domesticity of it all makes me long for something I didn't think I missed. After my mom died, I wasn't sure I would ever know what it felt like to have a family again. Then there were a few months when Kristy and I first got together, before she showed her true colors, that I thought maybe I could have something like it with her. But she never wanted this life.

The custody hearing is coming up, and I'm antsy, but Holland and I can't continue to live like this. Merely thinking about the situation she's put us in has my muscles tensing.

When I step into the master bathroom and see evidence of Vivienne there: her towel hanging on the rack, her overnight bag still visible on my bed, her toothbrush on my counter, that melts away. There's a woman downstairs who, regardless of labels, wants to be here—with us—and I hang on to that knowledge.

After a quick shower, I dry myself off, eager to get back to the two girls waiting for me, but first, I shoot off a quick text to my lawyer because I can't let go of the sense that I'm not doing enough to protect my daughter.

XAVIER:

No changes?

COLIN:

No. Still in Florida. I don't think she will show for the hearing. As far as I know, she hasn't retained a lawyer.

XAVIER:

And if I'm ready to pursue terminating her rights? Would that be . . . final?

COLIN:

Legally, yes. And based on her behavior since Holland's birth, I'd say it's likely a judge would agree even if she contests. For now, we should keep pursuing full custody and consider the next steps carefully.

XAVIER:

Holland deserves better.

COLIN:

And that's what the court will look at: Holland's best interests.

The idea of fighting Kristy on it sours my mood. Forcing her out was never the goal; I wanted this to be her choice. But maybe her silence *is* her choice and I'm just not ready to accept that.

Unprepared to face a decision of that magnitude and taint any more of this otherwise perfect morning, I slip my phone into my pocket and take the steps two at a time, finding the one thing guaranteed to make me smile, Holland and Vivienne, playing together on the living room floor like it's the most natural thing in the world.

I want to hold onto these moments—both the tiny baby who's growing too fast and the bond building between them. This time I don't get to take a picture, because Vivi hears my footsteps and lifts her head, still chatting animatedly about Tenley.

"Am I interrupting girl time? We can reschedule brunch if you want me to . . ." I thumb over my shoulder towards the front door.

Vivienne's hearty laugh erases any lingering annoyance from my text with Collin.

"Cute *and* funny." She's not talking to me, instead keeping her focus on my daughter. "You ready to brunch it up, my girl?"

My girl.

Yeah, I like that.

Logically, I know she doesn't mean it in a permanent way. But hearing Vivienne say it unexpectedly starts to mend cracks in my soul. When everything on our list is checked off, there's a chance I'll be left broken again.

But for now, she's exactly what I need and I know it's the same for her. She told me at the start of this that she was using me, but that's not true. We're willingly giving each other what we need most: friendship—a person who sees us for who we are without trying to change a damn thing.

"Her bag is packed. I hope that's okay. You can double check it." Vivienne rises from where she's sprawled, bringing Holland with her.

This damn girl, always doing more than she needs to. At this point, I'm pretty sure it's a compulsion.

"Vi. You didn't have to do that. I don't need you to manage my life."

"But I wanted to help."

"Wanted to or felt obligated to? There's a difference," I remind her.

She crosses the room, carefully stepping over the baby toys scattered across the floor. "Is this you trying to protect me from myself?"

Shit. Yes, that's exactly what I'm doing. Instead of admitting as much, I ask. "Do I need to?"

"Sometimes," she admits. "But you're one of the few people in my life that's never made me feel like I have to do something. And that's an elite list to be on, so you should feel special."

"Oh, I do," I say, twisting a strand of hair around my finger.

"I packed her diaper bag because I really want that eggs Benedict. And I really want to see my *friends*. Not because I feel like I need to. You're a capable dad—which I told you earlier. I knew you could and would do it, but it was faster if I did it."

"Okay, then. Just making sure." I release her, turning to grab the bag.

"Hey, Xavier," she says to my back.

I hitch the backpack over my shoulder. "Yeah, sweetheart?" Her vivid green irises double at the casual use of endearment outside the bedroom.

"Thank you for looking out for me. I can be my own worst enemy."

"Aren't we all?" I agree.

CHAPTER 41

VIVIENNE

My nonna had lots of sayings about the power of gathering for a meal around a table. But her favorite was, "Around the table, all hearts are nourished." Maybe I was too caught up in my own shit, or too young to understand it, but looking around this table, empty plates pushed back, I think it's finally sinking in. There's more love here than there is in some homes, and this is as much a family as those by blood.

Like it's done most of the last hour, my gaze flits to the man next to me and then to the baby in Lilah's arms. Xavier had a shitty childhood. He grew up in a house filled with the kind of resentment no one should have to endure. Yet, he's building a beautiful life for him and his daughter and it all starts right here.

Poppy drops her hand to Lilah's bump, rubbing it and smiling, before snatching Holland from her.

"I need the baby. Planning a wedding is stressful," she justifies, booping Holland's nose softly. "She's a human Xanax."

"What's stressing you out? We can try to help," I offer.

"The groom." She shoots Hendrix a look. "He wants to change the cake design so it's Bandits teal instead of cream."

"Dude, aren't your wedding colors super neutral?" Dom says, his brow crinkling. "Baby, your dress is sage, right?"

Dean huffs. "More like moss."

"It's all green. I don't see what the problem is. Sage. Moss. Teal. What's the difference?" Hendrix mutters, taking the baby from his fiancée. "My turn with the calming child."

Xavier leans over the table, taking Holland from him before he can settle her against his chest. "People who don't know basic color coordination don't get to self-medicate with my baby."

I laugh at the absurdity of it all.

"So, the bridal shower is coming up. You're coming right, Vi?" Indie, the maid of honor, asks, her voice carrying a playful challenge.

Busted. I haven't responded yet, but it's not because I don't want to be there. I just don't want a pity invite because of my situation with Xavier.

Harlowe would tell me to take it at face value and stop doubting I'm awesome enough to be included on my own merit. Tenley would probably roll her eyes and say something like, *"They invited you. Period. That's all the validation you need. Go have fun."*

But I haven't told them that the invite still sits unanswered on my desk at work. Overthinking is exhausting. So, drawing strength from the advice I know the two women I trust most would give me, I say, "Yeah, I wouldn't miss it." Oddly, I realize I mean it as soon as the words hit the air.

Poppy beams back at me. "Really? I was nervous you would think it was weird I invited you. We might not know each other *that* well but, when you know you *know.* And I can tell you were meant to round out this girl gang."

She says it with so much heartfelt honesty that I duck my head, embarrassed I ever doubted her sincerity.

"Let me know if I can help with planning or set-up," I offer.

"Are you kidding? You're a guest. We would never." Lilah speaks up.

"Hermosa, you're practically nine months pregnant," Cruz reminds her. "Maybe don't turn down help when you very well might be giving birth soon."

"Seriously. I don't mind at all." I smile, looking from Lilah to Indie.

Under the table, Xavier's palm closes over my thigh, a silent reminder of the conversation we had earlier. But I want to help and carve out my own space in this amazing family.

CHAPTER 42

XAVIER

The kid at the front desk of Double Play looks half asleep, scrolling his phone when the door jingles. He drags his focus from the device momentarily before it falls back to the screen and then back up again. Eyes wide, he practically trips over himself when he shoots out of the chair to get to me.

"Hey, man, I'm Xavier. Vivi said I could stop by and spend some time with the kids," I tell him, extending my hand.

He pumps it excitedly. "Of course. I'm Clay. Let me get you checked in and then I can take you back. They'll be so stoked to see you."

It's the last day of the All Star Break and I haven't been able to get the idea of stopping by to see some of the kids out of my head since Vivi mentioned it. She doesn't know I'm here yet.

After verifying that I am a registered volunteer, Clay leads me back to the gym, hands flailing as he gives me a tour. He's clearly reveling in having something to do, so I don't bother telling him I've been here before.

Squeaky sneakers skid across the gym floor as a group of teens play basketball. High-pitched giggles come from a group of girls collapsing into each other as they watch back a TikTok dance by the bleachers.

On the opposite end of the gym, the sharp slap of a ball against a glove calls to me. Two smaller boys, still teens but undersized, are playing catch, and damn, the one with the tight dark curls sticking out from under his worn baseball cap has a cannon on him.

No wonder Clay is disinterested in anything that isn't on a screen while manning the front desk. All the action is in the gym.

"Is it okay if I go talk to them?" I nod toward the pair.

He nods eagerly. "Totally, Mr. Kingsley. That's Elijah and Ezra—they're brothers. Both are crazy talented, but Ezra, the little dude, he's next-level."

"Do you know what position he plays?"

His brow draws together as he thinks about it. "Second."

Second.

Clay opens his mouth to say more, shutting it as quickly.

"What are you thinking, Clay?" I ask, curious if sees the same thing I do.

Next to me, his eyes follow the path of the ball a few more times before peering at me. "It's BS, is all. There's nothing wrong with second base, but they only put him there because he's the smallest kid on the team. He's sharp too, knows the game better than any of them. They're holding him back."

"Thanks, Clay." I pat him on the shoulder and head for the two brothers.

Elijah spots me first, and the ball his brother throws zips past his head and bounces off the wall behind him.

"What the hell!" Ezra hollers at his brother as the ball rolls back toward them. "Are you going to grab it?"

When Elijah doesn't answer Ezra shakes his head, jogging towards the ball and scooping it up in his glove. "Are you broke, bro?" He slams the ball into the outstretched glove in front of him.

Still staring over his brother's shoulder at me, the speechless boy lifts his chin in my direction.

"Wha—" Falling as speechless as his nearly identical practice partner, Ezra's mouth comes unhinged.

"Do you mind if I join you?" I hold up my glove, the corner of my mouth lifting with it. I watch patiently while they have a silent conversation that makes me envious of not having a sibling, until finally, both of their heads bob rapidly.

Closing the space between us I extend my hand. "Xavier Kingsley."

"Catcher for the Bandits." Elijah's voice comes out as a squeak while he shifts from foot to foot, his whole body practically vibrating.

When his brother is done manhandling me in an impressive handshake, Ezra cautiously takes my hand. Looking up at me from below the brim of his Bandits hat, his dark eyes double in size, like it's all hitting him at once.

"You've won two Gold Gloves and you've been voted into three All-Star Games," the smaller boy finally says.

"I better step up my game or you'll be coming for my spot. You were throwing absolute lasers."

Vivienne was right. Being here and seeing Ezra blink back shock is fun. But he looks like he might pass out from the praise, so I release his hand and take the spot Elijah was standing in earlier. The two boys form the wide end of our triangle, taking turns throwing with me for a while.

Around us, the gym starts to quiet as kids are picked up, leaving us with space to talk. Of the two, Eli, which he tells me he prefers over his full name, is more talkative. I learn that he's younger, although not by much. They're Irish twins—thirteen and fourteen.

"I hear you're a second baseman. Is that your favorite position?" I ask, nudging Ezra into joining the conversation.

He shrugs, palming the baseball against his thigh before he throws it back. The leather smacks hard against my glove with the extra heat he put on that one.

"Do you ever play catcher?" I send the ball towards his brother.

Another lift of his shoulders, and he mouths something I don't hear. When I cup my hand to my ear, he rolls his eyes, reminding me a little of Tenley, before repeating, "The gear doesn't fit."

Damn that's rough. I instantly know if this kid has any interest at all in playing catcher, I'll have new gear in his size waiting for him next week.

"He'd be such a good catcher. No one sees the field like him," Eli brags.

"Shut up," Ezra snaps back.

"You don't want to play catcher?" I can't get a read through his mask of anger.

"He wants to, he's too damn stubborn." Eli rats him out in classic little brother fashion.

"Elijah." Ezra's temper flares.

"No, E. I'm sick of watching pride get in your way." Eli's gaze flits to me, his jaws tight with frustration. "He wants to play catcher, and he'd be damn good at it, too. He played when we were younger, but the gear is too expensive and Ma would never . . ."

Ezra fires his glove at the ground and for a heartbeat I think I'm going to have to break up a brawl as he stares down his little brother. His nostrils flare, but instead of advancing on Eli, he turns and stomps out of the gym.

I give Ezra space, choosing to focus on Eli. When I turn toward him, I find him holding both of their gloves, his head down.

"Sorry," he mumbles, sucking in a shaky breath as I approach.

"You've got nothing to apologize for, bud."

"He'll be okay." Eli shakes his head like it's him that needs convincing. "He needs a minute. I wish he'd stop protecting her."

Alarm bells go off in my head and I look around for an adult who might be better equipped to deal with whatever Eli is about to unload. It's then that I realize the gym is cleared out and check the time.

It's six o'clock and the brothers are the only two kids still here.

Leading him to the bleachers, I fire off a text to Tenley, belatedly letting her know I'm going to be late. When she replies with a thumbs up, I sit the kids down and brace for the tough conversation.

Hoping to coax him into sharing, I keep my voice soft. "Who's your brother protecting?"

"Our mom." He sniffles back against the moisture building along his dark lashes.

"Are you guys safe?"

"Safe enough," he mumbles.

I don't like that answer. I've lived that answer and hearing him say it makes rage boil in my belly.

I grit my teeth hoping he offers more, knowing it needs to be shared on his terms.

After a few beats of silence, Eli pushes the heels of his hands into his eyes and shakes his head. "She's not abusive or anything; she works a lot, and when she's not working, she likes to go out. It's better that way. She's nicer when she gets *her* time."

Her time.

"Is Ezra afraid your mom will get mad if he asks for catcher's gear in his size so he can play?"

He rolls his tongue along his front teeth, nodding.

Having the supreme displeasure of being raised by an asshole myself I ask another question, not wanting to make things worse at home. "Those are nice gloves," I comment, testing the waters.

He looks at his lap, studying them before he says, "Yeah, these are from Double Play."

And there it is.

"Why hasn't Ezra asked Ms. Cardoza about catcher's gear?"

Eli huffs out a wet laugh. "Ms. Cardoza—no one calls her that. Why would you call her that, bro? Are you her favorite or something?"

I sure fucking hope so, but that's not the point. I push the errant thought away, focusing on Eli, who's smile has made a reappearance, but he's not done.

Eli looks much too eager to roast me over the formal use of her name when he opens his mouth to continue the assault. "Vi, or, Vivi, sure, but never *Ms. Cardoza.*" His eyes light up with mirth and I roll mine back at him, genuinely glad he's finding humor in this.

I must not recover fast enough because the next words out of Ezra's mouth are a teasing taunt. "You like her, don't you?"

I press my lips into a thin line, if only to mask my grin. "Hey, we're talking about you, not me."

"It's like that? Okay, I see."

I nudge him with my shoulder. "What if I talked to *Vivi* about the catcher's gear for your brother?"

He tilts his head, assessing me with the skepticism of a distrustful teen—looking more like his brother than ever. "Why would you do that?"

This is the part Vivienne was talking about where *I* can make a difference.

I wet my lips, looking up for help, direction, a *fucking* clue on where to start. But there's no one. At nearly six-thirty, the boys still haven't been picked up. *How often is this happening*, I wonder, still looking for my sign to continue.

I turn on the bleacher so I'm facing Eli head-on.

"My mom died when I was young and my dad was . . . well, let's just say he was a piece of work. I think if he'd stayed sober long enough to figure out how to hand me over to the state, he would have." The dark laugh that breaks loose takes me by surprise. "I don't know what's going on at home, but I know what it's like to have a parent who's not around much. Or who doesn't want to be. I've been there and it might not be much, but if this helps, I'll make sure you both have the gear you need."

"Okay," he says, quick to accept my reasoning. "Okay," he repeats.

That was easier than I expected.

"You know," Eli says, his hand landing on my shoulder and his lips flattening, looking serious beyond his years. "If you just, like, stop being dramatic about it and, I dunno, go outside and touch some grass, maybe this decades old trauma wouldn't weigh you down. Like, you've got all this stuff bottled up, and you're not even letting it out. Let it out like a big fart or whatever. You might feel better." He pauses, then shrugs. "Or, you know, take Vivi on a date. Hot girls fix everything."

Yeah, I knew it was too easy. "A comedian and baseball player. You remind me of my teammate, Dom."

"He's hilarious. I follow him on Insta. I'm thinking of turning my trauma into a side hustle someday. Gotta start now if I want to be good at it, right?"

"Right," I say, wondering how quickly we lost the thread of this conversation. I stand, tilting my head towards the lobby. "Let's go find your brother, and I'll talk to Vi about that gear."

Eli hops off the bleachers like we didn't just have a heavy-ass conversation and follows me across the gym, peppering me with questions about playing professionally.

Ezra sits in the lobby, his arms crossed, staring at the front door—watching and waiting. I open my mouth to say—I don't even know what. Clay gives me a slight shake of his head.

I look at Eli and he waves me off, falling into the chair next to his brother. Taking the hint, I veer off into the hallway behind Clay to look for Vi.

I find her still holed-up in her office, her head bent over her keyboard, phone to her ear. Her fingers make a mess of her hair as she nervously plays with it.

"Glenda. This is Vivienne Cardoza from Double Play *again*. It's six-thirty, and the boys are still waiting to be picked up. This is becoming an issue. Pick-up ends at six. Please call me back immediately to let me know when you'll be here."

A future where Holland deals with this kind of shit from Kristy flashes in front of my eyes and I make a note to follow up with Collin and make sure my testimony for the upcoming custody hearing is airtight.

"Does this happen often?" I ask when she ends the call.

"More than it should." She lifts her head, her mouth forming a little *O* when she sees me. "How long have you been here?"

"Long enough to know they're great kids. Eli's really something—funny as hell. Ezra . . . he's . . ." Too serious. Like someone who has the weight of the world on his shoulders.

"I worry about him. He takes everything so personally, like it's his job to fix things he can't control."

I nod. I round her desk, leaning over her chair and rubbing her shoulders until some of the tension she's carrying from the phone call ebbs.

We can talk about the catcher gear later.

Loud voices break through the silence of her office and she tips her head back, giving me a look I've seen before. The one she used to get right before she'd lay into me. Only this time it's not aimed at me and I'm extremely grateful to be on her good side.

And I hope I can convince her to come over later and work off some of the tension I can see building in her shoulders from dealing with the boys' mom.

CHAPTER 43

VIVIENNE

Of all the days Glenda could've picked to be late again, she picked the one that's supposed to be a happy occasion for the boys. The catcher's gear for Ezra and bat for Elijah that Xavier picked out himself, came in this afternoon. When I called them into my office a half an hour ago to give it to them, they were overjoyed.

They called Xavier on FaceTime together from my phone to thank him. It was a great distraction until they hung up and realized it was quiet outside my office. All the other kids had been picked up and their mom was late again.

I'm about to call her when the lobby door opens, and she bursts through.

"I'm so sorry, baby," Glenda coos.

Ezra rips his face from her grip. His jaw is tight as he glares at his mom. "You lied," he spits, his shoulders practically vibrating with tension.

Undeterred, she turns to Eli. My fingers flex around the edge of the desk as I watch her approach him. His stiff posture screams *don't touch me,* but she doesn't seem to notice—or she does but doesn't know what else to do.

"It won't happen again, promise," she pleads with her younger son.

Eli throws his hands up, breaking through hers as they reach for him, ducking under her arms and spinning out of her grasp.

"Another lie," Eli spits, his voice sharp enough to cut. Of the two boys, he's usually the more laid-back, the one who lets things roll off his back. But not now. Undeterred rage twists his face, his usual calm long gone. "I hate you," he snarls.

The words hit their mark like a physical blow, and Glenda's shocked gasp fills the lobby. Her hands freeze mid-air, her body trembling under the weight of his words.

"It's time to go. Grab your things," she says, her voice shaky as she sniffs, refusing to meet my eyes.

The boys don't need to be told twice. They grab their new gear and lead the way out the door, shoulders tense and heads down, their anger dragging them down.

"What's this?" Glenda asks, eyeing the gear, her eyes filled with accusation when they shift to me.

"Catcher's gear and a new bat. It was a donation from a player they met recently," I explain.

"Great, just what I need, more baseball shit cluttering up the apartment," she grumbles.

Please let the boys be out of earshot.

When Glenda stands in the doorway alone, she pauses. Her hand grips the edge of the frame, knuckles blanching. Finally, she looks back, her face drawn, the smile she burst in with gone.

"It's not easy, you know." Her voice breaks at the edges. "Doing it all on your own."

Her words linger in the empty space she leaves behind, and I let out a slow breath, the ache in my chest pressing a little harder as I think of the red-haired angel who's a perfect source of light for her dad and my niece. Will her mom walk back into her life someday and cause the same pain Glenda does?

I rub my temples, trying to push the thought away. It shouldn't cling to me this way, but Glenda's words echo through my head. *"It's not easy."* Maybe not, but the damage left behind isn't easy either—something I've seen working with her sons for the last three years.

Double Play gives these boys the stability they don't have at home. It's a lifeline for them—a place where they can be more than their anger and pain. I won't jeopardize that by saying the things I want to, even as the words press against my tongue. Some battles aren't mine to fight. My job is to preserve this space and give them steady ground here, no matter what.

As long as she doesn't show up here drunk or high and the boys are safe in her care, I'll continue to bite my tongue.

I lock up behind Glenda, spinning and letting my head rest against the door for a moment. My face tips toward the heavens and my eyes close. When I open them and see the time, I swear under my breath.

The girls are expecting me at the game tonight. Part of me is tempted to cancel, hole myself up in my apartment and take down a pint of ice cream to see if it helps.

I know it won't—it never does. But maybe being around other people will give me something else to focus on.

At least I had the foresight to bring a change of clothes for the game. With the office empty and my day done, I change in my office, rushing so I don't miss the first pitch.

Twenty minutes later I'm barely dropping into my seat when Poppy presses a cold beer into my hand. "Sounded like you could use this."

"You have no idea." I press the plastic cup to my lips, letting the cool bubbles pop on my tongue—a small reprieve after a long day. "Is it that obvious?"

"You look stunning, so no," she says with a grin. "But the shorthand text that you were *still* at the office gave you away."

Like last time, we are sitting on the net next to the dugout. She nods toward the field. "Hopefully, a little baseball therapy helps. Did the kids run you ragged today?"

"Try the parents—or one in particular." I take another sip, letting out a slow breath.

Poppy winces. "Oof. It's always the parents."

I laugh softly, though the edge of the day still lingers in my chest. "This one is really testing me lately and I wish there was more I could do . . ."

Mia nudges me from where she sits opposite Poppy. "Can we help?"

"Maybe." I hesitate for a beat, then fill them in—careful not to share any identifying details.

"Bringing the kids to a game before the season's over is an easy one," Poppy suggests first, her voice full of excitement.

"And what about dogs?" Lilah adds, leaning forward to look at me around her friend. "You could reach out to *Saving Paws* and have them bring some animals so the kids can play with them. Like cuddle therapy."

"And you could bring in an actual therapist," Indie chimes in. "Someone for them to talk to without any pressure."

As the ideas pile up, the knot I've been carrying inside my chest eases and I feel better than I have all day.

Especially when Xavier jogs over to the net before the game starts, crooking his finger at me with that signature grin peeking out from under his cage. When he gets to the railing, he works the zipper loose and my heart drums against my ribs.

This is the closest I've been to him in days, and knowing I can reach out and touch him after seven days apart has the thousands of fans fading into nothing.

"You better tell me to stop right now if you don't want everyone to see how much I missed you this week." His voice burns low and hot just for the two of us. I doubt even the girls, who I can feel staring a hole into the side of my head, can hear.

"What are you going to do?" I ask, as if his palm wrapping around the back of my neck and dragging me closer isn't a dead giveaway.

"I'm going to kiss my lucky charm."

"That's a bold statement," I manage to say, though my voice wavers as the warmth of his touch sinks into my skin.

"So fucking true." His lips hover inches from mine, making every nerve in my body stand on edge.

An edge I want to dive headfirst off of, no matter who sees and what they say; I can't bring myself to care with Xavier standing in front of me. The effect he has on me is dizzying. I thought after a few weeks it would wane, but we've been doing this for over a month and the pull to him is stronger than ever.

I barely make out Indie's voice somewhere behind me saying, "If he doesn't kiss her soon I think she might combust."

Xavier's deep laugh rumbles through me. "I'm glad it's not just me," he whispers.

Grabbing his jersey I pull him to me. "So kiss me," I challenge, meeting his need.

This kiss isn't like our others, it's soft and sweet, yet no less consuming and no less demanding. There's a tenderness in the way he takes my mouth with sure strokes of his tongue against mine, claiming me the way you would someone you care deeply about.

It's the kind of kiss you could lose yourself in forever, but like all the others it's over before I'm ready.

When he pulls back, his thumb brushes the corner of my mouth as if he's reluctant to let go. I blink up at him, dazed, and the roar of the crowd trickles back in, including the loud whistles and cheers of our friends.

"Lucky charm, huh?" I murmur, breathless.

His lips quirk into a grin, his eyes dark with something that makes my pulse skip. "Wait for me after the game and I'll show you just how lucky."

I nod wordlessly, my head still spinning from the buzz of our kiss.

If his kiss hadn't sealed the deal, the bounce of his perfectly round ass as he jogs back to the dugout for the National Anthem would have.

God, I love that ass.

"Tell us more."

I slowly turn away from the field, finding four knowing smiles waiting for me.

"I take it, I said that aloud." There's not a hint of regret over the kiss or my accidental admission.

"Kissed the brains right out of her." Poppy laughs.

"Seriously. I think it made me stupid by proxy," Lilah confirms.

"Are we still lying to each other about what this is between you?" Indie teases, rolling her teeth over her lips, like it's killing her to stop the laugh that wants to escape.

"Yes." That infatuation I was so sure I wouldn't develop is creeping in and I'm not ready to deal with the fall out from that. If I'm being honest, I think it's been building toward more from the start, but the last two weeks have shifted things between us. This isn't about the list or even being friends anymore. Somehow, as we've gotten to know each other, it became deeper than that. There's an emotional connection there that makes everything better.

Maybe if we'd fucked it out that first night things wouldn't have ended up here.

I have to press my hand to my mouth to stop the laughter that attempts to spill free. Now that I know what it's like to have Xavier inside me that idea is delusional at best. I'd just have been hooked sooner.

"We'll be here when you're ready to talk it out," Indie says, pulling me out of my thoughts and back into the game unfolding a few feet away.

Another thing that's become glaringly clear in the last five weeks is that the friendship I've built with this group of Bandits' WAGs is healing my soul in a way I didn't know I needed.

There's an unspoken understanding among us—like we've all been through the fire in our own ways and come out stronger for it. We show up for each other in the little ways that matter most: a cold drink passed across the stands, a gentle coaxing not to lock myself away, a group chat that's half memes and half support.

I didn't realize how much I was missing that kind of connection until I had it again. These women see me—*really* see me—and piece by piece, they're reminding me who I want to be as much as Xavier is.

Will I lose all that when I lose him? The thought hits me hard and it's almost too much to bear.

"I don't like that look on your face," Poppy says, her knee bumping against mine. "You look like your world is crashing down around you."

I force myself to sound nonchalant. "It's nothing. Pesky self-doubt."

The look she gives me tells me she doesn't buy it. "Well, knock it the fuck off. You're incredible, don't doubt that for a second."

"That was really cheesy."

"Cheesy but true." She holds up her half empty beer to me, knocking it against mine.

"Thanks for that. You're a good friend." I might not be ready to tell *everyone* how I feel, but those words come so natural I can't hold them back.

"Damn right I am, and you deserve good friends, Vi," she quips, taking a sip and nudging me again. "Just like you deserve a good man."

The man in question steps up to the plate for his at bat. I might deserve good things, but am I ready for them? That's the part I'm not so sure about. And if having them means giving up the pieces of myself I worked so hard to find over the past decade will it be worth it?

The worry is still lingering nine innings later as I'm waiting beside my friends for the guys after the game.

"Whatever you're feeling right now, don't let it ruin the good things in your life," Indie warns when she slides up next to me, popping her hip against the cement wall.

"God, I must be as transparent as a window," I mutter, shaking my head.

Indie snorts, not bothering to hide her amusement. "More like a glass door, babe. Everyone can see right through, but we're still knocking to make sure."

I roll my eyes, but I can't stop the grin tugging at my lips. "Great. Exactly what I needed."

"Hey," she says, her voice softening as she leans in, "being transparent isn't a bad thing. It means we care enough to notice when something's off. And, spoiler alert, you're allowed to have doubts—lord knows I did. But you don't have to carry it alone anymore."

"It's not exactly the same. From what I hear, Dom was obsessed with you long before you gave him a second chance."

"Our stories might be different, but Xavier looks at you the same way my husband looks at me. He only sees you and that says something." She sighs. "I'm not going to tell you not to hurt him, because I know you don't want that either. But don't forget that you have the power to. Be honest with him and yourself about what's in your heart"

Be honest. Such simple advice if I could make sense of it all. But my feelings for the man pushing through the door are all jumbled—messy and tangled with the expectations I've held for myself since I turned eighteen. They're knots I don't know how to untie, threads of fear and hope so tightly wound together that I can't pull one free without the threat of everything I've worked for unraveling.

And yet, when his gaze finds mine, something clicks into place. Part of me whispers that maybe I don't have to figure it all out right now. Being honest doesn't mean having every answer—only the courage to admit how I feel, even if I don't understand it.

But God, even *that* seems impossible.

CHAPTER 44

XAVIER

The usual crowd waits outside the locker room. Kids with their dad's jersey, wives and girlfriends exchanging hugs as players join them, but none of it registers. All I see is her.

And goddamn, what a sight. Vivienne's wearing a pair of ripped shorts that mold to her lush hips. She's leaning against the cement wall, one of her Nikes scuffing lazily at the shiny floor, her arms crossed like she has nowhere to be but here. I've had girls wait for me before, but this is different, and it might not seem so significant if I hadn't claimed her for the world to see before the game.

Her eyes lift and catch on mine. It's there too, in her steady gaze.

That kiss wasn't nothing.

I changed the rules of our arrangement without asking her and she's scared. But there's something in the way her lips twitch, giving me a hint of a dimple, as if to say, *You started this, now what?*

We have an audience for the second time tonight, but I don't care. Caging her in, I bring my lips to her ear. "There are a lot of places I like seeing you, but this might be one of my favorites." There's something about her being here on her own, for me.

"Why don't you take me back to your place and show me the other places you like having me . . . your bed, for starters?"

"Have something you want to cross off tonight?" I ask.

"No, I want you, nothing else."

Well fuck. That's more vulnerability than I expected from her.

Taking her hand, I lead her out of the stadium and to my car.

When we get to the house, warm light spills from the kitchen where Tenley's busy making freezer smoothies. She glances up as we walk in, her eyes darting between us. Even if she didn't know about her aunt and me, there's no chance she'd miss the heavy tension.

After a quick hello, I drop Vivienne's hand and continue through the kitchen to the nursery. I take the stairs two at a time. Checking on Holland when I get home is my favorite part of the day, but tonight I don't linger. She's safe and sound in her crib and I'm going to make the most of my night with Vivienne.

When I step back into the kitchen, Vivienne's barefoot and helping herself to a glass of wine while she and Tenley talk. The quiet conversation that was happening halts. Pretending to be oblivious to the fact that they were most certainly talking about me—or *us*—I grab a glass of water.

"I think I'll finish this tomorrow." Tenley grins, already putting the blender in the dishwasher and tucking the bag of frozen strawberries back into the freezer. "Leave you to your night. Holland's been asleep since seven—had a five-ounce bottle. It's all in there." She points to her trusty notebook.

"Thanks," I say.

Vivienne's cheeks flush a pretty shade of pink when her niece throws a wink her way. "Have fun and be safe, kids," Tenley adds, grabbing her bag and disappearing out the door to the garage with a bounce in her step.

"That was truly mortifying. She's never going to let me live it down," Vivienne mutters, her hands flying to her flushed cheeks as she leans into the island.

"Having regrets about coming home with me?" I lean casually against the opposite cabinet, arms crossed.

She looks up at me, her lips curving into a slow smile. "Absolutely not."

"Good." I push off and make my way to her, not willing to stay away now that we are alone. "Did you eat at the game?"

"I had a hot dog."

I raise a brow, fighting back a grin. "A hot dog?"

"Don't start," she warns, her tone laced with mock seriousness.

I chuckle, brushing a stray lock of hair behind her ear as I settle beside her. "I'll take that as a no. You need some real food."

"I thought you were taking me to bed."

"I've got a better plan." I grab the strawberries from the freezer and take the biggest, juiciest looking one from the bag. It's already half-thawed from sitting out earlier.

"You're going to feed me half-frozen strawberries?" Disbelief lifts her dark brow. "I think I prefer the original plan."

Her laugh is soft and warm, curling around the space between us.

"Patience," I counter, stepping closer. "Give me a minute and I'll change your mind. This isn't on our list but I think you'll like it."

I hold the strawberry between us, the cold fruit brushing her pouty lips—lips I'm dying to taste again. Her laughter fades into a stuttered breath as the icy fruit melts against her heated skin and her eyes lock on mine.

Pulling her lip down with the fruit, my mouth replaces it, and she shivers beneath me as I drag it down her neck and over her collarbone.

"Well?" My voice is rough.

She swallows, and I chase the bob of her throat with my tongue. "Not bad." Her voice breaks, betraying her. "V-very refreshing."

"Not bad?" My gaze slips from her lips, following the line of her sternum down to where her tank top dips low, teasing at what lies beneath the most perfect breasts I've ever seen. "You'll be begging for me to feed it to you in no time."

Her breath catches as my mouth descends on her, sucking up drops of juice before they stain the hem of her white tank top. The trail of red melds with the wetness from my tongue glistening against her skin.

"So fucking pretty." I press my lips to the top of each mound. "But I want more. I'm so greedy for you." Her lips part as I lean closer, the strawberry tracing slow, deliberate paths, back and forth, over her chest. "Still think the hot dog was a better choice?"

Her laugh is a shaky exhale, her cheeks flushing deeper. "I don't know. It's pretty hard to beat a stadium dog."

Well, that won't fucking do. My hands find the hem of her tank before she can take another breath. "Arms up." I hastily pull the ribbed tank top over her head, taking a moment to appreciate the way her bra pushes her breasts together."Game on, sweetheart. You're never going to look at a strawberry again without turning my favorite shade of pink."

I don't waste any time because seven days was more than enough. Flicking the front clasp of her bra open, I step back in awe. The way her heavy tits spring free almost does me in.

I swipe my thumb across my bottom lip. "This body drives me mad—*you* drive me mad. Now what the hell am I going to do about it?"

"I thought you were going to feed me?" she challenges. "Give me something more . . . filling."

Each time, Vivienne gets a little more bold in the bedroom, letting more of the woman I know outside of the bedroom shine. And the way she's talking to me right now has my dick harder than ever.

"So damn eager. Lose the shorts for me while I decide what part of you I want to start with." My voice comes out raspy, my mouth dry and my tongue heavy.

Without taking her eyes off of me, she shimmies her shorts down her hips, swaying as she works them off her body. Standing in front of me in nothing but a barely-there lace thong that sits high on her hips, highlighting the curves she wears so well, I know exactly how I want her.

But first she needs to come. I advance on her. In one quick step, I set the fruit aside, and put my hands on her waist, lifting her easily onto the counter.

A hiss of her warm breath hits my neck when her ass hits the cool marble counter. A split second later I'm removing that last barrier keeping me from what I so desperately want—no, *need*.

Definitely need.

I don't know how or when it happened, but I'm so fucking gone for Vivienne. And even though that's not what we agreed to, I don't fucking care. I'm going to keep being gone for her.

With her thong fluttering to the floor, I push her hips back. My palm coasts down her legs, banding around her ankle. Fuck, even those are pretty. I place a kiss on each, lifting them until her feet are flat on the counter.

"Jesus," she mutters.

"Look at you." My eyes rake over every inch of her, catching on all my favorite parts: the softness of her as she leans back on her elbows for support, the swell of her hip, and the glistening spot between her legs that is calling to me. "Open for me so I can see all of you," I praise, my elbow pushing her knees open further.

They fall wider, giving me what I want. I pick up the strawberry from beside her and trace the same path I did earlier. The warmth of her skin has it nearly soft enough to eat, and by the time I'm through it will be ripe for tasting, succulent and dripping.

I spend extra time circling her nipples into tight buds, alternating cold swipes of the strawberry and feverish kisses until she's clutching my hair and whimpering my name.

"It's been too long," she whispers, her voice sharp with need when my mouth pops free.

"I know, sweetheart." I reach below the counter, palming my covered cock.

"Why are you still wearing so many clothes?"

All my clothes in fact. She's delightfully naked while I stand over her with everything but my shoes on.

"If I weren't, I'd already be buried deep inside you." I reach around the island, grabbing a stool and sliding it between my legs. This late in the season I'm not too proud to admit my body hurts. Besides, it puts me at the perfect height to be able to devour her without getting an inconvenient cramp.

She squeaks out a surprised laugh when I lift her by the hips, cradling her back and pulling her closer to me.

My fingers are still cool from the strawberry and I swipe them through her searing center. Shivers rack her body when I push inside, slowly stretching the wall of muscle that's pulling me in.

"Your cunt is already begging for more."

"Yes. More." Her head lolls to the side.

"If I put my mouth right here"—I press my thumb firmly on her sensitive bud—"are you going to make a mess all over my counter?"

"Definitely," she murmurs, so breathy and distracted that I'm not even sure she knows what she's saying.

I can't help it. I chuckle against her apex, making her cry out.

"Your mouth—the things it does to me should be illegal. I want to keep this mouth forever."

She's babbling now, lost in the moment, but I covet the words she's giving me too much to stop her.

With my fingers inside of her, I press towards her belly button at the same time I clamp down on her clit. Each stroke against her front wall makes her glazed pussy drip, leaving a mess all over my face and counter as I drive her higher. "Get there for me, sweetheart. Give me your first one. There are so many more coming—lost time and all." Trembling, her thighs bump my shoulders, trying to close on me as she gets closer. The wet sound her pussy makes as my fingers continue to fuck her makes my cock swell even more.

"Stay open," I demand.

"Can't." She hums. The one word followed quickly by my name—sweet and broken, spilling from her lips. "It's . . . so much pressure. Oh god. I don't think . . ." Her words dissolve into a deep moan.

I work her harder, her hips nearly lifting with each jerk of my wrist. Her breath comes faster until the grip she has on my hair bites painfully. She could pull it all out and I wouldn't give a fuck if it meant my lips were on her sweet cunt.

"Xavier. Shit. Oh my—fuuucck." The word is drawn out as her walls seize around me so tight that they almost force my fingers out. I keep stroking her until she's shaking under me, soaking the counter with her release.

It's filthy and beautiful all at once.

Her grip on my hair loosens and she lets her arms drop to the counter. She's sweating and breathing hard, her body lax from the potency of it.

"Did I just—shit, what a mess," she groans.

"Fuck yes, I'm covered in you."

"Oh god." She covers her face, already flushed from her release.

I pull her hands away, standing from the stool and pulling her with me so we are face to face.

"Nothing—*no one* has ever turned me on more. You hear me?"

"That wasn't on the list." She laughs, a little manically, as she buries her face in my shoulder.

"It would have been a fucking travesty not to cross that off now that we know you can do it."

Once she's steady, I lift her from the counter, letting her feet land on either side of mine before spinning her around, pinning her hips between me and the counter. Pressing between her shoulder blades, I ease her forward, loving the way her body shudders when her skin hits the slick counter.

"Why is it so hot?" She turns her head, finding me over her shoulder.

"What?"

"This—all of it. You still fully clothed. Me lying naked in my own cum."

"Because it's messy. It takes away all of your carefully constructed control and puts me in charge." I pull my shirt over my head. "You get to be unapologetically yourself, and no one but me gets to see you like this, do they?" My belt clanks as it comes undone and falls to the floor with my pants, punctuating the question.

"You know they don't," she whispers, her sparkling greens eating up every inch of skin I give her.

My dick springs free, happy to be released from the confines of my briefs and aching to be inside her. I'll never get my fill of looking at Vivienne, especially when she's exquisitely bare for me.

The brush of my dick against her ass has me gritting my teeth when I lean over her, covering her back with my front. It's insane to me how deeply affected I am by her. No one else has ever made me crazy like this. It's borderline embarrassing how quickly she makes me fall apart.

"This is going to be fast and dirty." Everytime we're together I'm fighting to hang on a little longer to make sure it's as good for her as it is for me. "Tell me that's okay—that I can be a little rough with you tonight."

She's still drenched from earlier and I slide against her with ease. My teeth clamp down on her shoulder, stifling my groan.

"Yes. Fuck," she gasps. "That feels—it's so good—god, Xavier."

I let myself sink into the moment, flexing my hips and sliding my cock through her slickness again, soaking my cock. "I'm going to bury myself so deep that you'll carry me with you even when I'm not here."

"Do it," she begs.

My crown nudges her entrance and I'm about to push in when I realize there's a problem.

I don't have a condom.

"Shit," I groan, pulling my hips back.

"What—no."

"Sweetheart, I don't have protection. I need to . . ."

"I have an IUD!" she practically shouts, making me freeze.

CHAPTER 45

VIVIENNE

Words continue to pour out of me. I should shut up, let him process, but I can't. It feels too right. So I keep babbling like the idiot his dick has reduced me too.

"I've never gone without protection and I get checked regularly. Everything's good—I'm good," I rush out. God, this is stupid. He's got a baby upstairs—this was supposed to be just sex. And yet, I can't bring myself to take the offer back. Because that's what it is. I'm draped over his counter, the mess I made sticking to me, ass up, offering him every piece of me.

"You're killing me. Tell me you're sure you want me like this—that you're not wrapped up in the moment."

I twist as much as I can, finding those pleading baby blues in the dim kitchen lights. "I want this." And I mean it, what I feel for him *is* real, that much I'm certain of. I care deeply for Xavier, even if serious still scares the shit out of me.

Urgent need has my hips shifting beneath him, seeking out friction, but he stays still.

"Goddamn," he groans, his breath fanning over the back of my neck.

Past Vivienne would be shocked to see me like this. Sweaty, covered in my own release, and basically begging this man to fuck me raw. But she didn't know what it was like to want someone with every breath you take. She'd been so deprived for so long that she couldn't even imagine the rapture that takes over when he's near. It's potent and hot and I *need* him, now.

"Xavier. I can't wait any longer. Please give me your cock—all of it."

That does it. He lines himself up, pressing in with a feral groan. "Fuck— it's so good. You're so perfect. Never going to stop wanting you. *You* were made for me."

If I wasn't already a sopping mess, the praise he pours over my skin along with his kisses would ruin me. Without a barrier between us, I can feel *everything*. It's unreal.

With one quick snap of his hips, he buries himself deeper, and I'm clamoring for a grip on the edge of the counter. The sounds that leave me are incoherent.

"Shit. Ah. Xavier."

I slip against the counter as he draws out and drives back in, his hand wrapping around my hip to soften the force. This is the sloppiest, messiest fuck of my life and I love it.

"Vivienne. Fuck, sweetheart."

We are both half sentences and ragged breaths, reduced to the need between us.

With a gentleness that has no business being in the same room as his punishing thrusts, Xavier sweeps my hair off my face, gathering it in his fist before he tugs, bringing me flush with his chest.

"You're a fucking dream, the way you take my cock. This ass . . ." He releases my hip, drives up into me, and spreads my cheeks with his free hand. "I want this. Let me add it to the list."

"Oh god," is all I can manage. I've never considered it—never thought I would, but the trust I have in him goes beyond anything I've ever imagined. It's that damn emotional connection he's forged despite our rules.

"Can I have this part of you too? I want them all, sweetheart."

"It's yours," I pant, knowing I'll give him every piece of me that's available. On the edge of my fraying consciousness I realize that this entire night is very much encroaching on the parts of me that are off limits. Still, at *this* moment it all feels very right.

"That's my girl."

He rewards me with two fingers strumming my clit until I'm sure I'm going to crash to the ground, the twisting in my spine stealing my strength.

"Xavier."

"Yes."

"I'm there. Don't stop."

"Come, Vivienne. Give it to me. Give me this piece of you."

I come hard and fast, my knees knocking against the island as they tremble from the force of it. Slowing, Xavier works me through the waves before he pulls out, leaving me bereft.

I whimper and he laughs.

"Don't worry. We're not done yet."

He spins me until I'm facing him, one hand gripping the base of his cock. "I still want to fuck these." He pinches one nipple and then the other, slowly pumping his gleaming cock. "But I'm too worked up to make it to bed."

I lick my lips, unable to form words. My mind is too addled from the orgasms and the obscene sight in front of me. His forearms flex with each slow pulse as he fucks his hand. I can't stop looking, it's so hot. Finally, the lights click on upstairs.

"Come on them."

The smirk that creeps across his face is carnal. Still shaky, I lower to my knees in front of him, taking my tits in hand and pushing them together.

"You're already such a perfect fucking mess for me. Look at you on your knees, waiting for me to come all over you like such a good girl."

"Only for you."

He steps closer. With each long stroke of his hand, my breaths come faster. Somehow, at his feet like this, I feel powerful, when the dynamic should be the exact opposite. I make this man weak; I can see it in the strain on his face as his veiled restraint slips away, his hips flexing to meet his hand.

"Come, Xavier, mark me. I know you want to."

He gasps, my name rushing out, desperate and unforgettable. This moment and that sound will be etched on my soul. Hot cum hits my chest, clinging to my sticky skin.

"Don't move," Xavier pants, bracing a hand on the counter behind me. Still sucking in gulps of air, his knee hits the ground next to mine.

For a moment I'm at a loss and then the moonlight catches the crimson, heart-shaped fruit in his hand.

He doesn't explain or give me a warning before he swipes the fruit through my center, over my belly and up my chest to collect his release. A full body shiver shakes me before he lifts the fruit to my lips.

My mouth pops open and I, or maybe it's both of us, groan as I bite into the ripe strawberry. Juice beads at the corner of my mouth, rolling down my chin and Xavier's there in a heartbeat, kissing it away before he takes my mouth.

Holy shit.

He crowds me and when I feel him harden against my stomach, I'm seconds from taking him to the ground and riding him to another orgasm. Then he pulls back, letting his chest rise and fall against mine.

"Best snack ever, don't you think? Was it better than a hot dog?"

It's so off the cuff and real that I start laughing hard. "I give an eight and a quarter."

"You're a brat," he teases, making my laughter start again.

It takes me a minute to get it under control and when I do he kisses me sweetly. The strawberry and the way he's brought this all back to dirty filthy fun after something so incredibly intimate settles the nerves that were starting to work their way in, wondering what this all means.

"Let's go. I'm cleaning you up then fucking you again before we shower. You're mine for every waking second between now and when I leave again." The mention of his upcoming ten game road trip has my heart sinking. But it doesn't last long because next thing I know I'm soaring—literally. The man scoops me up bridal style and carries me to his massive shower where he makes good on his promise.

CHAPTER 46

VIVIENNE

Looking at the pile of clothes laid out on my bed, I feel every bit the chaos monster I look like. My hair is still in heatless curlers and under-eye masks are perched high on my cheek bones—but there's a good reason.

My annual spiral is starting.

It's like this every year before I go home, but I've decided it's time that I finally put the past behind me and talk to my parents. I thought what I was doing was working because I'm successful and content. But spending time with Xavier has shown me that running from this has actually kept me from moving on at all.

It's kept me at arm's length from anyone but Tenley and Harlowe. My work is fulfilling, but beyond that there's been nothing meaningful in my life. And that's not a life I'm satisfied with anymore.

But before I can overcome my past I need to pack this damn suitcase and I suddenly hate everything I own.

My phone, which is propped up on my shelf playing music, rings through with a FaceTime request. Harlowe's face pops up and I quickly answer it.

"You're falling apart already, aren't you?"

"Can you blame me? Look at this mess." I flip the camera and pan over the bed. "I can't wear any of this to HarvestFest."

"I mean you could," she says slowly.

Flipping the camera back to my face, I let her see my eye roll so she knows how much I hate her point. "This is my armor. I need to feel good and none of this is going to do that."

"Babe. *You* are your own armor. But I get it, I know how much coming home stresses you out. So how about this . . . I'll pick you up from the airport as planned but we make an afternoon out of it, grab drinks, and find something that makes that ass look even better than it already does before we take you back to the promised land."

"Yeah?"

"Of course. I took four days off to spend time with you. Did you think I was going to dump you on the doorstep and disappear?"

"I mean . . . you're staying with me . . . so no. But this is why you're my person. I love you, Harlowe Jean, say you'll marry me."

"And how would that make Ginger Daddy feel if I stole you away for our own happily ever after?"

No one can pick me up when I'm down like Harlowe. "First, my happily ever after was always going to include you. Second, a situationship is a long way from getting a happily ever after together.."

"Fun Fact: you don't blink when you lie."

This is the problem with a best friend that knows you better than anyone else: they call you on all your bullshit. "Maybe I'm lying about the first part," I deflect—or try to. It works about as well as I'd expect.

Harlowe tips her head back and laughs. "Fat fucking chance. You're so stuck with me. I'd stalk you if you tried to cut me out."

"Don't tempt me with a good time."

There's a mock gasp from her. "I didn't know you had a primal kink. Are you going to make Xavier chase you through the Rockies? Oh, is that on your list?"

"No. That sounds exhausting," I tell her honestly. "The only cardio I'm interested in is riding—him or my stationary bike, but mostly him."

"Now, see, that time you blinked."

I hum. "I'll never lie about how good it is with him."

"You hear yourself, right?" My friend smiles knowingly from where she's sprawled across her worn couch.

"Yes, and it's so fucking confusing. The things that come out of my mouth and the things inside . . ." I wrap my knuckles on the side of my head. "It's normally such a good brain, and I'm so proud of it, but lately it's been betraying me."

"Is it? Or is it telling you things that scare you, like maybe you need to stop pretending that you don't really like this guy?"

"I do really like him. And it's giving me the scaries because I didn't expect this when we agreed to our rules. So I need you to help me finish packing because I want to head over to see him before I leave." I riffle through the pile until I find the lingerie set I bought for tonight. "Can we save the blatant honesty until after I've talked to him and tell me how hot I'm going to look in this?"

"Holy shit." She blinks dramatically. "He's going to lose his ever-loving mind."

"There's one thing left on the list from early on that he's been dying to cross off. That felt like it deserved a little something special."

"And what happens after the list is done," she asks carefully.

The words choke me, forcing me to reach for my water before I can get them out. "I don't know, but I think that's why coming home this year is so hard. I want good things, and he is the very best."

"It sounds like you already have good things. All you have to do is hold on to them."

Is it really that simple? Do I get to just keep him after all? If I can get through this week at home could *they* be mine for real. I'm suddenly overwhelmed by that possibility because I've told myself I couldn't have this for so long, that being on my own was protecting myself. But I know now that wasn't true.

"I love you," I say, tears clawing at my throat.

"I love you too, babe."

NOTES
Vivi's Orgasm Wish List
Dry Humping
Phone Sex
Fingers
Oral receiving
Edging
Oral Giving
Multiples
Penetrative Sex
Semi-public Play
Shower Sex
Try New Positions
Food Play
Squirting
Titty Fucking

CHAPTER 47

XAVIER

There's an immediate sense of relief when I don't get picked for postgame interviews and all that stands between me and my girls is a shower and my drive.

Almost an entire month of only video calls, texts, and one rushed quickie with Vivienne has me more than a little messed up. It's no one's fault, but I still fucking hate the distance the end of season has put between us.

The night we were together after she came to the game with the girls was intense, to say the least. For me, it felt like we were on the brink of more—of everything. I think this loneliness that finds me on the road stings more now because I've grown so attached to her.

Forty minutes later, I'm stepping inside my house, kicking off my shoes, and racing up the stairs. A quick stop in the nursery to say good night to Holland and I'm stalking through the house, searching for my other girl.

Tenley is back in school and knowing Vivi was here waiting was one hell of a motivator to win and win quickly.

Dim light from my bedroom has me rushing for the door and I almost trip over my feet at the sight waiting for me on my bed.

Fuck me.

It's not my birthday, but the prettiest present I've ever seen waits for me. Vivienne lays coyly on my bed, her dark hair draped over my pillows in a lush curtain. The green lingerie she wears shimmers in the glow coming from the bathroom. Pressed together to create mouthwatering cleavage, her tits are wrapped up in a bra that looks like a damn bow. One tug and it would all fall apart.

My fingers twitch at my side. I want to take the silky fabric between my fingers and undo my perfect package. I don't stop moving until I'm standing at the foot of the bed. "I could get used to finding you in my room."

She hums, toying with the ribbons at her waist. "You've been so excited about that last thing on the list, I thought we could cross it off tonight."

With her tits tied up like that there's only one thing she could mean. Imagining what she has in store for me has a whimper slipping free. And when she confirms it with a short pull on the bow I have to stop myself from tackling her on the bed.

She disappears behind my hand for a second as I drag it down my face. Every time with Vivi is better than the last, but *this one* might be the one that pushes me over the edge. Sliding between these soft full breasts is going to be the highlight of my life.

"You come first," I tell her, because I'm not sure I'll survive this and I don't want to die without getting her off one last time.

"As I should," she says with a shimmy of her shoulders.

"Damn, sweetheart." This is a departure from the woman in the hallway all those months ago, or the one who told me I didn't have to eat her out.

Like it was it a fucking chore.

Gone is the woman who brushed aside her needs for everyone else's. The goddess in my bed would never. She's no longer polite about her pleasure.

Crawling up the bed I kneel next to her, cupping her face. "Tell me how to make you come."

She stretches away from me, toward the nightstand, grabbing a black drawstring pouch that I didn't notice earlier. It's one I've seen many times during our FaceTimes when I'm on the road.

"You're so fond of watching me use this, but I wanted to see you use it on me."

The bag swings from her finger, dangling between us. I take her lips, my hand closing around the toy simultaneously.

"You've planned this whole night out, haven't you?"

"Maybe," she admits coyly.

"We're going to need to find more things to add to the list," I tell her, straddling her and working the string loose before pulling the vibrator free.

"Sounds like something to keep you busy while I'm gone," she teases, knowing damn well I haven't had a single free second in weeks between practices, games, and Holland.

"You underestimate how motivated I am." That's a job I'll make time for, especially if it means I get to keep her for longer. "Besides, I can think of a few things off the top of my head that we've talked about but haven't officially added." Hovering my lips at the shell of her ear and clicking the power button on, I whisper my filthy ideas like the one she agreed to under the influence of my mouth and a strawberry.

"It seems like you're trying to stretch this out." Her tone is still light, but there's a strain in her voice like something is bothering her. I know she's nervous about going home and I hope that's all it is. And now hardly seems like the time to ask, not when I need to get lost with her. But she's not leaving for California without telling me what's going on in that pretty little head of hers.

Using the curved tip of the toy I trace the strap of her open bra. "I think I'll leave this on while I fuck your tits."

Her breath hitches as I follow the strap around to her ribs and further down, rounding the curve of fabric that sits below heavy breasts. I repeat the pattern on the other side, working her up slowly before I drag it over each nipple, turning them into tempting peaks and letting the vibration ripple her skin.

"Do you think this toy can fuck you like I can?" I ask circling her belly button, letting each sweep get wider.

"No, I've tried."

That has my cock jumping inside my pants. Because I've seen her try and she always comes, but never as hard when I'm deep inside her.

"That's right, sweetheart. No cock—real or fake—can replace me."

Her eyes flare with fear. "I don't want to replace you."

"Hmm . . . Why do I feel like I want to make you prove that?"

"Yes," she gasps as the bulbous head sweeps over her pubic bone heading north, where she needs it.

"That wasn't a yes or no question."

"Show me. Prove that I can't replace you," she pleads, reaching for my cock.

I push her hand away, pinning it to the mattress next to her and scoot lower on the bed. "After. We have other things to do first." Her back arches off the bed with the first sweep of the pulsing toy over her clit. "I never tire of making you feel good, of showing you what you're capable of."

"Xavier," she starts.

I cut her off, easing the toy in an inch.

"With or without the list, you're strong. Don't forget, Vivienne—the power has always been yours. You just have to claim it."

She blinks up at me for a moment, clearly not expecting that, then her hands wrap around the back of my neck, dragging me in for a searing kiss.

"Thank you for always reminding me of that," she says softly when she pulls back. "Now fuck me." It's a demand and I would expect nothing less.

The toy slips in with ease. "So slick for me. Is this all from waiting in bed for me?"

"Yes. I've been thinking about this all day. It's been—"

Her thought is cut off by the press of the toy against the spot that has her clinging to me. "Distracting?" I finish for her, smirking down at her before I take one of her hard nipples into my mouth.

"Yes, so much."

"Good. I've been in a daze since the day I found you in my hallway. This list, and you . . . you've been the ultimate distraction. There hasn't been a day since that you haven't occupied half my mind."

My heart lately too.

I pull the toy out in retaliation for how quickly she's made herself a permanent fixture in my life.

"God. No. Please," she whines. All one word sentences and thrashing legs. "I don't want to stop."

It's exactly the way I feel when our schedules or her hang-ups keep us apart.

"Are you going to think about me while you're home?"

"Of course," she breathes out too quickly.

"I'm always thinking of you. It wasn't supposed to be like this, but I'm helpless in this. I want you every second of every day, and that wasn't part of the agreement. I wasn't prepared for what you'd do to me."

"I know," she says, sagging into me, giving me the intimacy and honesty I'm looking for.

Fuck it.

I'm breaking our rules and I don't care. If we're honest with each other, we've been bending the rules we set for a while. This hasn't been just sex since she risked showing up in the locker room. Our day together during the All Star Break sure as hell counts as a date. And the kiss at the game was as public as it could get. We both said we weren't looking for a relationship and I meant it, but that last rule is quickly closing in on me. Every day the need for more with her gets harder to ignore.

I might not be outright asking for it, but the connection between us is real and pretending it doesn't exist is killing me. She's leaving tomorrow and I want to know where her head is at.

"Sounds like we might need to set some new rules."

She hums, taking my face in her hands and pressing her forehead to mine. "Can any negotiation wait until I get back from California? My family—spending time back there is all I can handle. Let me get my head on straight? Because I want this, I want you, but I need to fix things with them first."

Everything about the moment is real and intimate. She's being real with me. So I give her an inch of the toy like she gave me an inch of truth. "Promise not to avoid me when you get back."

Still connected, her mouth drops open and her lids drift closed. "I promise." She seals it with a sweet kiss.

I reward her with a flick of my wrist driving the toy inside her the way she needs.

"Shit!" she cries out, her grip on my face nearing painful. She slides her hands back into my hair and I let her pull me back to her chest.

I give her what she needs: a reprieve from the stress of getting on that plane tomorrow. It's not long before my marks are blossoming all over her chest and the toy between her legs has her singing my praises, trembling in my arms.

"Xavier. Oh god. So good. Don't stop."

"Don't you know by now? I never want to stop, sweetheart."

She shudders, the fake cock drags to a stop as her muscles clamp down around it.

I'm impossibly hard from watching her come, so I flick off the toy, handing it to her. She takes it wordlessly, her chest still heaving as she comes down from her release.

"We're not done with that," I tell her, rising to my knees.

Her laughter chimes through the silent bedroom as I strip out of my clothes at lightning speed.

"Someone is excited."

"Sweetheart, you wrapped yourself up for me like my favorite fantasy. Have you seen yourself? Stunning." My lips brush her neck as I stretch out next to her. "You waited for me, making it premeditated. And it got *you* hot. Other than the baby one door down, this is the coolest thing that's ever happened to me. So yeah, I'm fucking excited." I press my hips forward showing her how eager I'm to have her like this.

I kiss her and she hums against my lips. One sweep of my tongue over the seam of her lips and she lets me in. Taking my time, I explore, savoring the taste of her, absorbing the way it feels to have her like this: willing and pliant in my arms, her guard temporarily down.

She kisses me back, deepening it, putting her whole body into it and throwing her leg over my hip. I can't help but groan at how wet she is when she grinds her hot center against my thigh.

Our kiss continues to build and she rolls on top of me, holding on to me like I'm her anchor. The sharp bite of her nails scores my scalp. It's like she's committing every second of this to memory, taking as much as she can get before life forces us apart again when she leaves tomorrow.

I flip us again, putting her on her back and taking the toy from her hand. Slipping it between her legs on the lowest setting, I work it back inside her.

"Cross your ankles and hold there for me like a good girl while I fuck these perfect tits."

My cock is already weeping from everything leading up to this—finding her in my bed, the heated kisses and seeing her come. With her on her back, I straddle her hips. Watching her closely, I loop my hand under her back and around the waist. The toy is curved with some flex to it so it should hit her front wall with the movement, but I don't want to hurt her.

"Shit. Oh," she moans, dropping her head back as it shifts inside her.

I hold my cock, the grip on the base tight. "Spit on it. Make me good and messy." Her pupils dilate.

Watching her gather saliva in her mouth is so damn dirty I might come before I even get my present. Her gaze drops mine as she lets a thread of spit trickle from her mouth. Seeing it mix with the cum already leaking from my slit pulls another whimper from deep within my chest.

"That . . . I've never . . ." Her eyes flash back to mine and then drop to wear her spit rolls down my cock.

"Again." My voice is rough with need. "The sloppier, the better."

She shifts, leaning forward and letting another string of spit join the other, her thighs rubbing as the vibrator between her legs does its job.

"I love your cock. It's perfect. Thick and long. This vein . . ." She skims her finger up the plump line on the underside. "And my favorite thing is the way it's always so hard—ready for me." Her hand covers mine at the base as she lowers herself flat to the bed.

She hums and I imagine the pulsing toy has her floating right about now. It's enough to keep her body buzzing without tipping her over the edge.

"You good?"

"Very."

I take my dick back from her. "Not too good. When you come again, it'll be from my tongue."

That elicits a content little murmur that I take to mean she understands.

I scoot up the bed still in awe that she's not only letting me do this but enthusiastically onboard. I lower my head so that I'm closer to eye level with her letting spit gather behind the dam of my lips and slowly releasing it to coat her sternum.

"Push them together, nipples in," I instruct.

The first stroke through the valley of her breasts has me groaning out in relief. Her eyes flick from where I'm poking out her cleavage to my face and back again.

"Holy shit, Vivienne," I choke out.

I pull out, my dick rubbing over her nipples on the exit. "Oh." The exclamation floats out of her. "I didn't expect—mhmm."

"Yeah. Mhmm," I agree.

A smirk spreads across her lips as I drag slowly back through, using all the control I can muster. My hips pulse forward and she lifts her head, offering me her tongue.

"If you let me play with your mouth while I have your tits wrapped around my cock—fuck I'm in so much trouble."

She does it anyway, stretching her neck to wrap her lips around the head and sucking hard. I almost fold in half. There's a pop when she releases me and I pull back, tempting her with a shallow thrust.

"What kind of trouble?"

"The type where you end up with a mouthful of cum and no warning."

"And here I thought you promised me a necklace."

"I'd give you anything you ask for, sweetheart." Her mouth wraps around my head again and she suctions to it like she's trying to suck the soul out of me.

"So much trouble," I grit when she releases me. "You want a mouthful?" My hand collars her neck gently, not squeezing, just holding her as I thrust, keeping her from lifting to take me inside again.

She nods, wetting her lips.

I groan, heat licking down my spine. "First, tell me, do you like my hand here?" My thumb brushes her jaw lightly.

"Yes," she moans. "I want you to hold me there while I come."

She's brave and open-hearted with me, it's a connection I've never had with anyone else. The way she trusts me with her body is implicit. It's the same way I feel about handing my heart over to her.

"I'm close." My cock swells as I press my hips forward. Releasing her neck, she opens for me. I shorten my movements, and her mouth is all I need to tip me over the edge. She hums and that's it. I spill, coating her tongue.

When I pull back, a ribbon of my release hangs on to her plump lower lip. I swipe it away with my thumb, but her hand wraps around my wrist, pulling it back to her mouth and licking it clean.

It takes longer than it should for me to catch my breath considering I'm a professional athlete, but that's what it's like with Vivienne. She always leaves me feeling like I'm free falling. Once my breaths even out, I crawl down the bed and settle myself between her legs.

I hold up the black toy so she can see it. "Look what you did to this. Absolutely drenched."

I drop it on the bed before burying my tongue inside her, licking up every drop. When she pulses around my finger, I find her neck, holding her like she asked. Then she's calling out my name in that fractured way I love so much.

We shower off the mess we've made and crawl into bed together. Somewhere around three in the morning, after feeding Holland, I wake her up with my fingers before I sink inside her. If she's leaving me, even for a week, I want her to feel me while she's gone.

Sleep pulls her back under, but I stay awake, watching her until I lose the battle.

Morning comes too early, bringing with it a goodbye that has my stomach twisting after last night. I don't want her to leave.

It only takes a moment for the reality to sink in: I'm in bed, alone.

But when I see her suitcase still in the corner, the panic fades. She hasn't left yet.

Checking the clock, I know she only has a short time before she needs to leave for the airport, so I don't bother getting dressed. I slip on my briefs and go out searching for her.

Soft murmurs draw me to the open nursery door. Like last time, I stop in the doorway, watching her with my daughter. Vivienne drops her nose to Holland's head and her shoulders rise with a deep inhale.

"Goodbye, my sweet Estrela. I'll miss you while I'm gone." She holds her close, whispering to her. "Take care of your daddy until I get back."

The unexpectedly sweet moment hits me in the heart. This is everything I didn't think I had room for, but I want it more than anything and sooner or later I need to tell her.

I clear my throat from the door. "Do you have time for breakfast before you have to leave?"

She crosses the room to meet me, leaning into my side. "I can spare a few minutes for you."

I drop a kiss to Holland's head and press my palm to Vivi's back, leading her out of the room, down the stairs and to the kitchen.

CHAPTER 48

VIVIENNE

"How do you feel about omelets?" Xavier asks from the fridge.

"That depends, are you going to fold the veggies in or plop them on top?"

"Is this a trick question?"

I shrug, taking a seat at the island with Holland.

"Putting them on top isn't the right answer, is it?"

I sigh dramatically, looking down at the baby in my arms. "I think we found his flaw. And things were going so well."

He cracks the eggs, glancing over his shoulder. He looks so good like this—so comfortable and at home. It makes my heart skip a beat.

He clears his throat before he asks, "Are they going well?"

Nerves send my heart plummeting into my stomach. "What do you mean?"

"With us? Last night it felt like you weren't all there with me. Is it just going home that's bothering you. Or have I pushed for more than you can give me?"

"No, you haven't pushed. I want this. I meant that when I said it last night."

"That's good because this is so much more than our list. That this is as real as it gets for me."

How can words I'm so desperate to hear be so scary? I shift Holland in my arms so she's resting against my chest, somehow having her closer eases some of those fears just a touch.

"This trip home has me in my head. Last night I wanted to forget about what was coming at me once I get to California. That wasn't fair to you and I'm sorry if that made you doubt this, because I'm right there with you."

He lets out a deep exhale and turns back to the stove and adds the cut veggies to the hot oil.

"Is there anything I can do to make your trip home easier?"

"Let me keep holding Holland until it's time to leave. She reminds me a lot of Tenley as a baby, she was always happy too."

"Do you always get stressed like this when you go home?"

He whips the eggs, his muscles putting on a show with each turn of the whisk.

"Vi." He tilts his head grinning. "I asked you a question."

"You did?" I laugh nervously, dragging my eyes back up to his face.

"Do you always get stressed like this when you go home?"

"It's never my favorite, but this year is different. I've been holding on to things that I need to air and I'm nervous about how it's going to go over. My family suffered when Erica died and I don't want to dredge that up, but I'm realizing how much losing her and the fallout from it hurt me. It's held me back in ways I couldn't see until now."

He sets the bowl of eggs on the counter, moving to stand beside me. He bends, kissing the corner of my mouth and pulling back so that there's nothing but a sea of blue looking back at me. "You deserve closure, you deserve to be heard, you deserve all of it."

I almost break into a million pieces right there on his kitchen floor. If it weren't for his arms wrapping around me at that exact moment I might have.

"How are you doing with the hearing coming up?" I ask when he goes back to the stove. Guilt has plagued me that I'm leaving when he's facing this draining ordeal with Kristy.

He shrugs. "We deserve closure too and this brings us one step closer. I hate that it has to be this way."

"Yeah, me too." And I'm not only talking about his custody trial. I hate knowing that what I have to tell my family has the power to hurt them. "You'll call me and let me know how it goes?"

"I will. And when you get home we can talk about those rules. Because I meant what I said about this being real."

♥

I scan the baggage claim, searching for something outrageous—a giant inflatable dinosaur costume maybe, or some other off-the-wall embarrassment. With Harlowe, it's never a regular airport pickup.

Then, I spot her.

Even being a brat, with her sunglasses sliding down her nose revealing those bright blue eyes, she manages to look like a goddess. Her long blonde hair is woven into a braid draped over her shoulder, disappearing behind a sign that reads: *Ginger Daddy Detox Program*.

People make all kinds of assumptions when they see my best friend. She looks like a model—perfectly put together, sweet, and approachable. Until she opens her mouth. That's when her dark sense of humor knocks you on your ass.

Today, she's rocking a baseball cap, a short unitard, a sweater tied around her waist, and a pair of pristine white sneakers. She looks like she stepped out of an ad for an athleisure brand. Only she can out-climb, out-run, and out-lift anyone in the room.

When she spots me walking towards her, the sign drops to her side and her other arm opens, beckoning me in for a hug.

"You're still short," she says, throwing her arm around my shoulder and hugging me.

"You're still tall." I hug her right back, a little tighter than I know she'd like because if we have one thing in common, it's our aversion to intimacy.

"It's a damn good thing opposites attract." She laughs, turning us towards the exit and leading us outside.

"The sign's less dramatic than I expected." I take it from her, holding it up to examine it.

"Yeah, well, you seemed like you had plenty brewing without me shoving you over the edge," she quips, her tone light but laced with knowing.

"Shopping first and then we can delve into all my issues."

Harlowe leads us through the parking ramp to her rebuilt International Scout.

"I can't believe you drove your baby into the city for me. Does your dad know?"

She snorts, her smile bright. "Of course he does. I was going to rent a car for the trip and he told me if I didn't have faith in all the work we put into the old girl to take him out to pasture now." The sparkle dulls a little at the last few words.

I hook her pinky in mine and squeeze. The last few years have not been kind to Harlowe and I'm not talking about the superficial wound of heartbreak—that was the least of the damage her ex, Canyon, left in his wake. He destroyed Harlowe's entire world in the blink of an eye and walked away unscathed.

Good fucking riddance.

The tailgate swings out to the side, the dusty blue paint gleaming like it's brand new instead of a restored, off-road truck.

"Sounds like James." I slide my bag into the open back and step aside as Harlowe shuts the door, leaning against it. I take the spot next to her. "How's your dad doing?" I ask.

She shrugs. "Some days are better than others. Mostly for me. He's adapting better than I would have, but there's still a lot of pain after PT. Every time I catch those grimaces that he tries to hide, I want to track down Canyon and—"

I take her hand in mine, squeezing it gently to ground her.

Her dark laughter echoes off the concrete pillars. "I don't even know what I'd do—what I'd say if I saw him again. I'd like to think I have something truly devious and scathing to throw at him, but I'd probably punch him and end up with an assault charge. Wouldn't be so bad if I knew it wouldn't disappoint my dad."

"Let's hope he stays the hell away from Timberline Peak for good, and you never have to find out," I say, voice firm.

"His parents are still in Wyoming. I'm bound to run into him at some point. Hazards of a small town."

And I hate that for my friend almost as much as I hate him.

"Enough about him; he's not worth it. You're going to let me style you and I can't wait any longer. Get your sweet ass into Phantom. Let me know if you need a boost."

I roll my eyes dramatically. "It was one time, and I was wine drunk."

She laughs, sounding less burdened. I push off the tailgate and round the passenger side. As smoothly as I'm able to, I make the giant step up into her car.

"Look at you." she says, her voice teasing. "I could hardly see the panic on your face."

"I hate you."

"Nah, it's all love, babe."

We make the drive out of the city, heading inland, and stop in one of our favorite towns about thirty minutes from home. It's not as boujee as Napa, but still has an eclectic mix of boutiques and restaurants.

The inland heat is about ten degrees warmer, a noticeable shift from the cool coastal breeze of the Bay Area. I shrug off my jean jacket and let the heat from the sun warm me as we grab an open table in a quiet corner of Gott's.

Harlowe tilts her head, scanning my face with a mix of curiosity and warmth. "You look happy. It's in your eyes—they're softer. Your shoulders too. Like you finally put down some of the weight you've been carrying."

I tip my wine to my lips, stalling, hoping she won't press. But her gaze stays steady, patient, and far too knowing.

"It's him, isn't it?" A sly smile creeps across her face. "And it's not the sex. You really like him."

I hang my head, hiding my silly grin. I guess we're just diving right in.

"He's . . . *everything*." It sounds cliché, but I can't think of another way to explain it. Xavier makes everything in my past fade away, like he's the missing piece I didn't know I was searching for. "Being around him is disorienting. All the things I thought I wanted suddenly don't matter. He makes me forget, and all I see is him."

"What exactly does he make you forget?" my friend presses, and I stumble for an answer, fear clouding my mind.

"Uh . . . I guess, what I thought I needed and wanted to be happy. I thought I had enough with my job and focusing on myself. But he makes me want more and it's scary."

She raises an eyebrow. "Are you afraid it's going to be like before—that you're going to lose yourself?"

"No. It's the opposite. He takes care of me like no one else ever has. But the idea that I've already fallen hard when we agreed not to catch feelings is a bit nerve racking. I've been on my own for so long. What if I'm not good at really being with someone."

She tilts her head, lips quirked. "Seems like a real problem you've got there, Vi."

"Not helping."

"Are you sure this is about him? Or is it about"—she gestures around us—"being back here? All the stuff with your family you've been carrying for years?"

Good god. The questions throw me off. It's all jumbled up together which is why I wanted to come home and fix this first—sort through the two separately.

"Look. I've never met the man, but I know two things: he's brilliant at giving you orgasms, and he makes you happy. That seems like something you should grab onto with both hands."

I let another sip of wine ease some of my nerves over being home. It's the first time I've been here without Tenley. It's the first time I've been here with this much certainty over who I am and what I want.

"I think I needed this trip home. As much as it's got me rattled, it's a full circle moment. Like maybe it's time to put the past with my family behind me. Start fresh with them. Take back the power this place and my past holds over me."

"Forgive them," she suggests, her voice soft but firm.

I can't help the way my lips pull into a frown. "I don't think they even know they need to be forgiven."

She leans back, arms crossed, like she's about to launch into one of her no-nonsense speeches. "Talk to them first and when you get home, talk to Xavier. You don't let a man like him go."

I stare at my best friend, dumbfounded. "You don't even know him."

"But I know you." Her gaze sharpens. "And you're happy, Vi, that's a good thing."

"It's a start," I say, downing my beer. If Xavier's taught me anything it's that good isn't good enough. I want it all. "Now, let's go shopping"

And that's exactly what we do: shop all afternoon, slipping into laughter and leaving behind the heaviness of dealing with talking to my family for the day.

CHAPTER 49

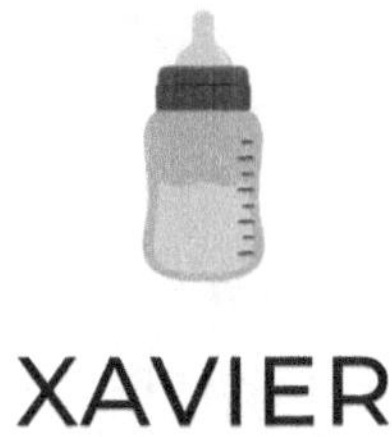

XAVIER

I'm not trying to snoop, but the notebook left open on my counter before I head to the courthouse makes it impossible. Brightly colored Post-It notes practically beg for attention, and the whole thing looks like one of those string diagrams you see in true crime shows. Except this one has hearts and arrows that scream twenty-year-old girl.

It doesn't take more than a glance to figure out the focus of this operation. Every line and doodle is centered on me and Vivienne. The words jump off the page at me.

Figure out how to get Ginger Daddy and Aunt Vi together.

We've been played like fucking fiddle and I couldn't be happier about it.

Tenley steps into the kitchen, freezing when she finds her notebook in front of me. "Well, shit," she tosses the empty bottle in the sink like she doesn't care—but her stiff posture gives her away. "How mad are you?"

I lean against the counter, holding up the notebook like evidence. "Why would I be mad?"

She smirks, folding her arms. "Maybe because I orchestrated your entire love life?"

"Orchestrated?" I scoff. "That's bold."

She tilts her head, unimpressed. "Look, you're welcome for the assist, but let's not pretend this wasn't my doing. I mean, *come on.*"

I laugh, setting the evidence down. If she only knew how her aunt and I really got our start. She'd probably beat me over the head with her notebook to shut me up. "I hate to break it to you, but this project only sped things up. Vivienne and I would've ended up together anyway."

"Really?" Her voice drips with sarcasm. "And *I'm* the bold one. How do you know that?"

I shrug, giving her a grin. "Because some things just work out. When the right person shows up, it doesn't matter how or why. It just . . . happens. You just know."

Tenley's smirk turns saccharine. "You'd have screwed it up if it weren't for me, Big Red."

I shake my head. "You're impossible, you know that?"

"And yet," she says, handing me Holland so I can say goodbye, "here we are. Don't forget to name your second kid after me."

I kiss my daughter and hand her back to Tenley, grabbing my bag with a sigh. Swallowing my pride, I glance over my shoulder. "Have you heard from her?"

"Only a few texts and a picture of her and Harlowe wine stomping," Tenley replies casually.

I nod. "I got that one too." She looked happy, her thrown back in joy as Harlowe clung to her. I hope she's feeling as good as she looked.

Tenley pauses, studying me as I head for the door. "Are you worried about her?"

"Honestly? Yeah. She's been stressed."

"It's like that every year when we go home," Tenley says, leaning against the doorframe. "But you're right—this year is different, and I can't figure out why. I should have gone with her."

It's not my place to tell her the things Vivi shared in private with me, but I can see this is eating at her so I stop, turning back to face her. "That would have stressed her out even more. Knowing you're here, handling your classes and helping with Holland, that's what she needs from you. She's got Harlowe to lean on out there."

Tenley nods reluctantly, her expression softening. "Yeah . . . I know. Hot and smart. Good for you."

"Jesus," I groan, exasperated. "You can't say that shit to me, Ten."

She laughs, and it's a touch evil, but I can tell she's trying to take my mind off the day ahead. "But it's so much fun seeing you squirm."

"Whatever. See you later."

"Good luck today. Everything is going to be okay." She lifts my daughter's tiny hand, forcing a wave.

She's a fucking weirdo, but we're lucky to have her. Knowing that Holland is surrounded by people that love her is more than I could have ever hoped for.

And I'm extra thankful for that today because when I arrive at the courthouse twenty minutes later to find that Kristy failed to show, it's a crushing blow. Part of me hoped she would at least acknowledge Holland today.

As if on cue, a text from Vivi lights up my screen.

VIVIENNE:

I wish I could be there with you today.
I'm thinking of both you and Holland.
Please let me know how it goes.

XAVIER:

She didn't show. I don't know what to think.
Can I call you when we're done here?

VIVI:

Please.
I need to hear your voice and know you're okay.

I slip my phone into the pocket of my suit pants and follow Collin into the courtroom. I'm no stranger to wearing a suit and tie, but today, this one feels like it's strangling me as I step forward when the judge calls me forward.

The judge starts by acknowledging Kristy's absence, then Collin steps up to the bench and provides evidence documenting that she was properly served with legal paperwork outlining all the details of today's proceedings.

After some back and forth, the judge determines that all paperwork is in order and continues as planned without Kristy.

In theory, I was prepared for this outcome. Collin had walked me through exactly what would happen. But being here, learning that my daughter truly only has one parent, it's nothing like what I imagined. It's gut-wrenching. Bile crawls up my throat, and it takes everything in me to keep my breakfast down.

The rest of proceedings are a haze as the judge and Collin go back and forth before calling on me to testify why I'm seeking full custody. Even though I'm well practiced, I couldn't tell you what I say—if the things Collin and I rehearsed come out of my mouth.

Affidavits from Wilson, teammates, friends, even Tenley are shared.

And when the judge rules, signing the custody order, granting me full custody of my daughter, I blink back the tears. Kristy has thirty days to contest the judgement, but Collin and I both know that won't happen. She's made her stance clear.

CHAPTER 50

VIVIENNE

Stars scatter across the night sky, their quiet brilliance mocking me because my mind is louder than ever and my soul feels like it's being ripped in half.

All day, my heart has been in Denver with Xavier and Holland. I hate that he was alone today in court. When we spoke earlier, I could hear the exhaustion in his voice. I wanted to crawl through the phone and hug him. At the same time, my head is spinning over what I need to do here.

My feet swing dangle beneath me as the porch swing creaks. The rhythmic motion does nothing to soothe me. I'm alone out here with the gravity of everything I've been avoiding to keep me company.

Harlowe leaves in the morning—her suitcase already half packed inside—and I have two days left before I head back to Denver. Just less than forty-eight hours to face the conversation I've been pushing aside for far too long.

The festivities are over and I'm waiting for my mom to come out and enjoy the swing like I know she does every night, hoping I can get through this without making a mess of things. I let out a bitter laugh—the irony of it isn't lost on me.

I've been carrying this uncomfortable truth with me the whole trip, too scared to disrupt anything or anyone.

Maybe I'm not as recovered from my people-pleasing ways as I'd like to believe.

The hinges on the door behind me squeak and I glance over to see my mom, still in the flowy maxi dress she wore to host hundreds of people for HarvestFest. She's still as beautiful as alway, her long dark hair with more pronounced waves than mine hangs loose down her back, gray woven through it, sparkling brown eyes, and two wine glasses dangling between her fingers.

"Mind if I join you, Stellina."

The nickname she uses for me, the same one Noni used for her, doesn't hold its usual comfort. "I'd like that." Any other night, I'd mean it. I love my family, but this resentment in my heart for my lost childhood is causing a rot that I can't continue to live with. The thing is I don't even know who owns the blame. It could just easily be me for letting this fester as long as I have. But I need to cut it out tonight. I want to go home from California with an open, unburdened heart. One that's free to be given.

"It's been so good having you home," she says, and I slow the swing so she can join me. "I wish Tenley could have come."

"She wanted to be here but school comes first."

My mom nods along and holds out the wineglass for me to take.

Taking it from her, I stall, saying, "Sometimes I forget how beautiful it is out here."

"It's the most beautiful place in the world to me, but I suppose Colorado holds its own wonder."

"Sitting out here, looking at the stars, makes me feel closer to Erica. There's not a day that goes by whether I'm here or in Colorado that I don't miss her."

My mother pauses with the wineglass halfway to her lips and then lowers it. "Losing Erica was hell. It changed us all. There's not a corner of this land or the houses on it that doesn't hold a memory of her."

"Sometimes I wonder if my life would've turned out very differently if she hadn't died. If *I* would've been a different person."

The wrinkles around mom's eyes deepen, and her lips pull down. "I think we all would've been different. She was a light in this family. The hole she left behind never fully healed and all of us have felt it for a very long time."

I rip off the Band-Aid. "Of course. And I'm not saying I was hurting worse than anyone else, but it changed me in ways that I'm only starting to realize. I was still a child, but I became a caregiver to a toddler. I threw myself into helping with Tenley—it was the only way I felt I could help. And it gave me a purpose. Something good in all the darkness. But it's like . . . after that, it became my job to take care of everyone. No one ever asked me if I was okay with it. I was a kid, Mom."

She looks stunned like my words are a physical blow. "What, no, you loved helping with the little ones."

Shaking my head I stand my ground. "I felt like I had too. And I let it go on for so long, speaking up felt impossible. I just wish someone would have asked, even once, if I was happy."

"After Erica died all you wanted was to be with Tenley." She sniffles.

I know this hurts her but I can't hold back now that I've started. Years of frustration and pain bubble out. "That might be true, I never asked for what came after. Anytime I wasn't at school I was watching Tenley, Cade, the twins. Then Luca and Levi had their boys and any hope of breaking free was gone. It became expected. I'd walk in the door and a baby would be dropped in my arms."

"That's . . . It's not true."

"Remember when I wanted to join the school newspaper?" I ask.

She squints like she has to think about it.

"The club met after school. When I brought it up you frowned and made a comment about not having anyone to get the twins off the bus so you could open the tasting room. They weren't my kids. Maybe I'm being a brat, but I just wanted *one* thing that was mine."

Her eyes widen, but I'm not done. "So I tried again a few months later. I wanted to go to the summer camp Harlowe went to every year. But Luca and

Levi didn't have anyone to watch their boys for the week and you couldn't close the tasting room to watch them because it was tourist season."

Her mouth opens like she wants to say something but I drive forward. The feeling of getting it out is cathartic. "I missed my senior prom because the buds were breaking and the shoots needed thinning. Even if I'd been able to go, Harlowe was the only person I was close with because all of my time was spent running a daycare. The only identity I had when I left here was caregiver. I was a teenager and I just wanted a little bit of normalcy."

My mom hangs her head. When she lifts it again, her eyes are brimming with tears. I almost take it all back—tell her to forget it and go back to pretending I'm a well-adjusted adult, when that couldn't be further from the truth.

"You were so good with Tenley—and with the others. You were thoughtful and responsible." She breathes, the first tear falling. "It made everything so much easier. We thought you wanted to help."

"I *did* want to help. This is not about being to entitled to contribute. But I didn't feel like anyone saw me as a kid with needs of my own. I was a commodity. Whenever someone needed something, they just came to me, they did ask . . . And I kept letting it happen because I didn't want to let the family down. The thing is, I was hurting. She was gone and was tasked with filling the space she left behind, but she was like a sister to me and that wound never healed because I never stopped to let it."

Her warm hand covers mine, pulling it into her lap. "I didn't mean for it to be like that. You were so strong, and we leaned on you—too much."

"Yeah. You did. And now? I've spent my entire adult life scared of getting close to anyone because I'm terrified of disappearing into their needs the way I did then."

A pained exhale leaves my mom, her hand tightening around mine. "I didn't know. I wish I would have seen it—stopped it." She looks up, realization striking her teary eyes. "Is that why you picked Maryland for school?"

I nodded. "I needed space to figure out who I was without all of *this*."

"And did you figure it out?" she asks.

"Yeah, I think I did."

"Thank you for telling me this, for letting me in." She takes my face in her hands. "My eyes are open now, Stellina, and I hope it's not too late."

I sniffle, feeling lighter than I have in years. "It's not."

"Are you going to talk to your dad and brothers?"

I bite my lip. Having this conversation with my mom is one thing. Having it with Leo, who never moved on from losing Erica, is another thing entirely. "Do you think they would want to know?"

She brushes a piece of hair from my face, tenderly tucking it behind my ear and cupping my face. "Yes, they would. *All* of them would want to know. You've been distant even when you're here. They miss their sister. Just like I miss my daughter."

I lay my head on her shoulder and we sit like that, watching the stars twinkle and sipping our wine in silence. It's healing.

Some time later, the door swings open and Harlowe steps out on the porch with a bottle of wine and an empty glass of her own. "Can I join you?"

My mom yawns, stretching out her legs before standing. "I actually need to get to bed. HarvestFest might be my favorite two days of the year, but boy does it tucker me out." She gives my hand a tight squeeze before she stands.

At the threshold she looks over her shoulder, grinning at how Harlowe's taken her spot and my head is in her lap as she plays with my hair.

"Goodnight, girls. Love you both."

"Night, Mrs. Cardoza," Harlowe says.

"Love you, Mom," I say, my voice carrying a tenderness I haven't felt in a while.

The door clicks shut behind her, leaving the rhythmic hum of the vineyard around us.

Harlowe glances down at me, her fingers still moving idly through my hair. "So . . . how are you holding up?"

I take a moment, letting the weight of the evening settle in my chest. "Better than I've been in a long time, actually."

"Yeah?"

"Yeah." A faint smile tugs at my lips. "Telling her was the right thing to do. It's like I can finally breathe again. Like I can start healing."

My fierce protector doesn't respond right away. Instead, she gives my hair a light tug, enough to draw my attention. "About damn time, Vi."

CHAPTER 51

XAVIER

The screen from my phone lights up the otherwise dim nursery. Shifting Holland in my arms to balance her bottle against my chest, I reach for the phone. When I see Vivi's name lighting up my screen anxiety cuts through me because it's three in the morning.

"Vivi. Is everything okay?" Her face is barely illuminated by the light from her phone, but it's enough that I can see she's smiling and happy. Somehow she looks lighter, more carefree than I think I've ever seen her.

"Mhmmm," she murmurs, sounding sleepy. "I just missed you." There's a drawn out yawn before she adds, "I couldn't sleep. Not without hearing your voice."

I hear it there at the end, a tiny slur in her words. "We talked earlier," I remind her. "Did Harlowe let you drink too much wine?"

"Actually I blame my mom," she says slowly.

The mention of her family strikes a nerve. "Did your conversation not go well?"

"Actually, it went okay. I mean it sucked. But we got through it. I needed to get through it. And I think I'm going to be okay," she adds absently. "She just left a bottle with Harlowe and I after we talked."

I try to make out where she is but it's too dark to see beyond her. It's not until she shifts, laying her head on her arm that I see the carpet.

"You're fucking adorable, but why are you lying on the ground?"

"Because it's late. And I wanted to talk to you." She shrugs one shoulder like that explains it. "Is my Estrela eating?" She puts more of an accent on the nickname than normal.

"She is."

"I miss her. I miss you too. How are you doing?"

When we talked earlier I was stressed about the outcome of the hearing, and I knew she could tell.

"Torn. I just want this to be over. But that means Holland doesn't have a mother in her life and even if it's for the best it still hurts." I glance down at her in my arms. "I wish she didn't have to deal with any of this."

"Me too," she says genuinely. "But she's got you. And you have a great support system. Holland will be okay. You'll be okay." Vivi bites her lip like there's more she wants to say.

And from thousands of miles away I'm willing the words out of her.

Say it, sweetheart. Let me hear it.

Her eyes lift to the screen. She might be tipsy but they are clear, filled with meaning when she says, "And you've both got me."

I groan, making Holland startle. "I want to kiss you right now."

"That sounds nice." She sighs. "You're a good kisser. And you're shirtless. That's my favorite way to kiss you."

"No phone sex. I'm right here, Vi," someone says in the background, sounding half asleep.

"Harlowe?" I ask, knowing it's got to be her best friend.

"Nice to meet you, Ginger Daddy," the distant voice answers, making me snort out an unexpected laugh.

Vivi's eyes go wide and the camera shakes as she grabs something out of the picture and hurls at her friend.

"That was our secret," she whispers-shouts, no longer talking to me.

"I'm never getting rid of that nickname, am I?"

Vivi settles back into the crook of her arm, an easy smirk curving her mouth. "Afraid not."

Holland finishes the bottle and I pull it from her slack mouth, propping her my shoulder, watching Vivi practically melt when she sees her propped against my shoulder so I can burp her.

"She's so perfect," Vivi whispers.

"She is, but I've got to get her back to bed," I say, not wanting to hang up even though I need to.

Like she feels the same Vivi says, "We're going to watch your game tomorrow. Can I call you after?"

"I'd be mad if you didn't. Sweet dreams—"

"You guys are giving me a toothache," Harlowe interrupts.

"Night, Harlowe." I chuckle.

Vivi yawns, this one deeper than the last. Like she's fighting sleep now. "Give her a kiss for me. I hope she lets you sleep until morning now."

We hang up and I put Holland back down for the night.

The four month sleep regression has been a bitch, but talking to Vivi makes the exhaustion I know I'll be feeling tomorrow a little less daunting. Seeing her was exactly what I needed. She didn't say much about the conversation with her mom, but what she gave me told me everything.

She found what she was looking for in California.

CHAPTER 52

VIVIENNE

After that middle of the night phone call I slept hard enough that Harlowe had to wake me to say goodbye.

When we get downstairs, Levi is already making coffee. All my brothers have their own places on the property, but they still meet my dad here every morning before work.

Harlowe pours herself a coffee for the road and I follow her out to Phantom, my feet dragging the whole way, not ready to say goodbye. I'd much rather she stay until I'm done facing my brothers.

"You can do this, babe."

"I know. And even if I can't . . . I think I have to."

She loads her suitcase up, slams the door shut, and turns to face me where I'm leaning against her truck. "You do."

"Okay. I got this."

"Call me later and let me know how it goes."

"I will. Text me when you make it back." The drive back to Timberline Peak is almost thirteen hours and I always worry about her when she makes the drive alone. But if anyone can handle it, it's Harlowe.

I hug her tight and when I let her go she pulls herself up into the driver's seat with ease.

"Show-off."

"Next year I'll bring you a step stool."

I flip her off and turn back towards the house in time to see my dad and three brothers heading out to the vines. The twins are probably both still hungover and will join them later.

I cut them off on their way to my dad's work truck.

"Morning, sweetie," Dad says, stopping to drop a kiss on my forehead.

"Hey, Dad."

I turn towards my brother, stopping him before he can get into the truck. If I don't do this now, while Harlowe's encouragement is still fresh, I'm afraid I'll chicken out.

"Leo, can we talk? It's important." His brow knits together.

"Everything okay with Tenley?" He pulls his phone out to check it, like he expects to see a call or text from her.

"It's not Tenley."

"Can it wait? We're about to head out."

Before I can open my mouth to tell him no, my dad steps in. "The vines will wait. Talk to your sister." I flash him a thankful smile and he returns it with a sympathetic squeeze to my shoulder. "Love you."

"Love you too, Dad."

Leo shuts the door to the truck and waits as my dad, Levi, and Luca pull away.

"What's going on, Vi?"

Erica was the first person to call me Vi, and it's the only way my brother refers to me to this day. Hearing him say it now is like the first blow in a long fight.

Standing in the driveway doesn't seem like the place to have this conversation. I glance around, my gaze snagging on the tire swing. It's not the same tire or rope Leo hung for Erica when they were in high school, but it still hangs in the same old tree. Her favorite spot to spend evenings with my brother and with me.

"Maybe we could . . ."

His gaze follows mine. When he looks back at me, there's fresh pain in his brown irises.

"I want to feel close to her for what I'm about to say."

Silently, he leads me to the swing, holding it by the ropes for me. I can almost hear the sounds of mine and Erica's laughs. He'd take turns pushing so high that my mom would come out to scold him. The two of us would be in fits of uncontrollable giggles while he took the heat.

I step in front of it, looking over my shoulder at him. "Is this thing going to fall apart on me?"

There's a tick at the corner of his lip, like maybe he's lost in the same memory as me. "Nah. Levi and I changed it out after Gus and Russo broke the rope at the beginning of summer."

Of course the twins would have been the ones to break it. "Think they will ever stop being such menaces?"

"Not if they can help it."

My hands grip the thick ropes and the swing sways back and forth. Leo gives me small pushes, keeping it slow enough not to interrupt the flow of conversation.

"Tenley really seems to enjoy working for that baseball player . . . What's his name again?"

"Stop acting like you don't know. Xavier's one of the best catchers in the league. Football might be your sport, but you know who he is."

"So, Tenley was right, you do like this guy."

"A trap? Maybe *you're* the family menace. God, no wonder your daughter is the way she is," I tease. It's been a long time since Leo and I have talked like this. Maybe it's the swing. Or maybe it's him.

"I don't know. She had some positive influences too, didn't she?"

"Erica was the best." I sigh.

"I wasn't talking about her mother." His whole tone changes, going from playful to the serious brother I've come to know. "I was talking about you."

"I did the best I could, but I was just a kid."

"Yeah." The swing stops and he rounds it, coming to stand in front of me. "You gave her more at twelve than I could give her, and I don't know if I've ever said thank you for that."

"You don't have to thank me. Tenley needed me and I was there."

"She did, but she also deserved her father, and I failed both of you." Hands on his hips, he looks up to the sky, dragging in a shaky breath. "I failed Erica too. She made me promise to take care of the kids, not to shut down. She knew she was dying, and she begged me not to die alongside her."

I watch my oldest brother fall apart and it's nothing like the way he crumbled twenty years ago. The emotions he held back then are flowing out of him like a river and I don't know what to do, where to look. I think he needs me to sit and listen. So I stay on the swing, my feet planted in the dirt.

"She would hate the way I handled losing her. I think she could see it in those last moments—I wasn't going to be able to move on. And fuck, was she right?"

"She always was."

Leo snorts out a wet laugh. "Yeah, just ask her and she'd tell you, too."

"I miss her so much." A tear dots the dirt at my feet. "Losing her changed everything. I tried to give everyone what they needed because there was so much pain. Helping with Tenley gave me an outlet I didn't realize I needed— until it didn't. Everything else piled on top of it and I got lost in helping everyone with everything."

"Then Luca had Gio, and Gabe came along a year later. The twins were always around, too, and Cade was still a toddler. Everyone looked to you to help. We'd leave to work the vines for twelve hours a day and Mom would be in the tasting room six nights a week. You went to school and raised kids while you were still one yourself."

"Yeah. So I ran as fast and far as I could when I got the chance. All the way to Maryland."

He shakes his head. "We chased you away. None of this would have been possible without you, and not one of us ever stopped to acknowledge that or check on you, did we?"

"No, not really." I kick the dirt, smearing the divot where my tears are drying. "I needed to see who I was when I was on my own."

"And did you like what you found?" Leo asks.

"For a decade I thought I did, but now I'm not so sure." I look up to find him studying me, like that doesn't add up to him. "Until I met Xavier, I didn't realize what I was missing. But before him, Harlow and Tenley were my only real friends. I've kept people at arm's length my entire adult life, all in the name of independence and finding myself. It might have gotten me a career I love, but I want more than that."

I look up the rope at the big branch above. I remember like it was yesterday, Erica screaming at Leo not to fall or she was going to kill him as he hung this swing for her.

"I want a life that Erica would be proud of," I finally say.

My brother steps to the back of the swing, pulling it back as far as he can, leaving me suspended. "Then live that life."

"Like you're doing?"

"This conversation is about you, not me." And he lets me go. When I swing back to him, he gives me another push. "Where are you going to start? With the baseball player?"

I tilt my head back, enjoying the ride. "You're a secret gossip, aren't you?"

"If I tell you, it won't be a secret anymore."

"Can you do me a favor?"

"Maybe."

"Try to do the same. Erica would hate this for you. Try to find some happiness."

"Tenley and Cade are my happiness."

"And what happens when Cade goes to Twin Falls for school next year?" My nephew has a full ride to play football in Idaho and Leo will be all alone, like I've been for the past decade. He gives me another push but doesn't answer my question. "Your happiness doesn't have to be another person. Just do something for you that has nothing to do with this vineyard."

The swing slows to a stop, and I stand turning to face him. His lips are pressed into a line. He takes off his baseball hat, running his fingers through his salt and pepper hair.

"I'll try." He holds out his arm, and I step into his embrace. "But you need to do the same. Keep showing my daughter what it looks like to go after the life you want."

"I will."

As soon as I get back to Denver.

CHAPTER 53

VIVIENNE

When the apartment door swings open, I nearly jump out of my skin. I clutch my hand to my chest, heart racing as I spin to find Tenley standing in the doorway, her expression guilty.

"Sorry," she says softly, not meeting my eyes. "I didn't mean to scare you."

I pause the music on my phone. "I was lost in the music." It's half true. I was lost, but more in my thoughts about Xavier and the wedding tonight than the music.

"Your awful dancing gave that away." The hint of attitude she gives me puts me at ease, but it's short-lived when the teasing smile falls off her face and she nods to the couch. "We need to talk. I know you don't have much time, and I feel bad for springing this on you right before the wedding, but it's been—" She blows out a long breath. "It's been really great, just busy." She laughs nervously.

Rambling from my niece is never a good sign. This girl doesn't get nervous, it's not part of her DNA. I take her hand in mine—it's as much to put me at ease as it is to encourage her.

"Tenley. Nothing you tell me could make me love you any less."

"Well, duh. I'm awesome."

Her smile isn't as cocky as I'd like, but it's a start. "Then why don't you just tell me what's going on?"

"I'm moving out."

My brows pull together in confusion. This isn't the first time I've heard her talk about getting her own place, but I thought she would wait until next semester. Housing near campus is going to be impossible to find this time of year, and I'm almost certain Xavier wouldn't offer to move her in as a nanny without giving me a heads-up.

"Does one of your friends need a roommate?" I ask, trying to make sense of the timing.

"Not exactly."

I run my thumb along the bridge of my nose. "Okay. Where are you going?"

"I'm moving to Spain."

My stomach bottoms out.

She's not just moving out, she's moving *out of the country.* I open my mouth to say something, but I can't form words. I don't know what to say.

"It's not forever, but I leave in eight weeks. And when I get back, I'm going to find housing on campus."

"What?" I finally choke out. "Why so fast?"

"It's a study abroad program. I'll be there for the spring semester and summer. I have plenty of money saved from working, and I want to go early and explore Europe for a few weeks before classes start."

I blink back the tears welling up at the torrent of emotions. Pride, confusion, and yeah, a little sadness. "Tenley, that's amazing . . . Can I ask how long you've been planning this? I'm thrilled for you even if I'm going to miss the hell out of you, but this is um . . . unexpected."

"My advisor and I have been meeting for months, but I finalized things last week. I wanted to make sure everything was set before I told you."

The back of my neck prickles with discomfort at what she's not saying. "What does that mean? Were you waiting to be accepted?"

Her eyes drop to her lap. "No, I had a spot, but I didn't want to tell you until I was sure I was going to take it."

Sure, my stomach sank when she first mentioned it, but I'm not too selfish to understand what a great opportunity this is for her. It breaks my heart that she thinks I'd be anything less than happy for her, even if I'm sad for me. "This is a life-changing opportunity. Why wouldn't you jump at it?"

"There was a lot to consider. My classes, the commitment I made to Xavier . . . and I wanted to make sure you would be okay without me."

I rub my temples, having a hard time understanding. "Did you think I wouldn't be happy for you?"

"No, that's not it." She pushes her shoulders back like she's getting ready to lay it all out there. "I couldn't leave if I didn't know you were going to be okay. You've only had me and Harlowe for so long . . . I needed you to find your people. And then I saw how you were with Xavier, and I thought he could be your person too. When I saw you two making googly eyes at each other the night of the gala, I knew there was something there."

My head spins with her words, a jumble of revelations that are both tender and cutting. It's like I'm hearing her, but I can't make it all fit. She's been carrying this all alone for months. Holding herself back for me.

That's the last thing I want.

"I needed you to see it too." Her tone shifts from nervous to hopeful. "So, I sent him to Double Play with cake."

Tenley keeps talking, sounding more relieved with each breath. Meanwhile, I'm stuck on one thing. She felt she had to make sure *I* was okay before she could live her life. She was so worried about me she was considering not going to Spain. The realization hits like a blow to the chest. I almost caged Tenley without even trying to, just like my family did to me.

"More than anything I want you to live a life filled with experiences and people you love. I would *never* want you to hold yourself back for me." My voice is choked with emotion. "Never, Tenley."

I pull her close, wrapping my arms around her, my nose pressed into her hair, and tell her what I need her to hear. "I'm so damn proud of you. Go see the world. Do great things. Be the incredible nurse I know you can be. And thank you for helping me find my people."

"You're going to be okay, Aunt Vi."

I laugh at the conviction behind her words. "Oh, yeah. How do you know?"

"Because sometimes you just know."

And I believe her. There will be moments of sadness when she's gone, but I have Xavier and Holland to help me through it. I have the girls and the comfort of knowing Tenley is doing what makes *her* happy. And for the first time in my life I have happiness that's all mine.

CHAPTER 54

VIVIENNE

The outdoor space at the hotel Hendrix and Poppy picked to host their wedding is breathtaking. Golden light filters through the trees and the laughter of guests fills the air, but all of that pales in comparison to Xavier standing at the altar with his chosen family.

The music changes and the girls come down the aisle, one after the other, each looking happy and beautiful. My chest fills with warmth reflecting on the day we shared and how they pulled me into the fold. I missed out on so much by shutting the world out, but they made it worth the wait.

All the guests shift, their attention drawn to the bride preparing to walk down the aisle alongside Janet. The James' family matriarch beams broadly at Poppy before they take their first steps down the aisle.

The breeze filters through the pines, ruffling the flowing fabric of her floral jumpsuit. She smooths a hand down Poppy's arm, leaning in to whisper something that makes her soon-to-be granddaughter-in-law throw her head back in laughter. Her joy echoes softly through the mountain clearing as they make their way to the altar.

Poppy is breathtaking in flowing lace, with intricate patterns glinting softly in the sunlight. Her red hair, swept up in a loose chignon that frames her glowing, freckled skin. She looks radiant—stunning—with the cascading train swaying gently with the breeze coming off the surrounding mountains.

They're still a few feet from the altar when Hendrix steps down, unable to wait any longer. He stops to embrace his grandmother first, leaning in as she talks into his ear. When he pulls back, he digs into his pocket for a handkerchief, gently dabbing Janet's cheek before wiping his own.

With a gentle pat to his chest, right over his heart, and a kiss to her grandson's cheek, Janet takes the open seat beside her boyfriend, Marv, in the row in front of me.

Hendrix turns to Poppy, his eyes softening as he plants a firm kiss on her lips, drawing laughter and cheers from the guests. His grin is brighter than the sun peaking through the trees as he takes her hand and leads her the rest of the way to the altar.

But my focus skips over the happy couple to find Xavier already looking at me. The openness of his gaze has tears prickling at my eyes again, and I have to pull my gaze down to check on Holland before I lose it.

Every detail of the ceremony is simple and poignant, focusing on the bond Hendrix and Poppy share. The officiant speaks of enduring love—the kind that transforms a partner into a home, a family, and a forever. It's a sentiment reflected in the way Hendrix looks at Poppy, unable to take his eyes off her as she stands beside him.

When Hendrix reads his vows, he's steady, his voice filled with devotion. He praises Poppy's patient love and creative mind, makes promises to always assume positive intent and never forget the way he feels right now.

Unlike her husband, Poppy's voice trembles with emotion as she recites her vows. She thanks Hendrix for giving her unconditional love and for being her champion at every turn. As they exchange rings, her hand shakes, but the warmth in his gaze as he encourages her steadies them both.

When the officiant announces them husband and wife, Hendrix doesn't wait. He sweeps Poppy into another kiss—this one lasting longer than the first.

When they pull apart, they join hands, linking them together as they beam at each other.

It's almost too much for me to take because I want that too.

The music dies down and the guests around me stand to rejoin the wedding party inside for drinks and dancing before dinner. Xavier steps down from the altar, taking Holland from me as I push up off the bench.

I grab the diaper bag and lean into him, letting him lead me inside. There's a private room off the reception space that's been made into a makeshift nursery for the two babies, so we drop Holland's stuff and Xavier takes advantage of the space, laying her in the swing and pulling me close.

There's a desperation in the way his mouth hovers over mine as he backs me into the wall. "I need your mouth." One soft brush against the corner of my mouth before he adds a pleading, "Can you give that to me, sweetheart?"

"Don't mess up my lipstick," I warn, my tone half serious, half playful.

Heeding my warning, he presses his lips to my neck—the delicate curve right below her ear. Lingering, he sucks gently on the sensitive skin there until my breath hitches and a soft, shaky laugh escapes.

His deep sigh washes over me. It's the sound of a man who doesn't want to stop but knows he needs to. Reaching between us, Xavier adjusts himself.

"Can we skip out before dinner? We're not alone enough for how badly I need you."

"We cannot. Unless you want to be the worst wedding guest in your friend group, we need to stay through dinner and at least one dance."

He groans dramatically. "I don't like it."

I pat his lapel. "You'll survive. And if you stay for cake cutting, I'll do that thing you want where I hang my head off the bed."

That gets his attention. Pushing off the wall next to me, he takes my hand, practically dragging me out of the room. "Maybe I can bribe the wedding planner to start dinner early."

I giggle because he's serious about it.

"Then, after dinner, I want a dance where I don't have to pretend like you're not mine."

When the nanny Hendrix and Poppy hired for the night walks in with Jarret, Xavier gives her the rundown of Holland's schedule and points out the diaper bag, never letting go of my hand.

Following Xavier, we rejoin the rest of the guests. The music in the reception area is soft as people wander, making small talk and grabbing drinks before dinner starts.

We find the wedding party gathered by the cake, getting ready to pour champagne for a toast with the bride and groom, who've just come in after taking pictures.

Well, everyone but Mia, who's got the cutest little bump rounding out her belly.

"Good, you guys are here."

I take a glass from Indie and Xavier takes one from Dean, holding them up as Hendrix clears this throat.

"Before things get crazy, I want to tell you all how much it means to Poppy and I to have you here. Since the beginning, you all have rooted for us—you've become the family that chooses us over and over again. I know that fifty years from now, we'll be standing together, surrounded by our kids and grandchildren, toasting each other for more big moments, because you can't break a bond like we have."

Poppy sniffles, and he pulls her in, brushing his lips across her forehead.

"So, here's to you. Thank you for your love, your loyalty, and, most importantly, making me see sense when it escapes me. We wouldn't be here without you. Let's raise a glass to lifelong friendships and making even more memories tonight."

Cheers of agreement ring out as glasses clink together.

Later, with our bellies full from dinner and my head slightly fuzzy from the elated atmosphere that permeates every part of the night, Xavier leads me out onto the dance floor. Familiar chords float through the room, meaningful and bittersweet. My feet stop working halfway across the dance floor. It's the same song—the one that played at the gala all those months ago, when everything felt simpler. It was the start of a friendship I never saw coming. My eyes well with tears that I don't try to stop as a velvety voice sings about a couple letting the world burn around them as they dance.

And now, here we are, dancing to it again, and I know, without a doubt, that Xavier would dance with me while the world was on fire.

His hand rests firmly on my waist, holding me close as he guides me through the rhythm. The song feels like a confession.

"How much longer do we have to stay?" Xavier asks, his eyes flicking between mine.

"You're not getting out of this dance that easily." My grip on him tightens because I want to guard this memory and never let it slip away.

Xavier closes the space between us, molding our bodies together, his roaming hands caressing every inch of exposed skin, running up my arms, sliding under the strap of my dress, cupping the side of my neck, my face, brushing his lips over my forehead. Anyone watching can see that he wants me—that he cares for me.

"I love being yours, Vivienne," he whispers softly, his lips grazing my neck.

Before I can catch my breath from that admission, the tempo shifts to something more upbeat—a classic wedding song with choreographed dance moves—and Xavier drags me off the dance floor toward the nursery.

I have to jog to keep up as he dodges people, pulling me closer to Holland. "They haven't cut the cake yet."

"Don't care. We can do that another night. It's been six weeks since we've seen each other for more than an hour at a time."

"I've stayed over," I remind him.

"Yeah, well, I hope you don't plan on sleeping tonight." My cheeks ache from how many times he's made me smile tonight, but the look he shoots me over his shoulder as he pushes through the door of the nursery shuts me right up.

The nanny looks up from where she's feeding Jarret, surprised to see us.

Xavier tips the nanny and gathers Holland's things while I walk to the portable crib and lift her out of it. Our sleepovers these last few weeks have given me extra time with Holland, so even if I haven't gotten as much time with her dad as I would like, the two of us have spent plenty of nights together in the rocker as of late.

"Shhh," I hum, swaying side to side with Holland in my arms as Xavier calls the elevator. The doors slide open with a soft chime, and we step inside, the space feeling impossibly small. Each ding of the floors as we climb toward our two-bedroom suite has my heartbeat kicking hard against my ribs.

Xavier leans against the opposite wall, ankles crossed and his gaze fixed on me with a heat that makes the air between us electric. His gaze burns me up, a mix of admiration and untamed want that sends a shiver down my spine.

"I don't care what we do when we get to that hotel room. Whether I'm inside you once or all night, I just want to be together," he says, his voice rough, like he's barely holding himself back.

I swallow hard, trying to focus on the glowing numbers above the doors, or the baby in my arms, instead of the magnetic pull to him.

The elevator dings one last time, and Xavier straightens, adjusting the strap of the diaper bag. "I didn't think it was possible, but you look even more beautiful tonight than you did at the gala," he says.

My cheeks burn, and I glance at him, trying to gauge how far he's going to push this tonight. His eyes don't waver, they settle over me with sincerity that hits me square in the chest.

"Xavier," I say, my lips curving into a warning smile.

"I'm done holding back," he replies, stepping closer as the elevator slows. "We've lost too much time already. If I have to leave you again to go back on the road next week, you're going to know where we stand and everything you're missing when we're apart."

The doors slide open, giving me an escape from the intensity of the moment. I want this man and I'm ready to tell him how much, but sweet baby Jesus, I need a moment.

"Vivienne," he whispers, my name hanging between us like a thread, his voice steady with his request. "I hope you're ready."

I nod, the simple gesture enough to make him join me in the hallway. His broad shoulders fill the narrow space, the sharp lines of his suit showing off his impressive figure as he walks ahead. The man is just as strong physically as he is emotionally, and that's something I'll never take for granted, again.

I follow in silence, the soft sound of our footsteps on the carpeted floor the only noise, the tension between us thick enough to drown out everything else.

Xavier steps into the room first, the diaper bag slipping from his shoulder onto the nearby chair—his suit jacket follows. With practiced ease, he takes Holland from me, laying her down in the portable crib, his movements careful. I linger in the doorway, watching as he removes the small blanket from earlier today and brushes his hand over her head. I've seen him in countless tender moments, but this one hits me harder than any other.

Once she's settled, he stands, taking a moment to look down at her sleeping face before turning to me. His gaze meets mine, and for a moment, neither of us speaks.

Wordlessly, he takes my hand, leading me to the other bedroom.

"I've missed you," I say, my voice barely above a whisper, though I'm not sure why I'm trying to keep it down—the door to the other room is shut.

He steps closer, his gaze steady, unreadable. "You don't have to keep missing me. Throw the rules out the window. Be with me for real."

My legs bump the soft edge of the bed and I sit, looking up at the only man who's ever come close to owning every piece of me. "I already have. The rules were gone the moment I came home from California."

"Which one went first?" His knees land on either side of my hips, straddling me and forcing me back. He's everywhere, his elbows on either side of my head, not letting me run yet.

"It was never about sex. The first time I let you inside me, it was already more."

His hand covers my heart, easing me backwards. "And the other rules."

"Well, there haven't been any other men." I laugh nervously, rambling in front of this man once again.

"And . . ."

"This is at least our third date, so that one is long gone, too."

"There's only one left. It's time to make you fall in love with me."

I blink up at him, not sure what to say because tonight that feels like a real possibility. I'm so close, it wouldn't take much at all.

I sit up, giving him a soft kiss.

"Before we go further, I need to tell you something."

I promised Tenley I'd let her tell him on her own terms tomorrow, but now it feels wrong. She might be mad at me, but she'll have to deal.

"Um, okay."

"Tenley is leaving for a study abroad in Spain. It starts in January. She's going to tell you herself tomorrow, and she's got a friend that's interested in helping with Holland while she's gone."

He looks at the door where his daughter sleeps on the other side, but when his eyes find mine again, they're filled with quiet compassion for me. "Are you okay?"

"I'm not sad she's leaving." I wipe my face expecting tears, but they come away dry. "Well, that's not entirely true. Obviously, I'll miss her, but I want her to go—to experience another culture. To learn, to grow, to flourish. I want all those things for her and she almost didn't go because she was afraid of how it would affect me."

"Oh." He sits back on his heels, still on top of me but giving me space.

Space I don't want.

"I should have told you when I came over earlier, but I was afraid it would ruin our night, but I . . . I needed to tell you. This whole 'being open' thing is new and I'm not sure exactly how it's supposed to work, but I listened to my gut."

"That's pretty much it." He pushes a head through his hair. "I'm really proud of you. Two months ago, that would have made you spiral and run. You would have self-destructed over it."

"Probably."

He lifts off of me and I grab hold of his shirt, fisting it and pulling him back. "Where are you going?"

"I'm not sure. I thought you might want a second."

"All I want is you."

He doesn't waste any more time. His lips meet mine in an urgent kiss. I claw at his shirt, tugging at the buttons, fighting to free them. When that fails, I pull the shirt free from his waistband, slipping underneath the white button down to find hot skin stretched over his toned stomach.

With more restraint than I can muster, Xavier undoes the top few buttons before pulling it over his head. Then he's dropping to his knees and slipping my heels off one by one. His hands brush under my dress, lifting it to my waist in one hurried tug.

I lift my hips and let him pull the dress over my head. Goosebumps prickle my skin as they bloom across it. Xavier steps back, my dress in his hand, wearing nothing but his black dress pants.

This moment is big and I want to memorize every detail—the hard lines of his chest, the way his free hand rakes through his red hair, leaving it deliciously disheveled. His expression mirrors my own, a mix of awe and something unspoken, something that steals the breath from my lungs.

"Show me," I say, my voice trembling, hoping he understands the plea buried between the lines.

You have to leave again, so show me what I'm missing when you're gone.

CHAPTER 55

VIVIENNE

The silence of my office after hours is broken by the sound of my phone vibrating on the corner of my desk. I almost ignore it because I'm fucking exhausted. Xavier came home from New York yesterday after the Bandits won their division. I waited up for him because he's only home for forty-eight hours before they leave again to face the Comets, and today I'm paying the price. I glance down at the screen before I send it to voicemail and see Tenley's name lighting up the screen.

The last time Tenley called me was when she got food poisoning and needed help with Holland. A pang of longing hits me at the memory of how that call changed my life. I pick up without another second of hesitation.

"Hey, Tenley. What's up?"

She pauses before she speaks, her voice hesitant. "Hey . . . um, I know this might be weird, but could you meet me at the house?"

My niece isn't timid, and hearing her sound so unsure sends a wave of concern through me.

"You know I will, but is everything okay?"

"I'm not really sure."

Panic spikes in my chest, and I'm moving before I can stop myself. "Holland?" I blurt, already grabbing my keys to go to them.

Her words calm me a fraction, but something's still off. "She's okay, but . . . I just . . . I don't know, Vivi. I feel like I'm being watched. Like someone's been following us, but I can't be sure."

A shiver runs down my spine and I grip the phone tighter.

"I don't know what it is. I just . . . I need someone with me tonight."

My heart is racing—her fear becoming my own. "I'll be there in twenty minutes, okay? Just hang tight. And if anything seems off—a car behind you, someone at the house—you call nine-one-one."

"Okay. Yeah," she agrees.

"And send me a pin so I can track you," I add.

I'm shaking when I hang up, running out the door, barely remembering to stop and lock up after myself. My fingers fumble with the deadbolt, my mind already running through all the worst-case scenarios. Fuck, I should've had her call the police. What if she's actually being followed?

Does Xavier know? He's in the middle of a game. Getting a hold of him is going to be difficult. We haven't exactly had time to go over emergency contact protocol during the postseason. Fuck, that seems like it should have been a priority given everything that's happened.

First, I need to get to Tenley and Holland to see what's going on. I can get there faster than him and I don't want to waste precious time trying to get in touch with him when I could be making sure the girls are okay.

Once I've checked on them, I'll figure out if I need to bring Xavier into it during his game, or if it can wait until after.

I jump into my car, dumping my phone in the cup holder with Tenley's location pulled up on the screen while I drive. My eyes dart down to it every few seconds until I see she's pulled into the driveway. I give her a minute and then I call her.

The dial tone rings through the speakers, each unanswered ring making my foot press harder on the gas. I'm only a few minutes away now.

Finally, she picks up.

"Jesus. Tell me you're inside," I say, my voice tight with nerves.

"Yeah. And I locked up behind me."

"Okay, I'll be there in three minutes. Keep the door locked until I'm there. I'll stay on with you."

Tense silence fills the car and three minutes seems to stretch into hours before I pull into the driveway, scanning the area quickly before stepping out.

"I'm here, let me in," I say, breathless, my heels clicking sharply on the pavement as I rush up the driveway.

As soon as I'm inside, I lock the door and glance out the window. "Let's go sit down and you can tell me what happened."

Tenley nods and follows me, clutching Holland to her chest.

"Want me to take her?" I ask

"Yeah, actually, that'd be great," Tenley says, handing her over. "I can't explain it. I didn't see anyone, but we were at the park earlier and I had this creepy feeling that someone was watching us. Every time I looked, there was no one that seemed out of place, but I couldn't shake it. And then when we were coming back from the store, I swear I saw a car from the park earlier, but it was empty. I don't know, it creeped me out. It was probably nothing, but I didn't want to be here alone until Xavier got home."

"You did the right thing. Did anyone approach you at the park?"

"No. No one. Like I said, it was just a feeling. God, this is silly," she says.

"It's not silly. I'm proud of you for trusting your gut."

I grab my phone from my pocket, googling the non-emergency number for the Denver police and hit the button to call. When the dispatcher answers, I explain the situation, give them Xavier's address and request additional patrols overnight.

I run a hand over her hair like I used to when she was little. "Why don't you relax and try to calm down a little? I'll get her ready for bed and put her down."

"Yeah, okay. Maybe some trash TV will help," she says, grabbing the remote from the coffee table.

I head to Holland's room and lay her down on the changing table and pull open the drawer to grab a fresh diaper and wipes.

With a clean diaper on Holland, I put away the wipes and blindly reach for her pajamas. I stop when my hand finds glossy paper instead of the soft fabric I expect. Looking down, I see a pile of pictures that cause me to gasp into the dimly lit room.

Scooping Holland up, I pull them out, along with a pair of pajamas that I pay no attention to and carry her to the rocker. Flipping through the handful of pictures, my heart swells and emotion clogs my throat. I've been in this drawer so many times and I've noticed this same stack of pictures tucked away for weeks, but I've never snooped because I didn't want to invade Xavier's privacy.

There's one from the first night I came over, with Holland sleeping in my arms. The three of us at the park. Me chatting with Holland early in the morning after our first sleepover. Holland clutching my dress at the wedding. And so many other random moments, some of which he wasn't present for, others which I didn't even know he was paying attention to.

This man has always seen me, from the very start.

I want him to know I see him too.

I pull out my phone, snapping a picture of Holland on my chest, and send it off to Xavier.

Vivi: I'm here helping Tenley. She's a little spooked today—felt like she was being watched. Everyone is okay, but she didn't want to be alone.

It goes unanswered, which I expected.

Rubbing Holland's back, I soak in the feeling of knowing that good things are coming, despite a scary night.

She goes down easy, like usual, and I slip the pictures back into the drawer, leaving them undisturbed before I go back downstairs to check on my other baby.

Tenley's curled into the corner of the couch, an episode of *Bluey* on TV.

"Interesting choice."

"Don't judge. I needed the dopamine hit."

"No judgement," I say, holding my hands up. When I sink into the couch next to her, I hold my arm out and she cuddles in.

"I was so scared, Aunt Vi, but now I feel silly."

"No. You're not silly. You did everything right. Always trust your gut."

"My gut told me to eat the gas station sushi that gave me food poisoning this summer."

"That's always the exception."

She doesn't laugh like I expect her to. Maybe she's still a little too shaken for a joke.

I switch topics. "Did you know about the pictures in the nursery?"

Her head bobs against my shoulder. "Yeah, why? You didn't."

"Nope," I say.

"Hmmm. They've been there for a while," she says it so casually that I almost let it slide.

"Did you pull them to the top so I would find them?"

"It's a possibility." She shifts, putting her head in my lap. "Now that you mention it, I vaguely remember doing that this morning."

"Vaguely remember . . ." I repeat slowly.

"Don't seem so surprised. I'm the reason you and Xavier are together," she says with a smile.

"Are you now?"

"Yes. We talked about this last week when I was telling you about Spain—the cake, bringing you to a game, getting sick."

"Wait, but you were really sick."

"A happy accident that worked perfectly into my plans to get you cuffed up before Spain."

I have no idea what she's talking about, but honestly, I can't bring myself to care. If she wants to take credit for getting us together, she can have it. All I care about is that I get to keep Xavier and Holland.

CHAPTER 56

XAVIER

They say there's a first time for everything.

I've never told my coach no—not once in my entire career. But one look at the text from Vivienne changed all that. After winning our division against our biggest rivals, the LA Diablos, Wilson found me in the locker room, still sticky from champagne to tell me I was up for postgame press and I looked him dead in his stony face and told him no before I grabbed my keys and bolted for the door.

There will be consequences to face in the morning, but I don't care. There is one place I need to be right now, and it's not in a room full of reporters.

XAVIER:

I'm on my way.

The drive home is a blur, my only focus locked on getting home to the girls.

Vivienne's on the couch with Tenley's head in her lap, stroking her hair. *She's okay. Tenley's okay.* My eyes linger for a second, and she gives me a sad smile, nodding towards the stairs.

With a glance back at Tenley and Vivi I take the stairs two at a time to get to my daughter. My whole body seems to go slack when I see her sleeping, completely oblivious to the panic around her.

She's fine. Everyone is okay.

My elbow propped on the crib rail with my hands braced on the back of my neck, I stare down at my sleeping daughter, safe and sound in her crib, her little chest rising and falling in perfect rhythm.

Soft footfalls pad up the stairs and then Vivienne steps up next to me, our arms brushing as she glances down at my daughter.

"She's okay. I called the police and requested extra patrols." Vivienne's hand lands on top of mine. I flip it, linking us together, because that's the only way we get through this. We don't step back from the crib, neither of us ready to let Holland out of our sight.

"Tell me what happened."

Vivienne breaks down everything she knows, patiently explaining it to me for a second time, when I ask her to go over it all again, and answering all my questions as best she can. Collin's going to be getting a text as soon as Vivienne leaves, so I can let him know what's going on and see if there's anything else we should be doing. "Tenley can fill you in on anything I missed before I take her home."

"You're not staying?" I ask.

Her mouth pops open and I'm hanging on, waiting for whatever she's about to say, only for her to press her lips together and glance back down at Holland. When she looks back up at me, I'm struck by the sadness in her eyes.

"I want to . . . more than anything, but Tenley was really rattled, and she asked if I'd take her home. I think she just wants the comfort of her own bed tonight," she says softly.

Selfishly, I want to tell her to ask Tenley to stay here in the guest room so I can have her for a few hours, but I need her back here to watch Holland when I leave for Cleveland. And if Tenley needs a minute on her own to process tonight, then I guess I can wait until tomorrow to spend time with Vivienne, because I have the day off and there's no way I'm letting this or anything else keep us apart.

"Take care of her. I owe her everything for making sure Holland was safe tonight." A flip twists my stomach thinking about what might have happened if Tenley hadn't followed her intuition. I have no idea if the threat she felt was real, but I intend to get to the bottom of it to make sure neither of them is in danger. Because as much as she gives me a hard time, she became part of our family over the summer. "And thank you for coming when she called."

"Of course I would come—even if it hadn't been Tenley that called." She looks down at my daughter and there's so much love radiating off her. I know she would do anything for her, just like I would. The urge to tell her how much that means to me—how much she means to me is overwhelming.

I turn to face her cupping her cheek. The words are right there, ready to spill out. "Vivienne . . ." There's a heaviness to her name that's never been there before. She must hear it too because her lips part on a gasp and her fingers encircle my wrist.

"Xavier, if you're about to say what I think you might, don't. Not tonight." She takes a step closer, her other hand covering my rioting heart. "I want those words when it's not fueled by fear. Please. We deserve that, don't we?"

"We do," I say hoarsely. It doesn't change anything, this woman owns me completely. But she deserves to hear those words when it's about us, about how far we've come, about everything we can be.

Vivi wraps her hands around my waist and whispers up at me, "Meet me for lunch tomorrow. I'll skip out of work for the afternoon and we can hang out—the three of us? Let's have a nice, normal day together."

"That sounds perfect. I'm going to need to meet with Wilson in the morning after my disappearing act tonight, and I've got to call Collin, too. But if you're willing to play hooky, you know I'm not going to turn you down."

"I've literally never done that before, so you should feel very special.."

"Oh, I do," I tease, pulling her to me for a too-short kiss. When her hips bump the crib we break apart, her resting against my chest, and me with my arms looped around her back, holding her because I'm not ready for her to go.

She looks up slowly.

"You need to get going, don't you?"

"Yeah, it's already late, and you kept me up late last night. If I stay any longer, I'll be completely useless tomorrow," she says with a big yawn.

"Text me when you get home." I steal one last kiss.

She nods, lingering for a beat before brushing a hand over Holland's hair and leaving us with a glance over her shoulder.

CHAPTER 57

VIVIENNE

The urge to throw up as I wait at Buns & Roses for Xavier is real. I'm nervous and out of sorts. Although, after last night I would be more worried if I wasn't. The whole night was a roller coaster.

Tenley and I went over everything again this morning and I can't shake the feeling that she had a right to be scared, and that this isn't over.

And then, when I think about the end of the night, and Xavier saying my name like it was his reason for existing . . . God, I want to hear those words, just not under duress. Now, my belly swoops for an entirely different reason.

Which is why I picked an outside table. Being trapped inside, with the sweet smell of baked goods fresh in the air seemed like a recipe for disaster. The only thing that's going to make me feel better is seeing Xavier and hearing about his conversation with Collin.

I smooth my hands down the front of the floral fabric of my dress—the one I hoped would give me some confidence to stay strong today. I threw a sweater over it for work this morning, but I left it in the car when I got here. After the last eighteen hours, Xavier deserves a little distraction.

I spot him parking and belly flips for him just like it did last night. He steps out of his SUV and I stand like I might meet him halfway because I'm nothing more than a hot mess today.

It should be an actual crime to look as good as he does dressed so casually in a pair of basketball shorts and a cutoff shirt. His biceps flex, giving me and the rest of downtown Denver a show as he lifts Holland's car seat.

For a second, I feel silly for dressing up, self-consciously adjusting the strap on my shoulder. Xavier's movements are unhurried. He shuts the car door, his eyes sweeping over me, slow and deliberate, tracing a molten path over every inch of me. He doesn't look away as he carefully adjusts the car seat in his grip. His lips quirk in a half-smile and it's a good thing I'm sitting with how my knees go weak.

Holland's sleeping soundly when he sets her car seat on the table and bends across it to kiss me. "Fuck, sweetheart, you look pretty in that dress."

After all these months he still makes me blush with the hoarse way he compliments me. Like I literally make his mouth go dry. I hope it's always like this: him looking at me like he's seeing me for the first time, and my body reacting like the man hasn't been inside me dozens of times.

"Did everything go okay with Wilson?" I ask.

He takes the seat across from me, covering my hand and pulling it toward him an inch. "Fine. I think he was more concerned that I didn't communicate with him last night, but after our call this morning, he understood."

"What did Collin say?" The need to know Holland is safe is overwhelming.

"He's having the private investigator look into a few things." He pats his pockets and swears softly under his breath. "I'm actually waiting for a call back from him but I left my phone in the car."

"Go grab it. I'll watch Holland."

His broad shoulders sag with relief. "Thanks. I can't miss his call. And sorry in advance if I have to step away." His eyes drop, taking in my dress again. "I promise it's not because I don't want to be here . . . I *really* do." Just like last night the feelings he's holding back are written on his face.

It's so intense that I have to shift my focus to the baby girl who's captured my heart right alongside her dad. Reaching into the car seat I take her tiny hand in mine. "Get your phone. I'm not going to be able to relax until we have some answers."

He nods, his chair scraping against the sidewalk as he pushes it back. The noise startles Holland awake and he pauses.

"I've got her."

"I know."

Unbuckling her straps, I take her in my arms pressing my nose to her head. That baby smell is fading and I never miss a chance to soak up what's left of it.

I watch Xavier lean into the car from the passenger side. Does it make me a creep if I check him out while holding his daughter in my arms? Probably. But the way the fabric molds to his rounded ass as he digs around for his phone has me utterly transfixed, and no amount of self-scolding can tear my gaze away.

Holland gurgles, tugging at a loose strand of my hair, bringing me back to reality. I glance down at her, a blush creeping up my neck as I silently vow to focus on *literally anything else.*

When Xavier straightens up, phone in hand, he shakes his head, looking frustrated. He looks back at us, a silent apology on his face, his thumb pointing towards the car.

I wave my hand trying to convey that we're fine here while he has a moment of privacy to do what he needs to.

"It's me and you, girlfriend," I say when he closes the door, closing himself inside.

She grins up at me, showing off a new white dot on her gum. She's changing so fast. With Xavier being gone, has he noticed? He didn't say anything and the idea that he might have missed her first tooth breaking through sits bittersweet in my chest. With the Bandits still in the postseason it means more time away and I know that's a heavy burden on him.

Lost cataloging every inch of Holland and taking stock of what else might be changing, I look up, glancing around. I expected to find Xavier leaning against his car watching with a coy smile, but he's not there. The goosebumps come in a rush, as if my body knows something I don't.

I tuck Holland in closer. Nothing seems out of place, yet everything feels very wrong. Heeding the alarms my body is throwing off, I stand, reaching for the car seat with a shaky hand to move inside.

I'm feet from the door when it opens and a stunning blonde walks out. She's tall, willowy, and heading right for us. I freeze, looking at the car, silently pleading for Xavier to open the door.

Whoever he's talking to can wait because his ex, the mother of his child, is walking towards me and I'm freaking the hell out.

Shifting Holland to the opposite side of my body, putting myself between her and Kristy I step out in front of the chair. The last thing I want is to get tangled up if I need to move quickly.

"Don't look so panicked." Her laugh is callous. "Do you think I'm going to try to take her?"

"I don't know what you're capable of, but we're sure as hell not going to stick around to find out."

"Cute. He already found someone else to play mommy." She tilts her to the side studying me like an art exhibit instead of a person. "Better you than me. This was never the life I wanted."

I round the table and she moves, blocking my path and cutting me off from Xavier and the entrance to Buns & Roses.

"If you don't want this life, why are you back?"

"Consider it a moment of weakness." Her hand digs through her purse and I'm a millisecond from taking off in the other direction when she pulls out a thick envelope. "I carried her for nine months. Annoying as it is, I couldn't shake the need to see her to make sure I was doing the right thing."

"Hey!" Xavier yells in the distance. I don't spare him a glance over my shoulder, not willing to take my eyes off Kristy.

Rapid footfalls sound behind me as he gets closer, but it doesn't stop me from telling his ex exactly what I think. "The right thing would be not scaring the shit out of her nanny yesterday. That was you, wasn't it, lurking around, watching?" I straighten my back, anger taking the lead. "Or not waiting until I was alone here to approach us?" Each ranting thought has my voice raising. "Or, I don't know, answering one fucking text from Xavier over the last six months and not putting him through literal hell wondering if you were coming back or not."

"Woah there, mama bear, simmer." She laughs. It's cold and I know she's Holland's mother, but I don't want her anywhere near us.

I almost laugh out loud at the absurdity of the situation, but my heart is still beating far too fast for me to do so. "Simmer!" I hiss, borderline deranged and giving no fucks who sees or hears it. "I absolutely will fucking not. You're selfish. You don't want to be a mother, fine, but why put them through months of wondering and court hearings you're not going to show up for? Walk away, but do it with some damn dignity."

"Like this?" she asks, sliding the envelope across the table. Still completely unaffected by the chaos she's causing, she crosses her arms over her chest.

I don't move to reach for it. I don't care what's in there. The only thing I want is for her to leave.

"Goody, you're here." She rolls her eyes as Xavier steps in front of me, easing me behind him.

He presses the keys in my hand. "Take Holland to the car."

"With pleasure." My entire body vibrates with rage as I leave them to figure it out.

"What are you doing here, Kristy?" I hear him ask as I walk down the block to where he's parked.

CHAPTER 58

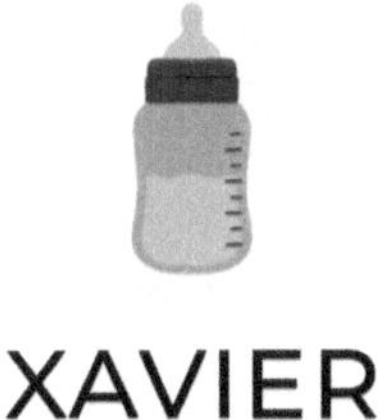

XAVIER

Sending Vivienne away so I can deal with my ex is the last thing I want to do right now. Especially considering I heard every word she said and all I want is to pull her to me and tell her exactly how much she means to me. The impulse is getting harder to ignore, and I'm not sure if I'll be able to quiet the call after that.

"Always so dramatic." Kristy scoffs. "But it seems you found what you were looking for, and it sure as hell wasn't me."

No, it wasn't, but telling her that won't do either of us any good. "We never would have worked. The fact that you're showing up here now, after six months, is proof of that."

"No, we wouldn't have. I would've hated this life." She glances at Vivienne's back and then picks up an envelope from the table, holding it out. "Call off your lawyer. I'm not going to contest terminating my rights."

I take it from her outstretched hand, sliding my finger through the seal and pulling out a thick stack of paperwork.

"Everything's signed and notarized. I'll show up to our hearing and leave with my life back. No more texts or tracking me down. I want to put this behind me and start over."

Her words cut like a knife. It's painful to hear how little she actually cares. But after today I can't say I'm sad she's walking away. There are no illusions left about Kristy or her intentions.

"All I wanted was stability for Holland." I clear my throat, trying to ease the ache there as the overwhelming emotion of all this being done washes over me. "Show up to court and you never have to hear from me again."

"Pay for my flight back here. You can start your happy little life and I'll find mine." The snark that I expect from Kristy coats every word and it makes me sad for her. I hope she finds what she's looking for someday.

Far away from me.

"My lawyer can coordinate everything, but you have to communicate with him," I say, slipping the signed paperwork into my back pocket to drop off with Collin.

With that, she turns on her heels, ducking between the parked cars before jogging back across the street where I lose sight of her.

As soon as she's gone, I run back to the car, pulling open the front passenger door. I'm prepared for an angry Vivienne, but I find her with Holland laying across her thighs, hand by her knees as they play the cutest game of peekaboo I've ever seen.

She turns in the seat, shifting Holland around and handing her to me. "That was not what I had in mind for my afternoon off of work. Are you okay?"

I step to the edge of the car and she lets her knees fall open, inviting me closer. "Yeah. Actually." I laugh, but it comes out hoarse. "She signed the paperwork to terminate her rights ahead of the hearing. Said she just wanted this to be over." I leave out the cruelness behind her words because it won't serve either of us.

Saying it out loud hits me hard. Relief pours from me in the form of a hot tear spilling down my cheek. Vivienne's soft hand cups my face, brushing it away with her thumb.

"That's good. Really good." The emotion chokes her too as she tries to stay strong for me.

"You don't have to hold back," I remind her. "Not with me."

"I'm glad she's gone. She's awful."

"She hasn't made things easy." He pushes a hand through his hair. "But I wouldn't change a thing. Not if it means giving up where we are today."

"The butterfly effect," she hums.

"The butterfly effect," I repeat. "She brought me the two best things in my life and taught me a lot about not settling.

I'm not settling anymore and I'm not letting Vivienne settle either. We are both getting the lives we deserve.

CHAPTER 59

VIVIENNE

"This is very sneaky. I'm proud of you," Tenley says when she lets me in the front door of Xavier's house. He's in Cleveland and doesn't know I'm here today. After everything that went down with Kristy, I wanted to do something for him. He's always taking care of me and doing something for him is overdue.

"It's just a little redecorating. It's not like I'm burglarizing the place," I say, lifting the bag of picture frames. After I found the pictures in a drawer last week, I got an idea that I haven't been able to put to rest.

Tenley arches a brow. "A little redecorating, my ass. You're peeing all over him and this baby."

"Ew. Am not."

"You so freaking are. This is you making your mark, in her nursery no less, and a week after Kristy showed up. You love him."

The rush of heat is unmistakable. Tenley takes the flush crawling up my chest as confirmation. "Oh my god. I'm right, and my plans worked."

"You're really going to take credit for this for the rest of your life, aren't you?"

"Heck, yes I am."

"I added some of my own. Is that creepy?" I admit sheepishly. "Pictures he doesn't know I took of him and Holland."

"No, it's adorable, and he's going to love it," she says with a laugh. "Just like he loves you."

"Stop," I beg, slipping past her toward the nursery. She's pushing buttons that she knows make me uncomfy. The words have been right there, swirling around inside my brain all week, but Xavier's not home, leaving me with nothing to do but overthink if it's too soon to tell him.

The smell of Holland's baby wash and Xavier blend as I step into the room, settling around me.

Home.

I kneel on the carpet, pulling the frames from the bag and laying them out. A starry print that I ordered that night with Harlowe on the swing. Candid photos of Holland and Xavier. One of me—that one feels like the biggest risk, but for them I'll take the chance that I could end up looking like a fool. Because ready or not, I'm the fool who fell for the guy I was only supposed to be getting orgasms from.

Starting with the art print—a navy and teal swirl of ink depicting the star alignment from the day Holland was born, with Holland Áine Kingsley and her birth date beneath it—I arrange the rest of the pictures around it, hanging them above her changing table. When it's all done, I ball up the painter's tape and gather the small level and hammer I brought with me, admiring my work.

"Xavier's gonna love this," Tenley says softly from the doorway, her eyes lingering on the art. "Going to Spain, knowing you're here with them, happy and fulfilled, is going to be so much easier now."

"Let me put her down and we can have a glass of wine and watch the game."

"I'm not going to have a job to come back to, am I?"

"Oh no, you will. I love her, but I've got a job that I love. And Xavier's got baseball. We'll need the help."

CHAPTER 60

XAVIER

I've never understood self-proclaimed masochists who claim to enjoy emotional pain. Maybe it's because I've already felt enough of it in my life to last a lifetime.

Yet here I am, standing in my daughter's room, looking at a wall with tears in my eyes. My gaze falls to the pictures she hung in the nursery for Holland. The art print of the star she had named after her, which feels even more meaningful after our day together at the planetarium. There's a note tucked under the corner of one of the frames—he one with Holland and I sleeping together in bed that's months old.

I reach for it, flipping it over in my hand before I open it. I don't know what's inside, but it feels momentous.

The paper is rough as my finger slides underneath the seal of the envelope. But the words on the paper are so fucking soft for a woman that doesn't show much vulnerability. She really outdid herself.

I see you too.

She's giving me something I didn't even know I needed—something I haven't had since my mom died. A small, quiet gesture to let me know she's choosing us.

Kristy always pushed, demanding something from me, while my dad never made me a priority. But Vivienne? She's here, offering me all of her with no conditions. Without even realizing it, she's healing parts of me I forgot were broken long ago.

We're home for our last two games of the World Series, and win or lose, the season is almost over. And no matter what happens on that field, I'm telling Vivi exactly how I feel.

XAVIER:

Your seats are right next to the girls. Security will be ready to get you guys out onto the field or down to the locker room after. See you soon.

VIVIENNE:

Why am I so nervous? Are you nervous?

XAVIER:

Not even a little.

CHAPTER 61

VIVENNE

Frustrated doesn't touch how I feel as I lock up the door to Double Play, thirty minutes behind schedule. If Xavier knew how late I was running, he might change his tune about being nervous. I've been busting my ass all week trying to figure out how to fund a transportation program so no one gets left waiting here like this. Now, of course, I'm the one stuck here because of that scenario occurring again.

Cole is out sick, otherwise I would have stuck him with the job of waiting for Glenda. I swear to god if she doesn't get the boys to this game I will never forgive her. Xavier got them tickets for tonight as soon as he found out they would be playing at home and they've been talking about it all day, their excitement palpable.

I'm a split second from risking my job to take them myself. They deserve to be there. And it's the biggest game of Xavier's career. *Nothing* is going to keep me away.

I'm grabbing my things, ready to round them up and tell them they're coming with me when the door swings open and Glenda hollers for them. The two boys are so excited for the game that they give her exasperated eye rolls instead of the full berth of their teen wrath and follow her voice to the door with a parting wave for me.

"Now I'm going to have to break about ten laws to get to the stadium in time. And parking is going to be a nightmare. My heart drops. There's no way I'll make it for the first pitch. My phone is already in my hand as I open the Uber app, hoping there's a ride nearby.

By some miracle, a driver is around the corner. I don't even flinch at the surge pricing. Totally worth it. I lock up the building and jog to the curb to wait for my ride.

Traffic is thick with people in the same predicament as me, the city frantic with the possibility that the Bandits could win it all tonight. I tap my foot nervously, my fingers gripping my phone as the minutes tick by and the tiny car on the screen creeps closer. By the time the stadium looms in front of us, my heart is racing, and it has nothing to do with how close we're cutting it.

Tonight is the night. Win or lose, I'm telling Xavier how I feel.

Once the driver pulls up, I leap out, practically throwing myself into the sea of people before he's stopped. Weaving through the crowd I hear the muffled roar of the stadium growing louder. The teams must have taken the field. But I can't focus on the excitement. All I can think about is getting to my seat.

When I finally make it inside, the game is about to start and Xavier is taking his spot behind home plate. I stop at the top of the stairs leading to my section. My chest tightens when I see Xavier's eye on the empty seat—my empty seat. His helmet is lifted and resting above the creased lines on his forehead, his shoulders tense.

The pang of guilt and urgency hits me like a freight train. Without a second thought, I'm dodging people, skipping down the stairs as fast as my legs can carry me.

Flying past the girls who are already there, I don't stop until I'm at the net, my fingers hooking into it. "Xavier!" I shout, my voice lost in the sea of cheers.

The security guard on the field spots me, his stern gaze locking in on me like I'm about to strip off my clothes and streak across the field. My stomach knots, certain I'm about to get kicked out before Xavier even realizes I made it. The guard takes two deliberate steps toward me, and I brace myself for the worst.

But Xavier's head snaps up just in time.

Those gorgeous blues meet mine. His eyes crinkle at the corners, his mouth curving into a slow, heart-stopping smile. God, he's so handsome it knocks the breath out of me.

He says something that makes the guard stop in his tracks, and Xavier tilts his head, lips shaping two unmistakable words.

"She's mine."

I can't tear my eyes away as he lowers his mask, still smirking, and drops low into his stance.

Someone behind me hollers, and I step aside in time to avoid a beer shower, realizing I'm blocking the view of the first pitch. Cheeks flushing, I make my way to my seat, nestled a few rows up and right next to Tenley, where he said it would be.

I'm surrounded by all the Bandits' WAG's who've taken me in as one of their own and there's no place I'd rather be. Draped over the back of the teal stadium seat is a denim jacket. I unfold it, ready to ask whose it is when I see the name and number.

I reach out and trace the stitching on the back, my breath catching. Looking around, I spot Indie, Mia, Poppy, Tenley, and Lilah all wearing matching jackets, their laughter and smiles making my own blossom.

That's when it hits me. He had this made for me.

My chest tightens, a mix of love and gratitude threatening to overwhelm me. He doesn't just see me, this man *loves* me. He left me a place, a piece of himself, and a sign that I belong here, with him.

Tonight is just the start for us. The Bandits are going to win the World Series and I get to go home with the man I love.

CHAPTER 62

XAVIER

Starting the most important game of my life with a scare wasn't ideal. But I'm playing in the World Series, something I've dreamed of since I was old enough to swing a bat. Little did I know I'd be eight innings in and stealing glances at a girl.

No—at *my* girl.

She's sitting in the stands, right where she's supposed to be, wearing the jacket I got her. Holland is on her lap, her tiny hands clutching a foam finger twice her size. Tenley leans in, saying something that makes her aunt laugh, and swear I can almost hear the sweet sound like it's meant for me.

Two more innings and I can have her in my arms. We're up four to three and the energy of the crowd is pushing us hard to hold the Comet's off and widen our lead. I pound my fist in my glove, giving our closer, Tyson, the symbol for a fastball with a two-one count. He nods his head once, winding up to throw, and a second later the ball cracks off the bat.

By the sound alone, I know it's not going far. My eyes track it up and over my head. I rip my mask off, but it's already out of play, sliding down the net and landing in the dirt. I pick it up and hand it the ump. Taking the new ball from his outstretched hand, I throw it back to Tyson, giving him a nod.

He's tense. He wants this inning over as badly as the rest of us. The pressure on the mound is over-the-top during a regular game, but I know the game—these players, better than most. Squatting low behind the mound, I watch as the Comet's first baseman grips his bat like he's trying to kill it. The nerves are getting to him. He's antsy and tense. It's a dangerous combo.

A signal for a slider. He's already on edge; let's see if we can make him chase.

It works. A second later, the ball smacks against my glove making my second favorite sound. I glance over my shoulder to see Vivienne on her feet screaming and pointing at me as the batter walks off the field, his head hanging and his shoulders slumped.

I jump to my feet and run to my dugout, flying high on adrenaline. There's only so much you can control in baseball and batting is one of those things. I zero in, more committed than ever to helping the team close out the season with a history-making win tonight. Because when I step off this field, it's going to be with more than just a new championship. It's going to be with the woman I love.

Trading out my catcher's gear for my batting gloves and helmet, I wait on the edge of the dugout taking the open spot between Hendrix and Dean.

"That's the smile of a man that knows he's about to win," Hendrix says, looking around me to Dean.

I don't pull my eyes from where Cruz is at home plate, stepping into the box. "I'm winning either way tonight."

The ump signals a ball and Cruz smirks.

"Yeah, but we're taking this," Dean says, his focus on the field.

"Hell, yeah we are," I echo as the pitcher throws another ball to give my teammate an oh-and-two count.

"The jacket was a nice touch," Hendrix comments offhandedly.

"Shhh . . ." Dean hisses, nodding to where Dom is warming up out in the on-deck circle. "He's got superhuman hearing and you know he'll never shut up about it if you tell him he was right."

Dom was the mastermind behind the jackets. He brought the idea to the team a few weeks ago and there was never a question if Vivienne was getting one. Even with the distance the end of the season and her trip home put between us physically, I knew I wanted her to be a part of this night as much as any of the other women.

We hold a collective breath as the pitcher finally throws a fastball worth swinging at. Cruz sees it too, planting his foot in the dirt and swinging. He connects with a power that vibrates through the stadium, sending the crowd and the dugout into a frenzy as the ball sails over the wall and into the outfield stands.

We pile out onto the field in a rush to get to him as he rounds the bases giving him high fives and pats on the back. The two point lead isn't a bow on the game, but in a situation like this, every run is celebrated because one is all it takes to change everything and shift the power balance. Being up two this late in the game is sure to mess with the Comets.

Their pitcher shakes his head on the mound, and the catcher runs out to talk him down.

Dean presses his helmet down tight and jogs up the stairs, bat in hand, to take his place in the on-deck circle.

It's not enough. Dom doesn't have the same patience as Cruz, especially knowing the man on the mound is shaken. He's got a knack for being able to chase down pitches that aren't quite perfect and he does just that, taking a chance on an outside curve ball, extending his hands and widening his zone to send it right center. It's not his best hit, but it's enough to get him on base.

I pat Hendrix's shoulder. "See you on the other side."

"Give 'em hell!" he yells at me as I run out onto the field in front of our dugout.

I nod, but the brunette waiting in the stands for me snags my attention. She's got her hands clutched in front of her face as she stands frozen in place.

"Breathe," I mouth.

Her shoulders rise and fall and she mouths back, "Thanks."

Ducking my head, I focus on finishing this inning.

Dean is usually one of our more conservative batters, but with the electricity coursing through the stadium, it's hard to hold back, even for the most disciplined player. He lets the first one go, and the ump makes a questionable call, shouting strike. Dean glares, his gaze intense as he resets his stance and stares down the pitcher.

Of all the guys in the league, Dean might be the most intimidating when he's at the plate. His hands twist loosely on the bat, combating the vibes he throws off. The guy is as calm and collected as they come, all the while mean mugging the pitcher.

Like he hoped it would, it throws off the pitcher and Dean swings at the sloppy slider, pulling it down the third base line. It lands shallow in the outfield, allowing Dom to take third and cover the corners.

Putting the fastest guy on the team right where we want him—in scoring position.

Now it's up to me and I've got options. As long as Dom comes in, that's all that matters—scoring a run myself would be a happy bonus. And not to be greedy, but I want it all today. The win, the girl, the run.

This is their pitcher's last chance. If he doesn't get me out here, his skipper is guaranteed to pull him and no one wants that, especially in the World Series. But I can't find it in myself to feel sorry for him today.

Before stepping into the batter's box, I grant myself one last chance to find Vivienne in the stands. Looking right at those deep greens I cover my heart with my hand and then take my stance.

This one is for her and I'm going to make it count.

The first pitch is trash, so I leave it, hoping for something I like soon. The pressure's on him, not me, and he's going to crack. It's clear in the tick of his jaw as he checks the bases.

Smart man. Give Dom an inch and he'll steal.

His attention refocuses on me, and he shakes off the first sign. He's playing a psychological game I know all too well, but it won't throw me off. Not with the motivation of winning the whole damn thing for the woman in the stands.

The corner of my lips tilts up in a smile just before he throws. It's a passed ball low in the dirt, sneaking past the catcher, exactly what we need. Immediately recognizing his mistake, the pitcher charges forward to cover and I step back allowing Dom to slide head-first, sneaking under the tag.

"Fuck!" the opposing pitcher bellows.

"Hell yeah!" Dom lets out a triumphant roar as I help him up and I dust him off, patting him off the back. "Finish this, Xav," he says as he charges towards the dugout, hands fisted, still shouting, getting everyone riled up with him.

"Our time." I say under my breath, shaking out my arms and getting back into place. Dean waits on second, giving me a quick sharp nod, a silent show of faith.

I fucking love this game. This is the most fun I think I've ever had playing ball, and it's all because I get to play with my brothers—the family that always chooses me. So, when the next pitch comes, and it's right down the middle, I give it everything I've got for her, for them, for me.

It's a solid hit over the infielder, dropping in front of the right fielder. It's enough to get Dean home, but the throw to first is clean and they pick me off, sending me back to the dugout to celebrate another run from the team.

There's no shame in a sacrifice.

Skipping down the steps, I gear back up to take the field and wrap this thing up. I'm still catching my breath when Cruz stoops down next to me, handing me my shin guard as I strap the other on one.

"That was a smart play. Not everyone can keep their head, but you did. Nice work."

The praise means everything coming from my captain because I know he's not only talking about the game happening on the field. "Thanks, Cap," I huff, still checking my breath.

"Watch Tyson. Keep him calm," he says, squeezing my shoulder as he stands to grab his glove. The bottom of the order is not faring as well against the Comet's pitcher.

The final Bandits' batter gets out, and Wilson's whistle grabs our collective attention before we take the field. "Men, baseball is a fickle sport. As easily as we took the lead, they can take it back. In a game this important, there's no giving up, no taking it easy. You get here by having grit. Don't for a second forget that they have just as much grit as you do. But I think you have more heart, and that's what's going to win you this game. Now get the hell out there and end our season the right way!"

A rumble of agreement rings through the dugout before we all take the field with the same determination. There's no false sense of security starting the ninth inning up three points, but there is a united sense of how we got here and what our goal is.

The ump sets a clean ball in my outstretched hand and I jog out to the mound, holding it out for Tyson. "You've got this. Everyone knows that. Give us three outs and we dog pile on the mound. Let's make it quick."

"What's the rush?" He laughs, as calm as a mountain breeze.

"There's a girl waiting for me in the stands and I need to tell her I love her." I nod to where Vivienne watches. She's not going to stop me tonight.

He follows my gaze, a smirk tilting his lips. "By all means, I'll win the fucking World Series so you can lock her down."

"I knew I could count on you." I press the ball into his hand and jog back to the mound.

This is it.

Tyson doesn't mess around, throwing gas and getting the first two batters out, throwing a total of eight pitches. The leadoff batter takes the plate with one out left and I don't envy him. This is do or die and he might be one of the best batters the Comets have, but it would take a miracle for him to change the direction of the game.

I keep a level head, calling on everything I know about Diego Rivera and pick my call carefully, Wilson's words ringing in my head. With a closed fist, I angle my arm away from my body. Tyson nods and puts it right in my glove. At the same time, the breeze of the bat washes over me.

"Strike." The bellow comes from behind me and I stand, throwing the ball back to Tyson and hold up two fingers for the stadium to see.

"Two more," I say to myself as the next batter takes his spot. He's a contact hitter, not a power hitter. We can take more risks with him, so I signal a fastball outside. The contact is weak and pops high, easily caught by Hendrix.

"One more to go!" I shout at Tyson, the sound getting lost in the deafening crowd noise. Taking another ball from the ump, I throw it to him and he nods, understanding even though there was no way he heard me.

I don't dare look at the stands where I know security is already waiting to get the girls on to the field. My focus stays on Tyson, knowing that I need to finish this so I can get to Vivienne and Holland.

The real test steps up to the plate. Anton Jones is consistent and powerful, but Tyson is the best closer in the league and one of the reasons we've made it this far. He shakes off my first call so I give him what he wants, a fastball.

Bending low at the waist, he checks the bases, glancing over his shoulder before rising and throwing a fastball outside for Jones to chase. And he does.

"Shit," he grits out.

I try to hold my smile because I'm not a total asshole. Two fingers pointing down and Tyson gives me what I want this time: a curveball that fools Anton into making the same mistake twice. One more pitch is all we need and I know what my pitcher is going to want: a fastball. Like the pro he is, he throws it high, tricking the batter into thinking it's another curve and checking his swing.

The split second it takes for the ump to say what I know is coming seems to drag on for minutes before I hear the five letters that set the whole stadium on fire.

"S-T-R-I-K-E!"

CHAPTER 63

XAVIER

World fucking champions!

Adrenaline surges through me as I drag myself out of the dog pile, grinning like a fool. The weight of the long season lifts in a single breath, replaced by unfiltered joy. My teammates are shouting, laughing, and slapping each other on the back, but my focus has already shifted. I'll celebrate with them later—pop the champagne, hoist the trophy, all of it—but right now, there are only two people I need to see.

Vivienne and Holland.

I scan the field, heart racing for a completely different reason. My eyes lock with them and I break out in a sprint, not stopping until they are both in my arms. Vivienne looks up at me, her irises sparkling with pride. I take Holland from her, and Vivi's hands lift to my face.

"You did it." She beams, her smile impossibly wide.

"And you're here," I breathe, my voice thick with more than just victory.

"Here," she says, her hands lifting to cradle my face. "And I'm not leaving. Not now. Not ever."

Holland coos softly, her tiny hand brushing against my jaw. For the first time since Vivi left for California, everything is exactly as it should.

"I think I like the sound of that," I murmur, my grip on both of them tightening a little.

"Good, because I see you, Xavier," she says, her voice steady but full of emotion. "The three of us together is what I want. It was always what I wanted. Watching Kristy walk in and threaten that . . . it put everything into perspective."

Her gaze drops for a moment before she looks back at me, her lashes glistening. "Before you, I was afraid of losing myself. Afraid of giving my life over to someone else."

"I'd never let that happen," I say, my throat tight.

"I know," she says with a small smile. "Maybe, with someone else, I would have slipped back into old habits and lost pieces of myself, but you and Holland have only ever *given* to me. You've never taken anything away."

Her hand shakes as it brushes my cheek. "Meeting you, going home, facing everything with my parents and then Tenley leaving showed me that life is better when you let people in. You've given me more than I thought I could ever have. Understanding, acceptance, patience, friendship. Getting to know you and Holland taught me to ask for what I want in life, instead of fearing what I might lose if I spoke up. "

"You did that. You found your voice on your own," I say hovering above her lips. Not kissing her is testing my restraint.

"Maybe," she says, her gaze locking with mine. "But you made me brave enough to use it."

I exhale, the weight of her words settling over my heart. "You've always been brave, Vivienne."

"In some ways, but not in the ways that mattered. Putting rowdy baseball players in their place at work is very different from the bravery it took to open up my heart after all these years," she whispers, a tear slipping free, though her smile is radiant.

My focus drops to her lips. "Can I kiss you now?"

The breath shudders out of her. "Please."

I close the distance between us, my hand sliding to the back of her neck, pulling her closer. Her lips part as I press mine to hers, soft and warm and everything I've missed while we've been on the road.

Her fingers curl into my jersey, anchoring us together, and I pour every ounce of what I feel—relief, love, longing—into her. She tastes like popcorn and my future. Like my everything.

When we finally pull apart, her forehead rests against mine, her breaths coming fast. "That was . . ." she starts, but her words trail off as a shy smile tugs at her lips.

"Yeah," I murmur, brushing a strand of hair from her face. "I missed your mouth."

"It's been three days." She chuckles against my lips.

"Too damn long. I'm kissing you everyday during the offseason. Try and stop me."

Holland stirs softly in my arms, breaking the moment.

A piece of confetti floats down, landing in Holland's hair and Vivienne brushes it away, both of us laughing.

The celebration continues around us, and after a while we hand Holland off to Tenley, her pouty lips smacking together before she yawns, shoving her fist in her mouth.

Vivienne captures my heart for the second time tonight when she brushes a kiss against her forehead, murmuring, "Sweet dreams, Estrela."

I press my lip to her cheek, adding my own, "Goodnight, Áine."

Tenley takes her, promising to get her home safely.

"You know . . . that should have been a sign from the beginning," Vivienne says.

"What should have been?" I ask, too distracted by having her alone to follow her logic.

"That we both used nicknames with similar meanings. Áine and Estrela. Estrela means star. Áine means radiance." She stares up at me. "Two names for radiance and light—for something that guides you when everything else feels dark."

I pause, the significance of her words hitting me with so much force they almost knock me over. "Maybe we were always meant to find our way to each other—to be a family."

She stops walking, her hand slipping into mine, her gaze steady as it locks on mine. "I like to think so."

"Did the boys make it?" I ask, suddenly remembering that Ezra and Elijah are supposed to be here.

Vivi looks around, pointing when she spots them at the net in a crowd of fans holding up a sign with my name and number on it. Hand in hand we cross the field to them and get pictures and hugs. They're beside themselves with excitement when some of the other guys come over.

From there, the rest of the celebration is a blur of high fives, hugs, and cameras flashing as the team pours into the locker room. Champagne sprays everywhere, soaking through my jersey as we celebrate like kids who just won their first game.

Vivienne waits with the rest of the girls in the family area, cracking open their own bottle of champagne.

Later, we head to a private party with family and friends at Draft. They've closed down the bar for us to celebrate, giving us the run of the place instead of just the VIP area where the team typically gathers post game. The energy is as electric as it was in the locker room. Laughter and cheers fill the bar, but I can't look away from Vivienne—at the way she fits here, among my people, as if she's always belonged.

By the time we step through the door of my house, it's just us. The quiet wraps around us, a stark contrast to the noise of the night, and I know this is the moment I've been waiting for.

CHAPTER 64

VIVIENNE

The silence between us as we stand in the entryway to Xavier's house is louder than any part of the celebration tonight. Every glance, every breath, feels laden with the words we've held back for far too long.

It's late, and the door to the guest bedroom is shut, a reminder that Tenley is still here. The house is still, but there's a buzz in the air that has nothing to do with the champagne I barely touched at the stadium. I want to savor the moment building between us.

Xavier leads me toward the stairs, and each step we take towards his room bolsters my courage until it's pumping through my veins, vibrating over my skin, reminding me that I've never been as certain about anything as I am about us. This man is it for me.

Our hands find each other in the dark as we climb the stairs and I take charge, stepping into his room. I shut the door with a quiet precision that I mastered so as to not wake the sleeping baby down the hall, because I love her, but I'd *really* like to be alone with her dad right now.

Large hands find my waist, turning me before my hand has left the door. Xavier presses me against the wall, raising his hand to find the opening in the jean jacket. Slowly he parts it, his hooded eyes not missing a thing as he watches it slip from my shoulders.

The heavy material falls to the floor with a soft thump, leaving me in his jersey and a pair of jeans. He's seen me in dresses, skirts, leggings and nothing at all. But right now, he's looking at me like the simple outfit is everything.

Having his attention on me is always intoxicating, but I can't afford to get swept up in his crystal blue gaze, not when I still have things to tell him.

Before I can open my mouth to say what I need to, his hands find the back of my thighs, lifting me and fitting us together like we were made for this.

Brushing my hand up his shoulder until it rests on his cheek, I stroke his lower lip with my thumbs. "Xavier." His name comes out on a huffy breath. I hate stopping us when all I want is to feel him everywhere.

"What is it, sweetheart?"

The words stick to my tongue, not because I don't want to say them, but because they've lived there for so long. But I know if I don't say it now, he will, and I need him to hear me. To know that it isn't a heat of the moment response.

"I love you."

Slowly, his tongue sweeps across his bottom lip before his mouth spreads into a full-blown smile. "Say it again."

"I love you, Xavier Kingsley. I love you and I love your daughter with everything I am. And it's not new, it's the most natural, perfect thing I've ever felt. It's not something I decided, I never had a choice in the matter. You and Holland stole my heart, piece by piece, until there was nothing left to give to anyone else. Loving you has made me stronger, fuller, more whole than I ever thought I could be."

"You don't know how glad I am to hear that," he says, his voice low and steady, the warmth of his words settling between us. "Because I've been unconditionally, hopelessly in love with you for months."

"Tell me."

"I never saw you coming," he begins, his hand joining mine where it still covers his cheek. "At first, I didn't think there was room in my heart to love someone so completely after Holland was born. She filled every corner of me, and I thought I didn't have anything left to give. But then you came along and filled spaces I didn't even know were empty. You healed the pain from my past I thought I'd put behind me. You gave me hope and fun back. You gave us all of you without even realizing it. I love you, Vivienne."

"I want to love you without rules, no bounds, just us," I say, leaning forward until our foreheads are touching.

"But we keep making lists because I have plenty of things I still want to do with you. This is only the beginning." He rolls his hips, reminding me how hard he is for me already.

Feeling bold from the declaration of love, I ask, "Anything in particular?"

Cradling me, he turns from the wall, taking us both down to the bed where his lips find my neck. "So many things. But tonight I want you in this jersey when I slide into you for the first time. Then I'm going to make love to you until we both pass out."

"That's a thing for you?" I ask coyly.

"Seeing you in the name I want to make yours someday? Yeah, it's a thing." He says it so casually, like there's no question where this is headed.

My breath catches, but he doesn't waste any time stripping my pants down my legs.

"What if I want to keep my name?" I challenge, pushing up on my elbows to watch him crawl back up my body, soft kisses falling all over my skin as he goes.

"A name doesn't make you any less mine. I'm going to put a ring right here." He sucks my finger into my mouth and I almost combust on the spot. "I'm going to put a baby right here." He splays his hands over my belly in a gentle caress, before they travel higher, one collaring my neck and the other stroking my cheek. "And I'm going to hold you like this so I can feel it when you call out my name— now and always."

"Xavier," I breathe out, sounding desperate.

"Yeah, like that, sweetheart." Swooping in, he takes advantage, stealing the air from me with a kiss that's filled with all the promises he just made. A sweet caress of love that's easy to get lost in because with him, every kiss feels like a first kiss. By the time we break apart, I'm clawing at his shirt and pants to get him closer, to feel his body slide against mine.

He stands from the bed. "On your knees, in the middle of the bed. Undo the buttons on the jersey, but keep it on."

I do as he asks, fumbling through it as I watch him slowly undress. He's been pushing himself hard all season and you can see it in every line of his body as the shadows highlight the deep groove of his abs and the defining swell of his quads. He catches me gawking and his smile doubles.

"Like what you see?"

"You know I do." I slip the last button free.

His leg brackets my calves and his hard cock bobs before it's pinned against my spine. "If I dipped my hand between your legs right now, would you be ready for me?"

"Why don't you find out—" My taunt is cut short when he dips his head, nipping at my shoulder.

"It only seems fair that I get a good long look, too." He takes his time, smoothing his palm down the back of his jersey until it wraps around the curve of my waist. With steady pressure between my shoulder blades, I sink lower. A hoarse groan rumbles deep in Xavier's throat, lighting me on fire like a candle burning at both ends as his thick cock drags over my ass until I'm on all fours.

The bed shifts beneath me as he takes me in.

His fingers slide under the waistband of my thong, pulling it down and leaving it stretched around my thighs. The cool air of his room hits my core. I look over my shoulder, finding his attention on my exposed pussy as his hand runs over his jaw. "This is what fantasies are made of, this cunt dripping for me. Show me how much you missed me, spread yourself for me."

Restricted by the underwear still looped around my thighs, my only option is to drop to one elbow and use my hand. My apex is slick with the evidence of how much all of this turned me on. And the thing is, I can't even pinpoint what's doing it for me—it's just him. It's always been him. He makes me feel comfortable in a way no one else could ever touch.

"It's almost criminal that you covered my jersey with the jacket. I swear, not even Wilson or the threat of fines could've kept me from you during the game if you hadn't. Do you know how many times I've dreamed of you like this, in nothing but my name and number as I slide inside you?"

"But it was your jacket," I manage with a strained laugh, my voice becoming more unsteady the longer he sits back watching me.

"Not the same thing." The roughness of his tone scraps over my skin.

"What's the difference?" I swallow, clinging to the fragments of my composure as he drags the tip of his finger over the curve where my thigh meets my ass, stopping short of where I want him.

He gives the jersey a gentle tug, making it slip free from my shoulder. "This is a symbol—validation of everything I've worked for. Seeing you in it, sitting with the other girls and holding my daughter makes me crazy. It's you claiming me. Telling the world you're mine."

Another trace of his finger along my sensitive skin has my elbow collapsing. I rest my cheek against my forearm.

"Is it?" he asks and this time it's the head of his cock running through my core that has me groaning in agreement.

"Yes. Yes. Yes," I chant.

"Did you wear this to tell everyone that I'm yours?" There's a teasing in his voice, but this doesn't feel funny. I get what seeing me in his jersey did to him— the primal instinct it brings out. That same desire is washing through me, making my head swim, and the only thing I know is I need him.

I shake my head and he shifts his hips back slightly. "I wore it because I'm yours—in every way. Your lover. Your friend. Your partner. Your biggest fan. Your future."

He pushes the jersey up and kisses a path up my spine, not stopping until his lips are at my ear and he is pressed hot and hard against me. "Are you saying you're mine to keep forever?"

"God yes." I try to grind back into him, but he holds me steady.

"Fucking finally." For a moment, he's gone, and I want to cry out in frustration. Because while we've seen each other, the last few weeks have been trying. If he's home, we're falling into bed, exhausted. Between postseason baseball and Holland teething, no one has been sleeping well, and sex has not been the priority, but that changes tonight.

Then he sinks himself deep in one claiming thrust.

"Ffuucckk. I missed this." His voice is as smooth as the snap of his hip as he fills me again and again. "I think I'm going to retire so I can do this every night."

"No, you're not." His thrusts turn my protest into a plaint moan.

"I'm not, but it's really." *Thrust.* "Fucking." *Thrust.* "Tempting."

The delicious build of pressure starts to take over and, like he always does, he knows exactly what I need before I can even tell him. Withdrawing, he flips me to my back, pushing the jersey off one shoulder and then the other.

"I hate to see it go, but I want all of you when I make love to you."

I want that too. Lifting my shoulders, I help him slip it off me. When he lines himself up again, his eyes are filled with a tenderness I'm not prepared for.

I'm so primed he slides right in, pulling a moan from me. There's a frantic tangle as we try to get closer, deeper, our mouths fusing and our bodies gliding together until I can't tell where he ends and I start.

With his hands in my hair and his heart pounding against my chest, he grits his teeth. "I need you to give it to me, Vivienne."

I throw my head back, grinding my hips against him, chasing. His slips his hand between us to find my needy clit and begins circling it, pressing down firmly with his thumb. "Come on, sweetheart. That's my girl. Show me how perfectly you shatter for me."

His words, the pressure, the rhythm, his hand cupping the side of my neck—all of it has me calling out his name, clinging to him as my orgasm shakes through me, taking him over with me.

There's a moment where our hearts pound in unison, still pressed close, before he shifts, rolling us gently to the side and softly captures my mouth. It's slow and sensual, the softest kiss we've ever shared, but filled with so much promise.

When he finally pulls back, his emotion is pouring off him and he looks as if he might break. My heart clenches with the overwhelming need to be the one who holds him together.

"That was . . ." His voice falters, his expression raw, and I brush my fingers against his cheek.

"I'll never forget the way tonight felt," I whisper, the words coming out on a sigh. Then, without hesitation, I add, "I love you," because it feels good to say it. The rest of the night is more of the same.

We take our time with each other, our love spilling over each time we come together before we drift off for a while. Sometime around sunrise, we shower, soaking up the last few minutes before Holland wakes up and we have to leave this bubble.

CHAPTER 65

XAVIER

I have a non-alcoholic beer in one hand and Vivienne in the other, her fingers laced tightly with mine and draped over her shoulder. Below us, a sea of people stretches across the streets as we ride atop an open-air bus, the celebration rowdy as we parade through downtown Denver. My teammates surround us, cheering, laughing, holding the moment high like the banners and signs that line the street.

World fucking champs.

And I feel every bit the champion that the commissioner's trophy says I am, but it's got nothing to do with baseball. No, it's her that makes me feel like I've conquered the world—the woman at my side. This victory, this life, is complete because of her.

One little thing is still bugging me: the bag at the end of my bed. She packed the afternoon after we won so she could stay the night and she's been living out of it for the last three days.

The bus rounds the corner and the Bandits stadium comes into view. The crowd is thicker here with families that have driven out from the suburbs to catch a glimpse of the team before we disappear inside the stadium. Parents hold children high on their shoulders for a closer look. We wave and smile and soak it all in before stepping off the bus and up to the barricaded area, where we stop to sign a few autographs.

Vivienne waits for me off to the side with our friends and I glance back at her, catching a breathtaking smile on her face. I take one last ball from a little girl with red hair and a gap tooth smile that can't be more than eight or nine.

I hand the ball back and jog over to Vivienne, sweeping her up in my arms and carrying her into the stadium.

When we step out onto the grass minutes later, confetti rains down around us. It's a lot like it was after the game, except I'm settled—more at peace. I pull her to the side to escape the fray of the celebration for a moment just the two of us.

"I love you so fucking much." My voice cracks. "After all this time, you've given me back what's been missing most of my life, a family. Me, you, Holland, that's all I need. And I don't want to go weeks without seeing you ever again. That bag on the floor isn't cutting it. I've only got one, maybe two years of baseball left, but that's too long to wait. Move in with us. Wake up with us every day. Be the family we choose."

"Seriously?" she asks, her eyes searching mine.

I'm sure her head is spinning because I've caught her off guard, but it feels right.

"You're it for me, so, yeah, I want you there with me and Holland."

She makes the happiest sound, her laughter spilling out as she squeals, "Yes!"

When she presses up on her toes, I lift her, sealing it with a kiss. "Thank god. I was nervous you'd think it was too fast or too much. I didn't want to push, but I want—"

"I want it too. All of it. The ring on my finger, siblings for Holland. Someday I want her to be mine, too."

"She already is. Just as much as I am." Legally, there will be paperwork and a hearing. The state of Colorado makes everything complicated, but the day she becomes my wife, she'll officially be Holland's mother. I'll make sure of it.

Until then, she's ours in every way that counts.

EPILOGUE

VIVIENNE

ONE YEAR LATER

Retirement looks good on Xavier.

Like, really good.

His red hair is styled in that intentionally messy way that always makes him look playful and sexy. The beard he was growing for luck during the postseason has been traded in for a five o'clock shadow that still makes my knees weak. And that body that's holding me close as he spins me around the dance floor is covered in the finest Italian silk money can buy.

Dean Harrison might have given up his inheritance, but he's still a rich boy from Boston and he's spared no expense to marry the love of his life. It's the pick-me-up we all need after the Bandits were eliminated in the League Championship series. There's no parade or trophy this year, but seeing all our friends together and celebrating Dean and Mia's wedding is its own sweet victory.

You know what else looks good? The ring on my finger. Just like he promised, the diamond he gave me a few weeks ago gleams brightly under the lights of the dance floor. Next to us, Cruz and Lilah dance together, and right next to them, Holland toddles around, attempting to force Jarrett to dance with her. At fourteen-months-old, he's still wobbly, but that doesn't stop her from trying to force her favorite person to keep up with her.

Another promise Xavier fulfilled—a secret no one knows about—is the sibling growing inside me. Not that we were trying. That one was a surprise.

Well, kind of. After watching Indie struggle through her egg retrievals last year, I took my IUD out. (Side-note, it should be illegal to do that to a woman without pain meds). So while we weren't trying, we weren't very careful.

"You've got that look on your face," Xavier whispers, his voice as smooth as the fabric under my fingers as I run my hands over his shoulders.

"And what look is that?"

"The one that makes me want to drag you out of here and up to our room to put another baby in you."

"We need to brush up on your biology. That's not how it works."

"Not going to stop me from trying."

"We can't leave early."

"Why not? Let's start a tradition."

I roll my eyes and he rolls his hips, letting me feel how serious he is. "My hormones are supposed to be the ones causing trouble, not yours."

Mia and Dean waltz over and he raises an eyebrow at Xavier. "I know what you're plotting over here."

"You can't possibly—"

"No one leaves early," he cuts him off.

"You would have thought he'd stop being such a groomzilla now that we're married, but here we are. He gave everyone the same warning." Mia laughs.

"Micah is finally over his colic. We survived the first six months as parents and you look stunning in this dress, wifey. Our friends can stick around until ten o'clock instead of running off to their hotel rooms to try to repopulate the world." Dean grumps.

My cheeks heat. We're not ready to share the news yet, and we both agreed that the wedding was not the place to do it.

"There goes that idea. We could always sneak into a coat closet. We still haven't crossed off sex in public."

"And we're not going to tonight." Just then Holland and Jarrett bump into our legs.

Xavier has the same idea I do, each of us bending to scoop up a baby.

"Momma, cake," Holland says, her two tiny hands grabbing my face and turning my head towards the table of cupcakes.

"You already had one, Estrela," I remind her.

"More."

"How about we go find your water?"

"Milk," Jarret squawks from Xavier's arm.

"Did all that dancing make you thirsty, little man?" Xavier asks, brushing a dark curl off Jarrett's forehead as he follows me off the dance floor to the stash of diaper bags behind the head table.

We set them down and they race, stumbling and falling into the bags before they fish their cups out and roll to their backs, side-by-side, on the floor.

I lean into Xavier's embrace, watching the two of them giggle. "I love this life."

"There's no one else I'd rather do it with. And someday very, very soon, when you're my wife and Holland's adoption is finalized, everything will be the way it was always meant to be."

I sigh, letting him hold me and kiss my temple. "How would you feel about a California wedding?"

"At your parents?"

"Yeah." A lot of healing has happened over the last year and when Harlowe suggested it the other day it just felt right. "It's what I always imagined. It's beautiful, and it's where I feel closest to Erica. I'll marry you anywhere, but my heart is leading me home on this one."

"California it is," he says.

There's a loud squeal from the floor and Holland pushes up, dropping her sippy cup, narrowly missing Jarrett's head and takes off in a run.

"Tenny!" she screams, darting towards the doors.

Xavier spins me around to see my niece standing behind me. His lips brush my favorite spot, the one below my ear that always takes my breath away. "Surprise."

The tears flow freely as she walks over with Holland in her arms.

"You smell like an airplane," I tell her, burying my nose in her strawberry hair as I wrap my arms around both of my girls.

She scoffs like she's offended, but I know she's not. "Has that baby stolen your filter?"

"Shhh . . ." I hiss, still holding her close.

"They're going to figure it out. Your boobs are huge."

"They've always been big."

"True," she admits.

"What are you doing here?" I ask, stunned to see her. Spain captured her heart during her study abroad and she came home for one semester before she transferred to school there to finish out her degree. I miss her every single day, but knowing she's living her life the way she wants to more than make up for it.

She shrugs. "I just wanted to see you."

"Yeah?"

"Yeah. I'm here for a week and then going back home to see Dad for a week," she says. "Ginger Daddy." She releases me, wrapping her arms around my fiancé's waist.

"Don't call me that," he groans.

"But you paid for my flights."

He rolls his eyes. "It's an advance for the babysitting you're going to do while you're here, so I can take little momma out on a proper date."

"Damn, a date night sounds perfect." I light up at the suggestion. I love Holland. Like really, truly, with all my heart, but chasing around a toddler in my first trimester while Xavier played baseball and I worked was exhausting. A night alone sounds blissful.

His voice is low, so only I can hear. "You're really going to like this one. I got us a hotel room and I'm going to do that thing you've been begging me for."

I clench everywhere because I know exactly what thing he's talking about and now that I'm in the second trimester and feeling better, I've been craving it.

"So glad to have you here," I say, extra thankful for her now that I know what Xavier has planned for me.

BONUS EPILOGUE

VIVIENNE

EIGHT MONTHS LATER

"Stop fidgeting with your dress. You look gorgeous." Xavier, peels my fingers off the straps, smoothing out the fabric.

"I want today to be perfect."

"It already is. You could show up at the courthouse in a plastic bag and Holland would still love you."

He's right. I know he's right, but this is the day we've been waiting for since Xavier officially became the sole guardian of Holland.

We've got our son, Haze. We're married. And now, with the adoption of Holland, we will all legally be a family.

It seems silly since we already *are* a family, but there's an extra layer of reassurance that comes with today—knowing that the little girl I've loved since before I realized I was falling for her dad is protected in case something awful happens.

"I'm nervous," I admit, my fingers finding the strap of my dress and adjusting it again.

"Hold the baby and tell me why." Xavier slips our two-month-old carefully into my arms and I instantly relax as I look down at his tiny, perfect face. Despite the head full of dark hair that he inherited from me, he looks a lot like his sister with his pouty little lips, blue eyes, and button nose.

"What if the judge doesn't think I'm fit to adopt her? He could rule against us."

"That's not going to happen. You're the only mother Holland knows. She loves you more than me most days. Collin has all the paperwork in order to show that we've gone through all the necessary steps," he reassures me, reaching out to stroke my face.

"But he could. What if we jinxed it by inviting everyone over afterwards?"

"He won't. It's uncontested."

I swallow the nerves still sticking to my throat, even though I know everything he's saying is true.

Xavier pulls his shirt up his arms, making all the worry flee my head. I step forward, running a finger down his happy trail.

"Keep touching me like that and we'll have three under four."

Nope. That'll do it. Do I want more babies with this man? Absolutely. Do I want them right now? Not a chance.

He laughs as I pale and step back. "What can I say? You looked hot pregnant, and I want more." He leans forward to button the white dress shirt he's shrugged on. "But you're in charge of when."

"Maybe, for today, we focus on surviving this hearing and party with the two we have."

Hours later, the four of us, along with Dom, Indie, Dean, Mia, Cruz, Lilah, Poppy, and Hendrix and their kids, are all scattered around the house. I've got a much needed glass of wine in hand and a very real smile on my face.

Everything is right in the world. I'm officially Holland's mother and I couldn't be happier. This life is better than I could have ever imagined and I owe it all to my husband. He gave me the courage to go after the things I wanted most in my life and he did it without me realizing what was happening. He tells me all of the time that I healed him, but that goes both ways. Without him, I'd still be living a half-life, in fear, instead of being surrounded by this beautiful Bandits family.

THE END

DON'T STOP NOW.
DOWNLOAD THE BONUS SCENE WHERE VIVI AND XAVIER CROSS OFF THE LAST THING ON THEIR LIST.

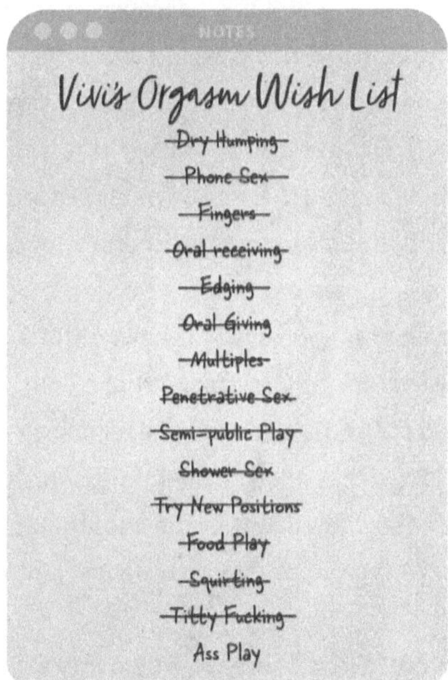

OTHER BOOKS BY LO EVERETT

MILE-HIGH HEARTS SERIES:
All on the Line - Poppy & Hendrix

All or Nothing - Delilah & Cruz

Calling it Safe - Mia & Dean

Force Play - Dom & Indy

ACKNOWLEDGMENTS

We fucking made it! One whole series under our (baseball) belts. And holy bananas, what a ride it's been.

J & Q, the older you get the more sure I am that when you dox me to your teachers, coaches, and friends' parents it's because you like to see me flustered. My game play and youthful lingo would be garbage without you two. Thank you for always loving me and supporting me through this series.

Allison, this series is just as much your baby as it is mine. You've nurtured each book right alongside me and there's no one else I'd rather plot with or meet at Epcot for a quick trip around the world. Thank you for everything. I hope you're ready for your small town era.

To my beta readers and support system. Ashley, Britt, Lib, Madison, Isabella, Mudge, Jessi—thank you for helping make these characters and this story stronger with your words of encouragement and reining me in when I'm off track.

To my author friends that answer my endless questions and just keep me from going off the deep end. Especially the ones that tolerate my audiobook length voice memos: Ambar, Ronnie, Rana, Hailey, Kat, Amanda, Sarah and SO many more.

To Cait, we survived. I wasn't sure we would make it out of this one alive but we did it.

Lastly, to my readers, I hope you've enjoyed your time with the Bandits. This isn't goodbye, it's so long. Whether it's back in Denver or maybe a cameo somewhere else, this isn't the end of the Bandits. Thank you for loving them the way I do and I hope you'll take a chance on Timberline Peak with me next!